MICHAEL VEY

RISE OF THE ELGEN

**MERCURY
INK**

**SIMON
PULSE**

MICHAEL VEY

RISE OF THE ELGEN

ALSO BY RICHARD PAUL EVANS

MICHAEL VEY
THE PRISONER OF CELL 25

MICHAEL VEY

RISE OF THE ELGEN

RICHARD PAUL EVANS

MERCURY INK

SIMON PULSE

NEW YORK   LONDON   TORONTO   SYDNEY   NEW DELHI

This book is a work of fiction. Any references to historical events, real people, or real locales are used fictitiously. Other names, characters, places, and incidents are the product of the author's imagination, and any resemblance to actual events or locales or persons, living or dead, is entirely coincidental.

SIMON PULSE / MERCURY INK
An imprint of Simon & Schuster Children's Publishing Division
1230 Avenue of the Americas, New York, NY 10020
First Simon Pulse/Mercury Ink paperback edition May 2013
Copyright © 2012 by Richard Paul Evans
All rights reserved, including the right of reproduction in whole or in part in any form.
Simon Pulse and colophon are registered trademarks of Simon & Schuster, Inc.
Mercury Ink is a trademark of Mercury Radio Arts, Inc.
For information about special discounts for bulk purchases, please contact
Simon & Schuster Special Sales at 1-866-506-1949 or business@simonandschuster.com.
The Simon & Schuster Speakers Bureau can bring authors to your live event. For more
information or to book an event contact the Simon & Schuster Speakers Bureau at
1-866-248-3049 or visit our website at www.simonspeakers.com.
The text of this book was set in Berling LT Std.
Manufactured in the United States of America
2 4 6 8 10 9 7 5 3 1
Library of Congress Cataloging-in-Publication Data
Evans, Richard Paul.
Michael Vey : rise of the Elgen / by Richard Paul Evans.   p. cm.
Sequel to: Michael Vey, the prisoner of cell 25
Summary: Fifteen-year-old Michael Vey, born with Tourette's syndrome and special
electromagnetic powers, joins his techno-genius best friend and an alliance of other
"electric" teenagers to battle powerful foes in the jungles of Peru, where Michael learns
the Order of Elgen's plan to "restructure" the world.
ISBN 978-1-4424-5414-9 (hc)
ISBN 978-1-4424-5462-0 (eBook)
ISBN 978-1-4424-7510-6 (pbk)
[1. Friendship—Fiction. 2. Electricity—Fiction. 3. Tourette syndrome—Fiction.
4. Peru—Fiction. 5. Science fiction.] I. Title. II. Title: Rise of the Elgen.
PZ7.E89227Mi 2012   [Fic]—dc23   2012022717

To McKenna
You have brought light and warmth into the world

PROLOGUE

A Hitch

"This had better be important," the man said. It was past two in the morning in the Tyrrhenian Sea and the man on the boat had been awoken for the call.

"There's been a . . . *hitch*," Hatch said, choosing the word carefully. He leaned back in the leather seat of his private jet. "The transition from our Pasadena facility didn't go as smoothly as we planned."

"What kind of 'hitch'?"

"We had a revolt."

"A revolt? By who?"

"Michael Vey. And the GPs."

"Did any of them escape?"

"All of them."

The voice exploded in a string of profanities. "How did that come about?"

"The Vey boy was more powerful than we thought."

"The Vey boy escaped?"

Hatch hesitated. "Not just Vey. We lost seven of the Glows."

The man unleashed another string of profanities. "This is a disaster!"

"It's a setback," Hatch said. "One that will quickly be remedied. We know exactly where they are, and we're gathering up the GPs as we speak. We've already recaptured all but three of them."

"What if they've talked?"

"No one would believe them if they did. After what we've put them through, most of them are babbling idiots."

"We can't take that chance. Find them all. Where are the electric children?"

"We've been tracking their movements. They're still together and driving to Idaho. We have a team in place ready to take them."

"Why should I believe you'll be successful this time?"

"*This* time we know what we're dealing with. And we have a few surprises they won't be expecting."

"I'll have to report this to the board," the voice said.

"Give it until morning," Hatch said. "The picture will be different. Besides, everything else is on schedule."

"And I expect you to keep it that way." The voice paused, then said, "I think it's time you released Vey's mother."

"That would be a mistake. She's our only guarantee that Vey won't just disappear again, and he may be the answer to our problems with the machine. Besides, in less than twenty-four hours Vey and the rest of the Glows will be back in our custody."

"You had better be right," the man said.

"You have my guarantee," Hatch said. "Vey will be back in our hands before the day's out."

PART ONE

My Story

In fifth grade my English teacher, Ms. Berg, was teaching about autobiographies and had us each write our life story on a single page of lined paper. I'm not sure which is more pathetic:

(a) That Ms. Berg thought our lives could be summed up on one page, or

(b) I could fill only half the page.

Let's face it, in fifth grade you're still kind of waiting for life to begin. Yeah, some of the kids had done cool things, like one had gone skydiving; another had been to Japan; and one girl's father was a plumber and she got to be in her dad's TV commercial waving a plunger, so she's kind of famous—but that's about as cool as it got. All I remember is that my autobiography was super lame. It went something like:

My name is Michael Vey, and I'm from a town you've never heard of—Meridian, Idaho. My father died when I was eight, and my mother and I have moved around a lot since then. I like to play video games. Also, I have Tourette's syndrome. I'm not trying to be funny, I really do.

You probably know that Tourette's makes some of us swear a lot, which would have made my story more interesting, or maybe got it banned, but I don't swear with my Tourette's. In my case, Tourette's just means I have a lot of tics, like I blink, gulp, make faces, stuff like that. That's about it. As far as life stories go, no one's called to buy the movie rights.

They might if they knew my secret—the secret I've hidden for most of my life and the reason my mom and I keep having to move.

I'm electric. So are you, of course. That's how your brain and muscles work. But the thing is, I have probably a thousand times more electricity than you. And it seems to be growing stronger. Have you ever rubbed your feet on a carpet, then shocked someone? Multiply that by a thousand and you'll get an idea of what it's like to be me. Or shocked by me. Fortunately, I've learned to control it.

I'm fifteen years old now and a lot has happened since the fifth grade. I kind of wish someone would ask me to write my life story now, because it would make a good movie. And it would take up *way* more than one page. This is how it would go:

My name is Michael Vey, and I'm more electric than an electric eel. I always thought I was the only one in the world like me, but I'm not. I just found out that there were originally seventeen of us. And the people who made us this way, the Elgen, are hunting us down. You might say we were an accident. The Elgen Corporation created a machine called the MEI (short for Magnetic Electron Induction), to be used for finding diseases and abnormalities in the body. Instead it created abnormalities—us.

My girlfriend, the way-out-of-my-league cheerleader with perfect brown eyes, Taylor Ridley, is also electric. I can shock people (I call it "pulsing"), but she can shock people's brains and make them forget what they were doing (she calls it "rebooting"). She can also read minds, but she has to touch you to do it.

One month ago the Elgen, led by a scary dude named Dr. Hatch, found us. They kidnapped Taylor and tried to get me, too, but ended up with my mother instead. A few days later I went to California with my best friend, Ostin Liss (he and I live in the same apartment building, and he's one of the few people who knows about my powers), and a couple of kids from my school, Jack and Wade, to save Taylor and my mother.

Things didn't go so well. In the first place, Taylor was there but my mother wasn't. Then we got caught. Jack and Wade were forced to be GPs, which is short for human guinea pigs, the name the Elgen give their prisoners they experiment on. Ostin and I were locked up too, though I was put in Cell 25, the place they put people to break their minds.

I managed to escape and rescue my friends. I was also able to rescue four of the other electric kids: Zeus, Ian, McKenna, and Abigail. They have some pretty cool powers too. Zeus can shoot lightning bolts, which is why he's named after the Greek god. (But he can't touch water without shocking himself, so he doesn't bathe much—actually, never—so he kind of smells.)

Ian's blind but he can see way better than any of us. He sees the same way sharks and electric eels do, through electrolocation—which means he can see things that are miles away, even through walls.

McKenna can create light and heat from any part of her body.

Abigail can take away pain by electrically stimulating nerve endings.

We also rescued Grace. She was one of the electric kids who were loyal to Hatch (who calls us Glows). I don't know much about her other than that she can download things from computers and she downloaded all the information from the Elgen's mainframe before we escaped. We're hoping she has information on where the Elgen have taken my mother.

There are ten of us now (including our nonelectric friends Ostin, Jack, and Wade). We call ourselves the Electroclan.

There's one more thing I would put in my autobiography, something that scares me but would make my story more interesting. I don't know for sure, but I may be dying. Hatch told me that four of the electric children have already died of cancer caused by their electricity—and I have more electricity than any of them. I don't know if it's true because Hatch is a liar. I guess time will tell. In the meanwhile we're headed back to my home in Meridian, Idaho, to figure out where my mother is and plan our next move.

Like I said, I think my story would make a pretty good movie so far. Maybe it will be one day. But not yet, because it's not even close to being over. And I have a feeling that things are about to get a whole lot wilder.

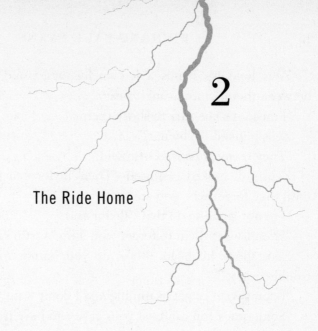

2

The Ride Home

"**I** am so freaking dead," Ostin said, rubbing the palms of his hands on his head so hard I thought he'd leave bald patches. "My dad's going to tear off my arms and beat me to death with them."

I looked at Taylor, and she rolled her eyes. Ostin had been talking for hours about how excited he was to be home again, and it was only as we exited the highway into Meridian that it occurred to him that his parents would be angry that he'd run off without telling them.

"Relax," I said. "They'll be so happy to see you they'll forget they're mad. Besides, you've never even been grounded before."

"I've never run away from home before either."

"I'll go with you," Zeus said from the front seat. "I'll be your wingman. If it gets ugly, I'll take them down."

Ostin's eyes widened. "You can't shock my parents."

Zeus held his hands a few inches apart and arced electricity between them. "Sure I can. It's easy."

"I mean it's *not okay* to shock them."

Zeus blinked. "Why not?"

"They're *my parents*," Ostin said.

Zeus still looked confused. "Then Taylor can just reboot them until they forget who you are."

"I'm not going to do that," Taylor said.

"I don't want them to forget who I am," Ostin said.

Zeus shook his head. "Make up your mind. You want to get in trouble or not?"

"I don't want to get in trouble *and* I don't want to hurt them."

"Sometimes you can't eat your cake and have it too," Zeus said.

"Technically," Taylor said, "you can *never* eat your cake and have it too."

"I wish I had some cake," Ostin said, leaning his head against the back of the seat in front of him.

A few minutes later we passed the 7-Eleven where we'd started our journey, then turned into my apartment building's parking lot. Jack put his Camaro in neutral and turned off the engine. "We're here," he said, even though it was kind of obvious.

"Where's Wade?" I asked.

"I don't know," Jack said. "Last time I saw him was about a half hour ago."

I didn't like the sound of that. "He was supposed to stay with us."

We'd left Pasadena with Jack's car and one of the vans from the Elgen Academy, which Wade had driven with Ian, Abigail, Grace, and McKenna. Jack drove his Camaro with Taylor, Ostin, Zeus, and me.

Zeus sat up front with Jack and helped drive while the three of us crowded in the back, which, since I was next to Taylor, wasn't the worst ride of my life. Around Barstow I fell asleep against her. When I woke up she whispered to me, "That was the strangest dream."

"You had a strange dream?" I asked.

"No," she said. "You did."

It's a weird thing sitting next to someone who can read your mind. At least she never has to wonder how I feel about her.

Our plan was to drive back to Idaho and hide at my apartment while we figured out how to rescue my mother from Hatch and the Elgen. But first we needed to find out where she was. The Elgen are global, which means my mother could be anywhere in the world. *Anywhere.*

As I said, before we left Pasadena, Grace downloaded the Elgen computers. We were hoping that somewhere in all that information was my mother's whereabouts. All we needed now was a computer powerful enough to hold everything Grace had saved.

Fortunately, the Elgen didn't know where we were. At least I didn't think they did. I couldn't be certain about that either. The only thing I knew for sure was that I was going to rescue my mother—or die trying.

3

The Trap

"I'm so dead," Ostin said again.

"We got it, Ostin," Taylor said. "Enough already."

"If they don't kill him, I might," Zeus said.

I looked at Ostin. "I'll come with you. They won't kill you if I'm there. Besides, they'll be impressed with how fit you look." Not surprisingly, Ostin had lost a few pounds in the Elgen prison.

"Yeah," Taylor said. "You're looking good."

Ostin's frown vanished. "Really? You think so?"

"The Elgen diet." Jack laughed. "Guaranteed to scare the fat away."

"Yeah," Zeus said. "Maybe you should go back and take the rest off."

Ostin frowned again.

Zeus and Jack opened their doors and got out, followed by the rest of us.

Taylor stood next to me in the parking lot. "Where do you think Wade went?"

I glanced back at the road. "I don't know. But it worries me."

Jack shook his head. "I'm going to pound him when he gets here. He knew he wasn't supposed to leave us."

"Maybe something happened," Taylor said.

"Yeah, maybe the Elgen captured them," Ostin said. "Or the van had a self-destruct mechanism."

Taylor frowned. "Or maybe they just got a flat. And besides, they have Ian with them."

With Ian aboard they were less likely to run into a trap than we were. His ability to see through solid objects had saved us more than once.

"I'm sure there's an explanation," I said, trying to sound calm. *Wait to worry*, I told myself. *Wait to worry*. I felt my face twitch. I could pretend to be calm, but stress always makes my Tourette's act up.

It was nearly fifteen minutes before Wade pulled the white Elgen van into the parking lot. He drove up next to Jack's Camaro and rolled down his window. "Hey," he said. "We're here."

Jack walked up to him and smacked him on the head.

"Ow!" Wade said. "Why'd you do that?"

"Where'd you go?" Jack asked. "You weren't supposed to leave us."

"The girls made me stop for doughnuts!"

"You wanted one too," one of the girls said from the back.

"I hope you got some for us," Ostin said.

"Sorry, man," Wade said. "We ate them all."

"They were *way* good," Abigail said.

"Thanks for sharing," Ostin said.

Everyone climbed out of the van.

"So this is Idaho," Abigail said, stretching her arms above her head. "Isn't this where they make potatoes?"

"*Grow* potatoes," Ostin said. "You don't *make* potatoes."

"You make french-fried potatoes," she replied.

Ostin shook his head.

Just then Ian said, "We're being watched."

I looked around but didn't see anyone. "Who's watching us?"

"There's a guy in the apartment building across the street with a telescope pointed right at us. I don't think he's seen us yet. He's sitting at the table eating a sandwich. But he's almost finished."

"What do we do?" Jack asked me.

"Is he alone?" I asked Ian.

"Yeah."

"Let's find out what he's doing here. Ostin, take my key and get everyone in my apartment. Taylor, Zeus, Jack, and Ian, come with me."

While Ostin, Wade, Abigail, Grace, and McKenna went to my apartment, the rest of us ran across the street. Inside the building I asked Ian, "Which apartment is he in?"

"He's on the third floor. I don't know which apartment, I'll have to look."

We quickly climbed the stairs. As we walked down the hallway, Ian commented on what he saw behind the walls, talking as if the residents could hear him. "Excuse me . . . Excuse me . . . Use a grenade jump . . . Don't eat that . . . Really, dude? Use a tissue. Oh, that's just nasty."

At apartment 314 Ian said, "There he is, he's back at his telescope. He just noticed the van. He's taking out his phone. Now he's dialing someone."

"Taylor, can you reboot him?" I asked.

"I'll try. Ian, where is he?"

Ian pointed left of the door. "Straight through there."

Taylor put her head up against the wall and concentrated.

"It worked," Ian said. "He put the phone down."

"What's he doing now?"

"He looks like he's thinking."

I tried the doorknob. "It's locked."

Ian examined the door. "Dead bolted and chained."

Zeus said, "Ring the doorbell and when he opens we'll shock him."

"There's a peephole," Taylor said. "He won't open the door with all of us standing here."

"He's dialing again," Ian said.

Taylor focused again.

"Got him," Ian said.

"You're right," I said to Taylor. "But if it's just you standing here, he'll open. Everyone against the wall."

Taylor looked at me. "What am I supposed to say when he answers?"

"You'll think of something. Just get him to open the door." I looked back. "Everyone ready?"

Jack nodded. "Bring it on."

I rang the doorbell.

A few seconds later, Ian said, "He's coming. He's got a gun."

Taylor looked at me fearfully.

"Is he holding it?" I asked.

"No," Ian said. "It's in his holster."

The peephole darkened. Then a gruff voice asked, "Who is it?"

We all looked at Taylor.

"Uh, good afternoon. I'm selling Girl Scout Cookies."

"Girl Scout Cookies?" I mouthed. Taylor shrugged.

"Not interested," the man said.

"He's leaving," Ian said.

Just then the door across the hall from us opened. An old man wearing a brown terry cloth robe scowled at us. "What are you kids up to?"

Before I could answer, Zeus zapped him. The man dropped to the ground like a bowling ball.

"You didn't have to shock him," Taylor said.

"What was I supposed to do?" Zeus said.

I put my ear to the man's chest to make sure he was okay. "His heart's still beating. Jack, help me get him back inside."

We dragged the man into his apartment, then shut the door behind us.

"The dude's back at the window," Ian said.

"Got him," Taylor said, rebooting him. She turned to me. "Let's try again. I think I've got something better this time."

I rang the doorbell.

"He's coming," Ian said.

We all leaned back against the wall.

"You're gulping," Taylor said to me.

"Sorry," I whispered.

"Who's there?" the man asked.

"Hatch sent me," Taylor said coolly.

"Who?"

"Hatch."

There was a slight pause, then the man began sliding the dead bolt. Jack leaned forward, ready to charge the door.

Suddenly the man stopped. "You're not supposed to use that name," he said. "How do I know you're with Hatch?"

Taylor swallowed. "How else would I know where you were?"

"What's the password?"

"The password?" Taylor said. She looked at me.

"Taylor," Ian whispered. "He's touching the doorknob."

"Oh," she said slowly, "the password." She grabbed the doorknob and concentrated. "It's . . . it's . . . Idaho."

There was a short, silent pause, then the man said, "All right." He finished unlocking the dead bolt. As he started to open the door, Jack rushed against it, knocking the man backward. The guy reached for his gun, but Zeus zapped him. The shock knocked Jack down as well.

"Man," Jack said, climbing to his knees. "Watch where you point that thing."

"Sorry," Zeus said.

We all scrambled inside, locking the door behind us. I knelt down next to the man. He was tall with a black mustache and beard. "Taylor, come see what they're up to."

Taylor crouched down next to me, put her hands on the man's temples, then closed her eyes. After a moment she said, "He's just the lookout. There are six Elgen guards waiting for us in one of the apartments across the street."

"Which apartment?"

"Just a minute." She touched him again. "One-seventeen."

"Are you sure?"

She nodded.

"That's not good," I said.

"What's wrong with one-seventeen?" Zeus asked.

"That's Ostin's place."

4

Home, Not Home

"What do we do with him?" Taylor asked, looking down at the guard. "We can't just leave him here. If he wakes up he'll warn the others."

I took his cell phone and pulsed. The phone lit up, then burned out, a wisp of smoke rising from its keypad. "He won't be using that again," I said, tossing the phone aside.

"He can still come after us," Ian said.

"We'll tie him up," I said. "Taylor, see if you can find some rope or something."

"Ian," Taylor said. "Help me look."

"Always using the blind guy to find your stuff," Ian said.

I stayed close to the man, prepared to pulse if he suddenly roused. A couple of minutes later Taylor and Ian returned.

"Found something," Taylor said, holding up a roll of silver duct tape. "Who wants it?"

"I'll do it," Jack said, kneeling down next to me. Taylor tossed him the tape, and Jack rolled the man over onto his stomach, then pulled his arms around to his back. "Hey, Zeus, make yourself useful and hold his arms."

Zeus pinned the guy's arms to his back while Jack wound the tape around his wrists and hands until they were cocooned. When he had finished, Jack looked at me and grinned. "He's not getting out of that."

"What about his legs?" I asked.

"That's next. Lift 'em, Zeus."

Zeus lifted the man's legs as Jack wrapped the tape around them.

"Save some for his mouth," Taylor said.

"I have plenty for his mouth," Jack said. He wrapped the last of the tape around the man's head, covering his mouth and eyes.

"Don't cover his nose," Taylor said. "He'll suffocate."

"I wasn't going to," Jack said.

I looked at the man. "No way he's getting out of that."

"My brothers did that to me once," Taylor said.

"Did what?" I asked.

"Wrapped me up in duct tape like a mummy. I was only seven. When they were done they went out to play and forgot about me for like four hours. They only remembered me when my mom asked them at dinner if they knew where I was. She was furious when she found me. They got grounded for two weeks."

"I would have shocked them silly," Zeus said.

"I wish I had known how to reboot people back then," Taylor said. "I was just figuring things out."

"Michael!" Ian said. "Ostin's walking to his apartment."

"What a time to get brave," I said. "Taylor, can you stop him?"

"All the way across the street?"

"Just try," I said.

She closed her eyes.

"Nothing," Ian said.

"It's too far," Taylor said.

"You need to eat more bananas," Zeus said. "The potassium in them will strengthen your powers."

"Come on," I said. "We've got to stop him."

"What about the old man across the hall?" Taylor asked.

"We'll be long gone before he wakes up. Maybe he'll think he dreamed it."

We raced out of the building and across the street. When we entered my apartment building Ostin was still standing in front of his apartment door, getting up the nerve to walk inside. He slowly reached for the handle.

"Ostin!"

He turned and looked at me. "What?"

Taylor put her finger over her lips. "Shhh."

I motioned him over.

He looked at us quizzically, then walked toward us. "What?"

Taylor shushed him again. I pushed him into my apartment, and everyone else followed.

When we were inside, Ostin asked, "What are you doing?"

"We're saving you," Jack said.

"From my parents?"

"No," I said. "There are six guards in your apartment."

"With my parents?"

Ian shook his head. "They're not there. Not unless they're dressed like Elgen guards."

Ostin turned pale. "They took my mom and dad?"

"We don't know that," I said. "But we've got to get out of here before the guards find out we're here. Ian, what are they doing?"

"Four of them are watching television. One's in the bathroom. The other's reading."

"Is anyone near the front window?"

"The guy with the magazine is."

"Then we better go out the back."

"Wade and I will get the cars and drive them around back," Jack said. "C'mon, Wade." He opened the window and climbed out.

"We can't just leave my parents," Ostin said.

"Your parents aren't here," Ian said.

"Then we need to find out where they are!"

"How?" Zeus asked.

For the first time that I could remember, Ostin didn't have an answer. "Well, they'll know."

"The guards?" Taylor said. "Sure, let's go ask them. They'll be happy to tell us."

Ostin looked down.

I put my hand on his shoulder. "If the Elgen took them, we'll find them. But if we get caught . . ."

"I know," he said.

A moment later the cars arrived around back. Zeus and the four girls climbed out the window, followed by Ian and Ostin. After everyone was gone I looked around my apartment. In the excitement of our return I hadn't let the emotion of being back home sink in. Over the last few weeks I had honestly wondered if I'd ever see my home again. But now that I was back, it didn't feel like home. Not without my mom.

I picked up a framed photograph of the two of us from the hutch next to the kitchen counter—a picture of us on the Splash Mountain ride at Disneyland. We had gotten soaked, and my mother had bought me a new T-shirt to wear. I still had the shirt even though it didn't fit anymore. My mother had sacrificed a lot for us to go on that trip. It was less than a year after my father died, and I think she was trying to make me feel okay again. She was always worried about me. I had no doubt that even now she still was.

Would our lives ever be normal again—the way they were before I knew about Hatch and Glows and the Elgen? After what we'd been through it was hard to imagine sitting at the kitchen table while my mother made waffles and talked about normal things like school and movies: the things other people talked about.

Ostin interrupted my thoughts, leaning in through the window. "Michael. We have to go. Everyone's waiting."

"Sorry." I slid the photograph from the frame, folded it into my front pocket, then climbed out the window, pulling it shut behind me.

Ostin was still standing there. He looked scared.

"You okay?" I asked.

"They took my parents."

I put my hand on his shoulder. "If they did, we'll find them. I promise. Everything will be okay."

I didn't really know if what I'd said was true, but just saying the words helped me believe they might come true. We checked to make sure no one was watching, then ran to Jack's car.

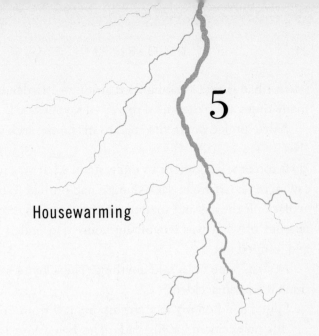

5

Housewarming

"Any idea where to go?" I asked Jack as I slammed the car door.

"We can go to my place," he said.

Jack's house sounded as good a place to hide as any—especially since I couldn't think of anywhere else. "Great," I said. "Your place."

"Don't mind my old man," he said. "He drinks sometimes." He rolled down his car's window, then pounded on his door to get Wade's attention. "We're going to my house."

"Got it," Wade said.

Jack drove around to the front of the building, waited for a car to pass, then pulled out into the street with Wade following closely behind.

Jack lived on the other side of Meridian High School, about two miles from my apartment. The last time I'd been to his house was when I had gone to ask him for a ride to Pasadena. I wondered how many times since then he'd regretted saying yes.

As we pulled down the road to his house, Jack suddenly shouted, "No!"

It took me a moment to understand what was wrong. But when I saw it, my heart froze. Jack's house had burned to the ground.

Jack hit the gas and sped down the street, slamming on the brakes in front of what was left of the house. He pulled his parking brake and jumped out.

At first, none of us said anything. Then Taylor said softly, "Do you think it was an accident?"

I put a hand on my face to stop my jaw from ticking. "No."

"It's no accident," Zeus said. "The Elgen love fires. It hides their tracks."

I got out of the car and walked to Jack's side. His hands were balled up in fists and his face was tight and angry. All that was left of his house were the concrete sidewalk and foundation. Even the cars in the yard had been torched. The area was cordoned off with yellow caution tape.

"I'm sure your dad got out," I said.

Jack thrust his hands deep into his pockets. "Unless he was drunk. Like he usually is."

I didn't know what to say, so finally I just settled on "I'm so sorry." My words sounded ridiculously inadequate. "This is my fault."

"Did you set fire to my house?" Jack asked.

"No. I just never should have gotten you involved."

"I made my choices," Jack said. "I'll stand by them." He turned to me. "It's not your fault; it's Hatch's. And he's gonna pay."

We stood there for another minute or so without speaking, the only sound was the whisper of a late afternoon breeze. Then I turned and walked back to the car. As I climbed in I looked back at Taylor. She was clearly frightened.

"Is he okay?" she asked.

I shook my head.

Jack returned a few minutes later. After he'd shut the door Zeus said, "Sorry, man."

Jack just grunted.

Then Taylor said, "I need to go home."

I turned to her. "If they were watching my place, Ostin's, and Jack's, you can bet they're going to be watching yours, too."

"I don't care!" she said. "I need to see my house."

"Taylor, think about it. If they capture us, your parents won't have a chance. The best thing we can do for them is be careful."

She turned away from me angrily.

"I'm sorry," I said.

After a moment she replied, "I know."

Jack started the car. Then he said, "We can drive by and see if Taylor's house is okay. If everyone stays down, they probably won't know it's us."

Taylor thought about this, then said, "Okay."

"Then we can go to my sister's place," he said. "She has a tanning salon about a mile and a half from here. She'll let us hide out." Then he said in a softer voice, "Maybe she'll know what happened to my dad." He looked back. "Any objections?"

Going by Taylor's house was risky, but she was so upset I couldn't bring myself to say no. "Let's go," I said.

Jack pulled his car around until his and Wade's windows were adjacent to each other. "Head over to my sister's tanning salon, we'll meet you there."

"Where are you going?" Wade asked. He looked as shocked as we did.

"It doesn't matter," Jack said. "Just go."

"Shouldn't we stick together?"

"No," Jack said, and rolled up his window. He turned back to Taylor. "Where do you live?"

"Behind the school," she said.

Taylor lived only a few minutes away, and none of us said a word the whole way over. As Ostin liked to say, the tension was as thick as good bacon. I knew Taylor was afraid of what she might find. *What if her house was burned down too?*

Jack turned onto her street, driving a little below the speed limit to avoid drawing attention to us. Ostin and I crouched down in the back, though I could still see out. I breathed a sigh of relief when I saw Taylor's house. Everything looked normal, though I noticed a white van with tinted windows parked at the end of the street. Taylor stared silently as we drove by.

After we had passed, Taylor said, "I think I saw my mom." There was longing in her voice. And pain. But at least she wasn't so afraid anymore.

"Seen enough?" Jack asked.

"Yes," Taylor said softly. "Thank you."

He picked up speed and headed off to his sister's tanning salon.

6

Bronze Idaho and the Voice

There are people in this world you don't really picture as having a sister, like, for instance, Hitler. (However, Ostin told me that Hitler did have a sister, named Paula.) Jack was one of those people. I wondered what Jack's sister would be like and how she'd respond to us all showing up at her tanning salon. I remembered what Jack had said about her on our way to California—that she didn't really associate with the rest of his family anymore. Maybe she'd throw us out. Where would we go then? And what if Jack's father was dead?

We drove to a small strip mall and pulled into the parking space next to Wade. The sign on the building in front of us read:

BRONZE IDAHO TANNING SALON

A red-and-blue neon sign in the salon's front window flashed
OPEN.

Wade started getting out of the van, but Jack stopped him. "You
guys better stay here for a minute. I need to make sure my sister's
cool."

"Okay," Wade said. "We'll keep watch."

The rest of us followed Jack through the front door. The salon's
lobby was decorated in a Hawaiian motif, with amateurishly painted
palm trees and hula girls on the walls and thatch covering the front
counter.

The woman standing at the front desk looked up as we entered.
She was a female version of Jack, though she was much smaller,
maybe only an inch taller than Taylor. She had long, blond hair
accented with a violet streak, and a nose ring and multiple ear
piercings. Not surprisingly, she was very tan.

"Hey, sis," Jack said.

"Jack," she said, her surprise at seeing him evident in her voice.
"Where have you been?" She looked at the rest of us with a confused
expression, then came around the counter and hugged her brother.

After they separated, Jack said, "I just came from the house, or
what's left of it. Where's Dad?"

I held my breath.

"He's staying with me until he can find an apartment," she said.

Jack's expression relaxed. I breathed out a sigh of relief.

"Where have you been?" she asked again.

"California."

"Who are these people?"

"Friends of mine," he said. "We need a place to hide out."

Her expression changed from curiosity to anger. "Hide out? What
have you done?"

"Nothing," Jack said. "We haven't done anything wrong."

She looked at me and I nodded in confirmation.

"Then why are you hiding?"

"It's a long story," Jack said. "And the less you know the better. We
just need a place to hang until we figure out what we're going to do."

She looked at him for a moment, then said, "Okay. But you can't stay up front. I've got a business to run. And you owe me an explanation."

Just then the front door opened and a tall, professionally dressed woman walked in. She looked around at us. "Excuse me, are you all in line?" she asked Taylor.

"No," Taylor said. "We're just visiting. We'll get out of your way."

"May I help you?" Jack's sister asked.

"Yes," she said, walking up to the counter. "Do you have a tanning bed available?"

"Yes, I do."

"Great," she said. "Do you have one a little more private—perhaps something near the back?"

"Yes. The last room has the Ultra Ruva bed. It's one of our best. Are you a member of our executive tanning club?"

"No. I'm just traveling through town."

"Very good. How long would you like me to set your session for?"

"Twenty minutes should be sufficient."

"Twenty it is." She handed the woman a key with a large key chain—a pineapple-shaped piece of plywood with the number six painted on it. "You're in room six. Just push the start button on the bed when you're ready."

"Thank you. Do you have lotion?"

"We have Coppertone and Beach Bum."

"Coppertone will be fine," the woman replied. She suddenly turned and looked at me, her gaze lingering a little longer than was comfortable. I twitched a couple of times.

"Here you go," Jack's sister said, handing her a bottle of lotion. "Cash or credit?"

"Cash. How much is it?"

"With the lotion it's twenty-nine dollars."

The woman handed her a couple of bills. "Keep the change," she said, stepping away from the counter. As she walked past me she dropped her cell phone on the ground near my feet. "Oh, I'm sorry," she said.

"No problem." I bent over and picked it up. "Here you go."

She made no effort to take the phone from me. "That's not mine."

I looked at her quizzically. "But, you just . . ."

"I believe it's yours, Michael." She looked right into my eyes, then handed me the tanning room key along with two other keys. "Take these into the room. Someone needs to talk to you."

My chest constricted. "Are you with Hatch?"

She touched her finger to her lips to silence me. "Room six," she said. "Turn on the tanning bed. I'll watch the door." She patted her jacket, making me think she was carrying a gun. I looked over at the others. No one was paying attention to me except Ostin. I could tell he was trying to figure out what was going on.

"Hurry," she said. "We haven't much time."

I looked back into her eyes. Something about her seemed trustworthy. "Okay," I said.

"Room six. Don't forget to turn on the bed when you get inside."

I walked back to the room and stepped inside, shutting the door behind me. I turned on the tanning bed and the sound of the machine filled the room. The phone she had given me rang immediately. I raised it to my ear. "Hello?"

"Hello, Michael. Are you alone?" The man's voice was deep and grave.

"Who is this?"

"One of the few people in this world who knows what you're up against. They're following everything you're doing."

"Who is?"

"You know who. We don't have much time. If we can find you, so can they. Now listen to what I say and follow my directions precisely. You have to leave immediately. As soon as you get in your car I'll text you an address. Drive directly to that location and abandon your vehicles. The Elgen van you borrowed has a tracking device, and I'm sure that by now they've identified your friend's Camaro."

"How do you know this?"

"I haven't time to explain," the voice said.

"How do I know this isn't another trap?"

"You don't. But think about it, if we wanted to capture you, we would have just done it. The building you're in right now is a death trap. It only has two exits, the front glass door and a back door that leads to a narrow alley. You're sitting ducks. You have to trust me. If you want to escape the Elgen, you're going to need our help."

"Why would you help us?"

"We have our reasons. And we know even better than you what the Elgen are planning and what they're capable of. The Elgen are rising. You should also know that there are more electric children. And they have terrible powers—worse than anyone you've met so far."

"Great," I said.

"You can defeat them, Michael. You might not be strong enough to face them today, but by the time you do, and trust me, you will, you'll be ready. But you'll need to act quickly to stop them."

"But we did stop them. We shut down the academy."

"They were going to close it anyway—you just sped up their timetable. I wish we had more time, but that's a luxury neither of us has, so try to understand what I'm saying. Now is the opportune moment to strike. The Elgen are divided. To most of its board members, it is just a business. To Hatch, and a few others, it's more. Much more. They're building a secret society, and they're growing fast. They've made inroads in government, police, and military. If you don't believe me, check the state records to see what happened to the man who robbed your mother."

"What happened to him?"

"He's not a worry to the Elgen anymore."

"How do I know you're not one of them?"

"Like I said, you're going to have to trust a little. I won't ask more of you than that."

"If we ditch our cars, how will we get around?"

"Where you leave your cars, there will be two other vehicles. My associate gave you the keys."

I looked down at the keys in my hand.

"I've programmed the address of a safe house into the GPS sys-tem of the yellow vehicle. Go there and wait for my call. But you must leave now. The police are already on their way to the salon."

"The police? Why?"

"To arrest you for burning down Jack's house."

7

Hummers

The phone went dead as the man hung up. I put it in my front pocket and walked quickly out of the room. Apparently Jack's sister hadn't made everyone go to the back, because they were all still in the lobby. The strange woman was gone.

I walked up to Jack, who was talking to his sister. "We've got to go," I said. "Fast. The police are on their way."

"How do you know that?" he asked.

I looked at the others, who were now all looking at me. "I just do."

"Who was that lady?" Ostin asked. It was the first thing he'd said since we'd left the apartment.

"I'll tell you in the car," I said. "We've got to hurry."

"Why don't we just wait for the police?" Taylor said. "They'll help us."

"No. They're coming to arrest us."

"Arrest us for what?" Ostin asked.

"We stole a van, Einstein," Jack said.

"It's worse," I said. "Someone told them that I burned down your house."

Jack frowned. "We've got to get out of here."

"You stole a car?" Jack's sister asked angrily. "You said you didn't do anything."

"We borrowed it," Zeus said. "And they owed us big-time."

She looked flustered. "What's going on, Jack? Why are the police coming?"

"I can't tell you right now. Just tell them that you don't know anything."

"I don't," she said.

"Good. It's better that way." He looked at her sadly. "We've gotta run. I'll explain when I can."

"C'mon, everyone," I said. "To the car."

When we were in the Camaro, Jack asked, "Now what?"

"I have an address," I said. I picked up the phone, but it was out of power. "I can't believe it, it's dead. It was perfectly fine a minute ago."

"Let me see it," Ostin said. He took the phone from me and examined it. "You just need to hold it."

"I was."

"Put out your hand," he said. He handed me the phone and this time it lit up.

"You were holding it wrong. See these metallic strips on the side? They're made of a silver alloy. The phone is designed to run off your electricity. That way it never runs out."

"And it won't work for anyone else," I said. I looked down at the address the man had texted me. "Thirty-eight South Malvern Avenue."

"I know that area," Jack said. "It's an industrial park. There are a lot of printing shops." Jack shouted to Wade, "Follow me!" Then he backed up and screeched out of the parking lot, followed by Wade, who also tried to screech but managed only a small chirp.

After we'd driven a few blocks, Taylor asked, "What's going on, Michael? And who was that woman?"

"I don't know who she was. But she knows who we are and who's chasing us."

"She knew about the Elgen?" Ostin asked.

I nodded. "She gave me the phone. A man called who says he's going to help us. He also told me that the van Wade's driving has a tracking device. That's how they've been following us. We need to ditch our cars."

"Wait a minute," Jack said. "No one said anything about ditching my car."

"Who is this man?" Taylor asked.

"Just . . . some man." I looked at her. "I know it sounds stupid, but I believe he's trying to help."

"I'm not ditching my car," Jack said.

"How do you know you can trust him?" Taylor asked.

"I don't. But do we have a choice?"

"Yes," she said, "we do."

I took her hand. "Here, read my mind. Listen to what he said."

She closed her eyes as I thought back on the call. When she opened her eyes she nodded. "Okay. I trust him too."

Jack was still upset. "You're saying that some dude I've never met wants me to ditch my car? I'm not ditching my car."

"They want us to *trade* cars."

"That's not going to happen," he said. "Do you know what this baby is worth?"

"The Elgen are following your car. They can either capture you and the car, or just the car. It's your call."

Jack shook his head. "This just keeps getting better."

We had driven about a half mile from the salon when two Meridian Police cars sped past us headed in the opposite direction. Their lights were flashing but there were no sirens.

"There they go," Jack said. "Looks like your man knows something."

"Maybe he's the one who called the police," Ostin said.

Possible, I thought.

The address on my cell phone led us to an abandoned industrial area near an automotive wrecking yard. I was nervous and twitching. I'm pretty certain everyone was nervous, because no one was talking. I looked over at Jack. His face was tight and his eyes were darting back and forth, searching for danger. The yard was surrounded by a tall fence topped with razor wire, and the sun had nearly set, leaving the yard dark.

"I don't like this place," Taylor said.

"Not a lot of escape options," Jack said slowly. "Keep your eyes peeled."

There was a loud snap of electricity from Zeus, and we all jumped. "Sorry," he said. "Just keeping sharp."

I did my best to control my tics. "I told Ian to have Wade honk if he sees anything that looks like a trap," I said.

We slowly drove around the corner of a weathered, aluminum-sided warehouse. There, next to a Dumpster, were two brand-new Hummers, one yellow, the other black.

Jack's expression changed when he saw the vehicles. "That's what they're giving us to drive?"

"Must be," I said. "I don't see any other cars."

"I've changed my mind," he said. "I'll trade."

We pulled up to the parked vehicles, and everyone got out of the cars.

"Are we safe?" I asked Ian.

"As far as I can tell. The only person around is a homeless guy sleeping in a Dumpster behind the building across the street."

I handed Wade a key. "You take the black Hummer. Follow us."

"Where are we going?" Wade asked.

"A safe house," I said.

"Are you sure it's safe?"

"I'm not sure about anything," I said, "except that the Elgen are hunting us and we just got some new cars."

Wade nodded. "Works for me."

"We're trading places," I said to Zeus, climbing into the front seat of the yellow Hummer.

"No problem," he said. "I'll sit next to Tara."

"Taylor," Taylor said.

"Sorry," Zeus said, sliding in next to her. "I keep confusing you with your evil twin."

"Well, you were with her a lot longer than you were with me."

Jack was in the driver's seat checking out the console. I handed him the key.

"Listen to that," he said, starting it up. "I've always wanted to drive one of these bad boys. My brother drove one in Iraq."

"Cool," I said.

"It was blown up underneath him by an IED."

"Not cool," I said.

"He survived, so it's even more cool. Where to?"

"The man said they programmed an address into the GPS system." I looked at the device. "I have no idea how this works. Ostin?"

Ostin leaned forward over the seat. He pushed a few buttons and a map appeared. "There are your coordinates," he said. "Just follow the arrow."

"Thanks," I said. "You good, Jack?"

Jack put the Hummer in gear. "I'm good."

As we pulled back out onto the street, Jack turned to me and said, "Hope it's not a trap."

I leaned back in my seat. "Me too," I said softly. "Me too."

8

The Safe House

According to the GPS our next destination was 7.3 miles from where we had picked up the cars, a distance we covered in less than fifteen minutes. The safe house was a small, ordinary-looking brick home in an ordinary suburban neighborhood. The yard was manicured enough not to warrant complaints, but simple enough not to warrant attention. The house was dark except for the front porch light.

Jack pulled into the cement driveway on the west side of the house. The drive was narrow but widened in back at the entrance of a two-car garage.

"I'll wait to pull in," Jack said. "In case we need to make a quick getaway."

"Good idea," I said, trying not to sound nervous. I realized that part of me was waiting for the worst to happen and I was ticking like crazy.

Wade pulled the black Hummer up next to us. In spite of our situation, he was grinning from ear to ear. "This baby is sweet," he said. "I never thought I'd get to ride in one of these, let alone drive one."

"I'm going to check things out," I said to Jack. "If it's a trap, just get everyone out of here."

"Warriors don't leave a man behind," Jack said.

"What are we doing?" Wade asked.

"Just keep your car running until we're sure it's safe," I said. I turned to Ian. "Can you give me a hand?"

"Sure, man. I'll give you both of them."

"It's your eyes I need."

"I'll give you both of those, too."

The two of us got out of the cars and walked to the edge of the driveway, looking cautiously at the dark house.

"What do you think?" I asked.

"It's empty," Ian said. He looked around at the neighbors. "Neighborhood looks legit. A mom helping a kid with homework, a family watching TV, a couple eating dinner."

"All right, let's go in." I rapped on the Hummer, and Jack pulled into the garage, followed by Wade. Everyone gathered in the driveway.

Taylor came up to my side. "You okay?"

"Yeah. Why?"

"You're ticking a lot."

"I'm nervous."

"But the house is okay?"

"It checked out with Ian."

We walked up to the back of the house, but as I reached for the storm door Ostin said, "Stop!"

I looked over at him.

"What if the door's booby-trapped? I saw this show where the bad guys had rigged all the doors with plastic explosives, so when the cops opened the door—ka-boom!" Ostin threw his arms out in demonstration. "Everyone's dead."

We all just looked at him.

Ostin shrugged. "It was a cool show."

"I'll open the door," Zeus said. He twisted the doorknob and pushed the door open, then stepped inside the dark house. "Hey, McKenna, how about a hand?"

"Sure." She lit up her hand, then stepped into the house behind him.

"There's the switch," Zeus said.

Taylor and I walked in, followed by everyone else. Jack was the last to enter. He still looked anxious and glanced around before shutting and locking the door.

The home's interior was as ordinary looking as its exterior, which, I suppose, is what a safe house is supposed to look like. I mean, if the place stands out like a zit on your nose, it's not going to be very safe, right?

We were standing in the kitchen. On the counter was a bulky, brown envelope, and I picked it up and pulled back its flap. It was filled with money.

"Check this out," I said, holding up the cash. "They left us money."

"That's some serious coinage," Jack said.

"I'll count it," Taylor said, taking the envelope from me. She riffled through the bills. "Ten grand," she said. "Even."

"That was fast," I said.

"I'm good at counting."

I took a handful of bills and put them in my pocket, leaving the rest on the counter.

From the front room Ostin shouted, "Michael, check this out! This is one sweet computer."

I walked into the other room. I was no expert on computers—I left that to Ostin—but it looked like a serious piece of technology. "Can we use it to get the data out of Grace?" I asked.

"I'm on it," he replied.

I was glad he had found something to distract him from his parents.

"Is there anything to eat?" Taylor asked. "I'm really hungry."

"Me too," Abigail said.

I opened the fridge. It was empty. "Nada."

"We passed a pizza place about a half mile back," Jack said. "Wade and I could go pick up something. What kind of pizza do you guys want?"

"Pepperoni and anchovies," Wade said.

"No anchovies," Taylor said. "They stink."

"I second that," Ostin said. "Who eats anchovies on pizza?"

"Only about a billion Italians," Wade replied. "And they're the ones who invented pizza, so they should know how to eat them."

Getting a history lesson from Wade, especially about food, was more than Ostin could stomach. "In the first place," Ostin said, standing, "no one knows who invented pizza. In the sixth century, Persian soldiers baked bread flat on their shields and covered it with cheese and dates. So you could argue that they did. Secondly, there are not a billion Italians in the world, not even a hundred million. In Italy there are—"

"Agh!" Wade shouted. "Will someone shove something into his mouth to shut him up?"

"Pizza would do nicely," Ostin said. "Without anchovies."

"Just get a bunch of different kinds," I said to Jack. "There are ten of us. How about three large?"

"I'll get some drinks, too," Jack said. "Everyone's good with cola?"

"I want lemonade," Taylor said.

"Me too," said Abigail.

"Diet cola," McKenna said.

"Write that down," Jack said to Wade.

Wade looked around. "With what?"

"Then remember it," Jack said. "All right, I'll be back. But not too soon. I need to test out the Hummer."

"Can I come?" Abigail asked.

Jack looked pleasantly surprised. "Sure."

"Thanks."

Taylor looked at me and grinned. Jack had told us earlier that he thought Abigail was hot.

"Wade," Jack said, "you don't need to come anymore."

"What?"

"Abi and I can handle it. Just chill here with everyone else."

"He can come," Abigail said.

"No," Jack said. "He doesn't want to." He looked at Wade with a threatening glare. "Do you?"

Wade frowned. "Nah, I'll just chill."

"Let's go," Jack said, opening the door.

"Okay, we'll be right back," Abigail said.

After they left I said, "C'mon, Ostin. Let's start uploading." I looked at Grace. "Are you okay with that?"

She nodded. "That's what I do."

Ostin powered up the computer, then turned to Grace. "So how do you transfer data?"

"First I need to touch a metal part on the computer." She glanced back at us. "I should sit down. Bringing it up is hard."

"Hard?" Taylor asked. "In what way?"

"I guess it's sort of like vomiting," Grace said.

"Oh," Taylor said.

Grace put both hands on the computer and began concentrating. Suddenly her eyes rolled back in her head and she began trembling.

"Holy cannoli," Ostin said. "Look at that."

Files suddenly began filling the screen. Grace continued until a screen popped up that said MEMORY FULL. She groaned, slumping forward.

"You okay?" Taylor asked, taking her by the arm.

She nodded. "Yeah. It just hurt a little."

"Wow. You filled the computer," Ostin said. "It has a terabyte of storage. You must have downloaded most of their mainframe." He looked at me. "We need a bigger computer."

"We got a lot of it, though, didn't we?" I asked.

Ostin nodded. "We got a boatload. Let's see if we can find your mom." He lifted his hands above the keyboard as if he were a pianist about to start a performance. He typed my mother's name into the computer's find function.

I held my breath. Taylor took my hand as we waited. A screen came up.

NO MATCHING FILES

My heart fell.

"I'll try 'prisoners,'" Ostin said.

NO MATCHING FILES

"Maybe they use a different word," I said. "Is there a GP file?"

"Let's see."

Ostin typed in "GP." About two dozen folders came up. "This one has the most information, let's see what's inside." He clicked on it. "Holy cow," he said. "Look at that."

There were thousands of records with names and mug-shot-type photographs.

"What are those numbers?" I asked, pointing to a series of numbers that appeared beneath each record.

Ostin glanced through the numbers looking for a pattern. "I'm guessing the first is the GP's serial number, like they give convicts in prisons. The second, based on the recurring sequence, appears to be a date, probably when they were admitted. I know how to verify that." He typed in a number. A picture of a terrified Wade appeared on the screen. "Yep. It's the day admitted. The third . . ." He hesitated, slowly rubbing his hand over his forehead. "Hmm. The list is sorted by the serial numbers, but you'll notice the last numbers seem to show up in clumped sequences. I'm betting it's where they're being held—they're just using a number instead of a location."

"That's not going to help us," Taylor said.

"On the contrary," Ostin replied. "It will tell us how many Elgen facilities there are."

"What's that?" I said, pointing to a folder that read:

CONFIDENTIAL MEMOS: STARXOURCE PLANTS

"No idea," Ostin said. He clicked on the folder.

MEMO

Mr. Chairman,

Please find requested report of Starxource development. Note: All countries with populations of fewer than 15,000 are deemed irrelevant unless there are recognizable political ties that may allow us future development in larger economies; i.e., Saint Barths—France. (Grid Infrastructure development will be detailed in alternative report.)

Beta Control Countries

Anguilla   *(Starxource Functioning 100%)*

Christmas Island   *(Starxource Functioning 100%)*

Cook Islands   *(Starxource Aborted)*

Falkland Islands   *(Starxource Functioning 96%)*

Saint Barths   *(Starxource Functioning 96%)*

**Operational Starxource Plants/
Combined Populations:**   **115,597,166**

Palau   *21,000*

British Virgin Islands   *28,213*

Gibraltar   *29,441*

Monaco   *35,881*

Saint Martin	36,824
Cayman Islands	54,878
Greenland	56,890
Bermuda	64,237
Dominica	71,685
Jersey	97,857
Aruba	101,484
Tonga	103,036
Grenada	110,821
Samoa	184,032
Finland	5,405,590
Zimbabwe	12,754,000
Taiwan	23,200,000
Peru	29,797,694
Tanzania	43,443,603

Plants Under Construction (PUC)/
Combined Populations: 32,623,410

Portugal	10,561,614
Greece	10,787,690
Chad	11,274,106

Under Negotiation/Combined Populations:	1,010,135,758
Poland	38,092,000
Sudan	45,047,502
Spain	46,196,278
South Korea	48,750,000
Italy	60,600,000
France	65,073,482
Philippines*	94,000,000
Pakistan	187,000,000+
Brazil*	192,376,496
India*	233,000,000

*Top 10 Populous Countries

Within 24 months we will be providing power to 19.89% of countries comprising 46% of the world's population. The current global economic stagnation provides an ideal political and socioeconomic environment to allow our entrance into these countries that might otherwise be wary of our global growth and Elgen control. It is our estimation that within 48 months we will control the energy and, subsequently, the economies of 78% of the world's population.

Dr. C. J. Hatch

"It's from Hatch!" Ostin said.

"It sounds like he's talking about global conquest," Taylor said.

Ostin clicked on another folder. "Check this out." He pulled up a video screen that showed a large logo.

"It's a news story about the Elgen," he said.

"Run the video," I said.

Ostin clicked the play button and an attractive, professionally dressed woman with a British accent began speaking:

REPORTER: *In global news, Elgen Inc., an international energy conglomerate, has announced a new source of cheap, renewable energy. Elgen's Starxource power plants promise to "light up the globe" by delivering economical, renewable, and environmentally friendly power to the world.*

The video cut to a shot of Dr. Hatch.

"Die, you pig!" Ostin shouted.

"Quiet," Taylor said.

REPORTER: *Dr. C. J. Hatch, CEO of Elgen Inc., told reporters that the Starxource project would revolutionize the world in more ways than just affordable power bills.*

The audio came up on Hatch.

HATCH: *Currently more than twenty-five percent of the world's population lives without electrical power. It is Elgen Inc.'s goal to remedy this problem within our lifetime. The benefits of our Starxource plants are innumerable, as will be the relief of human suffering . . .*

"Human suffering," Ostin said bitterly. "The man invented it."

"Shh," Taylor said.

HATCH: *. . . and other sociopolitical factors, such as freeing children in underdeveloped countries from gathering wood and fuel all day, so they can attend school.*

REPORTER: *The technology behind your Starxource plants is more confidential than the formula for Coca-Cola, but rumors are that you have created sustainable cold fusion.*

HATCH: *The process we've developed might best be compared to cold fusion; however, there is no environmental backlash. Starxource plants create no nuclear waste, and there is no danger of a nuclear core meltdown like that experienced in Chernobyl or during the Fukushima Daiichi nuclear disaster.*

REPORTER: *When will the first Starxource plants begin operating?*

HATCH (smiling): *They already are. Elgen Inc. has been operating mini–power plants in developing countries for more than three years now, and the benefits to the local communities have far surpassed our greatest hopes. We are now preparing to operate in more populated countries.*

REPORTER: *Tesla, Edison, and now Dr. C. J. Hatch. Clean, cheap, and renewable energy from Elgen Inc. Finally, some good news for a change. I'm Devina Sawyers. Back to you, Mark and Carole.*

After the video ended we all sat quietly.

"Hatch said the Elgen were going to control the world," I said. "If they control the world's power, they control the world, don't they?"

"But it doesn't make sense," Ostin said.

"What doesn't?" Taylor asked.

"Cold fusion's not their bag. The Elgen scientists are biologists, not physicists. It doesn't make sense that they would invent or discover something outside their field of research. It would be like a pizza chain building cars."

Taylor pointed to a folder next to the one Ostin had just opened: ER Protocol. "What's that?"

Ostin looked at it. "ER . . . Emergency room protocol?" Ostin clicked on the file.

MEMO

Dr. Hatch,

Due to your recent report of the likelihood of additional ER21 escapes, the board wants to know what protocol has been initiated in order to deal with a potential outbreak. There is concern that due to the organisms' short gestation periods, an epidemic of ER could quickly spread near one of our Starxource plants, jeopardizing our control. Do the ER20 and ER21 propagate outside the controlled environs, and if so, for how many generations? We have reviewed the press coverage you enclosed concerning the recent ER outbreak near our Puerto Maldonado plant. What is our status to date?

"What's an ER21?" Taylor asked.

"Never heard of it," Ostin said. "It sounds like a virus, which is something the Elgen would do. But what does that have to do with a power plant?" He turned to Grace. "Do you know?"

Grace shook her head. "I've never heard of it."

We continued reading the chain.

MEMO

Mr. Chairman,

The outbreaks of ER20 and, more specifically, ER21 in Puerto Maldonado have been contained. It was fortunate for us that this outbreak occurred during the rainy season, as the ER cannot withstand the direct application of water due to the specimen's biological mutations.

Dr. C. J. Hatch

MEMO

Dr. Hatch,

How can you be certain of the successful containment of the ER20/ER21?

MEMO

Mr. Chairman,

We have developed sophisticated el-readers for detecting ER20/ ER21 over large areas. Also, the properties of the living ER20/ ER21 make them highly visible in darkness.

Dr. C. J. Hatch

MEMO

Dr. Hatch,

Fortunate as it may be that the Puerto Maldonado situation has been contained, it is of concern to us that it was only by "fortune" that a near catastrophic situation was mitigated. Please respond to our initial inquiry. Do the ER20 and ER21 propagate outside the controlled environs, and if so, for how many generations?

MEMO

Mr. Chairman,

In regard to your inquiry about ER reproduction outside of captivity, the ER20/ER21 do, in fact, propagate the genetic mutation that is developmentally favorable for the rapid production and operation of Starxource plants. However, scientists at our Kaohsiung, Taiwan, plant have developed an ingenious solution. We have genetically altered the next phase, ER22, with a 92% iodine deficiency, far less than is available in any natural environment. The ER will die within 72 hours without the supplements we provide. Our beta test of ER22 in the Aruba, Puerto Maldonado, and Taiwanese plants has proven successful, and we will be neutralizing all ER21 as soon as we can replace them with the ER22, as not to disrupt our current power production and potentially damage our grids in those regions.

MEMO

Dr. Hatch,

Due to the short gestation period of the specimen, is it possible that some ER could survive longer than 72 hours and reproduce?

MEMO

Mr. Chairman,

*In response to your recent inquiry, the answer is no. It is not
possible.*

"Any idea what that's all about?" I asked.

Ostin shrugged. "I need to do a little detective work. The memo
said this ER escape made the news. We've got a date here and a gen-
eral location." He looked at me. "This might take a little while."

"Then I'm going to take a nap," I said. "Wake me if you find something."

"Will do," Ostin said.

I walked out of the front room to find a bedroom.

Taylor followed me out. "Michael. Can we talk?"

"Sure. Let's go in here."

We walked into a bedroom. I sat at the foot of the bed and Taylor
sat cross-legged on the floor.

"You okay?" I asked.

"Yeah." She looked down at her hands. "How long are we going to
stay here?"

"I don't know. The man didn't say."

"Can you call him?"

"I don't know." I lifted the phone from my pocket, and it immediately lit up. For the first time I noticed that it didn't even have a
keypad. "It's not designed to dial out—only to receive." I looked over
at her. "Are you sure you're okay?"

"No," she said. She lowered her head into her hands, her coffee-
brown hair falling in front of her like a veil. "All of this is my fault.
And now Ostin's parents are gone, and Jack's house is burned down.
If I hadn't looked for the Elgen online . . ."

I sat down next to her on the floor. "Taylor, you can't keep doing
this to yourself. You've seen how high-tech the Elgen are. It was just
a matter of time before they found us."

"What if they take my family?"

"Then we'll rescue them," I said. "Just like we're going to rescue my mother."

She looked at me, forcing a smile. "Thank you. I'm glad . . ."

I waited for her to finish but she didn't. "You're glad . . . what?"

"Can't you read my mind?" she asked sadly. "You could before."

"There's got to be a lot of electricity between us," I said.

She looked into my eyes. "And there's not?"

I smiled, restraining my impulse to tic. "That's a different kind."

She put her arms around my neck and laid her head on my shoulder. "What I was going to say was, I'm glad I have you for my boyfriend."

"Me too," I said. "Sometimes I have to pinch myself."

She pinched my arm and smiled. "You're so cute."

We sat there for several minutes, and my thoughts drifted to something I'd been hiding since my first meeting with Hatch. I forgot Taylor could read my mind.

She jerked back, her eyes wide. "Why are you thinking that?"

"Thinking what?"

"You know *what*. About dying."

"It's nothing," I said.

"Dying isn't *nothing*. It's a very big *something*."

"Why were you listening to my thoughts?"

"It just happens. Sometimes I don't even know I'm doing it." She squeezed my hand. "Why were you thinking that?"

"It's just something Hatch said. I don't know if it's even true. . . ."

"What did he tell you?"

"He said four of the other kids have already died from cancer caused by our electricity, and I have more electricity than they did." I looked into her eyes. "He said I might be dying."

Taylor looked as if she didn't know how to respond. "Was he lying?"

"I don't know. You know him better than I do."

Her eyes started to well up with tears. "You can't die, Michael."

"Believe me, it's not something I'm trying to do," I said.

She put her head back on my shoulder, and I held her for several minutes until Ostin barged into the room. "Hey, guys. You'll never guess what I just discovered." He stopped and looked at us. "What's going on?"

Taylor sat up, pulling her hair back from her face. "Nothing," she said, her eyes still red.

"What did you discover?" I asked.

He looked back and forth between us, then said, "I figured out what the ER20 and ER21 are. Dudes, you're never going to believe it."

9

ER20 and ER21

Taylor held my hand as we followed Ostin back into the front room. Everyone was gathered around the computer.

Wade was sitting in a beanbag chair, still looking angry that Jack had left him. "C'mon, already," he said. "What's the big announcement? What's an ER?"

One thing I know about Ostin is that it's impossible for him to just tell you the solution to a problem—he has to tell you *how* he solved the problem. It's annoying sometimes—actually, it's annoying all the time—but I'm pretty sure he can't help it.

Ostin's face was pink with excitement. "So I started searching for ER, ER20, ER21, ER22, but it just led to that old TV series and other stuff. Then I searched the location mentioned in the memo: Puerto Maldonado.

"Puerto Maldonado is a Peruvian city in the Amazon jungle near

Cuzco. The memo said that the outbreak occurred during the rainy season, which is between November and March, so I started to scan through their local newspaper for anything unusual. Look what I found." He clicked a link and an article appeared on the screen. The headline read:

Las Ratas Abrasadoras Destruyen El Pueblo

"Isn't that crazy!" Ostin said.

I looked at him blankly. "What language is that, Spanish?"

"Yeah, unbelievable, isn't it?"

"I wouldn't know; I don't speak Spanish."

"Oh, sorry," Ostin said. "I forgot."

Ostin was born in Austin, Texas (hence his name), where he had a Mexican nanny. Average human babies pick up second languages remarkably fast, but with Ostin's IQ, I'm sure he was reciting Shakespeare in Spanish by the time he was five.

"*Las ratas abrasadoras* is Spanish for 'fiery rats.'"

"What's a fiery rat?" Taylor asked.

"Exactly," Ostin said. "There's no such thing." His voice lowered. "Or is there?" He sounded ridiculously dramatic, like the host of some UFO show on the Discovery Channel. "Check this out," he said, scrolling down the screen. "According to this article, there was a plague of rats in Peru that nearly wiped out a small village. The town's mayor said that the rats started fires everywhere they went."

"What were they doing?" McKenna asked. "Smoking?"

Ostin didn't catch that she was joking. "No, I think they do it the same way you do. Or, at least, Michael and Zeus."

"They're electric?" I asked.

Ostin touched his finger to his nose. "Bingo. One eyewitness said that these rats glowed at night, like they were on fire. And when he tried to kill one with a crowbar, he said '*me dio una descarga como anguila eléctrica.*'"

"Translate," I said.

"It shocked him like an electric eel."

"Like an electric eel?" Ian repeated. "They've discovered a new breed of rat?"

"No," I said. "The Elgen have *made* a new breed of rat. They've electrified rats."

"It makes perfect sense," Ostin said. "They're having trouble creating more electric kids, but they've learned how to make electric rodents."

"Why would they do that?" Taylor asked.

"It was probably just an accident at first," Ostin replied. "I mean, we test everything on rats, right? Drugs, cosmetics, shampoo. Makes sense they were testing rats in the MEI. Voila, electric rats."

"Whoa," I said.

"Yeah, but what are they good for?" Taylor asked.

"That was my next question," Ostin said. "So I scanned the Internet for any other stories about fiery or electric rats. I came up with mentions in Saint Barths, the Cook Islands, and Anguilla." He looked at me, grinning. "Sound familiar?"

"No," I said.

"Remember what we read earlier? That's where the Elgen have built their Starxource plants."

It took me a moment to make the connection. "You mean their power plants are rat powered?"

Ostin was so excited he almost jumped up from his chair. "Exactly!"

"Why rats?" Taylor asked.

"Why not!" Ostin exclaimed. "They're perfect! The problem with most of our current energy sources is what?"

"They're expensive," Taylor said, turning to me. "My dad's always complaining about how much it costs when I leave lights on."

"Yes, but more importantly, they're exhaustible. They're limited. You can't make more oil, unless you can wait around a few hundred million years. Once it's gone, it's gone. The big search is for renewable energy, and the Elgen found it. Actually, they made it. Rats are super-renewable. They're practically breeding machines!

Think about it. Rats are mature at five weeks, their gestation period is just three weeks, and the average litter is eight to ten babies. If you started with just two rats and they had an average of ten offspring every three weeks, then they had babies, and so on, in one year you could have . . ." He did the math in his head. "Holy rodent. Under ideal circumstances and lacking natural predators, like in a laboratory, you could breed *billions* of rats in one year."

"That's crazy," McKenna said.

"And if each one of those rats could generate even a tenth the electricity that one of us does . . . ," I said.

"You could power entire cities," Ostin said. "Enough rats, you could power the entire world."

I shook my head. "They're making rat power. The Elgen are making *rat* power. That's why they're afraid of them escaping. If they breed, anyone could use them."

"They could also be like those killer bees that escaped from South America," McKenna said.

"You mean the band?" Wade asked.

"What band?" McKenna said.

"The Killer Bees."

McKenna shook her head. "I'm not talking about some stupid band."

"She means Africanized bees," Ostin said. "In the fifties some scientists took African bees to Brazil to create a better honeybee, but the African bees escaped and starting breeding with local—"

"Good job, Ostin," I said, cutting him off. "You did it."

"Thanks," he said proudly. "It's amazing, they're creating these power plants and no one knows how they're doing it, but the answer is right in front of them. Apparently the Elgen have a sense of humor after all."

"What do you mean?" I asked.

"The name of their plants . . . Starxource. It makes their power plants sound like they run off thermonuclear fusion, since that's where stars get their energy from." He turned around and looked at me. "But 'star' is just 'rats' spelled backward."

10

An Unplanned Visit

Rat power. In a bizarre way it made sense. Like my mother was fond of saying, "whatever works." The ramifications of this discovery made sense as well. If the world became dependent on Elgen energy, the Elgen would control the world.

"Man, all this thinking has made me hungry," Ostin said. "Where's the pizza?" I was glad to see he had his appetite back. He looked at the clock on the wall. "What's taking them so long?"

"They're probably kissing," Wade said, still bitter about being left behind.

"Hey, wait a minute," Ian said. "Both Hummers are in the drive-way. But they're not in them." His expression fell. "Oh no."

Just then something crashed through the home's front window. Before we could see what it was, there were two loud explosions, and the room was filled with an overpowering stench. My eyes watered

59

and I covered my nose and mouth with my hand and yelled for everyone to run.

Suddenly the door burst open, and a man shouted, "Everyone on the ground. Put your hands in front of you. Do it! Do it now!" He ran inside the front room, flanked by two other guards.

Zeus was the first to react. He extended his hands and blasted the man standing in the doorway, knocking him back against the wall. But before Zeus could hit anyone else, two darts struck him in the side. Zeus cried out and fell to the ground, screaming and writhing in pain. The darts were peculiar looking, fat like a cigar, tapered at one end, and yellow with red stripes.

Elgen guards poured into the room through the front and back doors, shouting as they entered. They were wearing black rubberized jumpsuits with helmets, masks, and gloves, which made them look more like machines than humans. Each of them carried a chrome weapon I'd never seen before. It looked like a handgun, only broader and without the barrel.

I pulsed while Taylor was trying to reboot the guards, but neither of us seemed to have any effect on them. Darts hit us almost simultaneously, one in her chest and one in her knee, and three on me, two hitting me in the side, the third just below my collarbone. We both collapsed, as if our bones had suddenly turned to rubber. The experience was similar to what we felt when Nichelle, one of Hatch's electric kids, would use her powers to drain the electricity out of us. Except this new machine was even worse.

I began to shake uncontrollably, and I wondered if I was having a heart attack. A moment later a man wearing a purple uniform walked in through the front door. He was followed by a guard nearly six inches taller than him. The guard in purple held an electronic tablet, which he studied as he approached Zeus.

"Frank," he said to Zeus.

"I'm Zeus," Zeus said.

"Yes," the man said. "Dr. Hatch said you suffered from delusions of grandeur. You know he's looking forward to your reunion. He has something very special in mind for you. He said a pool party was in order."

Zeus turned pale.

I looked over to see Ostin on the ground with one of the guards standing above him. The guard's boot was on Ostin's neck, pushing his face into the carpet. There were four darts in Ostin's back. "Captain, the darts don't work on him," the guard shouted.

"Idiot, he's not electric," the captain replied.

"What do I do with them?"

"Same as the ugly kid over there," he said, pointing at Wade. "Take them to the van."

The captain walked over to Ian, who had three darts in him. He was on his knees and holding his side. "So you're Ian," the captain said. "How's the vision?"

"Perfect," Ian said defiantly, turning toward the man's voice.

"Really? Perfect?"

"Yeah, I can't see your ugly face."

He kicked Ian in the stomach. Ian fell to his side, gasping.

"Too bad you didn't see that coming." He shouted to the guards, "Get them all into the van. Move it!"

At least Jack and Abi got away, I thought.

The captain looked over at Taylor and me, then walked up to Taylor, his stooge following closely behind him. "You must be Taylor," he said, looking her in the eyes. "The reason we wear these uncomfortable helmets. Let's remedy that." He turned to his guard. "Belt."

"Here, sir," he said, handing the captain a long strap with blinking green LEDs.

He cinched the belt over Taylor's head and chin. It looked like some kind of orthodontic headgear except with a lot of wires and lights. Taylor gasped. "It hurts."

"Does it?" he asked. He shouted to the guards who were still in the room, "You can take your helmets off now." Then he grabbed Taylor by the chin and forced her to look at him. "I heard Tara had a carbon copy."

"I'm nothing like her," Taylor said, wincing in pain.

"You're just as beautiful as she is." He ran his finger across her face.

"Don't touch her, you creep," I said.

The man turned to me, his eyes narrowing with contempt. "And you must be the famous Mr. Vey. Dr. Hatch was very specific about you." He touched something on the tablet he was carrying, and the pain in my body increased. I screamed out, gasping for air. If you have dental fillings and have chewed aluminum foil, you have an idea what it felt like—except spread throughout my whole body.

"Stop it!" Taylor shouted. "Please."

I rolled over onto my back, struggling for breath. The pain continued to pulse through my body—a wild, agonizing throb followed by a sharp, crisp sting. "Stop it!" I shouted.

"I don't take orders from little boys."

After another thirty seconds Taylor screamed, "Please stop it! Please. You're killing him. I'll do whatever you want."

"Don't be dramatic, sweetie. I'm not killing him. I'm just making him wish he were dead. Dr. Hatch gave us instructions to bring him back alive—like an animal to be put in a zoo. And yes, Miss Ridley, you *will* do whatever I want."

He pushed something on the tablet and the pain eased. "There's an app for everything these days, isn't there?" He looked at me. "We underestimated you, Mr. Vey. But it won't happen again. Trust me, there are worse things in this world than Cell 25."

11

The Ride to the Airport

I was carried by a guard out to the backyard, where the guards had parked their truck—a large van emblazoned with the name of a moving company. The darts were still in me, and the guards had special hooks with which they secured them. I don't know what the darts were, but they seemed to suck the life out of me, twisting my thoughts with pain.

Everything seemed to be happening around me in quick, staccato flashes, like I was surfing TV channels with a remote.

I saw Ian being dragged off by three men. McKenna was crying. Ostin had a bloody nose and was calling a guard a dumb gorilla. Two guards were standing near the garage taking pictures of the Hummers. I heard their conversation, or at least some of it—one guard was asking the other where we'd gotten the cars.

My mind flashed, and I remembered that Ian had said both Hummers were in the garage—where were Jack and Abigail? Then I noticed three pizza boxes on the ground.

Connected to the back of the truck was a motorized platform that the guards used to lift us into the cargo bay. The inside of the truck looked like a laboratory and was filled with long rows of blinking diodes and pale green monitors. On one side of the truck were horizontal cots, stacked above one another like shelves. Zeus and Ian were already strapped down on the bottom two cots.

On the opposite side of the truck was a white, rubber-coated bench with rubber shackles every three or four feet.

Jack and Abigail were both strapped to the bench, their arms fastened above their heads, with belts across their waists, thighs, and calves. Abigail was crying, and I could see that Jack was bleeding from his nose and forehead. He hadn't gone without a fight.

On both sides, near the center of the truck, were narrow, locker-like cabinets. Behind those was a console with digital readouts and rows of switches and more flashing lights. A guard was seated at the console, watching as we were brought in. Waiting for us.

One of the guards pulled a cot out like a drawer, and I was laid on it, then strapped down at my ankles, waist, chest, and arms. Last, a wire was fastened around my neck, holding me fast and making it difficult to breathe.

"C is connected," a guard shouted to the man near the console.

Through my peripheral vision I saw the man push a lever and I immediately felt a tingling in my neck followed by stinging pain throughout my body. I felt nauseous, as if I might throw up, but fought the urge.

"C is active," the man in back said. The guard pushed my cot toward the wall, into its slot. The empty cot above me was only six inches from my nose.

"What's this?" a guard said, holding up my cell phone.

"I got it off him," the other said. "It's dead. Take it back to the lab."

They stowed the phone in one of the cabinets. My mind was still racing, trying to figure everything out. Breathing was a challenge. Escape was impossible. Almost everything in the back of the truck was coated in plastic or rubber, which I figured was so we couldn't short things out.

Wade and Ostin were secured next to Abigail and Jack on the long bench across from me, their hands strapped over their heads. Taylor was brought in next and bound to the cot above me. I could hear her crying as they tied her down. The sound of her in pain hurt as much as the machine I was connected to.

"B is connected," the guard said.

Taylor moaned.

"B is active," the man in back said.

"What about them?" one of the guards said, walking up with McKenna and Grace. "They're electric."

"They're harmless," the voice said. "Put them on the bench."

McKenna and Grace were strapped to the bench, their arms lifted above their heads like the others'.

When we were all secured, the overhead door was brought down, leaving the truck illuminated in an eerie, greenish glow. Two guards were still with us, one sitting on a short bench across from Ostin while the other walked to the front of the cargo hold and disappeared through a door to the cab. The engine started up and the truck shook, then lurched forward, swinging everyone on the bench to one side.

I felt drugged. It took effort to maintain consciousness.

"Taylor," I groaned, the effort taking almost everything I had.

"Shut up!" the guard shouted, which, in my state, seemed to echo a dozen times between my ears.

Taylor never answered. I could hear Zeus breathing heavily below me. No one spoke. I felt like we were being driven to an execution, which was possible.

After a few minutes of silence, the guard stood up from his bench and walked over to the cots, squatting down next to Zeus.

"Hey, stinky. Remember me? It's your buddy Wes? I used to be on the electric children detail. I bet you're glad to see me again."

Zeus said nothing.

"Well, I'm excited to see you. I've waited a long, long time for our reunion—to catch up on old times. Maybe you remember when you and Bryan thought it would be really funny to shock me when I was in the shower?"

Zeus still didn't speak.

"Yeah, I'm sure you remember. How could you forget something that hilarious? Unfortunately, I almost forgot about it because of the concussion I got from hitting my head on the tile. And then I got distracted by the surgery it took to fix the slipped disk in my back. Not that they really fixed it, I still have chronic back pain. But no big deal, right? Everyone had a good laugh." His voice dripped with venom. "I guess we just don't go well together, stinky. That happens, you know? Some things don't go well together. Like, say, oil and water. They just don't mix." He turned around to the cabinets and brought something out. "Or should I say Zeus and water."

I caught a glimpse of what he'd taken from the cabinet. It was a child's plastic squirt gun.

"I brought this especially for our time together. Our special reunion. Oh, look at you. You look scared. What are you, a baby? It's just a tiny, little squirt gun. What harm could that do?"

He pulled the trigger and a stream of water showered on Zeus. I heard the crisp sparking of electricity. "Aaaagh," Zeus groaned.

"Oh, come on. It's just water, stinky. It's about time you bathed. You smell like an outhouse." He sprayed again. There was a louder snap, and Zeus cried out this time. He was panting heavily and moaning in pain.

"Ah, the stench. How do you live with yourself? Or don't pigs smell themselves. Maybe you like your own stink."

He sprayed again. Zeus sobbed. "Please . . ."

"Please? You want more?"

"Hey, be cool," Ian said.

"Shut your mouth, mole boy, or I'll turn up your RESAT." He leaned in toward Zeus. "Do you remember what you said to me after I got out of the hospital? You said, 'C'mon, Wes, where's your sense of humor?'" He began pulling the trigger over and over.

Zeus let out a bloodcurdling scream.

"C'mon, Zeus, where's your sense of humor?"

Zeus's screams rose higher still.

"Not so funny now, is it?" he shouted over Zeus's screams.

"Stop it!" Abigail yelled.

The man looked back at her. "Stay out of this, sweet cheeks."

"Please," she said. "Please. I'll take away your pain."

"What?"

"I'll take away your pain, if you'll leave him alone."

Wes stared at her, wondering if she was telling him the truth. "If this is a joke . . ."

"It's what she does," Ostin said. "She stimulates nerve endings. She can take away pain."

"I'll help you," she said. "Please stop hurting him."

Wes turned back to Zeus, then spit on him, which also elicited a sizzling spark. Then he walked back to the bench where Abigail was sitting.

"If this is a trick, I guarantee you'll wish you were never born."

"I can't hurt you," Abigail said. "I wouldn't if I could."

He studied her expression, then sat down next to her. "What do I do?"

"I need to touch you. If you unlock my hands . . ."

"That ain't gonna happen, baby face."

"Then put where it hurts next to me. Anywhere."

"Your knee?"

She nodded.

He crouched on the floor next to her, his back pressed up against her. After a moment he sighed. "Wow. I'm going to have a talk with Hatch about keeping you around."

Zeus was still whimpering below me, but Abigail had probably saved his life.

The truck continued on, but with few stops, which made me believe we were on the freeway. I turned my head as far as I could to look at the others. McKenna and Jack were shackled directly across from me. What was this thing I'd been hooked to? My body and my mind ached. My heart ached too, but that was my own doing. *What did I get my friends into? How could I have been so stupid to believe some stranger on a cell phone?*

Suddenly McKenna seemed to blur. It may have been sweat running down my forehead into my eyes, but something about her was different. Her skin color was changing. Was I hallucinating? Ostin looked at me, then he glanced over at McKenna. He got a strange expression on his face, and I wondered if he saw it too.

Ostin looked over at the guard, then suddenly began singing. "Ninety-nine bottles of beer on the wall. Ninety-nine bottles of beer. Take one down. Pass it around. Ninety-eight—"

"Shut up," the guard said.

Ostin swallowed. "Just thought . . ."

"Shut up."

Ostin clenched his jaw. He looked down for a moment as if thinking, then he said to the guard, "Those new gizmos you have rock. What do you call them?"

The guard didn't answer. But he didn't tell him to shut up either.

"Sorry, I didn't realize they don't tell you these things. Probably top secret. For the important guys . . ."

"It's a RESAT," the guard said.

Ostin nodded. "RESAT. Cool."

I looked back over at McKenna. I wasn't seeing things—her skin color really *was* changing. She was now almost glowing red. Ostin must have seen what she was doing and was trying to keep the guard distracted. I looked back at Ostin, who was nodding, carefully manipulating the guard.

"Clever. Clever indeed. RESAT is 'Taser' spelled backward."

The man suddenly scratched his chin. "I never thought of that."

"I'm sure you would have," Ostin said. "If they didn't work you so hard. I bet they work you like a rented mule."

"You got that right, cheeseball."

At that moment McKenna's arms melted through the bands. She was free.

"But I bet you get great health benefits with all those Elgen doctors around."

"You kiddin' me?" the guard said. "The dental plan has a five-hundred-dollar deductible."

"You're pulling my leg," Ostin said loudly. "Why even have it? That's a whole head of cavities."

"It's a joke," the man said.

McKenna slowly reached over and grabbed Jack's bands, immediately melting through them. Jack slowly lowered his arms, rubbing his wrists. Suddenly the guard started to look back. Jack put his hands up again.

"Hey!" Ostin shouted.

The guard stopped.

"Do you have kids?"

"What?"

"Kids. Rug rats, spawn, you got them?"

"No."

"Sorry, of course not. I'm sure you're married to your job. If you had kids, the dental thing might still be worth it."

"Family isn't allowed," the guard said. "It's a regulation."

"They regulate that, huh?" Ostin said. "You know, there's something I can't figure out."

Jack reached down and unclasped his legs, then slowly inched down the bench toward the weapons cabinet.

"What?" the man asked.

"I can't figure out how you'd go about getting hired for a job like yours. It's not like you could post it in the Help Wanted section."

"I can't talk about that," he said.

"I mean, what kind of ad would that be? Wanted: ugly, mean, smelly dudes with below-average IQs to kidnap and abuse teenagers."

The guy's mouth fell.

"What section would that be under anyway? Creepy Dudes?

The man scowled. "You watch it, you smart-mouthed little—"

"Actually," Ostin said, "you should watch it."

"What the—"

Jack cracked the guard over the head with a truncheon, knocking him out with one blow. The guard slumped to the van's floor.

"Man, that felt good," Jack said, stretching out his arms like a baseball player at bat.

"Not to him," Ostin said.

McKenna walked over to Ostin, who looked at her with admiration. "That was cool," he said.

"Careful, don't touch me," she said, kneeling on the bench next to him. "I'm still pretty hot."

"Yeah, you are *hot*," Ostin said, sounding smitten.

McKenna grinned a little as she grabbed Ostin's armbands and melted through them. "There you go."

"Like buttah . . . ," Ostin said, stretching his arm. He bent over and unclasped his stomach and leg belts. "Let's free Michael."

"We've got to take care of this guy," Jack said, standing above the guard, with the club.

"Let me loose," Wade said. "I'll help you."

Jack unloosed his bands, and they lifted the guard up and strapped him to the wall while McKenna and Ostin unfastened my collar. The intense pain immediately stopped, and I groaned with relief, though I still felt as dizzy as if I'd just ridden the teacups ride at Disneyland for an hour.

"Well done, McKenna," I said.

"Thanks."

As I climbed out of the cot, Ostin and McKenna unstrapped Taylor, then Ian and Zeus. I helped Taylor climb out, then Ian. Zeus hadn't moved. He was still in a lot of pain from the guard's torture. "Can I help you?" I asked.

"Just give me a minute," he said, rolling over in the cot.

"You okay, buddy?" I asked.

"Been better," he said. His skin was blistered where the guard had sprayed water on him. "I don't know what that new dart thing is," he said. "But it's like Nichelle in a can."

"That's exactly what it is," Ostin said. "The Elgen must have found a way to replicate her powers without her weakness."

"How's your vision?" I asked Ian.

"It's back," he said.

Across the aisle Jack unloosed Abigail. "Thank you," she said softly.

"You're going to be okay," he said. "I'll get you out of here. I promise."

As Jack freed Grace, Abigail knelt at Zeus's side. She put her hand on him and closed her eyes. After a moment he relaxed and stilled. "Thank you for stopping him," he said.

"You're welcome," she said.

I was leaning against the opposite wall, holding my head and trying not to throw up.

Taylor laid her hand on my back. "You okay?"

"Alive. How about you?"

"Me too," she said hoarsely. "I wonder where they're taking us."

"We just passed a sign for the airport," Ian said.

"What's our situation with guards?" I asked.

"There are two guards driving this truck, one Escalade in front, two behind us."

"How many guards in the Escalades?"

"Four in front, five and four in back."

"We need to take charge of the van," I said.

"Then what?" Ian said. "We can't outrun the Escalades. Not in this whale."

"We don't need to," Jack said. "We'll crush them. I saw this in a movie once. But first we need to commandeer this bad boy."

"That's a good word," Ostin said. "Commandeer."

Jack looked at him. "What? You don't think I know any big words?"

Ostin withered. "Sorry."

"Anyone got a plan?" I asked.

"I say we just storm the cab," Jack said. "Commando-style."

"Too risky," I said. "They'll crash."

Ostin's face lit up. "I have an idea," he said. "A good one, with three parts."

"Three parts?" I said. "That was fast."

"Yes. This is going to be epic," he said.

12

Riding the Whale

A couple of minutes later McKenna casually opened the door to the truck's dark cab. "Excuse me, guys. Can we stop to use the bathroom?"

Both men glanced back, their eyes wide with surprise.

"What are you—"

McKenna shouted, "Now!" All of us covered our eyes as she flashed to her full extent. A brilliant light filled the entire truck. Both men shouted and put their hands over their eyes. Jack and Wade rushed the cab, bringing clubs down over the guards' heads.

Jack knocked the driver out, but Wade only succeeded in dazing the other, so I put my hand on the guard's neck and pulsed, which took care of him. Wade and I climbed over the seat, and I held the wheel while Jack pulled the unconscious guard out of the way, then climbed behind the wheel.

"That was easy," Jack said, pressing down on the accelerator.

Zeus, Taylor, Ian, and McKenna dragged the men to the back of the truck and I used the van's passenger-side mirror to watch the two cars behind us. I hoped the other guards hadn't noticed the flash, but I was certain they had to have noticed our change in speed. This was confirmed ten seconds later when a voice came over the van's radio.

"Elgen Two, this is Elgen One. Are you having mechanical problems? Over."

I looked at Jack. "Don't answer."

"Wasn't planning on it," he said. "Time for phase two. We've got an exit a mile ahead of us, I'm going for it." He hit the gas, moving up quickly on the Escalade in front of us. I climbed back over the seat to see what was going on in the rear.

The two guards had been strapped to the wall, next to the guard Wes, who was now awake. "You're gonna pay for this!" he shouted angrily.

"Shut up, Wes," Zeus said fiercely. Then he blasted him. The guard's head jerked back so hard against the wall he knocked himself out again.

"Everyone, buckle up!" I shouted. "We're going for phase two!"

"Phase two!" Ostin shouted. "Everyone in place!"

Everyone sat down, strapping the waist belts around themselves. I went back up front and buckled myself into the passenger seat. "Ready," I said.

"Half mile," Jack said. "If this doesn't work, prepare for some crazy driving."

"Better work," I said. "We've only got a few seconds to hit phase three, so be ready. Everyone's strapped in."

"There's our exit," Jack said. "Hold on tight." He hit the gas. In spite of the van's size, it lurched forward, and Jack swerved into the lane left of the lead Escalade. We pulled up to the car's side, and I could see the guards looking at us with surprise.

"Here goes," Jack said. He spun the wheel to the right, forcing the moving van into the side of the Escalade. His timing was perfect as he pushed the car directly into the barrier between the exit and the freeway. The car smashed into the railing at nearly seventy-five miles per hour, flipping the car end over end.

Jack was grinning. "Just like Grand Theft Auto. Only better."

I unbuckled and climbed to the back. "Ian!" I shouted. "Are we good?"

"They're thirty feet behind us!" he shouted.

"Now, Taylor."

Taylor put her head down and concentrated on rebooting the driver of the car behind us.

"You got him," Ian said.

I braced myself against the wall. "Jack, now!'

Jack slammed on the brakes as hard as he could. There was a big jolt as the Escalade plowed into the van, followed by a second hit, when the rear Escalade plowed into the first. The force of the wreck jarred us, pushing our van partially sideways. All the lights in the back went out. Jack hit the gas again, pulling ahead of the collision.

"The first car is toast!" Ian shouted. "It's crumpled!"

"How bad are we?" Jack shouted over his shoulder.

"Not sure," Ian said, looking down. "But I see sparks." The truck was vibrating and there was a sound of something scraping. "Something's dragging. I think it's the lift."

"What about the second car?" I asked Ian.

"We're good . . . wait." His expression changed. "No way."

"What?" I asked.

"It's still running. They're coming after us."

"Jack, the second car survived the crash!" I shouted.

"I can see him in my mirror!" Jack shouted. He sounded worried.

"He's got a big gun," Ian said. "He's aiming it at us." He looked around. "Everyone on the ground. Now!"

Everyone unbuckled and dropped to the floor.

Jack shouted, "We can't outrun him. Are there any guns back there?"

"McKenna, we need light," I said.

She lit up the back of the van.

Taylor and I crawled to the cabinets and looked through them. "Nothing. Just those RESAT things."

"This just keeps getting better!" Jack shouted. "Hold on, kids!" He swerved to the right, and we all tumbled to the other side of the van. Bullets began ripping through the van.

"Ian, what's going on out there?"

"Nothing good. They've got a cannon-looking thing."

"A what?"

Suddenly we heard the gun again, though nothing came through the walls this time. The truck dropped and began veering.

"They shot out our tires!" Jack shouted. "Someone think of something."

"Taylor!" I shouted. "Can you reboot them?"

"It won't work," Ian said. "They've put their helmets back on." His brow furrowed. "What kind of gun is that?"

Ostin crawled to the back and looked out through a bullet hole in the back door. "It's an antitank gun," he said. "They'll blow us sky-high."

The truck dropped again as we lost another tire, and Jack swerved wildly trying to keep the vehicle under control. "Someone better think of something fast!" Jack shouted.

A voice came over the radio. "You've got ten seconds to pull the van over, or we will blow you up. Do you understand?"

"Don't say anything," Wade said. "They won't shoot us."

The voice returned. "Ten, nine, eight, seven . . ."

I looked over at Taylor, then took her hand.

Jack shouted back, "What do I do?"

"Four, three, two . . ."

"Pull over—" I started to yell, but before I could finish there was a loud explosion.

"Holy cow!" Ian yelled.

I looked around. We were all there. The walls were still there. The van was still there. "What was that?"

Ian was just staring at the back door in awe, shaking his head. "The Escalade . . ." He stopped in midsentence.

"Did you guys see that?" Jack shouted from the front. "That thing blew up like a bomb!"

"What blew up?" I asked.

"The Escalade. It, like, disintegrated. It's just a big ball of fire."

"What caused that?"

"I have no idea," Jack replied. "But I am *not* complaining."

"Good driving, man," I said. "Now get us off the freeway. Let's get out of this beast."

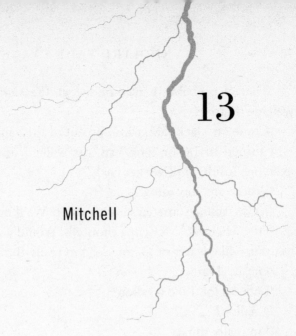

13

Mitchell

Jack pulled off at the next exit and drove to the far side of a Flying J truck stop. A long row of trucks was parked next to the mini-mart, and Jack parked the crippled van between two long semis and shut off the engine.

Jack smiled at me as I walked up to the front. "Just another day in the life of a superhero," he said.

I grinned. "You're having fun, aren't you?"

"As long as we're winning, bro," Jack said. "As long as we're winning."

"We've got to find somewhere safe to finish uploading Grace's info," I said. "Any ideas?"

Jack thought for a moment, then said, "I know where we can go. Do you still have that phone?"

"It doesn't dial out," I said. "Besides, I'm sure the Elgen would be listening in on it if it did."

"There's probably a pay phone at the mini-mart," Ostin said, walking up to us.

"Come on," Jack said, climbing out of the van.

I turned to Taylor, who had just walked up to the front. "Keep everyone inside until we get back."

"Where are you going?"

"Jack's calling someone to pick us up. We'll be right back."

"Hey, Michael!" McKenna shouted. "Would you get me something to drink—like water or Gatorade? I'm really thirsty."

"Got it," I said.

"I need a lot. Like a gallon."

"A gallon?"

"I'm really thirsty."

By the time I got out of the truck, Jack and Wade were already standing next to a pay phone outside of the truck stop. As I approached I heard Jack say, "I don't have time to tell you right now. Just shut up and listen. . . . I'll tell you when you get here. Get your mom's Suburban and come to the Flying J truck stop off I-Eighty-Four West. It's just south of Meridian. You can't miss it. . . . Hurry. Yes, I know it's late. Yes, Wade is with me. . . . Because you weren't invited, that's why. Consider yourself lucky. Now hurry. . . . No, I told you, bring the Suburban. . . . There's a bunch of us. I said I'll tell you when you get here." Jack hung up the phone. "Man, what a baby."

"Who was that?" I asked.

"Mitchell," Wade said.

"He's mad we left him," Jack said. "He has no idea what he missed."

"Lucky him," Wade said.

"Does Mitchell have a computer?" I asked.

"Mitchell has everything," Wade said, shaking his head. "His old man's loaded."

"He'll be here in fifteen," Jack said.

"I'm going inside the truck stop," I said. "McKenna needs something to drink. We might as well get something to eat. Everyone's starving."

"Yeah, the pizza didn't quite make it," Jack said.

Fortunately the guards hadn't taken my money. The three of us went inside the mini-mart, and I grabbed a plastic tote and filled it with six bottles of water and a six-pack of Gatorade. I also got two boxes of powdered jelly doughnuts, licorice, and a handful of Power-Bars while Wade put together a dozen hot dogs. Jack grabbed a bag of beef jerky and pork rinds.

We paid for the food, then brought it back to the van. Jack stayed outside to wait for Mitchell while Wade and I carried everything in through the front cab.

"Thank goodness," Ostin said as we came in. I handed him the box of doughnuts. He tore it open, shoved a doughnut in his mouth, coughed from the powdered sugar, then grabbed a second doughnut and passed the box along to Ian.

McKenna took two bottles of Gatorade from me and, to all of our surprise, downed both of them, stopping only twice to breathe. After she'd emptied both bottles she sighed with relief. "Sorry. Heating up dehydrates me like crazy."

I sat down on the bench and opened my licorice. I offered some to Taylor.

"Thanks," she said, taking a strand. She pulled her knees up to her chest. "So what's going on?"

"Jack called his friend Mitchell. He's coming to pick us up."

"Then what?"

"We'll hide out at his place until we've uploaded the rest of Grace's information. Once we know where my mother is, we'll make our plan."

"What if there's no information about her?"

I frowned. "I don't know. I have to hope there is."

"Hey," shouted a voice from the back of the truck. "How about some water?"

It was the guard Wes. Zeus stood up, carrying one of the bottles with him. "You want some water, Wes?"

The guard looked at Zeus in horror. Zeus poured what was left in his bottle over the guard's head. The guard sputtered a little as it washed over his nose and mouth.

"See, Wes. I haven't lost my sense of humor," Zeus said, electricity sparking between his hands. "And I'm going to prove it to you."

The guard's eyes widened.

"Zeus," I said.

Zeus looked back at me.

"Don't."

"What? You didn't see what he did to me?"

"Yeah, I did." I looked Wes in the face. "It was cruel. But we're not like them. We're better than them."

"Maybe you are," Zeus said. "But I'm not." He lifted his hands, and Wes shut his eyes, preparing to be shocked. But it never happened. Zeus had caught sight of Abigail, who looked horrified. Zeus sighed. "All right," he said. "All right." He looked at the guard. "You're lucky these guys are better than us."

I leaned back on the bench, closing my eyes.

"What's that?" Ostin asked.

"What's what?"

"That." He pointed to my butt.

Taylor started laughing as she pulled something off me. It was a refrigerator magnet in the shape of an Idaho Spud with the words IDAHO COUCH POTATO printed across it. "How is that sticking to you?" she said.

"Wait," I said, taking it back from her. I put it on my stomach. It stuck. Then she peeled it off me and placed it against my cheek. It stuck there too.

"Wow," Taylor said. "You're like a magnet."

Ostin stared in amazement. "Not *like*. He *is* a magnet. Doesn't surprise me with all that electricity running through him."

"But I've had electricity in me my whole life. Why am I suddenly magnetic, too?"

"You must still be getting more electric."

The words hit me like a bucket of ice water. I felt as if I'd just been told I had less time to live.

"But why is he becoming magnetic?" Taylor asked.

Ostin rubbed his chin. "Let's see," he said slowly. "How do I explain this to a cheerleader?"

Taylor bristled. "How would you like a *cheerleader* to permanently scramble your brain?"

"No, don't!" Ostin said, holding his hands in front of him as if he could block her waves.

"She's not going to do that," I said.

"Don't count on it," Taylor said.

Ostin still looked terrified. "I'm sorry. I won't do it again."

I shook my head. "Just explain the magnetism."

"Okay," he said. "It works like this. Electric currents are magnetic. When you coil an electrical current around a core, the magnetism becomes stronger. In your case, your body is the core, and as you have millions of nerves and veins, which are carrying your electricity, it creates a massive coil. So it makes sense that you're becoming magnetic."

"Great. So now I'm going to have things sticking to me?"

"Like me," Taylor said, taking my hand.

I couldn't help but smile.

Just then Jack shouted through the front door, "Come on, our ride is here!"

"What do we do with the guards?" Taylor asked.

"Leave them," I said.

"Tied up?"

"Yeah. Someone will find them eventually."

Outside, Mitchell was standing next to Jack, watching everyone climb out of the truck. "Who are all these people?"

"Friends of mine," Jack said.

He pointed at me. "You're the kid who shocked us."

"His name is Michael," Jack said.

He turned back to Jack. "You took him instead of me?"

"Listen, Mitch. I'll tell you what's going on later. But right now we've got to get out of here before they find us."

"Before *who* finds you?" Mitchell asked.

"I'll tell you when we get to your house."

"We're going to my house?"

"Yeah. We need a place to hide out for a few days. Are your parents home?"

"They're never home."

A large FedEx truck pulled in next to us.

"We gotta go, Mitch," Jack said. "C'mon, everyone. Get in."

Jack and Mitchell climbed in the front, and Jack rolled down the window. "Hey, Abi. Want to sit up here?"

She smiled at him. "Thanks, but I better sit next to Zeus. He's still in pain."

"Right," Jack said, sounding disappointed.

"I'll sit up front," Wade said. "The three amigos ride again."

"Nah," Jack said. "You're too big. How about you, Grace?"

She shrugged. "Sure."

Zeus opened the tailgate and climbed into the narrow space between the backseat and the door. Abigail walked up next to him. "Do you mind if I sit here with you?"

His eyes brightened. "No, of course not." He scooted back as Abigail climbed in.

As I shut the tailgate, I noticed that two truck drivers were standing in the dark near the back of the van, examining the shredded lift. One of them pointed to the bullet holes.

"Really, it's time to go, guys," I said, climbing into the middle seat with Ian and Taylor. Ostin, Wade, and McKenna were in the row behind us.

"Hit it," Jack said.

Mitchell pulled out of the truck stop and headed east toward the freeway.

As we were climbing the freeway on-ramp, I said, "Hey, McKenna saved the day back there. Give it up for McKenna."

Everyone clapped.

"Thanks," McKenna said. "But everyone helped. Ostin distracted the guard."

"Thanks," Ostin said, looking pretty pleased. "I just saw an oppor—"

"And how about Jack's driving?" Taylor said, interrupting Ostin's speech.

"All in a day's work," Jack said.

Ostin turned to McKenna. "That really was awesome how you did that. How hot can you get?"

"At the Elgen laboratory they measured me at about two thousand Kelvin."

"Holy cannoli," Ostin said. "Two thousand Kelvin!"

"Who's Kelvin?" Wade asked.

Ostin rolled his eyes. "Kelvin is a thermodynamic temperature scale. Two thousand Kelvin is more than three thousand degrees Fahrenheit. That's almost twice as hot as fire." He turned back to McKenna. "You *are* hot. In more ways than one."

"Thanks," she said, smiling.

I didn't have to turn back to know Ostin was blushing.

"So much for your 'voice,'" Jack said.

I frowned. "I know. I'm sorry, everyone. He seemed legit."

"I believed him too," Taylor said.

"I would have put money on it," Ostin said. "I mean, it still makes no sense. Why would they have gone to the trouble of getting us cars, leaving money for us, and then attacking us? Why didn't they just trap us at the salon or along the road?"

"Maybe it was too public," Taylor said.

"True," I said. "But they could have attacked us when we got the cars. There was no one around."

Ostin added, "And those guards acted like they'd never seen your cell phone before."

"And why did they ask where we got the Hummers?" Abigail said.

"What are you guys talking about?" Mitchell asked.

"You have no idea how much you don't know," Jack said.

14

Special Delivery

It was nearly midnight when we reached Mitchell's house. Even though Wade had said that Mitchell's dad was "loaded," I didn't realize just how well-off his family was until I saw his place. He lived in a massive, well-lit two-story Colonial-style house with tall gothic columns in front, wings on each side, and a cobblestone driveway that wound past a carefully manicured yard up to a fountain and front door.

"This is Mitchell's house?" I said.

"It looks like the White House," Ostin said.

"Is the butler going to answer the door?" McKenna said.

"We don't have a butler," Mitchell said. "He quit."

Jack said, "We're going to be hanging out in the pool house."

"You have a pool?" Ostin asked.

"He's got a pool *and* a pool house," Wade replied.

There was a four-car garage to the side of the house, and Mitchell opened the third door by remote and pulled in. When the door had shut behind us, Mitchell said to Jack, "Okay, what's going on? You said you'd tell me."

"Let's go inside first," Jack said. "We don't know if we were followed."

Mitchell looked afraid. "Who's following you?"

"Bad people you don't want to meet," Jack said.

"They won't come here, will they?"

"Only if they find out we're here," Grace said.

Mitchell turned to Jack. "She's kidding, right?"

Jack shook his head. "Nope."

We got out of the car, and I opened the tailgate for Zeus and Abigail. As they got out, Zeus put his hand on Abigail's back. "Thanks, Abi."

She smiled. "Anytime."

Jack was standing on the other side of the car looking at them. I could tell he was bothered.

"This way," Mitchell said. "The pool house is in back."

The pool house was located behind the main home, next to a large barbecue area with an atrium and a rock fountain. The backyard looked like something out of a *Better Homes and Gardens* magazine. I didn't know Idaho even had places like that.

The house had an electric keypad entry, and Mitchell pressed a few buttons, then pushed open the door. Inside, we all looked around in amazement.

"Your pool house is bigger than my whole house," Taylor said. "Way bigger."

The pool house was two stories high with a loft and an outdoor balcony. Mitchell gave us a quick tour. On the main floor was a large, open dining room, kitchen, bathroom, master bedroom, and two guest rooms. Upstairs, in the loft, was a television room with a fifty-one-inch plasma TV, two beanbag chairs, a long, wraparound sofa, and a foosball table. On the far side of the room, past the sofa, were two bedrooms connected by a bathroom. The walls were covered with paintings of lighthouses.

"It even smells good," Abigail said. "Like flowers."

"I could live here," Taylor said, still looking around.

"It's almost as nice as the academy," Zeus said.

"That would depend on which floor of the academy you're talking about," Ian said. Abigail and McKenna nodded in agreement.

"There are extra quilts, pillows, and sleeping bags in that closet," Mitchell said.

"The girls can sleep up here," I said. "We can stay downstairs."

"We only need two rooms," Taylor said. "Grace and I can share a room and McKenna and Abigail can take the other."

"I can sleep on the couch up here," Zeus said.

"That's okay," Jack said. "That's Wade's and my spot." He glanced over at Abigail, and she smiled at him.

Zeus looked back and forth between the two. "Whatever, dude."

"Anyone hungry?" Taylor asked. "That hot dog was gross."

"Can we order pizza again?" Grace said. "Maybe we'll get to eat it this time."

"I don't think we need to," Ian said with a curious expression.

"Why is that?" I asked.

He raised his hand. "Wait for it . . ."

A doorbell rang.

Mitchell looked at him quizzically. "That was the main house doorbell. How did you know it was going to ring?"

"Psychic," he said.

"Who is it?" I asked Ian.

"Pizza delivery. The guy has like six boxes."

"Did you order pizza?" Jack asked Mitchell.

"No," Mitchell said. "I didn't even know you were coming."

"Everyone better hide," I said. "Ian, Zeus, Ostin, and I will check this out. Mitchell, it's your house. You better get the door."

"I better come too," Jack said.

"No, you and Taylor should stay back with the rest in case it's another trap. They'll need you."

The doorbell rang again as we walked past the pool and in through the main house's back door.

"He's alone," Ian said. "It looks clean."

"How are you doing this?" Mitchell asked.

"I told you," Ian said with a grin. "I'm psychic."

Ian, Zeus, Ostin, and I ducked into Mitchell's father's office next to the front door, where we could see Mitchell but not the delivery-man. Zeus raised his hands, electricity snapping between his fingers.

"Take it easy," I said.

"Just being prepared," he replied.

Mitchell glanced over at us nervously, then opened the door. "Hey."

"Got your pizza," the voice said. "Also your garlic-cheese bread, a cinnamon dessert pizza, and two liters of soda."

"We didn't order any pizza," Mitchell said.

There was a pause. "Isn't this 2724 Preston Street? The Manchester residence?"

"Yeah. That's us."

"Then it's your pizza. And it's already been paid for. Except my tip. And this stuff was heavy."

"All right," Mitchell said, pulling out his wallet. "Just set them there."

We all moved back from the door as the guy stepped in and laid the stack of boxes on the foyer table. The deliveryman wasn't what I expected—he looked older than my mom and had hair longer than Taylor's. There were six boxes in all. Mitchell handed him a bill.

"Thanks," the man said as he walked out.

Mitchell shut the door. I watched out the window as the guy got in his car and drove off.

"Anything look suspicious in the car?" I asked Ian as we walked out to the foyer.

"No. It's a mess."

"Who do you think sent the pizza?" Zeus asked.

Just then something started to buzz in one of the boxes. "What's that?" Mitchell asked.

"It's a bomb!" Ostin shouted.

"Hit the deck!" Mitchell yelled, dropping to the ground.

Zeus, Ian, and I just stood there.

"It's not a bomb," Ian said. "It's a phone. Second box from the bottom."

Mitchell looked up from the floor. "How do you do that?"

Zeus lifted the top pizzas off, and I opened the box and took out the buzzing phone. It was identical to the one I'd received from the woman at the tanning salon.

"Are you going to answer it?" Ostin asked.

"Do you think I should?"

He shrugged. "Your call. Literally."

I pushed the answer button, then held the phone to my ear. "Hello?"

"Michael. It's me." It was the *voice* again.

"You tricked us."

"We didn't trick you. That was a safe house."

"You call that 'safe'?"

"We don't know how they found you. Someone in your group might be tipping them off."

"You're saying one of us is a traitor?"

"Maybe. An Elgen plant."

"I trust them more than I do you," I said. "I'm hanging up."

"Please don't hang up. We need to talk."

"What are you doing, tracing this call?"

"We already know where you are. We sent the pizza."

I felt stupid. "Oh yeah."

"If you look out the window you'll see two white, windowless service vans parked across the street. They're ours. They're guarding the house."

"Why should I trust you?"

"Do you know what happened to the third Elgen car?"

"What?"

"The third Elgen car. The one that was about to blow up the van you were in. You don't believe that car just blew up on its own?"

I didn't know what had happened to the car. None of us did. I wondered how he knew about it.

"We did it," he said. "You did an amazing job of escaping, Michael. All of you did. You just needed a little help at the end."

"If you're with us, why didn't you just stop them from capturing us to begin with?"

"Anonymity is our most valuable weapon. If the Elgen had gotten you to the airport, we would have been forced to attack. But it was our last resort. Thankfully we didn't have to. After you destroyed the first two cars, we knew they'd assume you destroyed the third."

My mind was reeling. I didn't know what to believe. "How do they keep finding us?"

"Like I said, we don't know. We knew that the Elgen were tracking your cars. We thought once you traded cars they'd lose you. Unfortunately, we were wrong."

"We noticed," I said sarcastically. "How are *you* following us?"

"The old-fashioned way. We've been following you since Pasadena." The voice paused. "Are there any GPs with you?"

"No," I said. "We let them all go in California."

"All of them?"

"Of course, we don't have room for . . ." I stopped. "Jack and Wade were GPs."

"That's how they're doing it," the voice said. "The GPs are all implanted with subdermal RFIDs. You'll have to get rid of them."

I didn't understand. "Get rid of Jack and Wade? Or get rid of the subthermal R-F-I . . ."

"Sub*dermal* RFIDs," the voice said quickly. "Your friend Ostin will know what they are. And the answer is either. I'm afraid my time's up."

"Wait. Do you know what happened to Ostin's parents?"

Ostin looked at me.

"They're safe, and we have a man watching over Taylor's house as well. You saw our van as you drove by her house yesterday afternoon."

"What about Jack's house?"

"We didn't know about him, so we weren't prepared." The receiver went dead. I put the phone in my pocket.

"What did he say?" Ostin asked.

"Your parents are okay."

"Where are they?"

"He didn't say."

Ostin looked confused. "That's good, right?"

"I hope so. What's a subdermal RFID?"

"'Subdermal' means beneath the skin. RFIDs are radio frequency identification devices." His eyes widened. "Holy cow, is that how they've been following us? Did they implant everyone with them?"

"He only said the GPs."

"What about the electric kids?"

"They tried," Ian said. "But our electricity interferes with the frequency."

"RFIDs," Ostin repeated. "So that's how they're following us."

"What do they look like?" I asked.

"You've seen them before," Ostin said. "Stores put them in books and video games to catch shoplifters. It's a little square foil thing, usually about the size of a postage stamp. But I've read that some new, high-tech RFIDs are the width of a human hair. They can almost make them like powder. There's even talk of making them digestible."

"Why would they do that?" Ian asked.

"Think about it," Ostin said, suddenly looking excited. "You could put them in restaurant food, then when you go to check out, they'll scan your stomach and charge you for what you ate."

"That's . . . weird," Mitchell said.

"That's the future," Ostin replied.

"How do they implant these things?" I asked.

"They inject them," Ian said. "In a shot. I've seen them do it."

"We need to get rid of them," I said.

"Jack and Wade?" Zeus asked hopefully.

"No," I said. "The tracking devices." I lifted half the pizzas. "We better get back to the others."

Jack, Taylor, and Wade met us by the pool.

"What happened?" Taylor asked. "Who sent the pizzas?"

"I'll tell you inside," I said. We carried the food into the pool house and set it on the kitchen table. "The voice sent the pizzas. And he sent us another phone."

"What did the *voice* have to say?" Jack said angrily. "Sorry we *almost* killed you?"

"He said they didn't do it. He said that they were the ones who blew up the third Elgen car so we could escape."

"Do you believe him?" Taylor asked.

"I don't know. I mean, the Elgen wouldn't blow up their own car, and we sure didn't do it. And if they know we're here, why didn't they just attack us?"

"Because we kicked their butts last time," Jack said.

"No," Taylor said. "If they're still trying to capture us, it would be better for them if we didn't know that they knew where we are."

"What?" Wade said.

"Precisely," Ostin said. "First rule of war, never give up the element of surprise."

I said, "The voice said he thinks they know how the Elgen have been following us." I looked at Jack. "They think that you and Wade were implanted with tracking devices."

Jack's brow furrowed. "Implanted where?"

"When the guards took you prisoner, did they give you a shot?" Ostin asked.

"Oh yeah," Wade said. "And that needle was wicked big. It stung worse than a hornet."

"Did they tell you what the shot was for?" Ostin asked.

Jack shook his head. "No, they weren't real talkative. Why?"

"GPs are implanted with a subdermal RFID so they can be tracked if they escape," I said. "That includes you and Wade."

"A what?" Jack asked.

"It's a radio frequency identification device," Ostin said. "They use them to track people. And they're small enough that they can be injected into the body."

"The voice told you this?" Jack asked skeptically.

I nodded. "He thinks the Elgen have been using the RFIDs to track us."

"Wait," Taylor said. "If that's true, then they can still find us."

Mitchell looked at her. "What will they do if they find us?"

"They burned down my house," Jack said.

Mitchell's eyes widened. "If something happens to the house, my parents will kill me."

"If the Elgen find us," Jack said, "they'll kill you for real."

Mitchell turned pale. "You've got to get out of here. All of you."

"No, just Jack and Wade have to get out of here," Zeus said.

"But they'll capture us," Wade said.

"It's you or *all of us*, moron," Zeus said.

"Watch your mouth," Jack said.

"We're in this together," I said. "There's got to be another solution."

"Wait," Ostin said. "There is. Mitchell, do you have any aluminum foil?"

"In the pantry."

"Get it. Quick. The thicker the better."

He started walking toward the kitchen.

"Run!" Jack said.

"Okay." He ran out of the room.

"Aluminum foil?" I said.

"We can wrap them in foil. It will block the frequency."

Taylor stifled a laugh. "They'll look like baked potatoes."

"I'm not going to wear foil," Wade said.

"Maybe you prefer the Elgen jumpsuits," Jack said.

Wade nodded. "Actually, I have always looked good in silver."

Mitchell returned with two boxes of foil. "Here."

"Someone help me wrap them," Ostin said.

"I'll help," Taylor said.

"Where did you get the shot?" Ostin asked.

"At the Elgen Academy," Wade said.

Jack shook his head. "In our arms. Our left arms."

Ostin and Taylor wrapped Jack's and Wade's left arms and shoulders with foil.

"I take it back," Taylor said. "You don't look like baked potatoes.

You look like the Tin Man from *The Wizard of Oz*."

"Yeah," Zeus said. "I'll get you a funnel for your head."

"And I'll shove your greasy head through it," Jack said.

The two of them glared at each other.

Abigail stepped between them, then said to Jack. "I think you look like a knight in shining armor."

Zeus shook his head and turned away.

"At least there are no more radio frequencies," Ostin said.

Jack smoothed the foil down on his shoulder. "We can't walk around like this for the rest of our lives."

"He's right," I said. "Can't we just run a magnet over it like you do with a credit card?"

"That won't do anything," Ostin said. "You've got to really crush it. Like hit it with a hammer."

"We can't hit anyone with a hammer," I said.

"Yeah," Wade said, looking pale. "That wouldn't be good."

"You're right," Ostin said. "It wouldn't be efficient. You'd crush bones long before it damaged the chip."

"Can we cut it out?" Jack asked.

Wade's eyes widened. "What?"

"You could do that," Ostin said. "If you could find it."

"What?" Wade said again. "You want to cut it out of my arm, like with a *knife*?"

Jack walked to the kitchen and returned with a steak knife. He handed it to me. "Cut it out."

Wade stared, his eyes wide with fear. "Please don't."

"Is there any other way to break them?" I asked.

"You can microwave them," Ostin said. "But even if Wade fit in a microwave, he'd probably explode."

Wade was speechless.

"What about an EMP?" Zeus said. "Quentin used to blow out RFID readers at toll booths just to cause traffic jams."

"What's an EMP? Taylor asked.

"Electromagnetic pulse," Ostin said. "A high-frequency electro-magnetic burst could overload the RFID's antenna and blow out the chip." He thought for a moment. "A quick electric surge could knock it out. But you'd have to be right above the RFID. And we don't know where it is."

"Ian can find it," I said, looking at him. "Can't you?"

"If I knew what I was looking for. What does it look like?"

"I've never seen one that small, but it would look like a tiny piece of metal," Ostin said. "Like a sliver. Embedded in flesh it shouldn't be that hard to find."

"What about the EMP?" Taylor asked. "Where do you get one of those?"

"A big blast from Michael," Ostin said.

"Why do all these solutions have to involve some form of torture?" Wade said. "Michael's done that to me before."

"He's shocked you before," Ostin said. "This would have to be much more powerful."

"I really don't mind the foil that much."

"Quit being such a wimp," Jack said.

"It's that or the knife," Ostin said.

"Enough of this," Jack said. "Let's get it over with. I'll go first."

"Ian?" I said.

Ian walked up to Jack. "Point to where they gave you that shot."

Jack peeled back the foil and rolled up his sleeve. He pointed to a spot a few inches down from his shoulder.

We were all quiet as Ian looked at Jack's arm. "I think I see it. It's about the size of a sesame seed."

"What does it look like?" Ostin asked.

He focused his eyes. "It has markings. Almost like . . . fingerprints."

"That's it," Ostin said. "We should mark where it is. Anyone got a pen?"

Mitchell retrieved a fine-tipped marker from a drawer next to the phone. "Here."

Ostin handed the marker to Ian, who drew a small dot on Jack's skin. "It's right there, about a sixteenth to an eighth of an inch in."

"The subcutaneous level," Ostin said.

I looked at Jack. "You sure about this?"

"Do I have a choice?"

"Not really," I said.

"Then I'm sure."

"You should sit down," Ostin said. "The shock might knock you out."

"Right." Jack walked over to the couch and sat back, his arm on the armrest.

I put my hand on his arm. "Ready?"

"I feel like I'm in the electric chair waiting for them to flip the switch. Don't count or anything. Just do it."

"Wait!" Abigail said. "I can help." She walked over to Jack's side and put one hand on his shoulder, the other on his neck. "Okay," she said.

Jack smiled. "Thanks."

I put my index finger on Ian's ink dot and closed my eyes. Then I pulsed.

Jack's body heaved and Abigail jumped back with a scream. The spot on Jack's arm was bright red and there was a blister where my finger had touched him.

"Sorry," I said.

It took him a moment to speak. "It was nothing," he said, still looking a little dazed. "I think Abi took most of it." He looked at her. "Are you all right?"

Her eyes were moist with tears, but she nodded.

"Thank you," he said. "I owe you one."

She forced a smile. "You're welcome."

Jack turned to me. "So, did it work?"

"Ian, what do you see?"

Ian looked at Jack's arm. "The thing looks . . . smaller than it was, kind of wrinkled, like it's melted."

"Perfect," Ostin said.

Wade stepped forward. "Guess it's my turn." He pulled the foil back from his arm.

Ian had to look a little longer for his. "What's up with this? You've got a *bunch* of metal in there."

Wade looked stumped for a moment, then said, "Oh. It's probably buckshot. I got in the way of a shotgun when I was little."

"His dad was drunk and took him duck hunting," Jack said.

"There it is." Ian marked the place with the pen.

Abigail put her hand on Wade's shoulder.

"You don't have to do this," Jack said to her.

"I know."

This time I didn't hesitate. I put my finger on the spot and immediately pulsed. The shock wasn't as strong as the first one, but it was strong enough. Abigail cried out as she pulled away, shaking her hand in pain. Tears were rolling down her face. McKenna and Taylor both put their arms around her to comfort her.

"I'm so sorry," I said.

"It's not your fault," she replied.

Ian examined Wade's arm. "It looks shriveled too."

Jack wadded up a piece of foil from Wade's arm and threw it at Mitchell. Then he grabbed Wade by the hand and pulled him up. "You're the man."

"That wasn't so bad," he said.

"Yeah, because Abi took it," Taylor said. "How about a thank-you."

"Sorry," Wade said. "Thanks."

"That's okay," Abigail said.

"Now that that's done," Ostin said, "how about some pizza?"

"I could go for that action myself," Zeus said.

"Looks like there's a little of everything," Grace said, opening the boxes.

"Pineapple and Canadian bacon," Ostin said. "Score."

I took a couple of pieces of sausage and pepperoni pizza for Taylor and me, then we sat on the floor in the corner of the room. After we'd taken a few bites she asked, "Now what do we do?"

"We get the information out of Grace." I looked over at Mitchell. "Hey, Mitchell. Do you have a computer?"

"Like six of them," he said, his mouth full.

"We need your most powerful one. We've got to upload Grace."

"What's grace?"

Grace was sitting on the arm of the couch next to him. "I'm Grace," she said.

Mitchell looked at her. "I don't get it."

"They're uploading me," she said.

"I'm so confused," Mitchell said. "Will someone please tell me what's going on?"

"I'll tell you," I said. "Remember when I shocked you?"

"Yeah, like I'd forget that."

"There are other kids like me with electric powers. Thirteen of them. The people who made us this way, the Elgen, are trying to get us back. That's why they kidnapped my mother and Taylor."

"You?" Mitchell said, looking at Taylor.

Taylor nodded.

"She's electric too," I said.

"You can shock too?" Mitchell asked.

"Kind of," she said. "Just your brain."

"Might be hard with Mitch," Jack said. "Small target."

Mitchell made a face.

I continued. "Jack and Wade drove Ostin and me to California to rescue my mother and Taylor."

"Where we were captured and put in cells and tortured," Wade said. "Still wish you had come?"

Mitchell looked at Jack. "The Elgen dudes captured you?"

Jack nodded. "They put these electric collars on us that would shock you if you even talked. But Michael escaped and freed us."

"And the Elgen dudes are the ones looking for you now," Mitchell said.

I nodded. "Yes."

Jack said, "We came back to Idaho to regroup. But the Elgen were waiting for us. They burned down my house."

"Then they recaptured us," Wade said. "But we got away."

"That's where you come in," I said. "The truck you saw us climb out of, that was what they were holding us in."

"You're really not making this up?"

Jack scowled. "Don't be an idiot. You saw the truck, dude. You saw the bullet holes."

"So what are you going to do now?"

"We're hoping Grace has information about my mother," I said. "That's why we need a computer."

Mitchell just stared at me for a moment. "But what if these Elgen guys find us?"

"That's why we had to get rid of the RFIDs," Jack said. "So they won't."

"There's no way they'll find us now," Ostin said.

Just then my phone rang. Everyone turned to look at me as I answered. "Hello."

"Get ready, Michael," the voice said. "The Elgen are here."

15

A Second Visit

"**W**here are they?" I asked.

Taylor grabbed my arm. At first I thought she was frightened, then I realized she was just listening in.

"They're one street east of you. There are about a dozen guards in three vehicles. Did you get rid of the GPs?"

"No, but we destroyed the RFIDs," I said. "At least we think we did."

"You must have succeeded or else they would have already surrounded the house. They were probably closing in on you, then lost the signal. They've got a helicopter and listening devices, so stay inside and no loud talking. Turn up the radio or TV. They're also going door to door with remote el-readers. They're sensitive up to thirty feet, so stay away from the front door and outer walls."

"What are el-readers?" I asked.

"They pick up erratic electrical signals like yours."

Taylor looked up at the ceiling. "I hear a helicopter."

"What should we do?" I asked.

"Prepare yourself for battle. Is there someone they won't recognize who can answer the door when they arrive?"

"Mitchell can," I said. "It's his house."

"*What* are you volunteering me for?" Mitchell asked.

Taylor shushed him.

"We're positioned on both ends of the street, but we're outnumbered. We won't move in unless we have to. It's best that we don't engage them, unless you want to turn the whole area into a war zone. I'm guessing they have enough ammunition that they could level the block if they had to. Or at least the house." The voice paused. "Did you hear that?"

"No."

"I need to go before they intercept this signal. I'll call back when it's clear. Be strong. Good luck." The phone went dead.

Taylor looked at me, her eyes dark with fear. Everyone else was staring at me as well.

"What?" Ostin and Zeus asked simultaneously.

I lowered my voice to a whisper. "The Elgen are in the neighborhood."

"They're in my *neighborhood*?" Mitchell said.

"Quiet," Taylor whispered. "They have listening devices."

"Someone turn the TV on," I said.

"What channel?" Wade asked.

"A noisy one," I said. "They don't know where we are. They lost our signal. So they're going door to door." I looked at Mitchell. "If they come here, you're going to have to answer the door."

He turned white. "Why me?"

"Because they have machines that can detect us and you're not one of us."

"How about we just don't answer the door?" he said.

"Then they'll search your place, and if they pick up our el-waves . . ."

"But what's going to stop them from forcing their way in?"

"Look," I said. "They have a lot of houses to check. They won't attack if they don't think we're here. So just act normal and nothing will happen."

Mitchell just stared at me blankly. "Act normal? They're going to kill us!"

Jack put his arm around him. "Listen, Mitch. It's cage time in the Octagon. Wipe that fear off your face. You're a warrior. No fear."

Mitchell took a deep breath. "Right. No fear."

"Jack, you're going to have to be his backup."

"Wade, Mitch, and I got it," he said. "And you." He pointed to Ostin.

Ostin looked around. "Me?"

"Yes, you. We might need your smarts."

"We'll need to know what's going on," I said.

"I'll be watching," Ian said.

"I know. But it would be better if we could hear what they're saying." I turned to Mitchell. "Does your house have an intercom system?"

"Yeah, but I'm not sure how to work it."

"I'll figure it out," Ostin said. "Just show me where it is."

"Set it so we can listen from the loft in the pool house."

"Done," Ostin said.

"All right," I said. "Good luck, everyone."

Ostin turned the front door's intercom on so we could listen to what was happening. It was about twenty minutes before the doorbell rang. We heard the door open.

"Whassup, guys?" Mitchell said.

"We're sorry to disturb you at this hour, but we're from Homeland Security. There's no need to panic, but we've received a report that there is a radiation leak in the area. For your safety, we need to check the radiation levels of your house."

"Liars," Taylor whispered.

Mitchell said, "Radiation? Someone got a bomb around here?"

"No, sir. It's not a bomb. It may be nothing at all. May we please come in?"

"Uh, my parents are out, and they'd freak if I let strangers in. You got a warrant or something?"

"No, sir, Homeland Security doesn't need warrants. This is for your safety. We don't need your permission to enter your home."

There was a long pause. "Come on, Mitchell," I said. "Think of something."

"Look, I just got my little sister to bed. Why don't you come back tomorrow?"

"It will only take a few minutes, sir."

"Come on, guys. It took me an hour to get her down."

We heard a high voice say, "Mitchie, who is it?"

"Mitchie?" Zeus whispered.

"Was that Ostin?" I asked.

Taylor shrugged. "He kind of pulled it off."

"Just some government guys!" Mitchell shouted. "Go back to sleep!" Pause. "Really, guys. I'm sure there's no radiation around here, or I'd be glowing or something, right? Just come back in the morning."

"Do you mind if we check around back?"

Taylor and I looked at each other.

There was a long pause. "No problem," Mitchell said. "Help yourself."

A different voice said, "I'm not pulling a reading."

"Nothing?"

"No."

"All right. Looks like you're good. Thank you, sir."

"Yeah. No problem. Come back when my parents are here."

We heard the door shut and lock.

"He handled that surprisingly well," I said.

"You think that girl's voice was Ostin?" Taylor asked.

"Probably Jack," Zeus said.

"You're so mean," Abigail said.

I looked at Abigail. She was smiling at Zeus.

"I don't like where that is headed," Taylor whispered to me. "I see a collision coming."

16

Uploading Grace

Ian watched the guards until they left Mitchell's street and started on the next. A few minutes later Jack and the rest walked back into the pool house. Jack had his arm around Mitchell, who was beaming like a conquering hero.

"How'd I do?" Mitchell asked.

"You should win an Academy Award for that performance," Taylor said. "So who was the girl calling for 'Mitchie'?"

"That was me," Jack said.

"Told you," Zeus said to Abigail.

Jack scowled at him.

"Okay," Abigail said. "Can we go to bed now? I'm exhausted."

"Me too," McKenna said.

I looked at Taylor. She grinned. "Me three."

"Someone's got to stand watch." I looked around the group. "Anyone not tired?"

No one said anything. Finally, Jack looked at Zeus. "If no one else is going to man up, I'll do it."

"I'll do it," Ostin said.

I looked at him in surprise. Ostin was one of those guys who always went to bed at the same time and always before ten.

"Really?" I asked.

"If we can upload Grace, I'll stay up and go through the files."

Grace had been so quiet I'd almost forgotten she was there. She took a deep breath. "Let's get it over with."

While everyone else got ready for bed, Ostin, Grace, Taylor, Jack, and I followed Mitchell to his room on the second floor of the main house. Not surprisingly, his room was huge—larger than my room and my mother's combined. It was also a mess, strewn with clothing, cracker boxes, and candy wrappers. The walls were covered with magazine pictures of cage fighters and *Sports Illustrated* swimsuit models.

There was a large, beige computer next to his desk with a huge monitor on the desktop. Ostin was drawn to it like a moth to a flame.

"That's a custom Alienware Aurora," Ostin said. "Maybe the best gaming computer ever built. It looks brand-new. Have you even used it?"

Mitchell shook his head. "Nah. My dad bought it for my birthday. I'm not really into computers that much."

"He means he doesn't know how to turn it on," Jack said.

"Neither do you," Mitchell said.

"I would kill for one of these," Ostin said, sitting down at the keyboard. He fired it up and the screen's glow lit his face. "Let's go, Grace."

"You're not going to break it, are you?" Mitchell asked.

"Would you even know if we did?" Ostin said.

Mitchell just looked at him.

Ostin rolled his eyes. "No, we're not going to break it."

Grace sat down in a chair next to the computer. She took a deep breath, put her hands on top of the CPU, then closed her eyes and began to concentrate. Files began filling the computer as sweat beaded on her forehead. Just a minute into the upload she began to shake and her eyes rolled back into her head like before.

"That's creepy," Mitchell said.

"No it's not," Taylor said indignantly.

"Shh," Ostin said. "You're slowing her down."

It took nearly five minutes for Grace to upload everything. When she was done she fell forward onto her knees, panting heavily like an athlete just completing a sprint.

Taylor put her hand on Grace's shoulder and knelt down next to her. "Good job."

Ostin just stared at the screen. "Mitchell, do you have a pen and paper?"

"We've got some downstairs."

"I'm going to need a whole pad. Actually a couple. Is there paper in your printer?"

"What printer?"

"Just get the pen and paper, Einstein," Jack said.

I checked the printer drawer. "Looks full."

Ostin continued examining the file names, shaking his head in wonderment. "That's a lot of data. It's going to take me all night. At least."

Mitchell returned. "Here's your pen and paper," he said, setting two yellow writing pads on the desk next to Ostin.

"You're sure about this?" I asked. "I can stay up if you want."

"I'm good," Ostin said. "Everyone can go to bed."

"This *is* my bed," Mitchell said.

"Not tonight it's not," Jack said. "Ostin's got work to do."

"A few terabytes' worth." Ostin said this more to himself than us, and I could tell that he'd already started to slip off into his own world. I don't think he even noticed when we left.

17

Ostin's Discovery

"**M**ichael."

I opened my eyes to see Ostin standing over me. I had fallen asleep on the couch on the main floor of the pool house, and sunlight was streaming in through the blinds above me.

"What time is it?" I asked.

"Morning," Ostin said, looking very tired.

I rubbed my eyes. "Did you stay up all night?"

"I found your mother."

Suddenly I was wide awake. "You found her?"

"She's in Peru. I found her file on the computer."

"Peru? Show me." I pulled on my T-shirt and grabbed the cell phone.

We were walking to the front door when Taylor called to me. "Michael."

I looked up. She was leaning over the loft railing. "What's going on?"

"Ostin found my mother," I said.

"I'll be right there." Taylor hurried down the stairs and joined us at the door. "Are you sure?"

"I'm sure she was there when Grace downloaded the information," Ostin said. "They could have moved her."

"How did you find her?" I asked.

"I tracked her through their internal travel logs. I started with the date she disappeared, then went from there."

Taylor and I followed Ostin back to Mitchell's room.

"Is anyone else awake yet?" I asked Taylor.

"No. Everyone was exhausted."

"They should be," I said.

We walked into Mitchell's room.

"I've got a feeling things are going to get even crazier," Ostin said, pointing to a picture of my mother on the screen.

My heart froze at the sight of her. She looked tired and frightened and was wearing an Elgen jumpsuit.

"She's being held at the Elgen Starxource plant in Puerto Maldonado, Peru."

"Isn't that where the fire rats escaped?" Taylor asked.

"Exactly," Ostin said. "It's a jungle town in the Amazon rain forest."

"How long has she been there?" I asked. I noticed I was ticking but didn't bother to try to control it.

"The travel records show that she was transported to Peru directly from Idaho."

"How do we get to Peru?" Taylor asked. "Can we drive?"

"I'm not sure. We'd have to go through Mexico, Guatemala, El Salvador, Honduras, Nicaragua, Costa Rica, Panama, Colombia, and Ecuador and halfway through Peru."

Taylor just stared at him. "How do you know all that?"

"Geography is my strong subject," Ostin said.

"Everything is your strong subject," Taylor said.

"We're going to have to fly," I said.

"All of us?"

"We might have enough money," I said.

"You can't just fly into a foreign country," Ostin said. "There's customs and border control. Do you even have a passport?"

I had never traveled outside the country, so I hadn't thought of any of that. "That will be a problem."

"Not our biggest one," Ostin said. "The compound she's being held in is a fortress. It's more prison than energy plant. It's built on a twenty-five-thousand-acre ranch, and it has hundreds of guards. At least ten times more than what we faced at the academy."

All the excitement I felt at locating my mother vanished in a puff of impossibility. What good was knowing where she was if we couldn't reach her? She might as well be on the moon.

I put my head in my hands.

"What do we do now?" Taylor asked.

"I don't know," I said. I turned to Ostin. "Do you have any ideas?"

"I think . . . ," Ostin said. He thought for a moment. "I think I need some sleep."

I exhaled heavily. "Yeah, get some sleep. Thanks for staying up."

"No problem," Ostin said. He lay down on Mitchell's bed. A feeling of despair permeated the room.

Taylor said, "I know what we should do."

"What?"

"Get bagels. I need to get out of here."

After all we'd been through, something as normal as going out for bagels sounded fantastic.

"Maybe Jack or Wade are up by now."

I looked at Ostin. He had already shut his eyes.

"Do you want something from the bagel place?" I asked.

"Sleep," he said.

"Wow, you are tired," Taylor said.

"And a blueberry bagel," Ostin added. "Or chocolate chip if they have it. With strawberry cream cheese."

"You got it," I said. I started for the door, then suddenly stopped and turned back. The picture of my mother was still on the screen.

Taylor took my hand. "Things have a way of working out."

I looked at her. "My mother used to say that."

18

The Bagelmeister

When we walked back into the pool house, Jack was sitting at the kitchen table holding a spoon and eating from a carton of vanilla ice cream. "Where were you guys?"

"With Ostin," I said. "He found my mother."

He set down his spoon. "Awesome. Let's go get her."

"It's not that simple," Taylor said.

"She's in Peru," I said.

"Is that in Idaho?" he asked.

Taylor covered her eyes.

"No," I said. "It's in South America. They have her locked away in a huge compound."

"Good," he said. "I like a challenge."

"Well, you've got one. The first is how we get there."

"Maybe the *voice* can help us," he said.

Taylor looked at me. "He's right. I bet they could fly us there."

The thought gave me hope. "If they call again."

"They'll call," Taylor said. She turned to Jack. "In the meantime, we're hungry for bagels. Will you drive us?"

Jack stood. "Sure. I'll get the keys from Mitchell."

The three of us drove about six blocks to Taylor's favorite bagel shop—the Bagelmeister. I had never been to the place before, but I knew it was a hangout for the popular kids.

"Let's go inside," Taylor said. "It's faster."

"Wait," I said. "What if someone recognizes you? They've probably been hanging 'missing girl' posters around town."

"We'll just be a second," she said. "Besides, all my friends are in school right now."

"All right," I said. "But we can't stay."

I held the door for her as she walked inside. As we walked into the store, Taylor froze. There was a shrill scream. "Guys! It's *Tay*!"

I looked over Taylor's shoulder to see a group of girls. Her friend Maddie was pointing at her. "OMG! It's really you! Where have you been? You are in so much trouble."

Taylor just stared at them like a deer in the headlights of an oncoming car.

"Reboot them," I said. "Quick!"

Taylor closed her eyes.

Immediately the entire room froze. I grabbed Taylor's arm and pulled her to the door. As we ducked out of the shop I heard someone say, "I think I just had, like, an aneurysm. . . ."

We ran back to the car. I opened the door and pushed her in.

"That was fast," Jack said. "Where are the bagels?"

"We've got to get out of here," I said. "Taylor's friends are inside."

He looked at Taylor. "Did they see you?"

"Yes, but I rebooted them."

"Hope it worked." Jack put the car in reverse, backed up, then squealed out of the parking lot. When we were a couple of blocks away he asked, "Where to now?"

"There's that other bagel place over on Thirty-Third," I said. "Next to the theater. I think they have a drive-through window. What do you think, Tay?" I looked over. "Taylor?" Her head was down, her eyes covered by her hands. She was crying.

"What's wrong?"

She kept crying. I put my hand on her shoulder. "Taylor?"

She wiped her eyes, then looked up at me. "I just miss my life," she said. "I miss my family. I miss my friends. I miss my mom hiding my Easter basket in the same stupid place every year for the last ten years. I even miss my dad yelling at me for being gone all the time."

I wasn't sure what to say. Jack glanced at me in the rearview mirror with a helpless expression.

After a moment I breathed out heavily. "Maybe it's time you went home."

Her expression turned from sad to angry. "You're trying to get rid of me?"

"No. I just don't want you to be so unhappy."

"We're in this together. All of us are. Besides, we both know the Elgen aren't going to leave me alone just because I gave up. It makes me an easier target."

I held her hand. "I don't know what to say."

"You don't have to say anything. I just needed someone to listen." She wiped her eyes. "Do you have a Kleenex or something?"

"There are some napkins up here," Jack said.

"That works."

Jack handed her a stack of napkins, and she blew her nose and wiped her eyes again.

Just then the cell phone rang. I picked it up, and Taylor took my arm to listen in.

"Hello?"

"Well done last night, Michael," the voice said. "Another potential catastrophe averted."

"We found my mother," I said.

The voice paused. "Are you sure?"

"She's being held in Puerto Maldonado, Peru."

"Their Starxource training compound," the voice said. "Of course. It's their most secure compound—especially as far as Hatch is concerned. He has complete control over the personnel. How do you know she's there?"

"I can't tell you," I said.

"Are you certain your information is correct?"

"We know that she was sent there after she was kidnapped. I've seen her file with a picture of her."

"So you either hacked into their system or, more likely, downloaded the files at the academy."

I could have kicked myself for divulging so much. I didn't confirm his guesses, but I began gulping.

"You're right not to tell anyone," the voice said. "If Hatch knew that Grace had downloaded those files, he would stop at nothing to hunt her down."

His words filled me with fear. "I didn't say anything about Grace."

"You didn't have to, Michael. She's the only one who could have accessed that information before it was destroyed."

"How do you know it was destroyed?"

"Elgen protocol," he said. "Does Hatch know that Grace is with you?"

"I don't know."

"Even if he does, he clearly doesn't know what she's carrying. How much of their mainframe did you get?"

"We think all of it."

"This is a fantastic stroke of luck," he said. "That information is invaluable to our cause. Where is this data now?"

"It's on one of the computers at the house."

"We need to get that information. We'll send someone over this afternoon to retrieve it. The van we send will be disguised as some type of service vehicle."

"I didn't say you could have the information," I said.

There was a long pause. "What do you mean?"

"I need a ride to Peru."

"You want to try to rescue your mother?"

"Yes."

"You do realize that you're walking into a trap and that Hatch is holding your mother as bait."

"Probably."

"Not probably, he is. And once you're in the compound there's nothing we can do to help you."

"I wasn't planning on your help. I have to take a chance. I have to save her."

There was another long pause. When he spoke his voice was softer. "I just wanted to make sure that you know what you're up against. I'll make the arrangements. It will take me a while. We'll get you to Peru and provide you with all the information we have on the compound in return for Grace's information. But we want one more thing. We want Grace."

Taylor looked at me. She mouthed, "Grace?"

"I can't turn her over to you."

"If Hatch catches her, he'll probably kill her. But he'll break her first. Then he'll know exactly how much we know. It will render the information useless."

I thought over his warning.

"You know I'm right, Michael. Grace can't help you. Her powers aren't what you'll need. And you'll be putting her life in terrible danger. If you won't do it for the cause, do it for her sake."

After another minute I said, "Okay. I'll ask her. But it's up to her."

"Fair enough. Do we have a deal?"

I looked at Taylor and she nodded.

"Okay," I said. "We have a deal. Send your guy."

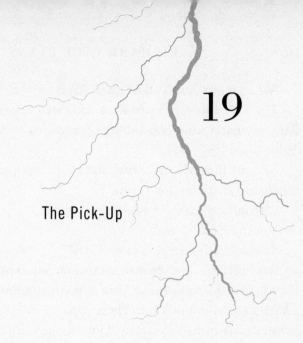

19

The Pick-Up

"**W**e're going to Peru?" asked McKenna, her mouth full of blueberry bagel.

"Isn't that in Africa?" Wade asked.

"Did you even go to school?" Ostin said.

"Same one you did, loser."

"Same school, different planet," Ostin said.

All eleven of us were gathered in the loft eating bagels. I stood in front of the TV with Taylor by my side. "Yes, we're going to Peru. The voice has promised to take us there." I looked around the room. "This is going to be very dangerous—even more dangerous than what we risked at the academy. I don't want you to go unless you're positive you want to."

"I'm in," Jack said immediately. "Wade?"

"I already committed," he said. "I owe you, Michael."

I nodded. "Thanks."

"What about you, Mitch?" Jack asked.

"Uh . . ." His eyes darted back and forth between Jack and me. "I think my parents are . . . I think we're going to be out of town. My dad—"

Jack cut him off. "It's okay, Mitch. It's not your battle. It's probably better that you don't come."

Mitchell looked relieved. "If you say so."

"I'm there," Zeus said.

"In with both feet," Ian said. "Girls?"

Jack and Zeus both looked at Abigail. She shrugged. "I'm coming."

"Me too," McKenna said. "You're going to need me."

"You can count on that," Ostin said.

McKenna turned to Grace. "How about you?"

She looked at us. "I guess I'm in too."

"Actually," I said, "it might be better if you stayed back."

"Why?"

"If Hatch catches you, he'll force you to reveal how much you downloaded. That will jeopardize all the information we already got from them. Plus, you know he won't hold back on your punishment. It's probably best if you're not with us."

"Where will I go?"

"With the voice."

Grace looked at me nervously. "But we don't know who they are."

"I know," I said. "Either way, it's a risk. It's your decision. But if Hatch catches you . . ."

"You know what Hatch does to traitors," Zeus said.

I looked at Zeus. I was afraid for him as well.

Grace looked down for a moment, then said, "All right. I'd probably just be in the way anyway."

"I think it's the smart choice," Taylor said.

"So when do we go?" Zeus asked.

"I don't know."

"Then I have a suggestion," Zeus said. "We need to better prepare ourselves."

"How do we prepare for the unknown?" Ostin asked.

"By practicing our powers."

"Practice?" Ostin said.

"We practiced using them every day in the academy. When I first got there, I could only shock things less than a yard away. Now I can shoot more than fifty yards."

"How do we practice our powers?" Taylor asked.

"By using them. Our powers are like muscles. They get stronger with use. And we need to eat right. We need to eat more bananas. More potassium."

"There are things with more potassium than bananas," Ostin said. "Spinach has nearly twice the potassium as bananas."

"The Elgen scientists would have known that," Ian said. "There must be something special about bananas."

"To begin with, they taste a lot better than spinach," McKenna said.

"Mitchell," I said. "When do your parents get back?"

"Not until two weeks from tomorrow. They decided to stay an extra four days in Hawaii."

"By then we should be gone." I looked around at the group. "So, I guess that's that. I'll let you know as soon as I hear something. In the meantime I suggest we take Zeus's advice and prepare ourselves. Zeus, can you coach us?"

Zeus nodded. "I'm your man."

Later that afternoon a white, windowless appliance repair van pulled into Mitchell's driveway. A husky man wearing a blue jumpsuit came to the door. "I'm here to check your washer," he said.

"What?" Mitchell asked.

"You know why I'm here," he said.

"Oh right. Come in."

The man stepped inside, and Mitchell shut the door behind him. I stepped forward. Zeus, Ian, and Jack stood by my side while Taylor and Ostin stood on the opposite side of the foyer.

"Why are you here?" I asked.

He looked at me apprehensively. "I've come for the computer."

"You can't have the computer," I said. "We need it. But we've copied the information to a hard drive."

"That will do," the man said. "Where is it?"

"Before we give it to you, we need you to sit down." I pointed to the upholstered chair we'd dragged from the den into the foyer.

The man looked at us suspiciously. "What is this about?"

"We're protecting ourselves," I said. "Now sit down."

His eyes darted back and forth between us. "I'm not sitting any-where." He started toward the door.

Zeus shot a blue bolt of electricity to the door handle, the sound of which filled the room. The man jumped back. Zeus held up his hands and electricity arced between his fingers. "Try that again and I'll light you up like a Christmas tree."

The man glared at us.

"He's got two guns," Ian said. "One in a shoulder holster, the other on his ankle."

"Put your hands in the air, now," I said firmly.

Zeus stretched his hands forward. "You've got three seconds to comply, man. You go for the guns it's the last thing you'll ever do."

The man looked exasperated. "Look, guys, we're on the same side."

"Then you won't mind if we check your story," I said.

The man hesitated, then slowly raised his hands in the air. "Okay. Do it your way. Whatever you say." He sat in the chair. I walked over and put my hand on his shoulder. "Don't move."

"You know he's got enough amps to make sure you never move again," Ostin said.

"We know what Michael can do," the man said. "Let's just get this over with. The longer I'm here the riskier."

"Jack, take his guns," I said.

Jack pulled the man's guns from the two holsters. "Nice," he said, examining the pieces. "A Glock and a Walther P99."

"I want those back," he said.

Taylor and Ostin walked over to the man. Taylor put her hands on his head while Ostin held out the list of questions he'd written.

"I want you to answer these questions in your mind," Ostin said.

He began reading from the list we'd put together as a group, asking each question twice and pausing between each question until Taylor nodded for him to continue.

"Who sent you?"

"Why are you helping us?"

"Did you know we were going to be attacked at the safe house?"

"Did you really blow up the third car?"

"Are you going to help us get to Peru?"

"Are you allies with the Elgen?"

"Are you helping the Elgen?"

"How do you feel about the Elgen?"

"How do you feel about Dr. C. J. Hatch?"

When Ostin had finished reading his list, I looked over at Taylor. "What do you think?"

"I think he's on our side."

Mitchell brought down the hard drive, and I handed it over to the man. "We've lived up to our side of the bargain. When do we go to Peru?"

"We'll call," he said. "There's a lot of preparation that needs to happen first."

"How long?"

"I don't know. Could be a few days, could be a few weeks."

"A few weeks?"

"This will take some planning. We need to get you as close as possible without them knowing. Be ready and wait for our call."

He put the hard drive in his bag and locked it. Jack returned the man's guns. He put them back in their holsters, then walked to the door. "Be ready."

He saluted me, opened the door, then walked out to his van.

20

The Call

The days we spent waiting for the phone call felt like an eternity. Ian, Zeus, McKenna, Abigail, and Grace didn't have to worry about being recognized in public, but we were pretty sure the Elgen were still lurking about, so they hid out as well. For the next week we mostly sat around the house playing cards and video games or watching television.

We also practiced our powers. My electricity had, as Ostin theorized, continued to increase. So had my magnetism. I was doing things that surprised me. After my first full day of practice, I pulled a bicycle over to me in Mitchell's garage from more than twenty feet away and, even more difficult, opened the refrigerator door from the kitchen table. I have to admit that magnetism was way more fun than shocking people, because it looked like magic and no one got hurt. By carefully varying my power I was even able to levitate objects. I started moving everything I could and quickly learned my own limitations. Magnetism is not like in the superhero movies. I couldn't pull a car toward myself, because a car weighs more than I do. I just ended up pulling myself to the car.

I wasn't the only one practicing my powers. One day McKenna got hot enough that she burned through some carpet and got a lecture from Mitchell, who was certain his parents would think he was smoking.

Taylor was practicing too. We were sitting around the pool when she showed me one of her new tricks.

"Are you still going to kiss me?" she asked.

I looked around, feeling a little confused. I couldn't remember what we were talking about or even offering her a kiss. "Sorry." I leaned forward and kissed her.

She laughed as she pulled away. "I'm sorry, but you said you wanted a demonstration."

"I wanted a demonstration of what?"

She cocked her head to one side.

"Did you just reboot me?"

She nodded. "You asked me to. I'll remind you of what we were talking about. Watch." She turned to Wade, who was standing a few yards from us holding a piece of pizza in his hand. She put one hand to her temple. Wade paused midbite, then looked up with a dazed expression.

"Well?" Taylor said to him.

He looked at her with a blank gaze. "What?"

"Are you still going to give me that piece of pizza?"

He glanced around. "Oh, yeah. Sorry." He walked over and held out the piece to Taylor.

"You can keep it," she said. "I'm not hungry anymore."

"Thanks," he said, looking even more confused than before.

She turned to me and grinned. "See? That's the second time I've made him do that. You just don't remember the first time. And that's how I got you to kiss me. I've discovered that people are especially vulnerable to suggestion after I reboot them. The more confused they are, the more willing they are to believe others."

"That makes sense," I said. "Like, if you're lost, you'll trust a complete stranger to tell you where to go."

"Exactly. I'm also getting better at rebooting too. Watch this."

She focused on Mitchell, who was standing next to Jack on the opposite side of the pool. Suddenly he put his hands to his temples and groaned. "Ow."

"I can fill their heads so they can't think at all. It gives them a little headache. I think if I did it really hard, I could make someone faint."

"That could come in handy," I said.

"I'm going to keep working on it."

"I've been working on something too," I said. "Want to see?"

"Yeah."

I held my hand out toward Mitchell. My hand began shaking. Mitchell started to walk sideways toward the edge of the pool, as if he was being dragged, which, incidentally, he was.

"Hey, what the . . ."

Then he fell into the water. He popped up to the surface, sputtering and flailing. "Who pushed me?" he shouted. "Who pushed me?"

Jack was laughing. "No one, you idiot."

Taylor burst out laughing. "You really just did that?"

I was grinning. "I locked onto his belt buckle. Cool, right?"

"Way cool."

"Kylee can do that," Zeus said.

I looked back, unaware that Zeus had been watching.

"She can climb metal walls too."

"Climb walls?"

"It's just timing. Like using suction cups. Lock onto the wall with magnets, then release one hand and the opposite leg at the same time and move them up, lock on and repeat."

"That would be cool," I said. "If I could find some metal walls."

While we practiced our powers, the nonelectrics did too. Jack did like a thousand push-ups a day, went on a strict diet of raw-egg-and-protein drinks, and practiced hand-to-hand combat and ultimate fighting techniques with Wade and Mitchell, who seemed more like punching bags than opponents and every day sported fresh bruises.

Ostin researched. He dug through Grace's information like a gold miner at the mother lode. Within days he had pulled up everything the mainframe had on the Peruvian compound, including an early architectural drawing of the facility.

He spent most of his time looking for a way in. What made breaking into the compound especially difficult was that it was surrounded by a lot of land and ringed by tall electric fences. It was clear that the Elgen had built a large buffer around the facility to prevent unwanted guests.

When a week had passed, I began to worry again about the voice, particularly because of all the information we had handed over. Could the man we had interrogated somehow have tricked Taylor? They knew about her powers; maybe they had been prepared to deceive us. Maybe they had technology we didn't know about. Eight days from the man's visit, my phone finally rang.

"I understand you gave my man some grief," the voice said.

"We were being careful," I said.

"Good," he said. "You should be. You leave for Peru tomorrow morning at six. Drive to the same place you picked up the Hummers. Do you remember the place?"

"Yes."

"There will be two black Ford Excursions waiting for you. They will drive you to the airport. What did Grace decide?"

"She's decided to stay behind with you. Keep her safe."

"We will."

"Okay," I said. "I'll let everybody know. Anything we need to take with us?"

There was a short pause. "Courage," he said. "Lots of courage."

I gathered everyone together to tell them about the call. Afterward, Ostin took a moment and briefed us on what he'd learned about the compound. Things got quiet fast. For the first time, the reality of what we were attempting set in.

I asked if anyone had questions, and no one did—at least none they wanted to share. I had no doubt there would be plenty to come—more than I had answers for. At the end of the briefing I said, "If you've changed your mind, it's not too late to back out."

"We're not backing out," Jack said. *"Semper Fi."*

"What does that mean?" Taylor asked.

"Always faithful," Ostin said. "It's the Marine Corps motto."

"We're all in," Ian said. Everyone else nodded their heads in agreement.

"Thanks, guys. Get some sleep. We've got a long day tomorrow."

As everyone got ready for bed, I slipped out alone by the pool, settling into one of the vinyl lounge chairs. The pool area was dark, lit only by the solar lights in the corner of the yard and the blue, shimmering luminescence of the pool's light. The only sound was a symphony of crickets.

I needed to get away and think. Or maybe to *not* think. I had too many thoughts to effectively corral and too many fears to accompany them. I had been gulping all day, and I took a few deep breaths to calm myself.

I cupped my hands together, like I was making a snowball, and pulsed. To my surprise a ball of electricity formed, almost like a soap bubble, except with more weight, like a Ping-Pong ball. Out of curiosity, I tossed it away from me. It hit the ground and popped loudly with a crisp electric snap.

I made another and threw it into the pool. It exploded in the water, lighting the entire pool. "That is so cool," I said.

I made another and threw it across the pool. I hadn't noticed there was a cat on the other side, and although the bubble didn't hit it, the cat screeched and ran off.

The glass door slid open and Ostin walked out. "There you are," he said. "I was wondering where you went."

"Come here," I said. "I want to show you something."

I pulsed as I had before, and a glowing orb about the size of a golf ball rose from my hand. I threw it into the pool. This time the pop was as loud as a firecracker. I thought Ostin's jaw was going to fall off.

"Pretty cool, isn't it?"

"Do you know what that is?" he said.

"A ball of lightning," I said.

"That's exactly what it is! Scientists have been arguing for centuries about whether or not ball lightning exists. You just solved a centuries-old debate. Do it again."

I was about to make another when Taylor walked out of the house. "Michael?"

"I'm over here," I said.

She walked over to my side. "I was wondering where you'd gone. What are you guys doing?"

"You gotta see this," Ostin said.

Taylor sat down in the lounge chair next to me. "See what?"

"Do it, Michael."

I pulsed, forming another ball. This one was larger than my first, about the size of a baseball.

Taylor leaned forward to look at it. "It's kind of beautiful. Can I touch it?"

"It will definitely shock you," Ostin said. "It's lightning. Just in a different package."

Taylor pulled back.

"Watch this," I said. I threw it at the pool. It came off my hand like a softball and exploded in the water, briefly illuminating the entire surface.

"That's so cool," Taylor said.

"I wonder how I could measure the amps of one of those," Ostin said, settling into the lounge chair to my left.

I made a few more while Taylor and Ostin watched.

Taylor said to Ostin, "Hey, Tex. Would you mind going inside for a moment? I need to talk to Michael."

"You can talk to him," he said.

"Alone," she said.

He looked at her, then me. "Okay," he said. He stood up. "For how long?"

"I don't know," Taylor said. "Until we're done."

He walked inside, sliding the glass door shut behind him. I looked at Taylor. Her eyes were soft.

"You okay?" I asked.

She nodded. "It's you I'm worried about. How are *you* doing?"

"I'm fine," I said. "Why? Was I ticking a lot?"

"Some," she said. "How can you be just fine? Your mother's gone, the Elgen are hunting us, we're about to fly to a strange country, and everyone's depending on you for answers. I don't know how you handle all the pressure. I know I couldn't do it."

I exhaled. "I don't know. What else am I going to do?" Suddenly my eyes began to tear up. I looked away so she wouldn't see.

Taylor got up and pushed her chair next to mine. "Come here," she said.

I looked back at her and she smiled. "Come closer," she said.

I leaned in to her and she put her arms around me. She put her chin against my forehead and gently stroked the back of my head. It felt so good.

"You don't have to be strong all the time," she said. "Even heroes need to be taken care of."

"I'm not a hero," I said. "I'm a fifteen-year-old who has no idea what he's doing."

She was quiet for a moment, then she kissed the top of my head and said, "You're *my* hero."

I didn't know what to say. Maybe there wasn't anything to be said. I just closed my eyes and felt her warm face against mine and, for the first time in weeks, felt peace.

PART 2

21

The Board's Decision

"I hate boats," Hatch said, wiping his forehead with a gold-monogrammed handkerchief. The boat he was *hating* was a superyacht with all the luxuries befitting a $450 million vessel: a helipad, two current-jetted swimming pools, and an art gallery that included two van Goghs, three Escher lithographs, and a Rembrandt (the chairman had a penchant for Dutch artists). There were luxury suites for eighteen and an exclusive dining room with crystal chandeliers and scarlet wool carpet interwoven with twenty-four-karat gold thread. The yacht also featured some less luxuriant but interesting add-ons, including radar, sonar, and surface-to-air missiles.

Hatch was prone to seasickness, and although he understood the necessity of moving the Elgen corporate headquarters to international waters, he would have preferred the ship to remain docked in some obscure bay off the coast of Africa or the Philippines. The two electric teens seated next to him in the waiting room looked at him sympathetically.

"Would you like me to help?" Tara said, tapping her temple. "I could make you feel better."

Hatch shook his head. "No. I've got to keep my wits about me. I'm sensing trouble."

Tara had traveled with Hatch and the rest of the kids from Pasadena to Rome, where they left the others behind, helicoptering to the Elgen's yacht a hundred miles north of Sicily—in the Tyrrhenian Sea. The other teen, Torstyn, had joined them in Rome. Torstyn had spent the last nineteen months on assignment in Peru and, at Hatch's command, had flown directly to Italy.

Tara knew Torstyn—all the Elgen teens were familiar with one another—but she hadn't seen him in a long time and he had changed. His skin was darker from the South American sun, and his hair was long and wild. His personality had changed as well. Something about him frightened her.

"How long will we be here?" Torstyn asked, his hand extended toward the hundred-gallon saltwater aquarium built into the wall in front of them.

"Only as long as we need to be," Hatch said.

"Stop it!" Tara said.

"Stop *what*?" Torstyn asked, grinning.

"You know *what*. You killed the fish."

Torstyn had boiled the water in the aquarium from fifteen feet away. Two exotic angelfish were now floating on top of the water.

"They're just fish," Torstyn said. "Same thing you ate last night."

"Actually," Hatch said. "They were rare peppermint angelfish, found only in the waters of Rarotonga, in the South Pacific. I gave them to the chairman as a gift last year. They run about twenty-five thousand dollars apiece."

Torstyn frowned. "Sorry, sir."

"Ask next time."

"Yes, sir."

Hatch looked at him coolly, then asked, "How long did it take you?"

"About forty seconds."

"Good. I want you to get it down to twenty."

"Yes, sir."

"Then ten."

"Yes, sir."

Hatch nodded. "At ten you'll be unstoppable."

"Yes, sir. Thank you, sir."

Hatch went back to his e-reader. He'd been reading a book on mind control written in the late fifties by William Sargant, a British psychiatrist. He had already read the book several times. He was fascinated with the subject and had studied all aspects of mind control from hypnosis to suicide cults.

A slender, well-dressed woman in her midthirties walked into the waiting room. "Excuse me, Dr. Hatch?"

Hatch looked up.

"The board is ready to see you now."

Hatch stood, tossing his reader on the sofa cushion next to Tara. "I'll be right back," he said.

"Do you want us to come with you?" Torstyn asked.

"No, you're not invited." He walked to the conference room door, then turned back. "But stay alert."

"Yes, sir," they said, almost in unison.

Hatch straightened his tie, then walked into the conference room. An Elgen guard stood on each side of the door. Neither of them saluted him. The guards on the boat were the only ones in the company who never saluted Hatch. He walked past them into the room.

The boardroom was bright and the walls were covered with stainless steel tiles. Recessed directional lighting illuminated the art on the wall—large, black pictures with red, abstract silhouettes, images that looked more like inkblot tests than art. The shape of the room was trapezoidal; one entered in at the smaller end and broadening out in the rear. The outer wall, to Hatch's right, was made of thick, protective glass, forming an eight-foot-tall window looking out over the crested waves sixty feet below.

The table in the middle of the room was twenty-seven feet long and made of rare Brazilian rosewood, with brushed stainless steel trim around the edge. The table was surrounded by twelve high-backed chairs upholstered in black Italian leather and spaced every few feet. All of the chairs were filled except for two, one next to the chairman and one at the opposite end of the table, which was usually reserved for visitors.

The board was split evenly between men and women—all over fifty, a few gray with years. Anonymity was essential to the Elgen, and board members used numbers instead of names, the numbers corresponding to their term of service and place at the table. The chairman, Giacomo Schema, was Number One and the only member of the board who used his name.

Every eye was on Hatch as he entered the room. Although he had, at one time, served as CEO of Elgen Inc., the company had been reorganized after the original MEI machine was discovered to be dangerous. Hatch had been removed from the board, but had served ever since as the executive director, overseeing the daily affairs of the company. His relationship with the board had been volatile, and more than once there had been motions to remove him as director. But the company's growing profitability and status had, at least to that moment, ensured his longevity.

"Chairman Schema, board members," Hatch said, slightly nodding.

"Welcome, Dr. Hatch," the chairman said. "I trust your flight wasn't overly taxing." Chairman Schema was a broad, barrel-chested Italian who dressed impeccably in Armani suits with silk ascots.

"No, thank you. I'm used to the flight."

"Take a seat, please," Schema said, motioning to the chair at the opposite end of the table.

"Thank you." Hatch pulled the chair out and sat down.

"Tell us about the disaster in Pasadena," Schema said, no longer concealing his anger.

"As I wrote in my report, one of the electric children—"

"Michael Vey," Six, one of the board members to his left, said.

Hatch looked at her. "Yes," he confirmed. "Vey managed to

overpower one of our youths, the one you know as Zeus, and recruited him to help him free the others."

"How did he accomplish this? Was Vey left unguarded?"

"On the contrary. He was actually strapped down and being watched by three guards and Zeus. We believe that Vey may have telepathic powers we were unaware of—powers like Tara's or her sister, Taylor. Shall I continue?"

Chairman Schema waved his hand in an angry flourish. "By all means."

"The surveillance cameras in the room were blown out, so we've had to deduce much of what transpired. From what we've gathered, after Vey overpowered Zeus, he freed two of his accomplices who were locked down and the four of them attacked the guards in the hallway outside. They then released three more of the children who had been kept in seclusion—Ian, Abigail, and McKenna. Together, the seven of them attacked the academy and freed the GPs. The GPs managed to arm themselves, and for the protection of the rest of the children, we were forced to flee."

"What is the status of the freed GPs now?"

"The GPs are all accounted for except three. Two of them are with Vey, the other one, we believe, committed suicide in an aqueduct. His RFID tags are no longer registering. We are awaiting a report on the body."

"What about the children?" Three asked.

"We lost seven. . . ."

There was an audible groan from both sides of the table.

Hatch looked around, then said in a softer voice, "We lost seven. Vey; Zeus; Tara's twin, Taylor; and the three from Cell Block H—Ian, Abigail, and McKenna."

"Please, remind us of their gifts," Four said.

"Ian sees through electrolocation. . . ."

"Which means?" Chairman Schema asked.

"He can see through solid objects that humans cannot. McKenna can generate heat and light. Abigail can eliminate pain by stimulating nerve endings."

"I could use her for my headache right now," Eight said wryly.

Hatch ignored the comment. "Then, as I mentioned, Zeus, who can throw electricity."

"That's only six," Chairman Schema said.

"We also lost Grace."

"They captured her?"

Hatch interlaced his fingers in front of him. "Yes, we think so."

"What is it that Grace does?"

"She can hack into data systems and store information like a hard drive."

Six asked, "Did she hack into our system? Does she have confidential information that could compromise our security?"

"She was never given access to our mainframe."

"Were the children still in the building when you fled?" Three asked.

"Yes. They were."

"Then may we presume that she had access to the mainframe after you left?"

"The mainframe was set on self-destruct, so all the information was destroyed. But there was a short window of opportunity, so it is possible she downloaded *some* information, but even that is highly unlikely. Especially if she was taken against her will."

"What makes you think she was taken against her will?" Six asked.

"As we gathered up the other youths, we were not able to locate her. We believe she was on one of the other floors when the attack occurred."

Eight shook his head in disgust. "What a nightmare."

Chairman Schema leaned forward, pressing his fingertips together. "You had reported to me . . . actually, you had *promised* me, that the children would be back in your custody two days ago. But they are not."

"No. Vey and his associates have eluded two of our traps."

"Two?"

"They were tipped off to the first one. They attacked and tied up our watch, then fled the scene. We tracked them down to a home where they were hiding, and they were all captured. But they managed to overpower the guards and escape."

"This seems to be part of a pattern, Dr. Hatch," Chairman Schema said angrily. "I am beginning to doubt your ability to capture Vey and his friends."

"These are very powerful youths. The combination of their unique powers makes apprehending them, as Eight so aptly put it, a nightmare. Especially since our objective is to bring them in alive."

"What provoked Vey's attack in the first place?" Three asked.

"Vey was looking for his mother. We captured and held him for more than three weeks before he attempted his escape."

Three leaned forward. "And did he find his mother?"

"No. She wasn't being held in Pasadena. She's currently detained in our compound in Peru."

"So now we are holding hostages too?" Eight said.

Hatch replied, "She's the bait we need to recapture her son."

Chairman Schema slammed his hand on the table. "Dr. Hatch, your missteps continue to compromise this organization. First you were abducting children, now you are abducting their parents. These are crimes for which the board may be held accountable."

"Which is why we reside in international waters," Hatch said. "Mr. Chairman, may I remind the board that we were all complicit in much greater crimes with the death of forty-two infants. It was our cover-up of that incident that revealed the phenomenon of the electric children in the first place."

"Strike that from the record," Chairman Schema said to the board member taking notes. "Yes, we are aware of our complicity in that matter. And every time you pursue additional lawlessness, you further endanger this board. Are you mindful of this?"

"I do not take any of our actions lightly, Mr. Chairman. What has been done is part of our ongoing Neo-Species Genesis program, a program that has been unanimously approved by the board, not once but repeatedly, over the past decade."

"Which is precisely what we wish to discuss this morning," Chairman Schema said. "Dr. Hatch, in the last decade you have spent two hundred and forty-six million dollars in the Neo-Species program. Other than the 'accidental' creation of the original seventeen children, have you successfully replicated an electric human?"

"No, sir. But we believe we're close."

"What evidence would you have to support what seems to me a rather optimistic assessment?"

"As you're well aware, we've now successfully altered the electric composition of other mammals, and we are about to begin testing on primates. Also, there have been many other worthwhile discoveries and advancements that have come as a result of the program. The Starxource initiative wouldn't exist if it wasn't for the Neo-Species program—surely that alone warrants its continuation."

"Dr. Hatch is right," Four said. "The Starxource program is of inestimable value."

"Thank you," Hatch said. "And we don't know what other beneficial advancements the program will generate in the future."

Board member Two spoke up for the first time. "I am the first to commend you for your success with the Starxource program, Doctor. Our power plants have been even more successful than we envisioned or hoped for. My question is, now that we have found a commercially viable use for the technology, why should we continue pursuing an end, which, after more than a decade, appears to be a dead one?"

"I would second that argument," Nine said. "Even if we are successful in achieving your Neo-Species goals, I see no commercial application."

"Commercial application?" Hatch blurted out. "We're talking about creating a new species of human beings. We are altering the very course of human history."

"Exactly," Nine said. "And how do you propose we monetize that? These are people, not machines. If we create an electric person, they are free to do whatever they want with that power. What is to keep them from sharing their gifts with the highest bidder?" Nine turned to the chairman. "It is not our objective to create history, it is our mission and corporate objective to create profits. If the doctor's goal is a worthy one, and I have no doubt that he intends it as such, I suggest he create a charitable organization to pursue these ends—but separate it from the corporate body."

Hatch didn't answer, though some of them noticed his hands trembling with anger.

"At any rate," Two said, "whatever good may come from electrifying people, it certainly will not generate more profits than the already proven Starxource initiative. We have a very real opportunity to become a force of global power, larger than OPEC or any of the oil-producing countries of the world."

This started a discussion among the board members. Chairman Schema raised his hands for silence. When the room was quiet he turned his attention to Hatch. "Dr. Hatch, you should be aware that this discussion on the continuance of the Neo-Species program is more than a hypothetical one. Several months ago a motion was brought before the board to shut down the program entirely. At that time we tabled the motion until you could join us in person and be given the opportunity to defend your work."

Hatch turned red. "Shut down the program? That would be ludicrous. The power of this corporation exists because of this program."

"That is incorrect," Twelve said, speaking out for the first time. "The MEI was developed prior to the Neo-Species program. Unfortunately it is still too dangerous to use. The only part of the machine we can duplicate is the part that kills people. I agree with the commercial assessment proffered by Nine. I believe we should focus our efforts on the propagation of the Starxource initiative, to the exclusion of all else. Future discoveries will still come, just from the Starxource labs."

"I have a question," Three said, looking over a document. "Please explain this twenty-seven-million-dollar price tag for our facility in Peru. It's nearly double the cost of our other plants."

"We added a new guard training facility as well," Hatch answered.

"What are we training them to do? Fly?"

Several members chuckled. Hatch looked at Three, concealing his fierce anger behind a controlled demeanor. She had been against him from the beginning.

"Elgen security is of utmost importance," Hatch said. "Just one leak of our information or the theft of one pair of breeding rats could endanger our entire operation. Security is no place to count pennies."

"Twenty-seven million dollars is hardly pennies," she retorted.

"Dr. Hatch has a valid point," Chairman Schema said. "But why Peru?"

"Peru gives us a certain latitude to train in privacy and in the manner we consider best practice."

"Very well," the chairman said. "Is there anything else you would like to say, Dr. Hatch, before we vote on the future of the program?"

Hatch glanced around the room. "What you are considering . . . to shut down the Neo-Species Genesis program is to turn our backs on the future."

"Wait, wait," Three said. "What future are you speaking to? Certainly not the Starxource program. The future could not be brighter." She turned to the other board members. "I sound like the slogan, don't I?"

"Please," Hatch said. "Just give me another year. We are on the verge of a breakthrough. With the finding of Vey and the twin, Taylor, we expect critical advancement."

"But you don't have Vey or Taylor," Three said.

"We will soon. I promise you, you won't be disappointed." Hatch turned to Chairman Schema. "Just give me twelve more months."

"We've been hearing a lot of promises but seeing few results," Three said. "You ask for another year, I would maintain that we've given you five years too many. At least."

"Mr. Chairman," Four said, "I move that we suspend discussion for a vote."

"Do I have a second?" Chairman Schema asked.

Three hands went up.

"Very well. Doctor, if you would please leave the room while we conduct a vote."

Hatch slowly stood, looking over the board members. "Shutting down the Neo-Species Genesis program would be a huge mistake, one I believe you will live to regret."

"Noted," Chairman Schema said. "If you would please wait in the reception area, we will momentarily notify you of our decision."

Hatch walked outside the room, shutting the door behind him. Tara and Torstyn watched him enter. They could see from his expression how angry he was. Torstyn started to speak, "What's—?"

Hatch held up his hand to silence him. "They are voting on our future." He sat down on the couch. Nothing was said. Less than a minute later the door opened.

"Dr. Hatch, you may come in now."

Hatch returned to the conference room. Few of the board members were looking at him, and from the sympathetic expression of those who were, he knew how the vote had gone.

"The vote was not unanimous," Chairman Schema said. "But there was a majority vote in the affirmative to dissolve the Neo-Species Genesis program. To avoid further expenditures we are asking you to fly immediately to Peru, where you will relieve the scientists who are involved with the program."

"But . . ."

Chairman Schema raised his hand. "You will relieve these scientists of their current duties. Obviously we cannot just release them back into society, so they will be assimilated into the Starxource program. Their expertise led to the creation of this program, so we expect that their talents will be put to good use in maintaining and improving the program. At our current rate of growth and demand we will certainly need their specialized knowledge.

"The GPs, of course, are no longer of use to us. For obvious reasons, we can't just release them, as that would cause serious problems and inquiries into our activities. We trust that you will find a creative *solution* to this problem. We don't want to know about it."

"What about the electric children?" Hatch asked.

"It is also the decision of the board that the electric children should be reintegrated into normal society. An endowment will be established for each one allowing them to pursue further educational or vocational opportunities.

"As for Vey, you will reunite the boy with his mother with sufficient monetary remuneration to guarantee that there will be no lawsuits filed. We expect you to work with Legal to ensure that this delicate situation is handled discreetly."

Hatch was speechless.

"This is not a censure, Doctor, this is simply a change in course. We appreciate your devotion and the success that your efforts have brought to our company."

Hatch clenched his hands behind his back, his jaw tightening. "Do you have a time frame for this action?"

"We desire an immediate shutdown. We expect you to be in Peru within two days to begin the process. We realize that your relationship with the children is as personal as it is professional, so your timeline for that transition is up to you and the children to decide; however we expect that all business related to this matter be finalized before the end of this calendar year. We ask to be kept informed in all aspects of the transition. We thank you in advance for your expeditious handling of this matter, and we trust that it will be more successful than the shutdown of the Pasadena facility."

Hatch looked around the room, veiling his contempt for most of the gathered body. "Yes, sir. I'll see to it immediately." He turned on his heel and walked out of the room.

Tara and Torstyn stood as he entered. "Come on," he said. "We're leaving."

Walking to the helipad, Torstyn asked, "Where are we going?"

"To Rome to gather the others. Then we're headed back to Peru."

Within minutes the three of them were hovering over the Tyrrhenian Sea on the flight back to Rome.

"What did they say, sir?"

"They want to dismantle the NSG program."

The kids looked at each other.

"What?" Torstyn asked. "How come?"

"What about us?" Tara asked.

"I'll tell you on the plane," Hatch said. He glanced down at his satellite phone. "No! No! No!" he shouted. He pressed a button on his phone. "Get me Dr. Jung immediately."

"What is it?" Tara asked.

Hatch looked at her with a dark expression. "Tanner just tried to kill himself."

22

More Bad News

The Elgen helicopter landed around 7:00 p.m. atop the six-story Elgen building just outside of Rome. Bright orange lights flashed at the corners of the structure, silhouetting the waiting guards dressed in the Elgen black uniform.

"Welcome back, sir," one of the guards shouted over the sound of the helicopter's rotors.

Hatch shouted to Tara and Torstyn, "Get something to eat, then gather up the rest of the family in the conference room by eight." He turned to the guard. "Where is Tanner?"

"He's in restraints in the basement detaining cell, sir."

"Where is Dr. Jung?"

"He's in the basement with him, observing, sir."

"Come with me."

They took an elevator from the roof. Tara and Torstyn got off on the second floor while Hatch and the guards went all the way down to the basement level.

The marble-tiled corridor was dimly lit and the only sound was the echo of their footsteps as they walked. The observation room and detaining cells were at the end of the hallway. One of the guards opened the door, and Hatch stepped in.

Dr. Jung, the resident psychiatrist, was sitting in a chair facing a two-way mirror that looked into the adjacent room. He stood as Hatch entered.

"Dr. Hatch, I was just—"

Hatch raised his hand, silencing the psychiatrist. He leaned forward toward the glass to better comprehend what he was seeing in the next room.

Tanner, one of the seventeen electric children, was cuffed and curled up in bed in the fetal position, softly whimpering. His long, red hair was tangled up around his face.

Hatch studied him for a moment, then turned back toward the doctor.

"You incompetent worm. I told you to fix him. Do those letters before your name even mean anything?"

The psychiatrist was red in the face. "I'm doing my best."

"And your *best* is in restraints curled up in the corner of his room."

"He's not a machine, sir. He's a boy. You can't just go in and change out a few parts and make him better."

"But I can change out a few doctors," Hatch said.

The psychiatrist took the threat seriously. He'd heard rumors about what happened to those dispatched from the Elgen service. Most became GPs. Some of them just disappeared. He began stuttering, "W-w-what do you want me to do?"

"Why are you asking me? You're the shrink. Give him a pill. Give him a hundred pills, just fix him."

"He has a conscience. If you killed a thousand people, you'd have trouble sleeping at night too."

Hatch leaned in toward him, his eyes narrowing. "I *never* have trouble sleeping, Doctor. And if you ever insinuate anything like that again, I'll see to it that you never have trouble sleeping either."

The doctor swallowed. "I didn't mean to imply . . . Tanner's just really stressed right now. He's been worked too hard. Children need downtime. We need to let him spend some time with the other teenagers. And his parents."

"His parents?" Hatch said softly. "You think he should see his parents?"

The doctor looked terrified. "He said he misses them."

"Of course he *misses* them, you idiot. That's why he's been taken from them. So you think he should spend a little quality time with them? And what if he tells his parents what he's been doing, and they tell him they would rather die than have him drop another plane from the sky? Add that to your list of mental problems." Hatch walked across the room. "You're on probation, Doctor. Don't disappoint me again."

"I'm sorry, sir. I'll figure him out."

"You better. I'm taking both of you with me to Peru. I expect the boy to be heavily sedated. Heavily. I don't want to be along for the ride when he decides to take his life again. We leave first thing in the morning, oh five hundred hours."

"Yes, sir."

Hatch looked back at Tanner for a moment, then turned and walked out of the room. On the way to the elevator Hatch's phone rang.

"Dr. Hatch, Captain Welch is on the line."

"Put him through." Hatch paused in the hallway. "Did you capture Vey?"

"No. We lost him."

"How do you lose a tracking device?"

"He must have discovered the RFID tracers in the GPs and disabled them."

Hatch's anger reached a new high. "Find them now!"

"Yes, sir. We'll find them, sir."

Hatch threw his phone across the hall. "Vey!"

The guard retrieved his phone and held open the elevator door. "Your phone, sir."

Hatch took it from him. "Fifth floor."

23

The Family Meeting

Quentin, Tara, Kylee, and Bryan were sitting in the Elgen dining room waiting for Hatch to arrive. Torstyn was on the opposite side of the room, looking through a stack of *Soldier of Fortune* magazines.

"What's Torstyn's power?" Bryan whispered.

The kids rarely talked about one another's powers, and Torstyn had been separated from them for so long that some of them had forgotten what he could do.

"He's like a human microwave oven," Tara said.

"That could come in handy," Bryan said.

"Yeah," Quentin said dryly. "Around lunchtime."

Torstyn suddenly looked up from the magazine he was browsing, and Bryan quickly turned away. Torstyn stood up and walked over to the group. "Hey, Tara," he said. "Do that thing again."

"What thing?"

"You know, what you did on the helicopter with your powers."

Quentin looked at Tara, and she blushed. "I don't know. . . ."

"Oh, come on. You said you needed to practice."

Quentin's eyes narrowed. "Whatever it is, she doesn't want to do it. So leave her alone."

"I wasn't talking to you, pretty boy. Mind your own business."

"I'm the student body president of the academy, so Tara is my business."

Torstyn grinned. "That is pathetic. Never before has so little power gone to somebody's head. And in case you didn't get the memo, school's out, loser."

Quentin turned red in the face. "Don't push your luck, Tor-Stain."

Torstyn pushed his face into Quentin's. "Do you think I'm afraid of you? While you've spent the last year and a half lounging around California in designer jeans and polo shirts, drinking girlie drinks with little umbrellas in them, you know what I've been doing for fun? I hunt anacondas alone in the jungles. No gun. No machete. Just me." He rolled up his sleeve to show a ragged scar across his biceps leading to two large puncture wounds.

All the kids stared, and Torstyn was pleased by their response. "Last January, during the rainy season, I was wading through a patch of jungle when a thirty-foot anaconda shot out of the water and grabbed me by the arm. It tried to drag me into the river."

"No way, dude," Bryan said.

Torstyn smiled. "As it was wrapping its coils around me, I looked it in the eyes and cooked it. Its brain exploded out its ears."

"Whoa!" Bryan said. "Awesome!"

"I had some of the servants drag the snake back to the compound, and I had boots made out of its skin. The thing was a monster. I could have made a dozen pairs." Torstyn looked at Quentin and sneered. "I'm guessing the scariest thing you've faced in the last year was too much starch in your shorts, pretty boy."

Quentin didn't back down. "You want to see how much you scare me, Tarzan?" Quentin said. The air around him began to crackle with electricity.

"Don't start what you don't want me to finish, tough guy," Torstyn said.

"C'mon, guys," Tara said. "This isn't cool. Someone could get hurt."

"Shut up," Bryan said. "I want to see them fight. Battle of the Titans."

"There better not be a fight," Hatch said sternly, walking into the room. "Stand down. Both of you." He looked at Torstyn. "You weren't thinking of using your powers on another family member?"

Torstyn fidgeted. "Uh, no, sir."

"And you, Quentin?"

"No, sir. I was protecting Tara's honor, sir."

"That sounds noble," Hatch said facetiously. "You were going to protect her 'honor' with your powers?"

He swallowed. "It hadn't come to that, sir."

"You both should be glad for that. Remember my rules, gentlemen. Then remember the penalty for breaking my rules."

"Yes, sir," they both said.

"Now listen up. We are flying out first thing in the morning. So pack up tonight. We'll be gone awhile and where we're going there are no shopping malls and no concierge desk. You're going to be roughing it. So bring extra necessities. Especially you young ladies."

"How long will we be gone?" Kylee asked.

"More than a month. Possibly as long as a year."

"A year?" Tara said.

Quentin raised his hand. Torstyn rolled his eyes.

"May I ask where we're going, sir?" Quentin asked.

"No, you may not. I will fill everyone in on the details during the flight. Now go to bed. We have a long day tomorrow, and I need you all to be sharp. Everyone's excused except for Torstyn and Quentin. You two stay."

"Yes, sir," Quentin said.

Torstyn breathed out heavily. "All right."

When everyone had left Hatch looked at the two young men. Quentin's head was slightly bowed; Torstyn was slumped down in his chair.

"Sit up," Hatch said to Torstyn.

"Yes, sir," he said, straightening himself up. "Sorry, sir."

"You thought you were going to fight? What were you thinking? This isn't a schoolyard playground. With your powers, any fight is to the death. Or have you grown stupid in the last two days? Who gave you permission to kill each other?"

They sat quietly, avoiding Hatch's fierce gaze.

"I asked you a question!" Hatch shouted. "Who told you that you could risk your life without my permission?"

"No one, sir," Quentin said.

Torstyn shook his head. "No one, sir."

Hatch leaned forward. "Let me make myself perfectly clear. I don't care what you think of each other. But if either of you lets your ego get in the way of what's about to happen, you'll spend the rest of your life guarding a Starxource plant in Outer Mongolia. Do you understand?"

"Yes, sir," they said in unison.

"There will be order and strict obedience. Do you understand me?"

"Yes, sir," they repeated.

"Good. Quentin has been in charge of the group for the last five years in Pasadena and has done an adequate job of keeping the Elgen youths in line. I see no reason to change that. Quentin will remain my number one."

Quentin crossed his arms triumphantly over his chest, giving Torstyn a satisfied look. "Thank you, sir."

"Don't get smug, Quentin. You're number one over the rest of the youths, but not Torstyn. Torstyn answers only to me."

"Thank you, sir," Torstyn said, glaring at Quentin.

"Where we're headed is no Beverly Hills vacation, and none of you, except Torstyn, are ready for what you're going to encounter. Torstyn knows what it takes to survive in a hostile environment, don't you, Torstyn?"

"Yes, sir."

"Now hear me and hear me well. Whatever you do, you will not get romantically involved with any members of the family. We do not need any complications right now—a house divided against itself cannot stand. Do you both understand?"

"Yes, sir," they said again.

"What we are facing will test everyone. We've lost half the youths already, and now Tanner is on the verge of cracking. In fact, he already has. I need both of you one hundred percent. Now shake hands."

Quentin reached out his hand. "My apologies."

Torstyn gripped his hand. "Okay," he said. "Me too."

"Good," Hatch said. "I'm not surprised that you're at odds. You're both alpha males and you're both warriors—which is exactly what I need right now. Warriors." He leaned forward. "Gentlemen, the pieces are in place and we're about to make the first move. The war has begun. But first we must cleanse the inner vessel."

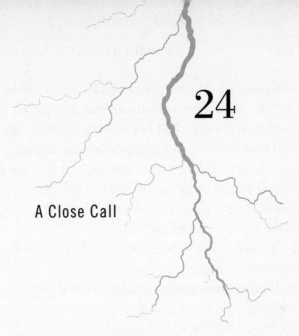

24

A Close Call

The sun was just starting to rise in Rome as Dr. Hatch and the electric children drove in a small convoy of Mercedes-Benz vans to the Leonardo da Vinci–Fiumicino airport to board the Elgen's private jet. Only Tanner traveled alone, strapped to a gurney and heavily sedated. He was attended by his doctor and one guard.

Hatch was in the lead car with three guards and the driver. He was wearing his dark, custom glasses and wrote in a notebook the entire ride, speaking only when they reached their destination.

He didn't talk to the youths at all, except to hurry them onto the plane. They each took their own row of seats except for Tara and Kylee, who sat next to each other. Tanner and Dr. Jung were behind the others, near the back of the aircraft. Tanner's gurney was fastened to the wall next to Dr. Jung's seat and a screen was drawn around them. After the jet's cabin door was closed, Hatch disappeared into his private quarters, in the back of the plane.

The flight attendant distributed a breakfast parfait to the passengers, then offered a full hot breakfast, which only Torstyn took. Bryan and both of the girls fell asleep as soon as they were airborne.

About two hours after the jet had left the ground, Hatch came out of his quarters and walked to the front of the main cabin. He grabbed a microphone from the wall and spoke. "All right, everyone. Give me your attention."

He waited as the kids stirred. Quentin woke Tara and Kylee. "Dr. Hatch is speaking."

"Is everyone listening?" Hatch asked.

"Yes, sir," Quentin said.

"Show me the Elgen salute."

Everyone made the sign, touching the three middle fingers of their left hands to their temples, their thumb and little finger touching.

"Listen carefully. What I'm about to tell you is C10."

"Whoa," Bryan said. He glanced over at Quentin, who raised his eyebrows.

Hatch labeled messages to the teens in levels of confidentiality—the more important the message, the higher the level. C10 was the highest. Even Quentin had only heard a C10 once before. The consequence of divulging information was proportionate to the level of confidentiality. Revealing a C10 message to outsiders would carry the highest punishment—death by torture.

"We are flying to Peru because I have been ordered by the Elgen board to shut down and dismantle the Neo-Species Genesis program—the very program that brought you to me in the first place, the program that you and I have spent our *lives* on for the last twelve years. I have been instructed to reallocate the scientists to different Starxource operations, quietly exterminate the GPs, and then send you all off to lead your own lives as private, normal citizens of whatever country and school you choose, never to hear from us again." Hatch leaned back, waiting for the teens to react.

"What?" Quentin said, clearly stunned.

"They can't do that!" Tara said.

Kylee started crying.

After a moment Bryan said, "Does this mean no more family trips?"

"No more family trips," Hatch said calmly. "No more *family*. You're on your own."

Hatch stoically watched them as the reality settled in, his own emotions concealed behind his glasses. The teens were clearly upset, glancing back and forth at one another in disbelief, hoping that Dr. Hatch was playing some kind of a horrible prank.

Finally Hatch said, "So tell me, what do you have to say to that?"

Quentin was the first to speak. "With all due respect, sir. I think I can speak for all of us and say we don't like it. We want to stay with you."

Hatch glanced up and down the rows. "Is that true? Kylee?"

Kylee wiped her eyes. "Yes, sir. I don't want to be an orphan."

"Tara?"

"Me too, sir."

"Bryan?"

"I think it's the dumbest thing I've ever heard."

"Torstyn?"

"Sucks."

Hatch nodded a little. "Then I take it you disapprove, Torstyn?"

"Yes, sir. I disapprove."

Hatch paused for a moment. "Then the real question is, perhaps, what exactly would you be willing to do to keep the family together?"

"Whatever you tell us to do, sir," Quentin said. "Right, everyone?" He was answered with a chorus of affirmations.

Hatch studied their expressions for a moment, then nodded approvingly. "Exactly what I thought you would say. Now let me remind you that what I am going to tell you, every word of it, is C10. What is the punishment for disclosing a C10 secret? Tara."

"The punishment for disclosing a C10 secret is death by torture."

"That is correct," Hatch said. "If you understand, show me the salute."

They all put their fingers to their temples again.

Hatch looked down for a moment, then removed his glasses, carefully folding them and sliding them into his jacket's inner pocket. "I'm pleased to hear that you don't like the board's plans, because I have no intention of following them.

"Imagine, letting you go. You beautiful, powerful youths. Cast out as pearls among the swine of humanity. You, my eagles, are not to spend your lives pecking among the chickens. The chickens are for your amusement only.

"The board will not decide our fate. *We*, not them, are in charge. *We*, not them, carry the burden of history. Their rejection is not a surprise to me. I knew that the day would come when we would reach this impasse. Why? Because we have different motivations. Their motivation is profit. But our motivation, our cause, is nothing less than a new world.

"Those idiots on the board want to put a new coat of paint on the house. I say burn the house to the ground and rebuild it! No government but *our* government. No religion but *our* religion. No gods but *our* gods. We will tear down the human foundation brick by brick and construct our own.

"These chickens have lost their way. And we are going to lead them into a bright, new coop." His eyes carefully studied the excited expressions of the youths. He spoke his next words very slowly and deliberately. "Are you with me?"

The youths cheered.

"The war has begun, my eagles. First the Elgen corporation, then the world. I have been preparing. We are going to Peru, not to shut down the compound, but to consolidate our power. Peru will be our headquarters for mounting our overthrow of the misguided corporation. You will be my war council, my generals, and my personal guard. Make no mistake, the stakes are high. If we lose, you are on your own, no money, no privilege, just a life of quiet desperation pecking out an existence with the rest of the chickens."

Hatch looked around the cabin, judging the effect of his words by the terrified and indignant looks on their faces.

"But we are not going to lose. That is not your destiny. That is not my destiny. And the Elgen are just the first speed bump on our journey. After we have conquered them, we shall, one by one, overthrow nations. I have taught you from your childhoods that you were royalty. You shall soon see how right I am. But you are not just royalty. You will be royalty's royalty. Kings will be your butlers and queens your maidservants. They will bow in your presence.

"Some of you are likely wondering how we are going to accomplish this. Our plan is perfect and already begun. We will take control of the world's electricity. Electricity is the mother's milk of civilization. When we control the electricity we will control communications, health care, and the production and distribution of food.

"If a country tries to take over our plants, we will shut down their businesses. We will shut down their communications. We will cripple their economies, and they will crawl back to us for help. And we will help them—but on our terms and at our price. If they do not surrender to us, we will threaten other countries' power until they fight for us. And *they will* fight for us. Survival is always the first rule of politics."

Quentin raised his hand.

"Yes?" Hatch said.

"How do we *make* electricity?"

Hatch smiled. "Except for Torstyn, none of you have been briefed on our Starxource project, even though you were, indirectly, a part of its development. Now is the time for you to know. How do we make electricity? The same way that you do. When we are in Peru you will have a full tour of the facility. Our Starxource plants use a renewable, bioelectric source of power production.

"We are currently opening Starxource plants at the rate of a new facility every two months. Soon we will have that down to one plant a month. Then two plants a months. Then a plant a week.

"Countries are already begging for us to come in with our power. Why wouldn't they? We offer them clean power at a fraction of the cost. It's practically free. No pollution, no economic strain. Those who don't turn to us will be at an economic disadvantage to those who do.

"Of course, this begs the question, why would we give away our electricity? Because we are like the drug dealer handing out free drugs on the schoolyard playground. Once the world is hooked, we will, of course, raise the prices and increase our demands until we own them."

"We rule!" Bryan shouted.

Hatch smiled. "Yes, we will."

Quentin raised his hand again. "Sir, how will we fight the Elgen? They have thousands of guards."

"Which we will use to our advantage. In fact, we will soon be quadrupling our number of guards, all of whom will be trained by us in Peru. As for our current force, I have summoned all the guards from Elgen facilities around the world. In two days they will be arriving in Peru for a two-week rehabilitation conference. The board believes this conference is to train our forces for their new roles in the Starxource plants, which, ironically, is true—just not in the roles the board expects.

"Our Peruvian force is our largest and is completely loyal to us. Soon *all* the Elgen guards will be loyal to us. We will choose our leaders and purge the rest of the force. When we are done, we will control the security forces within each plant. Anyone who does not follow my orders will be punished. Any questions?"

Suddenly the plane took a huge dip, knocking Hatch to the ground. Several of the teens screamed. An alarm began beeping and oxygen masks dropped from the ceiling.

"What's happening?" Hatch shouted to the pilots. There was no answer. Hatch crawled to the cockpit and pulled open the door. "What's happening?"

"We don't know," the copilot shouted. "We've lost power. Everything just went . . . ."

Hatch didn't wait for him to finish. He rushed to the fuselage, shouting to the guard. "Pull the screen!"

The guard, who was still belted in his chair, reached back and pulled the screen. Tanner was awake, his dark blue eyes looking at them.

"Shoot him!" Hatch shouted to the guard.

The guard didn't move. He just stared, as if frozen.

"Shoot him before he kills us all. Now!"

The guard still hesitated.

Suddenly Tanner started screaming. "I'll stop! I'll stop!"

Hatch looked over to see Torstyn, his lip curled in anger, his hand extended toward Tanner. Then the guard hit Tanner over the head with his pistol, knocking him out.

The jet dropped again, then leveled out. Kylee and Bryan both threw up. It took several minutes for everyone to settle. After the plane was back on course the captain's voice came over the PA system. "Sorry for the turbulence, everyone. We should be fine now."

Hatch stood again, composing himself. "Well done, Torstyn," he said. "A round of applause for Torstyn, who just saved all of our lives."

Everyone clapped, even Quentin.

"You will be handsomely rewarded when we arrive in Peru."

"Thank you, sir," Torstyn said.

Hatch pointed at the psychiatrist. "You."

Dr. Jung was pale with fear.

"Sedate the boy until anesthetic flows from his tear ducts." Hatch's eyes narrowed. "Do not let him wake again until we're on the ground. Do you understand?"

"Yes, sir. He won't. It won't happen again. I promise."

"I should hope not. If he wakes again, I'll have both of you thrown out of the airplane. Are we clear on this?"

The doctor blanched. "Yes, sir. Very clear."

"Close the screen," he said to the guard.

"Yes, sir," the guard said, pulling the screen around the pair.

"We'll deal with your insubordination after we land."

"Yes, sir."

Hatch looked back at the youths. "Where were we?"

25

Retribution

The plane landed in Rio de Janeiro to refuel, then quickly took off again, finally touching down at a small airfield near the Elgen's Peruvian compound, in the town of Puerto Maldonado.

The asphalt runway was surrounded by walls of trees that spilled outward from the burgeoning forest. The jet taxied to a small hangar where a contingency of Elgen guards and a bus were waiting to transport the group to the compound.

The plane stopped and a stairway unfolded from its side. A guard climbed to the top of the stairs and knocked on the door.

Bryan was the first one out, followed by the rest of the youths.

"Whoa," Bryan said. "It's hot. Like a furnace hot."

"And humid," Tara added. "My hair is going to be frizzy."

Torstyn rolled his eyes. "This is nothing. Wait until summer."

A moment later the guard walked out, followed by Hatch. The

six Peruvian guards at the bottom of the stairs saluted Hatch as he emerged from the plane and descended the stairway. Hatch stopped at the bottom and returned the Elgen salute.

"Captain Figueroa," he said.

"Yes, sir!"

He pointed to the guard from the plane, who was not standing at attention. "This man disobeyed a direct order. His inaction nearly cost us our lives. Put him under arrest."

"Yes, sir," the captain snapped. "Guards at attention."

The Peruvian soldiers pointed their guns at the lone guard, who, in spite of his many years with the Elgen, was still caught off guard. He looked on in horror.

The captain stepped forward with his gun drawn, his other hand out. "Guard 247, surrender your gun. Slowly and by the barrel."

"Yes, sir," he said, his voice trembling. He slowly removed his gun from its holster and, holding it by its barrel, handed it to the captain.

"Put your hands behind your back. Now!"

He quickly obeyed.

"Secure this man," the captain barked.

"Sir, yes, sir." One of the soldiers ran up behind the guard and handcuffed the man's hands behind his back, fastening the metal belt through a buckle in the back of the guard's uniform.

The captain turned to Hatch. "Prisoner is secured. What are your orders, sir?"

Hatch scowled at the handcuffed guard. "Captain Figueroa, detain this man for now in maximum security. For the benefit of the visiting guards we're going to make an example of him. We're going to put him in the chute."

The condemned guard's face turned pale. "No, please, sir. Not that. I beg you!" He fell to his knees, bowing his head to Hatch's feet. "Please, sir. Anything but that! Shoot me. Please, shoot me."

Hatch sneered. "Show some dignity, man." He kicked the guard away from him. "Captain, keep him alive until I give you further instructions."

"No!" the man screamed. He tried to get to his feet to run, but he was knocked down before he could stand.

The teens watched the exchange with amusement.

"What a wimp," Torstyn said.

"What's the chute?" Tara asked.

"It's where they feed the rats," Torstyn said.

"What rats?"

He looked at her with a snide grin. "They really don't tell you much, do they?"

Several guards carried Tanner's gurney from the plane, escorted by Dr. Jung.

"Let's go," Hatch said to the captain. "Captain Figueroa."

"Yes, sir."

"Also detain Tanner and the doctor in maximum security until further notice."

The doctor turned white. "But, Dr. Hatch—"

"Don't speak to me," he said. "Or I'll send you to the chute as well."

The doctor froze.

"To the bus, please," Hatch said to the teens.

Tara said to Torstyn, "They're going to feed him to rats?"

"Yeah. It's a cool thing to watch."

"You've seen this before?" Quentin asked.

"Of course. Hundreds of times. Feeding time is better than the movies. I've seen the rats strip the meat off a two-thousand-pound bull in less than a minute."

"Awesome," Bryan said.

"Yeah, this guy will be a snack for them."

As Hatch and the kids approached the bus, a man wearing a white jacket and Panama hat, holding a spider monkey, walked up to Torstyn. "Here is your *mono*, Señor Torstyn."

"Hey, Arana," Torstyn said, taking his pet. He put the monkey on his shoulder, and it climbed up onto his head.

"Cute," Tara said, reaching out her hand.

"Yeah, wait until she bites you," Torstyn said.

Tara quickly pulled her hand back, and Torstyn laughed. Suddenly the monkey began screeching, then jumped off Torstyn's head and ran off toward the jungle.

"Arana!" he shouted after it. When it had disappeared into the jungle he turned back to Tara. "What did you do?"

Tara just smiled. "Nothing. You think I can get in an animal's head?"

"Yes," he said.

Quentin grinned. "Bad news for you, Torstyn. You thought you were safe."

Torstyn glared at both of them. "That was my pet," he said, turning away from them.

Quentin laughed. "We're definitely going to have fun in the jungle."

26

Puerto Maldonado

The Elgen's Peruvian Starxource plant was situated near the southeastern city of Puerto Maldonado, a jungle town in the Amazon Basin. It was the largest of the Elgen's compounds and built on a twenty-five-thousand-acre ranch hemmed in by jungle on all sides. Hatch and his team had selected the city for three reasons: First, it was remote, many miles away from curious eyes. Second, there was plenty of water, as the Río Madre de Dios, a tributary of the Amazon River, passed through the town; and third, it had an abundance of labor. Puerto Maldonado had once been a thriving logging and gold-mining camp, but both the gold and lumber were long gone, leaving few employment opportunities for the natives and guaranteeing an abundant workforce.

The compound had three main structures. The largest building was the Starxource power plant, called *el bol* by the natives, or "the bowl." The bowl was a massive, redbrick building with stainless steel casings that bulged out in the middle. Most said the bowl looked like a flying saucer had crashed into it. Just east of the building were three smaller buildings: the water house, the ranch house, and a food production plant.

West of the bowl was the Elgen Reeducation Center, or "Re-Ed," as it was known by the guards, a rectangular building without windows used to rehabilitate uncooperative employees.

Connected to the Re-Ed by a brick corridor was the assembly hall, a massive building that could house more than two thousand people and served as both a cafeteria and an educational facility.

North of the assembly hall was residential housing, three long, rectangular buildings where the guards, scientists, and employees slept. Hatch, the electric children, and the Elite Guard—twelve men personally selected by Hatch to oversee the Elgen security force— had their own housing facilities on the west side of the Re-Ed.

The bus passed through two checkpoints during the drive into the compound, and even though the bus entered the gates only ten minutes from the airfield, it took a little more than thirty-five minutes for them to reach their housing facilities.

The youths were each assigned a guard and two personal assistants, all Peruvians who spoke English. While the assistants prepared their suites and oversaw the delivery of their luggage, the teens ate lunch in their private dining room. Afterward they gathered in the lobby of their new home, where Dr. Hatch was waiting for them.

"I know it's not Beverly Hills," Hatch said. "But I trust your suites are satisfactory."

All of them agreed that their Peruvian accommodations were as luxurious as the academy in Pasadena.

"Then it will be my pleasure to give you a tour of your new home. I think you will be rather impressed with what we've built in the jungle. I know I am." Hatch ushered them outside to a twelve-seat golf cart with a flashing amber light on top. The driver was a guard dressed in the standard uniform, except for a bright red patch featuring a condor, symbolic of the Chasqui, a special Elgen military order in Peru.

The teens boarded the cart and Hatch climbed up front with the driver and took the microphone. "Everything you'll see on this tour is C9."

The difference between C9 and C10 was that C9 could be discussed with other Elgen associates while in a secure Elgen facility. Unlawful disclosure, however, carried the same punishment as C10.

"Onward," Hatch said.

The cart made a sharp U-turn, then glided silently down the smooth, resin-coated cement floor past the Re-Ed and toward the Starxource plant. Two guards stood at attention as they approached, and the metal doors behind the guards opened.

The inside of the building looked similar to the lower laboratory of the Pasadena academy, only on a much larger scale. The building was more than a hundred yards from end to end, the length of a football field. The corridors were lit with bluish-white indirect lighting, giving the hallways a futuristic, eerie look. It took several minutes for the cart to reach their destination—the elevator to the bowl's observation deck.

As they approached the room Hatch said, "What you are about to see is the heart of the Starxource program—the very core of our power and our future." A grim smile crossed his face. "I guarantee you won't soon forget it."

The elevator opened to reveal a sealed door guarded by two Elgen guards dressed in black with red armbands. The guards stood stiffly at attention and saluted as Hatch stepped from the cart. One of the guards opened the door, and the kids filed in after Hatch.

Bryan was the first to comment on what they saw. "No way!" he shouted.

27

Beware the Stranger

The teens had seen remarkable things in their lives, far more than normal teenagers, but nothing could have prepared them for the bowl. The observation deck was sixty feet long, and the inner wall, slightly convex, was made of glass, which allowed them a view of something few would ever see: nearly a million electrified rats.

The swarms of rats crawled over one another, creating an undulating, massive orange-and-gray carpet, and in parts of the bowl they looked like molten lava.

"What you're looking at is almost a million rats, each of them capable of generating two hundred and fifty watts and two amps of electricity an hour; that's five hundred watts a second, nearly identical wattage to the electric eel. Combined, that's three hundred seventy-five million watts a second, more than enough to light downtown New York City.

"You can't see it because of the rodents, but beneath them, the floor is a delicate, silver-coated copper grid, the largest ever constructed. Its purpose is to conduct electricity to the capacitors below. We also use the grid to solve the problem of waste, as the rats' excrement drops below and is conveyed out to be processed into manure, more than twelve tons a day."

"That's a lot of crap," Bryan said, punching Torstyn in the shoulder.

"Do that again and I'll melt your head," Torstyn said.

"What's that big arm thing in the middle?" Quentin asked.

Connected to the center of the bowl was a curved metallic blade about three feet high and a hundred and forty feet long. The arm slowly swept the bowl like the second hand of a clock.

"That's the sweep," Hatch said. "The rats only generate usable amounts of electricity when they're active, so the sweep makes a complete revolution of the bowl every ninety-six minutes, forcing the rats to continually move. If we need more power we simply increase the speed of the arm, generating more electricity. The sweep has another purpose as well. The angle of the blade forces anything on the grid to its outer rim—so it disposes of animal bones and dead rats, pushing their carcasses off the grid."

"With the poop?" Bryan asked.

"No. The outer rim falls into special troughs that convey the dead rats into an electric grinder. There, the meat and bone are milled into powder, mixed with an iodine supplement and a glucose solution, then stamped and baked into biscuits, which our scientists call Rabisk—short for rat biscuits. We then feed them to the rats."

Tara grimaced. "You mean they're cannibals?"

"Rats are naturally cannibalistic, but ours are a little different. The electric rats won't eat their own. Our scientists believe that they learn this from shocking each other when they're young. So they won't eat a rat, even a dead one, until it no longer looks like a rat, or until it's been processed into Rabisk. It's an extremely efficient way of feeding. When we first started this process we had some problems with the rat version of mad cow disease, but our rats only live nineteen months on average, so by genetically altering the rats we were able stave off the disease for their lifespan. Our rats die earlier than other rats because of their constant state of motion and the electricity that flows through them."

"Where did you get so many rats?" Tara asked.

"The old-fashioned way," Hatch said. "We bred them. Rats are one of the most efficient breeders of all the mammals on the planet. They are capable of producing offspring within six weeks of birth—compared to twelve to thirteen years for humans. It's been speculated that two rats in an ideal breeding environment could produce more than a million offspring in their lifetime.

"Of course, until now, that has just been speculation. But we've proven it. We are able to create thousands of rats a day, far more than we need." Hatch pointed to the far edge of the bowl. "See that small door there? You can just make out the outline. That is where new rats are delivered to the grid. We introduce about seventy new rats every hour, twenty-four/seven. In addition, we keep a twenty percent surplus of rats at all times, in case of disease."

"What if they escaped?" Bryan said. "That would be awesome."

"No," Hatch said coldly. "That would not be *awesome*. In fact, it's one of our greatest concerns. They would spread throughout the world like an epidemic. Rats are already the world's leading cause of extinction. Electric rats like ours could destroy entire ecosystems.

"It would also allow anyone to breed our rats and create their own power source, something that would forever end our monopoly. So, as I said, it *would not be awesome*. And it will never happen. Our rats have been bioengineered to die outside of captivity. However, accidents happen. We had a few dozen rats escape before we reengineered them. It might have been an utter disaster, but fortunately the rats have a weakness. Water applied directly to their bodies kills them."

"Like Zeus," Kylee said.

Hatch spun around, his face twisted in fury. "What did you say?"

Kylee flushed as she realized what she had done—they were not allowed to speak Zeus's name. The other youths looked at her with anger and sympathy.

"I—I didn't mean to. . . . It just came out. I'm sorry. . . ."

"To your room," Hatch said.

"I'm so sorry, sir. It will never happen again."

"Indeed it won't," Hatch said. He turned to the guard. "Take her back. Punishment B."

Kylee grimaced but dared not complain. Punishment B consisted of a full week of room confinement on a bread-and-water diet. During that time she would be required to write *I will not disobey Dr. Hatch's rules* ten thousand times.

Bryan grinned. "Have fun."

Kylee shot him a look as she walked away with the guard.

Quentin slowly shook his head. "That was dumb."

"It was just a mistake," Tara said softly. "Anyone could have made it."

"I'm just glad it was her and not me," Quentin said.

Just then an alarm sounded from inside the bowl.

"Hear that?" Hatch said. "We're in luck. You're going to get to watch the feeding."

"You're going to love this," Torstyn said to Tara. "The guards usually come up here on their breaks to watch."

Thirty yards to their right, a chute, about eight feet wide with metallic rollers, suddenly protruded from the wall. The feeding chute was connected to hydraulic lifts that extended it about twenty yards out from the bowl's side, slowly lowering it until the end of the chute dangled less than ten feet above the rats, which had already begun congregating around it. A door opened from the wall.

"Watch," Torstyn said. "Here it comes."

Suddenly a massive, long-horned bull slid down the chute. The animal's feet were tied together and it struggled against its bindings but was able to move only its head.

"What is that?" Bryan asked.

"It's a bull," Hatch said. "Raised on our own ranch. We passed many of them on our way in."

"It's still alive?" Tara asked, slightly grimacing.

"Always," Hatch said. "Fresh meat produces more electricity. Or, more accurately, struggling meat."

A spiked-wheel mechanism caught the animal near the bottom of the slide, and the end of the chute snapped in the middle, slowly tilting farther down until the animal was about six feet above the grid. The animal was desperately trying to free itself.

"The chute can't touch the grid or it will damage it," Torstyn explained. "The grid, as a whole, can hold more than a thousand tons, but square by square it's actually pretty fragile."

In anticipation of their meal, the rats clambered to the chute, climbing on top of one another in a massive wave of fur that glowed a dull red like a hot plate. For the first time since they'd arrived, the glistening copper grid was partially visible, as the rodents were all gathered beneath the chute. When the bull was lowered within a yard of the grid, rats began jumping up onto the animal.

"I didn't know rats could jump that high," Quentin said.

"They look like spawning salmon," Bryan said.

"Rats can jump up to forty inches vertical," Hatch replied. "That's the equivalent of a human jumping three stories."

Within seconds the bull was completely covered by the rodents in a wild feeding frenzy. The rats increased in brightness like a filament. Blue, white, and yellow electricity arced around the carcass, and steam and smoke rose around the bull. The arcs and colors, highlighted by the steam, were, in a peculiar way, beautiful to look at—like the aurora borealis.

"The vapor you see comes from the rats' electricity against the bull. They're actually cooking the meat with their bodies," Hatch said. "That's a rat barbecue."

"Look!" Bryan said excitedly. "They've already stripped its legs to the bone."

Within three minutes the bull was reduced to nothing but skeleton. Even its internal organs were eaten.

"They're like furry piranhas," Quentin said. "I'd hate to be down there."

"Wait," Tara said. "You mean, that's what they're going to do to that guard on our flight? Put him on *that* chute?"

"Yep," Torstyn said.

Tara covered her mouth. "I'm going to be sick."

The chute began to retract and lift, dropping the animal to the floor of the grid as it moved. Then the door at the top of the chute opened again and another bull slid out.

"How many bulls will they eat?" Tara asked.

"Our rats are a little more voracious than your average house rat," Hatch replied. "Still, they don't eat that much. About an ounce to an ounce and a half a day. But with this many rats, that still equates to twenty-nine tons of food a day. They're omnivorous, so they eat a combination of grains and meat. Every day we go through about ten tons in raw meat, about five bulls, and the rest are in Rabisk and grain. But they prefer the meat, especially since fresh food helps quench their thirst and drinking water can be a little tricky for them."

"How do they drink?" Quentin asked.

Dr. Hatch smiled. "Very carefully." He pointed to the vacant side of the bowl. "See those white ceramic disks? They're drinking fountains for rats. They're exactly one tenth of a millimeter beneath the grid—just close enough that the rats can lick water off them."

After the second bull had been devoured, Hatch ordered the teens back to the elevator. "There's more to see," he said.

They made the rounds through the laboratory and corridors around the bowl. The MEI room and breeding labs were connected directly to the bowl for ease of operation. They toured the Rabisk plant, which smelled so bad they had to wear nose plugs. Men in white coats walked back and forth between different machines, measuring output, then sending the small biscuits to the oven, then back to the feeding rooms.

"This side of the facility is our meat processing center and next to that is our ranch house, where our *gauchos* live."

Before they left the facility Hatch pointed out one last section of the building. "These are the cells where we inter our traitors and GPs who have outlived their usefulness. You might also call this a meat processing facility. Our guards call it death row. You'll recognize our newest guest." They looked in to see the guard from the plane.

"You should show him the bowl," Bryan said.

Hatch replied, "If we were trying to get information from him or instill a behavioral change, the fear would be of some value. But, as it is, his course is set, so to show him the bowl would serve no useful purpose."

They walked from the cells back out to the lobby, where the cart was waiting. As they climbed aboard, an overhanging door rose ahead of them, and they drove out into the yard. The walks of the compound were all open but covered, as the weather on Puerto Maldonado was usually temperate, though subject to a heavy rainy season. The guard drove around the building to the south, the transmission substation.

"Nothing here you haven't seen before," Hatch said. "This is where the power that comes from the plant is dispersed. It feeds from our transmission substation over high-voltage transmission lines to local power substations and then to homes and businesses as far away as Lima.

"You can compare our system to the human body. Our power plant is the heart. The high-voltage lines are major arteries, which break down into veins, then capillaries, eventually feeding into individual homes and businesses. Electricity is truly the lifeblood of civilization.

"Over the last two years we've helped the Peruvian government lay miles of high-voltage power lines. If we were to shut down, all of Puerto Maldonado, Cuzco, and the surrounding cities would also shut down. Even more impressive is that two of Peru's largest cities would also be majorly impacted: Eighty percent of Arequipa and almost half of Lima would go dark. Within a year, we will be powering ninety-five percent of the country." A smile crossed his thin lips. "At which point, we'll own the country." He looked out over the station with satisfaction.

"They should have been more cautious. 'Beware the stranger offering gifts, as true for man as it is for fish,'" Hatch said slowly. "So it is."

* * *

The next building the cart stopped at was the Reeducation Center. The cart pulled up to a door made of thick steel and attended by two guards who, like the guards at the bowl, stood at attention and saluted Dr. Hatch.

The doors opened, and the group walked into a holding area with a second set of doors.

"This looks like a prison," Tara said, her voice echoing.

"It's much more than that," Hatch said. "This is our Reeducation Center. It's here that we help our enemies change their minds."

"You brainwash them?" Quentin asked.

Hatch gave him a disapproving glance. "This is where we *teach* these misguided souls the error of their thinking. Sometimes it takes a while, but you would be surprised at just how malleable the human brain can be. In the right environment the mind can be molded like clay. Men and women walk in here as enemies and come out as devotees, willing to lay down their lives for our cause."

After the first door had locked behind them, the second door clicked, then opened, and the teens walked into the main hall. The floors were smooth, resin-coated concrete, and the walls were dark red brick.

Hatch spoke as they walked. "Pavlov taught us the rules of conditioning—but he also taught us that the human mind can be quickly converted from years of training to a new way of thinking by a single traumatic experience.

"We can induce that kind of trauma through punishment—but we've also discovered that the mere *threat* of punishment can be just as effective. So, of course, we show them the rats."

Through Plexiglas windows the teens could see rows of men in pink, flowered jumpsuits sitting on long benches watching films.

"Why are they wearing pink?" Bryan asked.

"Everything you see has a reason. They are dressed in clothing that embarrasses and humiliates them. How strong can you be dressed as a little girl?"

Tara and Bryan snickered.

"You would be surprised at how powerful something as simple as changing someone's clothing can be. Psychologists and fashion designers have long known that changing someone's appearance can alter their self-perception. And when you change someone's self-perception, you change their behavior.

"Of course, we also change their names. In our case we give them numbers. When they no longer can identify with who they were, they begin to doubt their own thoughts and feelings. It is then that we can implant them with our truths.

"We didn't discover all this, of course—we had the Korean War and Vietnamese reeducation camps to learn from—but I'm proud to say we've significantly advanced the science. We have the benefit of using procedures they never dreamed of." He put his hand on Tara's shoulder. "Like emulating Tara's gifts. We can make them doubt their own sanity within minutes. And, like their identity, once they doubt their sanity, we're most of the way there.

"What we discovered is that the more people think they can't be controlled, the easier subjects they make. What the masses don't realize is that they're looking for a shepherd. Those who don't think they can be influenced or call themselves 'independent thinkers' are usually the biggest conformists of all—and the easiest to turn. Why do you think cults prey on college students? Easy picking."

"You make it sound simple," Quentin said.

Hatch looked at him and smiled. "It is when you know what you're doing." He stopped near an open door to a theater room. Nearly two dozen inmates were seated quietly on the ground even though there were enough seats for everyone. "Take a seat, everyone," Hatch said to the youths. "Everyone except Tara." The group quickly found seats. Tara stood anxiously, unsure if she'd done something wrong. "While I speak to Tara, I'd like you to view one of the films we've produced so you understand how the newly reeducated think and act. In the meantime I have an errand. I'll be back when the film is over. Tara, if you'll come with me."

"Yes, sir." Tara followed Hatch out of the room. In the hallway

Hatch turned to her. "We have a little visit to make. I need your help."

"You need my powers?" she asked with relief.

"No," Hatch replied. "I need your face."

28

Sharon Vey

Thirty-four marks. Sharon Vey had counted the days of her captivity by scratching marks into the concrete floor of her cell. Her room was only ten by ten, two-thirds of it occupied by her metal cage.

She was sitting back against the bars when Hatch walked into the room. "Hello, Sharon." A buzzer went off and he typed in the required code. Mrs. Vey turned away from him.

"Miss me?" Hatch asked.

Still no answer.

"I trust your accommodations are to your satisfaction."

"You can't keep me here."

"Of course we can."

"You won't get away with this. They'll find me."

Hatch's brow furrowed with mock concern. "*Who* will find you?"

Mrs. Vey didn't answer. She knew it was a stupid thing to say.

No one would find her here. She wasn't even sure where she was.

"Surely you don't mean that inept little police department in Meridian, Idaho. In the first place, we own them. Secondly, you, my dear, are a long, long way from Idaho. And the only way you're ever going to get back there is if you no longer wish to return."

"I know who you are," she said.

"Do you?" He sat down in the room's lone chair, an amused grin blanketing his face. "Don't make me wait, tell me."

"You're Jim Hatch."

"I prefer Dr. Hatch, but yes, they used to call me that."

"My husband told me about you."

"And what, exactly, did your late husband have to say?"

"He said you are an unstable, diabolical, delusional man with megalomaniac tendencies."

Hatch smiled. "Did he also tell you that I'm dangerous?"

Mrs. Vey looked at him coldly. "Yes."

"That's the thing about your husband, he always called a spade a spade."

"Where is my son?"

"We have him safely locked away as we reeducate him."

"I want to see him."

"When we're done, you'll see him. When he's broken and subservient, you'll see him. You may not recognize him anymore, but you'll definitely see him."

"You'll never break him."

"On the contrary. If psychology has taught us anything, it's that everyone has a breaking point. *Everyone*."

"I want to see my son!" she shouted.

"Poignant. Really, I'm moved. A mother crying out for her son. But what *you* want is of no relevance. All that matters is what *I* want. Besides, he's not ready. He's a special boy. And when we're done, he'll be of great value to our cause."

"You have no cause except your own lust for power."

Hatch grinned darkly. "You make that sound like it's a bad thing." He leaned toward the bars. "The lust for power is the only way the world has ever changed. Of course we dress it up in noble intentions, but in the end politics and religion are like sausage—it may be good, but it's best not to know what goes into it.

"Trust me, the day will come when I will be honored as the visionary I am."

"You're delusional," Mrs. Vey said.

Hatch smiled. "All great men are delusional. How else could they be crazy enough to think they could change the world?" He leaned back. "The day will come when I will be as celebrated as George Washington is today. And the electric children, including yours, will be held up and worshipped as the pioneers of a new world order. You should be pleased to know that your son will be held in such high esteem. You cling to the past only because you fear change. But nothing good comes without change. *Nothing.* Change is evolution, nothing more. And if it wasn't for evolution you'd still be living in a tree eating bananas."

Mrs. Vey just looked at him.

"Speaking of eating, has anyone told you what *you've* been eating for the past month? Those tasty little biscuits are called Rabisk. They're made of ground-up rats: meat, fur, and bonemeal."

Her stomach churned.

"There's someone I'd like you to meet." He walked to the cell door and opened it. "You may come in now."

Tara walked in. "Hi, Mrs. Vey."

Mrs. Vey looked at her with surprise. "Taylor?"

Tara smiled. "It's so good to see you."

"What are you doing here?"

"I came to help. What Dr. Hatch is doing is wonderful. For all of us."

"Have you seen Michael?"

"Of course."

"How is he?"

"He's great. He's having a good time."

Mrs. Vey couldn't believe what she was hearing. "A good time? Has he asked about me?"

Tara shook her head. "No. I mean, he knows you're okay and we're all just so busy and going places. But I'm sure he'll find time to visit before too long."

Mrs. Vey knew her son better than that. Something was wrong with the situation. Something about the girl's eyes was different—not the color or shape of her eyes, but something less definable. It was the light in them. Or lack of it.

"Does Michael still wear the watch you gave him for his birthday?" Mrs. Vey asked.

Tara hesitated. "Uh, most of the time. Not when he plays basketball or stuff."

Mrs. Vey nodded. "So, Taylor. What do your parents think of you leaving home?"

"They're really happy for me."

"Really?"

"Oh, yes. They're so proud that I can make a difference in this world."

"Even your dad?"

"Of course. Why wouldn't he be?"

"Well, you know how schoolteachers worry about kids. Especially their own."

"No, he's good with it all. He's good."

Mrs. Vey stared at her for a moment, then breathed out slowly. "No, he's not. Your father's not a schoolteacher, he's a police officer. And you didn't give Michael that watch for his birthday. I did."

Tara glanced nervously at Dr. Hatch.

"Who are you and why do you look just like Taylor?" Mrs. Vey asked.

Hatch slowly shook his head. "It was worth a try. Sharon, this is Tara, Taylor's lost twin. And she's going to be your new best friend. Every day until we bring Michael in, she's going to make your stay a little more . . . interesting. Just like she did for your son."

"What did you do to him?"

"You'll find out soon enough. Tara, Mrs. Vey likes rats. She's been eating them for weeks now. So, for your first session," Hatch said, tapping his temple with his index finger, "I think you should give her a few hundred to keep her company."

"Yes, sir," Tara said.

"Thirty minutes' worth."

"Yes, sir."

Hatch smiled. "Very well. I'll go now and let you two get better acquainted."

Hatch walked back to the others, who were still in the theater. "Let's go," he said.

The youths immediately stood, unnoticed by the others in the room. When they were outside the theater, Bryan asked, "How many times do they have to watch that movie?"

"As many times as they need," Hatch replied. "A few of these prisoners have seen this particular presentation more than a thousand times. Remember, repetition breeds conviction.

"When the prisoners are brought in for reeducation, they go through our boot camp, a carefully orchestrated psychological assault guaranteed to drive them to submission or madness. We'll take either. First they are shown a rat feeding, then told that they will be fed to the rats the next morning. While they await their fate they enter phase one: They are locked naked in a three-by-three cell without food or water. We call this 'think time'—time for them to contemplate the fragility of their own mortality and their own powerlessness.

"In their cell there is no sound, no darkness, just a bright light and their impending death. Since there is neither a clock nor contact with the outer world, they do not know when it is night or day, and minutes begin to feel like days. On the third day they are given two cups of water and three Rabisk biscuits. They are told that their fate is still being considered.

"They then enter phase two. During the next seventy-two hours loud music is piped into their cube, nonstop. We usually choose something primal with a heavy beat, like heavy metal or grunge, as we find that it has a decidedly *unsettling* effect. Believe me, it works.

"After those three days comes phase three. The music stops. They are told that due to the mercy of the Elgen and because we believe that they still might be saved, their life has been temporarily spared. This is when their education begins. We start by playing a looped audio presentation we call *The Scold*. This recording consists of different voices screaming at them, condemning them for their crimes against humanity. After three days of *The Scold* they are usually reduced to whimpering idiots. They are then invited to confess their crimes, real or imagined." Hatch grinned. "You'd be surprised what they come up with.

"They are then reviewed by one of our therapists, and if they are sufficiently penitent, they are moved to a cell and allowed brief interaction with others—in supervised group therapy, of course. It is here that they are given a new identity. They are allowed to confess and seek forgiveness. All this time they are allowed only four hours of sleep a night, and the rest of their time is filled with studying the Elgen plan of forgiveness and our new global order. Every moment is planned, and they become deeply dependent on us. By the end of the process, they belong to the order and we reinforce their condition by allowing them to help reeducate others. It's a beautiful thing to watch."

Tara appeared in the hallway.

"How did it go?" Hatch asked.

"Good. She's strong, but not that strong. She passed out."

"Next time tone it back so she experiences the full therapeutic effect."

"Yes, sir."

Hatch looked back at the group. "It's time for dinner. I want you to go to bed at a reasonable hour. The guards begin arriving early tomorrow. We have a special few days ahead, and I want you at your best for all of it. This is the time for you to show them who you are." Hatch smiled. "My eagles."

29

The Future

The next morning the Elgen guards began arriving from the thirty-eight Starxource plants around the globe. There were more than two thousand Elgen guards worldwide, and they made up an fierce, well-trained, and well-equipped security force.

They were met at the airport by Hatch's Peruvian guards. The men were disarmed, then led immediately into orientation.

One of Hatch's Elite Guards informed him of the first arrival. "The guards are arriving, sir."

"How many?"

"Three buses, a hundred and forty-seven men."

"What condition are they in?"

"Exhausted."

"Good," he said. "Don't let them sleep."

"A few have already lain on the ground."

"Then get them up and run them. Has there been any insubordination?"

"Some."

"Good," Hatch said. "We need examples. Arrest them. We'll be showcasing them tonight. You know my plans, make sure they are followed to the letter."

"Yes, sir."

Hatch had organized the guards' flights to be as long and tiring as possible, so they would be exhausted upon arrival. When the guards landed, they were also given drinks lightly laced with Trazodone, a mild antidepressant that is often used as a sleep aid, causing drowsiness, light-headedness, and confusion. Hatch's plan was first to break the men down physically through drugs, labor, lack of sleep, and hunger. Then, when they were near collapse, he'd break them mentally. In their weakened condition, the guards would reveal their true loyalties and Hatch would divide them into "sheep" and "goats." The sheep, those who would enthusiastically follow Hatch, he would train and advance to leadership rank, repositioning them to take control of Starxource plants or Elgen compounds. The goats, or those who did not cooperate, would be reeducated. If after several weeks they were still troublesome, he would extinguish them. There was no room for defiance.

Upon their arrival, the guards were put to work digging a large trench on the far side of the ranch. The trench had absolutely no purpose but to keep the men working. When darkness fell, the exhausted guards were driven back to the compound and assigned to their barracks. They were instructed to put on their guard uniforms and report to the mess hall for dinner.

The men were served small meals; peas and carrots, salad, and *cuy*—a local Peruvian delicacy of fried guinea pig. Many of the men complained about the food, and there was a small uprising at one table that was immediately quelled by the Peruvian guards. The two most demonstrative protestors were arrested and taken away.

At 9:00 p.m. the men were sent back to their barracks and told to sleep, as their day would begin early the next morning. It was only a ruse, as less than two hours later a shrill buzzer rang throughout the compound and all lights came on. Armed Peruvian guards walked into each barrack, waking the men and marching them to the assembly hall, where they were told to stand quietly at attention in front of metal chairs. A few more complained of their treatment and were quickly taken away by the Peruvian guards.

The room they had been congregated in was large enough to hold all two thousand men. The metal chairs faced a raised stage at the front of the hall. There was a podium in the middle of the stage flanked by twelve guards, six on each side, dressed in black, with purple and scarlet chest emblems and armbands on the right arm. The Elgen logo was projected on the screen behind them in letters twenty feet high. At exactly midnight a loud bell sounded and the guard to the right of the podium walked up to the microphone.

"Elgen Force. Salute."

The men gave the Elgen salute.

"The weak among you may sit."

The men looked at one another. A few sat—collapsed, really—but most, in spite of their exhaustion, remained standing.

"Many of you have flown from halfway around the world. I have heard complaints from the weak that you are tired. I would expect such complaints from weaker men. But you are not men. You are Elgen."

This was followed by applause among the standing.

"It is my distinct privilege to bring to this stage our supreme commander and president. A true visionary the world will someday acknowledge. The weak who are sitting will rise with the strong for President C. J. Hatch."

The room broke into applause as Quentin and Torstyn walked onto the stage, taking their places on each side of the podium, in front of the Elite Guards. Then Hatch walked in from the side of the stage to the podium. The guard who had introduced Hatch quickly stepped back as he approached. Hatch saluted him, then stepped up to the microphone. The audience stilled while he looked them over.

Hatch spoke in a soft voice. "Sit down. Sit down, please. All of you." He waited for everyone to sit. "Greetings, my friends. It is just past midnight. A new day, literally and figuratively. Today is the beginning of a new day for each of you. When you came into our employment you were fully aware that this was not merely a job but a cause far greater than any mission you ever will have or ever will bear—a cause of greater importance than even your own life. Today the fullness of our cause is revealed. Today you will begin to understand the depth of our campaign and the level of your own commitment. Yesterday you were mere men. Today you are Elgen."

The hall echoed with loud applause.

"The sleeping minions of this world may not have heard of the Elgen yet. But they will."

More applause.

"The sleeping minions of this world may not yet be trembling at the mention of our name and power. But they will."

More applause.

Hatch pounded the podium furiously. "Presidents, prime ministers, and kings may not be bowing to us yet, but mark my words—they will."

The audience rose to their feet in wild applause.

"I now introduce the new order. These soldiers standing next to me, wearing the Elgen uniform of purple and scarlet, are my Elite Global Guard. *You* will refer to them as the Elite Guard. You may have noticed that their acronym is EGG. Like eggs, there are a dozen of them. Only I will affectionately refer to them as my EGGs. You will not.

"You will obey their commands as if they came from me. To disobey their orders is tantamount to disobeying me.

"In the first three rows, directly beneath the Elite Guard, wearing scarlet armbands, are the Zone Captains. The ZCs are the leaders of a global zone of Squad Captains.

"Now hear me and hear me well. Your previous chain of command no longer exists. From this moment on, you will no longer take orders from weak-bodied scientists and weak-minded bureaucrats!"

Hatch's pronouncement was met with loud applause.

"You will answer only to me, the EGGs, your Zone Captains, and, most often, your Squad Captain. Squad Captains wear the purple Elgen uniform and are responsible for each and every one of the members within their squad, which will number between six and twelve. Let me repeat the hierarchy. Your Squad Captain will answer to a Zone Captain, who will answer to one of the twelve Elite, who answer only to me.

"In addition to your Squad Captains, there will be one or two Elgen Secret Police, known to us as ESP, in each squad. These men are primarily informants. You will not know who they are. This force constitutes the eyes and ears of our organization and will communicate directly with the Zone Captains and, if necessary, the Elite Guard. Any sign of insubordination within a squad will be dealt with swiftly and severely.

"It's a brave new world, gentlemen. Those of you who are with me will prosper far beyond your wildest imaginations. Governors and magistrates will bow at your feet and clean your boots with their tongues." His voice lowered threateningly. "But those who defy me will learn suffering they never imagined possible. I would like to demonstrate what I mean. You are all familiar with the Starxource energy grid. Captain Welch, please take us live to the bowl."

The image on the screen behind Hatch changed, revealing a close-up of the bowl's chute, which had already started moving out from the wall. When the chute reached its extremity, the door in the wall opened. A man's black boot appeared, followed by the rest of his body as he was pushed out and the door shut behind him. The guard was fully dressed in Elgen uniform and bound at his legs and wrists. As the chute lowered, he desperately tried to hold on to the sides of the chute, but it was impossible. He slid on the metal rollers to the bottom of the chute, where he was caught by the cog, which was hanging just a few yards from the grid.

Within seconds the guard was covered with rats. His amplified screaming echoed through the entire hall for less than a minute, leaving the men silent. After just ninety seconds the man's skeleton was ejected from the chute. The camera zoomed in on the shredded uniform and the bone remains of the guard.

"They go much quicker than the bulls, don't they?" Hatch said without emotion.

The room was silent as Hatch looked over the audience. Hatch nodded to one of the guards, and three men dressed in pink girls' party dresses were led out, bound and shackled. Their mouths and chins were covered with tape. They all had large bows on their heads.

"Cute, aren't they?" Hatch said.

The men in the audience laughed loudly.

"These so-called men arrived at our conference with the wrong attitude. How unfortunate for them. They will not leave us with those attitudes, simply because they will not be leaving us at all. If you once knew these men, you will be doing yourself a favor to disassociate with them, as they are traitors and fools. And they are part of tomorrow's entertainment, for they are all headed to the chute. But first you will be allowed the privilege of letting them know how you feel about traitors.

"Elgen Force, do not make their fate yours. Over the next two weeks we are going to introduce a new food group to our rodents' diet. Every day, for the next fourteen days, one of you will meet these men's fate. One of you each day."

The men were all silent, none daring to move or speak.

"We will select our fourteen 'meals' by monitoring your level of cooperation and performance. Each day we'll nominate three of you, but only one of you will be chosen, and that will be my decision. If you are nominated twice, then you will automatically be selected. Our informants are already in place. From this moment on, anything and everything you say and do *will* be used for or against you."

Hatch paused for emphasis. "If you think you can beat this system, think again. For those among you who have seditious thoughts, remember that the friend you invite to join you will rejoice in your treachery, because, and excuse the pun, to 'rat out' a disloyal guard is the fastest way to ensure your own survival.

"Each of you will be given a new Elgen rule book. It looks like this." Hatch held up a navy book with gold embossing. "This is your new *Bible*. It is only thirty-six pages long. Over the next five days you are to memorize the entire book. Every line. Every word. And yes, there will be a test. Two of them. The two guards with the lowest score will automatically be included as two of the fourteen meals. So, for your sake, I recommend that you know the book well."

Hatch nodded to one of the EGGs standing by the side of the stage. The guard saluted, then gave a hand signal, and twelve other guards—the ESP Captains—walked to the front of the stage. They wore scarlet berets and sashes across their chests.

Each of the captains had an assistant at their side, a guard dressed in black, with yellow and black striped armbands. The assistants wheeled a stainless steel cart with a black, metal box on top that resembled a large toaster. The box had several dials and knobs and a white meter with a needle. Two long red wires protruded from the side of the box leading to finger clamps. On a lower shelf on the cart was a box of books.

The ESP Captains sat down at black, plastic chairs while the assistants assembled the apparatus, then stacked the books on the ground next to them. The preparations were carried out quickly and sharply.

At the same time the three men in dresses were led from the stage down to the auditorium's exit. The men were forced to their knees and shackled together, facing outward in a triangle.

"This is how you will receive your Elgen rule book," Hatch said. "Each of you will have the opportunity to take the Elgen oath of loyalty. Should you choose to make this commitment, and I strongly advise that you do so, you will come up to the front and stand in the queue until it is your turn. When you are summoned to the podium, you will have sensors placed on the fingers of your right hand. The administrator will be reading his monitor as you take the oath. If you are lying he will know it.

"You will put your right hand on the Elgen rule book, raise your left arm, and repeat the oath after the administrator." Hatch lifted a paper from the podium and read, "'I swear on my life, breath, and fortune to prosper the Elgen cause, to advance its mission until every man and woman on earth have sworn allegiance to the *Novus Ordo Glorificus Elgen*, our new glorious order. I offer up my life and death to this endeavor and will follow all rules contained in this book and those that will come, with fidelity, honor, and exactness. I swear this oath on my life.'"

He set the paper down and looked over the group. "You will then make the Elgen salute and bow to the administrator and remain bowed until he accepts or rejects your oath. If he accepts your oath he will hand you the contract to sign. You will then be given your rule book and you will go to the adjoining hall to await further instruction and, if you are wise, start memorizing your rule book."

A guard stepped forward and whispered something to Hatch.

"Of course," Hatch said. "Let me remind you that as you pass out of this room you may make known your disdain for the three men who have shamed us all with their weakness. Elgen are not weak. When you are through with these pitiful little girls, what is left of them will be fed to the rats.

"Now, back to you. If your administrator rejects your oath, you will be sent to the end of the queue for another opportunity. If you fail your oath the second time, you will be taken to a separate hall. I will not tell you what will happen there. Those of you who merit that placement will learn soon enough."

He stopped talking, looking out over the silent audience. "I ask those of you who do not wish to take this oath to remove yourselves from our company immediately. If any of you wish to leave, you may raise your hand at this time."

There was a pause, then one lone hand in the crowd went up. Guards in red immediately surrounded the man and escorted him out of the room, amid the whispers and buzzing of the remaining men.

After he was gone Hatch smiled. "Gentlemen, I think we just found our first meal."

Nervous laughter skittered through the crowd.

"It is now time for you to make a decision that will affect your life, the lives of billions, and history itself. Time for you to choose your paths. Gentlemen, welcome to the future."

PART 3

30

Another Arrival

Our plane landed at night at the Cuzco airport. I had never left the United States before, and standing in a foreign airport where all the signs were in a different language filled me with anxiety. We walked out of the terminal. The air was warm and moist.

"My head is killing me," Wade said, grimacing.

"I have a headache too," Taylor said. "It started as soon as we landed."

"It's altitude sickness," Ostin said. "Cuzco's elevation is eleven thousand feet, more than double Idaho's."

"Does it go away?" Taylor asked.

"Not always," Ostin said. "I read that the best remedy is to drink coca tea. In fact, that's what that lady is selling over there."

Everyone glanced over at a brightly dressed native woman who was holding a plastic bag filled with green leaves.

"Now what?" Jack asked.

"Someone's supposed to meet us," I said.

"Who?"

"No idea."

"Anyone speak Spanish?" I asked.

"Yo hablo español," Ostin said.

"Besides you, Ostin."

"I know a little," Abigail said. "My uncle is Mexican. He used to teach me words. But it's been a few years."

"Beautiful *and* bilingual," Zeus said.

"Suck-up," Jack said under his breath.

"But you can still speak some?" I asked hopefully.

"A little," Abigail said. "And I can understand a lot of it."

"So it's Ostin and Abi," I said.

Just then a man walked up to me. He was poorly dressed and held out his hand. *"Tiene dinero?"*

"What did he say?" I asked Ostin.

"He wants money," Ostin said.

I took a dollar out of my pocket and handed it to him. "I only have American dollars."

Ostin translated. *"Yo tengo sólo dinero americano."*

The man nodded. *"Gracias, Señor Michael."*

I looked at him. "Did you say . . . ?"

"Sí," the man said. "Mr. Michael, the bus is for you and your friends." He cocked his head toward a medium-size tour bus that was parked next to the curb. The bus had dark tinted windows. When I turned back the man was already walking away.

"Guys," I said. "Over here."

We started toward the bus.

"What do you think?" I asked Ian.

"It looks clean," he said. "The driver has a gun, but nothing you, Taylor, or Zeus couldn't take out if you had to."

"I expect him to be armed," I said. "Where we're going, he probably needs it."

The bus shook as its engine started up, and the doors opened as we approached. From the curb I looked inside. The driver was a Peruvian man, stocky, and at least twice my age. He watched us carefully as we climbed aboard, counting or mumbling something as each of us got on. The moment we were all inside, the driver shut the door and pulled away from the curb, clearly in a hurry.

Taylor and I sat together about four rows from the front. Everyone else was behind us.

"He kind of reminds me of my grade school bus driver," Taylor said. "About as friendly, too."

"Do you think he speaks English?" I asked.

She shrugged. "No idea."

I walked up to the front, crouching down in the aisle next to the driver. "Excuse me," I said. "What's your name?"

He kept his eyes fixed on the dark road. "It is not important," he said with a thick accent.

"Where are you taking us?"

"Chaspi," he said.

"Chaspi?"

"You will see."

"How far are we from Puerto Maldonado?"

"Far," he said. "Far."

I guessed he was being purposely vague, so I went back to my seat.

"What did he say?" Taylor asked.

"As little as he could," I replied. I looked out the window. We were traveling away from the city lights into dark, forested hills.

"Do we even know where we're going?" she asked.

"Yes," I said. "To the Elgen."

Elgen. The name filled me with dread. In spite of how hard we had worked to get here, I was still having a difficult time controlling my fear. My tics were going crazy.

When we were in the middle of nowhere, the driver lifted the microphone. "Amigos. We are going off the highway up ahead onto a small side road so you can sleep. There are many trees overhead so the helicopters or satellites cannot see us. We cannot take the chance of staying at a hotel. The Elgen are very careful to know who is coming near them. This bus has a bathroom and there is food for you. The seats lean back most of the way, and there is a pillow and blankets above you. I am sorry it is not a real bed, but I know where you are going and it will be the best bed you will have for some time.

"You will start your journey in a few hours. We will hike a small distance to the river, where there is a boat waiting for you."

Zeus was already asleep, which I was glad about. I didn't think he'd like the idea of being in a boat.

"Can't we just take the road?" I asked.

"No. The road is not safe. The Elgen make many roadblocks and checkpoints. You will ride the boat up the Río Madres de Dios, a tributary of the Amazon River, and will be let out in the jungle near the Elgen compound. You will arrive a little before morning. There you will be on your own. So please, get what sleep you can."

31

Into the Jungle

That night I had a nightmare. I dreamed I was being chased through a dark maze by a beast. I never saw it, but I could hear its snarls and growling behind me, always just at my heels. The maze I was running through had hundreds of doors, but every one I tried was locked. I kept hearing my mother shouting out my name, but I couldn't tell where her voice was coming from. I just kept running. When I was in center of the maze, I heard her voice coming from the very last door. Relieved, I opened it. Dr. Hatch was standing there. He started laughing. When he opened his mouth, his tongue was a snake, and its body curled around me, constricting me. That's when I woke up.

It took me a moment to remember where I was. I could hear voices—two men speaking in Spanish. I looked out my window. In the moonlight I could see the men standing near the front of the bus. One was our driver, his face illuminated by a cigarette. The other was a man I hadn't seen before. I glanced over at Taylor. She was still asleep, and I could hear Ostin snoring behind me. I got up and walked to the front of the bus.

The man speaking to our driver looked up at me. He was carrying a machete. *"Buenos días, señor,"* he said.

"Buenos días," I repeated, which was pretty much the extent of my Spanish. I stepped outside with the men. "I'm Michael."

"Yes, Michael. I know you from your picture. I am Jaime. Are your friends ready?"

"They're still sleeping."

"You must wake them now. They can sleep on the boat. We must soon go. Timing is everything."

"Now?"

He nodded.

I climbed back on the bus and woke everyone. It was probably two or three in the morning, so, not surprisingly, no one was happy about the wake-up call.

As I headed back to my seat, the man with the machete walked onto the bus carrying a large sack over his shoulder. "Amigos," he said. "We are going to hike through the jungle. There is much water. You must put on the galoshes."

"How much water?" Zeus asked.

"You will not drown," the man said. "It is just a few inches of water."

"Drowning isn't the problem," Zeus said.

"Oh, yes, you must be Zeus. Forgive me. I have special boots for you." He brought out a pair of waders that would reach nearly to Zeus's chest.

Jaime walked down the aisle handing out boots, which we pulled on over our shoes. Then, following the man's directions, we grabbed our packs and hurried off the bus to the trees on the other side of the road.

Stepping under the cover of the forest canopy, the man pointed his flashlight under his chin, illuminating his face. "I am Jaime, your guide. I will go much of the way with you. As we walk through the jungle, keep your eyes paled for animals."

"Paled?" Ostin asked, yawning.

"He meant 'peeled,'" I said. "What kind of animals?"

"The vipers, jaguar, and the anaconda. The big snakes like the water. I am told that some of you are more powerful than these things—I do not doubt it. But your electricity will not save you from a viper strike, so please follow me. I was born in the jungle. I know its ways."

He pointed the flashlight ahead of us, and we lined up behind him in single file. I brought up the rear with Zeus, who was moving cautiously. Jack and Abigail were in the front, behind Jaime, who had given Jack a machete to help widen the trail. McKenna walked in the middle of the group. She lit up her head to illuminate the path for us but stopped after a few seconds because of the millions of insects attracted to her light.

About five minutes into the hike Taylor asked, "What's that sound?"

"Crickets?"

"No, it's a buzzing sound. Like electricity."

"It's me," I said. "I'm like a human bug zapper."

We were walking under a canopy of leaves so thick that we might as well have been inside a building. Our group made for an interesting sight, our glow lightly illuminating the forest around us.

After twenty minutes or so, Jaime stopped for us to rest. We gathered in a small half circle. As Jaime looked at us he said, *"Increíble."*

"What?" I asked.

"You, you . . ." He struggled with the word in English. Finally he said, *"Son fosforesentes."*

"You glow," Ostin said.

"I wish to show you something," Jaime said. He pointed to a nearby tree with his flashlight. It was maybe twenty feet tall, slender, with narrow leaves.

Wade walked up to it with his hand outstretched. "This one?"

"Don't touch it!" Jaime said.

Wade stopped.

"It is the tangarana tree. You will notice that there are no trees around it."

"That's kind of weird," Jack said.

"I'll show you why. Watch." He tapped his machete against the tree's trunk. Immediately a swarm of red-and-black ants covered the tree's limbs. "The tangarana ant," Jaime said. "They have a friendship."

"A symbiotic relationship," Ostin said. "The ant's a symbiont. Like Dr. Hatch."

The man glanced at him, then continued. "The ants protect the tree and the tree gives them shelter. The ants will attack animals who come too close. They will even kill any plant that tries to grow near it. The natives used to tie their enemies to the tree. The ants would eat them alive."

"That's horrible," Abigail said.

Jaime shrugged. "War is horrible."

He turned and we started walking again. A few minutes later there was a loud screech, which echoed around us.

"What the heck was that?" Ostin said, his eyes wide with panic. "It sounded like a pterodactyl."

Jaime smiled. "That is the *mono aullador*—the howler monkey. It is loud, yes?"

Suddenly something swung from the darkness toward us. A bolt of lightning flashed across our heads, and the animal dropped to the ground.

"You electrocuted a monkey," Ian said.

"I didn't know what it was," Zeus said. "It attacked us. It had it coming."

"You shocked a cute, furry little monkey," Abigail said.

"He's not little," Zeus said.

Jack laughed, and Zeus looked at him. "You going to give me grief too?"

Jack shook his head. "No, dude. I would have roundhouse kicked it back into the tree. You just got to it faster."

The jungle was alive with noise, and the sound of rushing water became more pronounced the closer we got to the river. The trail started to decline, and once we reached the riverbank, the trail dropped steeply to a dark, slow-moving river. The river bubbled at its crests, illuminated by a half-moon's glow.

Below us was a riverboat with a striped canvas top, the sides covered in plastic. A Peruvian man was sitting at the back of the boat, manning the engine.

"This boat is what the gold miners use," Jaime said. "It will not cause suspicion in the night. But you must all stay quiet. We do not know who we will encounter on the river."

"Do the Elgen patrol the river?" I asked.

"Not yet," he said.

One by one we boarded the boat. Jack and Jaime helped everyone on, except Zeus, who stood alone on the top of the embankment looking down at the boat. "Really, man. I don't do boats."

"Quit being such a prima donna and get on the boat," Jack said.

Jaime hiked back up to see what was keeping Zeus.

"I don't do boats," he said to Jaime. "I'll take my chances on the road."

"You have no chance on the road," Jaime said.

"You don't understand. If I fall in the water, it will electrocute me." Zeus looked into Jaime's eyes to make sure he understood the seriousness of his circumstance. "My electricity will *kill* me."

Suddenly Jaime started laughing, softly at first, then louder, growing into a great, echoing chuckle.

Zeus's eyes flashed with anger. "Shut up! Why are you laughing?"

"Amigo," Jaime said, "I do not mean to disrespect, but look." He held the flashlight out over the water near the bank, revealing several bright orange reflections, slightly oval like cat eyes. "You see, amigo? Many caiman. The river is full of caiman and piranha and anaconda. If you fall in the water you die anyway!"

Zeus looked at him for a moment, then said, "Oh." He walked down the bank to the boat.

Taylor swallowed. "Caiman, piranhas, and anacondas?"

I just shrugged. "Come on. This is the easy part."

Zeus carefully climbed over the bow, sitting at the opposite end from Jack and Abigail. I thought we all looked miserable and afraid.

I remember once seeing a World War II picture of paratroopers sitting inside the fuselage of a plane waiting to jump, wondering if they would live to see the morning. I guess that's how we felt.

Jaime unlashed the rope from the tree, then pushed us out from the shore while the other man revved up the outboard engine, pulling us backward into the flow of the river. Taylor laid her head on my shoulder. No one had anything to say.

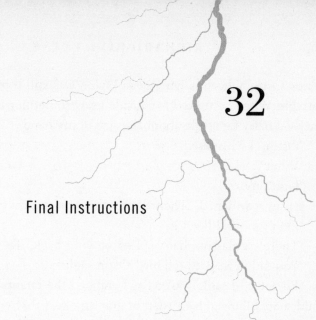

32

Final Instructions

The journey up the river seemed like a strange dream. It took two men to operate the boat—Jaime, who lay across the bow watching for drifting logs, and Luis, who sat back at the engine, quietly watching over us. Both banks of the river were walls of trees, creating a narrow, overgrown corridor that stretched for hundreds of miles through rain forest until reaching into the heart of the massive Amazon itself. There were occasional breaks in the trees, revealing small clearings for huts or illicit mining camps.

The boat's long benches were covered with dark vinyl pads and the ten of us stretched out on them, overlapping our heads and feet. The inside of the boat was lit with a warm, green luminance from our glow. I looked around at my friends. McKenna, Wade, and Abigail were asleep. Jack was awake, sitting near the engine, opening and shutting a pocketknife. Ian was leaning over the side watching the water. Ostin, who was lying near Taylor, was still trying to get comfortable. When he turned to his side I saw something move across his back—a hairy tarantula about the size of my hand.

"Ostin," I whispered.

"What?"

"Don't move."

His eyes widened. "There's something on me, isn't there?"

"Don't move. I'll get it."

"There's a massive, hairy spider on your back," Taylor said.

"You didn't have to tell me," Ostin said.

"I'll get it," I said. I pulsed as I grabbed the tarantula. There was a loud snap, followed by a wisp of gray smoke. I threw the spider over the side of the boat into the dark water.

"Spiders," Ostin said. "I hate spiders." He shuddered, then lay back down.

I slid to the front of the boat near Jaime. "How did you get involved with us?" I asked.

He leaned back a little. "Let's just say I do not like the Elgen. They come to my city and they change everything. We live in fear now. Their guards walk our streets. They have all the power. If they want something you have, they take it. There is nothing you can do. Even our policemen fear them. We know danger. The jungle is dangerous. It will take your life, even your family. But it is fair. It only takes from those who do not respect it. The Elgen take what they want."

"Did the Elgen take something of yours?" I asked.

Jaime slowly nodded, his eyes dark with gravity. "They took my son."

"Why?"

"I don't know. I wasn't there. The Elgen need no reason."

"I'm sorry," I said.

"Me too," he said softly. "I am very sorry I was not there to protect my son. I was working for the Elgen. It was my right to die before my son." Jaime looked at me with a deep sadness. "I must tell you something I learned as a boy." He looked around. "We are jungle people. From my boyhood I was taught its ways. My father taught me the vines and roots that will save your life from a viper bite. And he warned me never to go into the jungle without a machete. There are many dangerous animals in the jungle. In the water, the electric eel, the caiman, and piranha. On the land, there are the vipers and the jaguar and puma. But the most dangerous lives both on land and water, it is the anaconda. They grow ten meters and longer, yet they are fast. Even the caiman and jaguar fear the grown anaconda.

"One day my father taught me this lesson. He said, 'Jaime, if you are ever in the jungle without your machete and you are to meet an anaconda, do not run, it will catch you and eat you. This is what you are to do. First, you must look directly at the snake. It is frightening, but you must look at it. It will freeze like a tiger does as it stalks its prey. While it is frozen, you must slowly move yourself, very, very slowly, to where the sun is directly above your head. The jungle is on the equator, so the sun is often high in the sky. The snake will not want to lose its dinner, so it will keep following you, slightly turning. But the snake does not have eyelids, so as it looks up at you it is also looking into the sun and it will burn out its eyes. When its eyes are white with blindness, you may just walk away.'"

I looked at him for a moment, then said, "You're not just talking about snakes, are you?"

He shook his head. "No. I have not met the one they call Hatch. But I think he may be like this snake. If he wants you too much, that may be his weakness."

"I hope that's not his only weakness," I said softly. I exhaled slowly. "I better try to get some sleep."

"Yes," said Jaime.

I lay back on the bench next to Taylor. But I couldn't sleep. After a while I sat up, looking out over the dark, moving landscape.

It was maybe an hour later when Ian whispered, "Michael, look." He was pointing toward the riverbank.

"I don't see anything," I whispered.

"Look carefully."

As my eyes focused I saw the silhouette of a man standing on the bank looking at us.

"I see him. Is he . . . Elgen?"

"No," Ian said. "He's dressed like some kind of tribesman."

"He is of the Amacarra tribe," Jaime said. He had walked over to see what Ian was pointing at.

"Amacarra?" I said.

"Yes. The Amazon once had many such tribes—more than ten million people. But now there are few left in the forest. The shamans and medicine men are growing old. The ancient knowledge of the Amazon and her healing will soon be lost."

"Are they dangerous?" Ian asked.

"Not as dangerous as some of you, perhaps. But they have blow darts tipped in the poison of the blow-dart frog—very, very dangerous."

"*Dendrobates leucomelas,*" Ostin said in his sleep. "The poison dart frog, indigenous to South America. A frog the size of my fingernail has enough venom to kill ten full-grown men." Then he smacked his lips and was quiet again.

I looked at Ian, and we both shook our heads in wonder.

"The Amacarra have something in common with us," Jaime said.

"What's that?"

"They hate the Elgen. They call them *'bai mwo gwei.'* The white devil."

We watched the man fade into the inky blackness of the forest as our boat slowly slipped past.

"He is a holy man," Jaime said. "Once when I was fishing, my boat engine had problems, and I paddled my boat to the shore. The holy man was standing there at the bank. I told him I was having problems with my boat. He said, 'Yes, last night the Great Spirit told me to wait here for you.' Then he blessed my boat, and the engine started. I made it all the way home."

I wasn't sure what to say to that. "Now sleep," Jaime said, and went back to the bow.

* * *

As badly as I needed sleep, I couldn't find it. I lay quietly, listening to the steady sound of the boat's whining chug.

As dawn came, Jaime left his post at the front of the boat to talk to me. "Señor Michael. You are not sleeping?"

"No. I can't."

"Too much on your mind, I think."

"Probably."

"You are a very brave young man."

"No," I said. "I'm very afraid."

"You cannot be brave without fear." He sat back. "Luis at the engine is mourning. Last summer his son was in this river playing with his friends when he vanished. A caiman pulled him under. Or perhaps an anaconda. Luis was on the bank. He jumped in the river to save his son. But it was too late. His son was already gone."

I sat up and looked at Luis. No wonder he was so quiet. "That was very dangerous for him to jump in after his son," I said.

"Yes, but he did not think of the danger to himself because he loves his son."

I nodded.

"You and Luis have much in common. You also jump in the water with the Elgen caiman. You too are brave." He slapped his chest. "But more than brave, you have love. And love is brave." He patted me on the shoulder, then went back up to the front of the boat.

About a half hour later the engine cut back, and Luis shook Jack to wake him. He then pointed at the dirty, oil-stained blankets Jack was lying on. Jack handed the blankets to Luis, who began wrapping them around the outboard motor. Everyone but Wade and McKenna awoke.

"What's going on?" I asked Jaime.

"Luis is quieting the motor. Just ahead is the beginning of the Elgen compound. Their land comes close to the river here."

I peered up over the side of the boat. Through the trees I could see the light of a clearing in the forest and the glistening of a metal fence.

"How big is the compound?"

"Ten thousand hectares," he said. "It will take you an hour to hike to the compound, if that's the route you take. But I don't think that will be possible. There are cameras everywhere."

"The Elgen love cameras as much as I love Oreos," Ostin said, sitting up.

"It would be like walking three miles in front of their faces and them not seeing you. It is impossible."

"Then how do we get in?" I asked.

He shook his head. "I do not know. But I am instructed to give you this." He handed me a bulky envelope, which I quickly opened. Inside were several documents, a satellite map, and a letter. I extracted the letter and began to read it out loud.

> *Michael,*
>
> *If you are reading this letter you are already near your destination. Through satellite surveillance we have gathered some information about the Elgen compound that may be of help to you. The Elgen compound is built in the center of a twenty-five thousand acre ranch surrounded by two high-voltage electric fences. The fence may not be a problem for you, but it will be for some of the other Electroclan members. How you get into the facility will be up to you. It won't be easy. Crossing the ranch will be difficult, if not impossible, as there are hundreds of surveillance cameras, some visible and some not, and nowhere to hide. You will be utterly exposed. There is only one entrance into the compound, the main road, and it is heavily guarded and entered only at the checkpoint. All vehicles are searched by dogs, even the Elgen vehicles. Again, it is up to you to find a way into the compound.*
>
> *The facility consists of four main buildings and a power transformer. This is the largest of the Starxource plants. We know that your primary goal is to find your mother, but if you can knock out the compound's grid you will do great damage to the Elgen's credibility as you will shut down all power in a*

*two-hundred-mile radius and affect the major cities of Lima
and Arequipa. After you leave the compound, we have made
transportation arrangements for you. Enclosed in this package is
a transmitting and global positioning device.*

I reached into the envelope and pulled out what I thought was
the device but turned out to be only an iPod nano.

"It looks like an iPod," Taylor said.

"That's definitely an iPod," Ostin said. "Maybe they rewired it into
a GPS."

"Keep reading," Taylor said.

*For your and our safety the GPS device has been hidden inside
an iPod nano.*

"Told you," Ostin said.

"Shh," Taylor said.

*To use the GPS go to the Colby Cross album and click on the
song "I'm Lost Without You." A map of the area will appear,
leading you to us. When you have reached your destination you
can use the device to signal us. Again, go to the Colby Cross
album and click on the song "Come and Get Me, Baby." As
the song plays it will send us a signal, and we will dispatch
a helicopter to pick you up at the location we installed on
your GPS, a clearing in the jungle about ten miles east of the
compound. We're sorry it cannot be closer, but once you've
attacked the base, nowhere in the vicinity will be safe. Traveling
through the jungle will not be easy, but the Elgen will have
difficulty following you.*

*We have just received some unfortunate news. We have learned
that Dr. Hatch is now at the Peruvian compound. For reasons
unknown to us, he has summoned all of the Elgen guards from*

around the world. We believe there will be more than two
thousand guards on the premises. Had we known this earlier
we would have postponed your arrival. If you wish to delay, it's
your call. Tell Jaime and he will continue to drive you up the
river to our rendezvous.

Good luck.

"Hatch is there," I said.

"Good," Jack said, making a fist. "I have a present for him."

I looked over at Taylor. "What do you think?"

"Not good," she said softly. "Two thousand guards?"

"That's an army," I said. "Maybe we should delay." I looked at Ostin. "What do you think?"

Ostin thought for a moment, then said, "Where's the best place to hide a penny?"

"Really?" Taylor said. "We're about to face our deaths and you're telling riddles?"

"I'm making a point," Ostin said indignantly. "The best place to hide a penny *is in a jar of pennies.*"

Taylor just looked at him.

"Think about it. The more people there are, the easier it is to blend in. The huge influx of guards might be creating the very distraction we need. Besides, if it comes down to a gunfight, what does it matter if there's fifty guards or two thousand? Either way we're dead."

"Wow, I feel so much better now," Taylor said.

"He might be right, though," I said. "What do you all think? Do we go?"

"Your call," Jack said. "I'm game either way."

"Zeus?"

He looked nervous but said, "Whatever you decide."

I turned to Taylor, who was still looking anxious. "What do you think?" I asked.

"I don't know," she said. "It's up to you."

I put my head in my hands. "Why does everyone keep saying that? I have no idea what the right thing is."

Jack said, "Look, you got instincts. You rescued us from the academy, didn't you? You didn't know what you were doing then, either."

I sighed. "Okay, I think Ostin's right. If we can figure out how to get inside the place, I say we do it. As far as taking out the power station, I wouldn't know how to do that if I were alone in the building with a ton of dynamite. I say we find my mother, then get out of there."

For the next half hour Ostin and I carefully studied the map of the compound, trying to get an idea of where we were. About the time the sun rose above the tree line, Luis cut back the boat's motor and we began moving closer to shore.

"Señor Michael," Jaime said. "We are close. You should all eat before we dock."

"Ostin," I said. "Wake Wade and the girls."

"No problem," he said.

Jaime had brought bananas, tamales wrapped in corn husks, and a pastry that looked a little like something my mother used to make called a tiger roll.

"*Pionono de manjarblanco*," Jaime said as he handed it to me in a pan. "It is filled with *dulce de leche*."

I knew only a few words in Spanish, *leche* being one of them. "Milk?"

"Sweet milk," Ostin said. "Caramel."

I took a bite. It was airy and good. *"Bueno,"* I said.

"Eat many," Jaime said. "Eat many."

"Everyone eat a lot of bananas," Zeus said. "We need to be at our best."

"Hand me a couple," Ostin said.

"Not you," he said. "The electric ones."

"I do have electric powers. The brain . . ."

"We know, Ostin," Taylor said. "A hundred gazillion electric synapses-thingies." She smiled at Zeus. "He won't give up."

"Here is something to drink," Jaime said. He opened a cooler filled with cartons of milk and bottles of Inca Kola. I took one of each, popping the cap off the bottle with the bottle opener Jaime handed me. The Kola tasted a lot like bubble gum.

"What's with tamales for breakfast?" Taylor asked.

"It's Peru," I said.

The tamales were stuffed with eggs, cheese, and shredded chicken.

"Think we can heat these?" Ostin asked, peeling back the husk.

"Sure," Taylor said. "We'll just throw them in the microwave."

McKenna reached over and took the tamale from Ostin, holding it gently in her hands. Within a few seconds steam began to rise from between her fingers. She handed the tamale back to Ostin. "Careful, it's hot."

Ostin stared at her with bright eyes. "I'm so going to marry you someday."

She smiled as she sat back.

A half hour later Jaime and Luis began arguing. Jaime was pointing ahead toward the bank and Luis was shaking his head. *"No aquí."*

"Sí, aquí," Jaime said.

Finally Luis relented, steering the boat closer to the bank.

"Ian," I said. "I think we're about to dock. Do you see anything up ahead?"

He looked toward the bank and shook his head. "Nothing but jungle."

Luis guided the boat into a small inlet that was overhung with thick canopy, and again we were obscured in shadow. Jaime climbed out onto the bow as Luis ran the boat up onto the shore, startling several small caimans and sending them scurrying back into the water. Jaime jumped out onto dry ground with a coil of rope. He pulled the boat farther up onto the bank and lashed the end of the rope around the trunk of a peculiarly shaped tree. "Amigos, hurry," he said.

We grabbed our packs and one by one climbed out of the boat. Ostin and I were the last out. As I was stepping down Jaime put his arm on my shoulder, stopping me. "Señor, do you have your device?"

I held up the packet. "It's in here."

"I'm sorry, you cannot take the packet."

"What?"

"It is too dangerous. If the Elgen find it they will know we are helping you. Do you remember the instructions for the device?"

"Colby Cross. Yes. Can I at least take the map?"

"No, señor."

"It's okay," Ostin said, tapping his temple. "I've got it all right here."

I took the iPod out of the envelope and handed the rest back to Jaime. He unlashed the boat.

"*Dios esté contigo,*" he said.

"God be with you," Ostin translated.

"*Gracias,*" I replied.

Jaime pushed the boat off the bank, jumping into it in one fluid motion. He gave us a salute, then the boat pulled back out into the river, reversed direction, and sped back the way we had come.

33

Teasing Bulls

"How far is it to the compound?" Wade asked.

"I think it's about the same distance as our hike to the boat," I said. "Everyone ready?"

Everyone looked tired and anxious, but they all nodded.

"Okay," I said. "Let's go."

Jack held up his machete. "I'll take the lead."

We all followed him back into the jungle. Insects continued to flare off my skin in bright blue flashes. Ten minutes into our hike Jack stopped.

"What is it?" I asked.

"Look."

A jaguar was standing in our path, about fifty feet ahead of us, its green eyes pale in the distance.

"Zeus," I said. Zeus quickly stepped up. "We might need you.

Just in case it decides to hunt one of us."

"Nobody run," Ostin said. "We should be okay."

"Why are we okay?" Taylor asked.

"We don't look like what they usually eat. But if you run, it triggers the chase instinct."

"Good to know," Wade said.

The cat looked more bored than hungry. After a few minutes it turned away and lumbered off into the thick foliage.

We breathed a collective sigh of relief, then continued hiking.

Ostin said to Taylor, "I hope we don't have to deal with those rats. I hate rats. Even without electricity they're bad."

Taylor sighed. "You're going to tell me everything you know about rats, aren't you?"

"Rats," Ostin said, "are the most successful survivor of any mammal on earth. They can live almost three weeks without sleep, keep themselves afloat in water for three days, and fall fifty feet without getting hurt. That's the equivalent of us falling off a twenty-six-story building.

"They're also breeding machines. In ideal conditions a single pair of rats could produce, in three years, three and a half million offspring. That's why nearly ninety percent of the world's islands have been overrun by rats. They cause about half the extinctions of reptile and bird species."

"You're not making this any easier," Taylor said.

"Did you know that rats are ticklish and actually giggle?"

"No."

"And they have belly buttons but no thumbs?"

"Why would I want to know that?"

"Did you know that a group of rats is called a mischief?"

"No. Really?"

"Did you know that rats regulate their temperatures through their tails because they can't sweat?"

"Nope. Didn't know that either."

"Did you know that there's a temple in India where rats are worshipped?"

"No," Taylor said. "Maybe you should go there."

"Did you know that rats can't vomit?"

"Okay, enough. No more rat trivia."

"I'm just passing time."

"Then talk about something besides rats."

Ostin thought about it. "How about snakes? These jungles are slithering with them."

"Michael, your turn," Taylor said, pulling me next to Ostin.

We hiked another forty minutes before we saw light ahead of us—the edge of the forest. I stopped everyone. "All right, everyone, stay alert."

We cautiously approached the forest perimeter. The Elgen fence was only thirty feet from the clearing, and we could see dozens of bulls on the other side. The fence was about twenty feet high with horizontal wires eighteen inches apart. The fence was marked with DANGER: HIGH VOLTAGE signs in both English and Spanish.

"It looks like a ranch," McKenna said.

"It *is* a ranch," I said. "Ostin, how far do you think we are from the gate?"

"It's about three miles southwest."

I stared ahead at the animals. "Can you see the compound?" I asked Ian.

"Barely. There's a lot of electrical interference. There are also a lot of security cameras between here and the compound."

"A lot?"

"More than a hundred."

I shook my head. "The Elgen and their cameras."

"What now?" Taylor asked. "How do we get in?"

"I think I could lift the wires high enough that everyone could climb under, but then what do we do?" I asked. "With all those cameras, we'd be surrounded by Elgen guards before we got within two miles of the place."

Zeus said, "Ian could spot the cameras and I could blow them out."

"Yeah, like they're not going to notice that?" Jack said snidely.

"Shut up," Zeus said. "I don't hear you coming up with anything."

"C'mon, guys," Ian said. "Quit fighting all the time."

"Maybe if he'd quit being such a jerk," Zeus said.

"You watch your back," Jack said.

"Is that a threat?" Zeus asked.

"Please, stop it," I said. "We've got enough to worry about." I sat down to think.

"We need them to come get us," Ostin said.

"Sure," Wade said. "Why don't we just call them and ask for a ride."

"Ostin, tell us your idea," I said.

"If we can somehow damage the fence, they'll have to send out a repair crew. While they're trying to repair the gate we'll jump them, take their uniforms and vehicle, and drive to the compound."

"How do we damage the fence?" Taylor asked.

McKenna was looking at the top of the fence. "We could drop a tree branch on it," she said.

"Brilliant," Ostin said. "We find a tree that hangs over the fence, then one of us climbs up with a machete and hacks a branch off so it falls on the fence."

"I could do that," Jack said.

"It's worth a shot," I said. "Let's find ourselves a branch."

We walked about a half mile along the fence line concealed in the shadow of the jungle until we found a tree with a large branch that hung over the fence. The branch provided enough shade that six large bulls were grazing beneath it.

Jack shimmied about forty feet up the tree, his machete slung through the back of his belt. He climbed out on the overhanging branch, then, straddling it, began hacking away.

"Be careful up there," Abigail said.

Jack smiled and pounded harder.

"That's a really big branch," Ostin said.

"It will have to be big to damage that wire," I said.

"Yeah. I'm just saying, it looks really heavy. I just hope when it breaks off, the tree doesn't flip back and catapult Jack through the jungle."

"We should be so lucky," Zeus said.

It took Jack almost fifteen minutes to hack through the branch, and he was soaked with sweat. With each slash of the machete he rained down perspiration.

When the branch began to crack Jack shouted, "Watch out. Here it goes." He gave the branch a few more whacks, then jumped onto another tree limb as the branch fell out from under him, directly onto the fence. Sparks shot out in a bright cascade but the branch just flipped off the top wire, doing no damage. We stood there speechless.

"Crap," Ostin said.

I looked up at Jack. He was shaking his head. "That fence is a lot stronger than it looks."

"And it looks pretty strong," Taylor said. "Any other ideas?"

"Watch out," Jack shouted. He let the machete fall. It stuck blade first into the marshy ground about ten feet from Ostin, who wasn't paying attention and jumped when it hit. Then Jack slid down the tree's trunk and joined us. "Didn't work," he said.

"You need a shower, dude," Zeus said.

Jack wiped his forehead. "Yeah, I'm starting to smell like you."

The two glared at each other.

"What we need," Ostin said, "is a car to drive through the fence."

I looked over at the fence and the bulls behind it. "How much does a car weigh?"

"That depends," Ostin said. "Are you talking about a Volkswagen or a six-wheeler?"

"Something big enough to break through that fence."

"A ton should do," Jack said.

Ostin nodded in agreement. "That's about right."

"How much do you think one of those bulls weighs?" I asked.

Ostin smiled. "A ton. At least. The problem is, how do you get a bull to charge an electric fence?"

"Easy," Wade said.

We all looked at him.

"Oh yeah, my uncle had bulls on his farm. Those things are crazy.

I've seen videos of them charging a train head-on. You just have to get them mad enough."

"How do you do that?" Taylor asked.

"Call them names," Ostin said.

Everyone looked at him.

"You're kidding, right?" Taylor said.

Ostin blushed. "Yeah, of course."

"Actually, it's easy," Wade said. "Those things are born mean. You just have to throw things at them. It always worked for us. Once we were throwing apples at them and one of my uncle's bulls got so mad it broke through the fence. He had us up a tree for almost an hour."

"Let's try it," I said.

We all went into the jungle looking for things to throw. McKenna found some softball-size seed pods on the ground. We loaded up with them, then picked out the largest of the bulls and started throwing things at him. We managed to pelt him a few times—I even knocked him once in the head—but he was pretty tranquil as far as bulls go. He didn't even look at us.

Finally Zeus got impatient. "I'll do it," he said. He walked up to the fence and began waving and shouting at the bull. "Hey, want a piece of me? Come and get me, you ugly cow." The bull looked at him, then suddenly began hoofing the dirt, like it was preparing to charge.

"I told you they don't like to be called names," Ostin said.

Then Zeus stuck out his hand and shot a bolt of lightning at the bull. The bull stiffened, then fell to its side, rolling all the way to its back, then onto its side again, its legs sticking straight out the whole time.

"I think you killed it," Ostin said.

"Way to go, genius," Jack said.

Suddenly the bull climbed to its feet and charged at us.

"Run!" I shouted.

The bull hit the fence with the force of a car crash. There was an electric snap, like the sound of a moth on a bug zapper, except a hundred times louder. The bull didn't break through the wire, but had lodged itself halfway through the fence, and sparks continued to fly all around it. Suddenly the sparks stopped. I looked at the top of the fence. The orange flashing lights affixed to the posts had gone dim.

"He shorted out the fence," Ostin said.

I walked over and touched the fence to make sure the power was really out. It was.

"Perfect," I said. "They'll have to come out to free the bull."

"Which will take at least a half dozen men," Ostin said.

"All right!" I shouted. "Everyone back to the jungle!"

As everyone walked back, Ostin grinned at me.

"What?"

"I don't know," he said. "That 'everyone back to the jungle' just sounded kind of funny."

"Glad you liked it."

"I'm going to use that sometime."

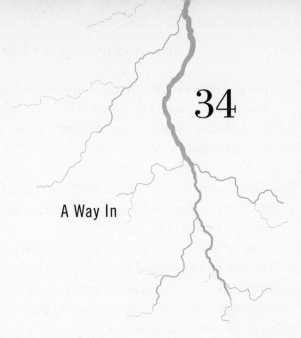

34

A Way In

It didn't take long for the Elgen to respond to the damaged fence. Less than ten minutes had passed when Ian said, "Here they come."

"The guards?"

"No. They look like ranchers or something. They're driving the fence looking for the problem."

"How many are there?" I asked.

"They've got two trucks. Three in each of them."

"Any guards?"

"Doesn't look like it. At least not in uniform."

"This is perfect," Ostin said. "They'll have to get close to the fence to free the bull."

"And while they're freeing the bull, we'll take them down," I said. "Then we'll take their clothes and trucks."

"We should tie them to one of those tangarana trees," Wade said.

Abigail looked at him. "What a horrible thing to say."

"What were you thinking, man?" Jack said, glancing at Abigail.

Wade flushed with embarrassment. "I was just joking. C'mon, can't you guys take a joke?"

The Elgen ranch trucks were larger than regular pickup trucks. And quieter. They looked like a cross between a pickup and a Sno-Cat, without the tank treads.

"They're electric of course," Ostin said, before I asked.

The first truck stopped just a few yards from the struggling bull. The men, all of them Peruvian and wearing boots, jeans, and white rancher shirts, got out of the truck and walked around the animal, trying to decide what to do with it.

They talked for about five minutes, then one of them went back to his truck and retrieved a rifle. He pointed it at the bull's head and fired. When the animal had stopped moving, the men took rope from the truck and tied the bull's legs together. Then they let out the wire from the truck's winch, wrapped it around the bull's torso, and began pulling it from the fence.

As the animal was being dragged to the truck, one of the men pointed to the branch that Jack had cut. All but two of them walked over to examine it. One of the men crouched down, running his finger over the machete marks. He began speaking excitedly. They looked up to where the branch was cut from, then in our direction. One of them pointed directly to where we were hiding.

"They're on to us," Jack whispered. "We've got to attack."

"We've got to get them closer to the fence," I said. "That guy's still holding his gun. Ostin, any ideas?"

Before he could answer, Abigail stood. "I've got one."

"What are you doing?" I said.

"Get down!" Jack said. They'll see you."

"I'm counting on it," she said, stepping from the shade of the canopy. "I'm betting they won't be expecting a blond American girl to come walking out of the jungle."

Abigail began sauntering toward the fence with a big smile.

"Zeus," I said. "Be ready to hit the guy with the gun."

"I'll try," he said. "But he's pretty far."

"*Hola*, amigos!" Abigail shouted.

The men all stopped what they were doing and stared.

"Excuse me," she said. "I'm lost. I'm looking for the beach."

The men looked at one another in amazement. One of them translated, then they all started to laugh.

"Hello, how do you do?" said one in broken English. He started walking toward the fence. The rest followed.

"Pretty girl," another said. "Come close."

"*Es un ángel?*" one man said. "*De dónde vino?*"

"They think she's an angel," Ostin said.

"Taylor, now," I whispered.

Taylor concentrated, and the men suddenly stopped talking. Some of them looked around as if they were confused; two fell to their knees, their hands on their heads.

"Now!" I shouted.

Jack, Zeus, Wade, and I sprang from the bushes. Zeus began firing, first hitting the man with the rifle, then knocking three others to the ground. I knocked out the two on their knees with lightning balls.

I tested the fence to make sure it was still dead, then all four of us climbed through the wire. Wade and Jack grabbed the man closest to the fence and dragged him over to Ian.

"Grab that guy's rope," Ian said. "And his knife."

"Got it," Wade said. He took the man's bowie knife from its sheath, then grabbed his coil of rope and threw it through the fence. "Here's the knife to cut it," he said, handing it to Ian.

McKenna began stretching the rope in long, straight pieces. "How long?"

"About five-foot lengths," Ian said. "Here's the knife."

"Don't need it," McKenna said, her hand burning red. She easily melted through the nylon rope.

Zeus, Wade, and I worked together dragging the men over to the fence within reach of Ian and the girls.

"I'll check the truck for weapons," Jack said, running toward the first truck. He returned holding two cans in the air. "Check this out. Bull mace."

We carried the men into the jungle, where we removed their rancher uniforms, leaving them in their underwear. Suddenly one of the men jumped up and ran.

Zeus shot at him but was too late, as the man was already in the trees.

"Get him!" I shouted. Jack and Zeus ran into the jungle after him.

We finished tying the rest of the men, then I said, "Ian, we better go help them. McKenna, you better come too. We'll need some light." I looked at Taylor. "Can you guys make sure they don't get away?"

"They're not going anywhere," Taylor said.

Wade held up one of the cans of bull mace. "I guarantee they're going nowhere."

Ian, McKenna, and I ran into the jungle in the direction Zeus and Jack had taken in pursuit. Even in the middle of day the jungle was dark enough that a person could hide, at least until McKenna lit up, illuminating everything around her like a great torch. After a few minutes of running we heard shouting in the distance.

"They're over there," Ian said.

When we caught up with them, the rancher was lying facedown on the ground between Jack and Zeus; Jack was pointing a can of mace at Zeus, and Zeus had his arms outstretched toward Jack, electricity arcing between his fingers.

"Stop it!" I shouted. They both turned to me. "What's going on?"

"Lightning stink shocked me," Jack said.

"It was an accident," Zeus said. "He was standing next to the dude."

"I *had* the dude pinned down, you stinking—"

"You say 'stink' one more time and I'm going to fry you—"

"Stop it!" I shouted again. "Are you guys crazy? We're about to walk into a camp of two thousand Elgen soldiers who want to kill us and you're fighting with each other?"

They both lowered their hands.

"If we can't do this together, we don't stand a chance. You two have got to stop fighting."

After a moment, Jack sighed. "All right. You're right." He put out his hand.

Zeus just looked at Jack angrily.

"I'm not offering it again," Jack said.

Zeus turned away. "It was an accident."

"Whatever you say, bro," Jack said. "Whatever you say."

"You guys have got to solve this. If we're not together, we're dead." I lowered my head, fighting my despair. "We're probably dead anyway. But if we're going down in flames, it's not going to be because we made it happen." I looked at the man on the ground. "Come on, we need to bring him back with the others."

"I got him," Jack said. He knelt down and lifted the man over his shoulders in a fireman's carry, and the five of us walked back to the fence in silence.

As the others came into view, Ostin shouted, "Good work, dudes. You got him."

No one answered him.

"What happened?" he asked McKenna.

"Don't ask," she said.

"What's wrong, Michael?" Ostin asked. "You'll feel better if—"

I held up my hands. "Just . . . stop. I don't want to talk about it. And I don't need you analyzing me right now."

Ostin stepped back. "Sorry." He glanced at McKenna in embarrassment, then walked away.

Taylor just stared at me.

"What?" I asked.

"Are you okay?"

"Oh yeah, I'm doing great," I said sarcastically. "My mother's being held captive by a sociopath, we're hopelessly outnumbered, and our friends are turning on each other while I lead them to certain death."

Taylor looked at me for a moment, then asked softly, "Do you really believe that?"

I suddenly realized that everyone was looking at me. I swallowed, embarrassed at my outburst. "I don't know what I believe."

Taylor took my hand. "Come here." She led me deep enough into the jungle that we were away from everyone else. When she looked at me her eyes were filled with tears. "You can't give up now. We're all here because we believe in you. If you really believe this is hopeless, we might as well turn ourselves over to Hatch right now."

"I didn't mean to say that," I said.

Her expression didn't change. "Michael, I'm terrified. Six months ago the most frightening thing I had ever done was try out for cheerleading in front of the student body.

"I need you to believe, Michael. Because I'm holding on by a thread—and you're that thread. If I don't have you to hold on to, I don't have anything. None of us do. I know it's not fair putting that much pressure on you, but it's the way it is."

"I didn't ask any of you to come," I said defensively.

"I know. But we're here. And we came because we believe in you. And because we care about you."

I looked down for a moment, then rubbed my eyes. "I'm sorry. I guess I'm terrified too."

"I know." She hugged me. After a minute she leaned back and said, "I've never told anyone this before, not even my best friend Maddie. I used to get severe panic attacks before I tried out for cheer. My first year, on the morning of the final cut, I pretended to be sick so I didn't have to go to school. My dad said to me, 'Are you afraid?' I said no but he knew I was lying. He said, 'Let me give you some advice. As long as you remember the whys, the hows will take care of themselves.'" Taylor looked into my eyes. "Your mom is a pretty big why. We believe in you because we believe you're doing the right thing. So let me ask you again . . . Do you believe that we can do this?"

"You're holding my hand," I said. "You already know."

"I want to hear you say it."

I straightened up. "I believe in what I have to do. That's what matters. My mother always said that if you do the right thing, the universe comes to your aid, and look what's happened so far: we escaped two Elgen traps, we found my mother, we got to Peru, and now we have a truck and a way into Hatch's stronghold. It's too big of a coincidence. I don't believe that whatever brought us this far brought us to fail."

Taylor smiled. "That's what I needed to hear. I'll follow you wherever you go and slap Hatch in the face if you tell me to. Now you need to let everyone else know."

I took her hand. "Come on."

We walked back to the group. The ranchers were all awake, lying on their stomachs with their hands bound behind their backs. Sadly, the Electroclan looked about as subdued as the ranchers did, their shoulders slumped in despair. Every eye was on us.

"I need to say something," I said, walking in front of the group. I looked at them all, then slowly started. "First, I'm sorry, Ostin. I shouldn't have gone off on you like that."

"It's okay, buddy," he said.

"It's not, but thank you. Second, I believe with all my heart that we're going to rescue my mom and get out of here. I'm sorry I was so negative. You've put your faith in me, and I should have been stronger."

Everyone was quiet for a moment, then Zeus said, "No, it's not your fault. We've been acting like jerks. Especially me." He looked at Jack, then stood and walked over to him.

"I'm sorry," Zeus said. "I really didn't try to shock you, but I didn't try not to either. You were right to be angry. I know you said you wouldn't offer your hand again, so let me do it." He put his hand out.

Jack looked at Zeus's hand for a moment, then he took it. "Forgotten. *Semper Fi.*"

Zeus nodded. *"Semper Fi."*

Taylor squeezed my hand.

I continued. "Third, it's time to do what we came here for. We're going to take the trucks right into the compound. Ian, I need you to stay next to me and tell us what you see as we get closer. Look for others dressed like us, and we'll head for their building. I'm hoping they might have a separate ranch entrance."

"Why don't we just ask them?" Ostin said.

"They're not going to tell us the truth," Zeus said.

"Maybe not with their mouths, but Taylor can read their thoughts."

"Except I don't speak Spanish," she said.

"I'll ask yes-or-no questions," Ostin said.

"Good idea," I said. "Is everyone ready?"

"Let's go, team!" Taylor shouted, sounding a lot like a cheerleader. In spite of the gravity of our situation I had to smile. "Sorry," she said, blushing. "Habit."

We put on the ranchers' uniforms. There were only six of them, so Abigail, Taylor, and McKenna didn't wear them. The men weren't big people, so the uniforms fit us fairly well, except for Jack, whose pants legs fell above his ankles.

"How do I look?" I asked Taylor.

"Like an Elgen ranch hand," she replied.

"Great. Now let's get some information." I looked at the men, on their stomachs. "Who should we talk to?"

"*Hombres,*" Ostin said. The men looked up. "Show them a little electricity, Michael."

I held my hand up, separated my fingers, and pulsed until electricity arced between my fingers.

"Let's talk to that one," Taylor said, pointing to a young man with fearful eyes. We walked over to him. He didn't look much older than us, and his back was marked with long, thick scars, as if he'd been severely whipped. The three of us dragged him away from the others, laying him in a small clearing near a termite nest.

"No!" he pleaded. *"Por favor!"*

"He thinks we're going to hurt him," I said. "Ostin, tell him we won't hurt him."

"You really want to tell him that?" Taylor said.

"You're right, he doesn't need to know that." I turned back to Ostin. "Tell him we won't hurt him if he cooperates."

Ostin relayed the message in Spanish.

While Taylor and Ostin interrogated the man, I sat down with Ian and showed him the photograph I'd taken from our apartment. "That's my mother."

"She's beautiful," he said.

"Can you remember what she looks like? She's probably not going to look exactly the same after all she's been through."

Ian put his hand on my shoulder. "Don't worry. If she's in there, I'll find her."

A few minutes later Ostin and Taylor returned to the group.

"Here's the four-one-one on the Peruvian dude," Ostin said. "His name is Raúl. His family is from Puerto Maldonado, and he was forced to work for the Elgen after they took his family's land. He says it's the same for all the ranchers."

Taylor nodded. "It's true. Those scars on his back are from the guards. The Elgen lost some cattle to a jaguar, so the guards whipped him as an example to the other ranchers. He says the Elgen treat them like dogs."

"Sounds like the Elgen," I said.

"He says that he can help us," Ostin said. "The compound has a double electric fence around the entire property, with guard nests on each corner. Close to the compound the fence is narrower, so you can't crawl through it like you can here. There is one main road with a checkpoint that everyone has to go through, except for the ranchers. The ranchers have their own gate on the southeast side of the compound near the building they call the 'bowl.' That's where they bring the cattle in to be slaughtered.

"He says there are guards above the wire but they don't pay much attention to the ranchers, and he knows this because some of the ranchers sneak their wives in. There's only one guard on the ground, but he's not always there and he's sleeping half the time. We can get into the bowl through the ranchers' entrance or the cattle entrance. From the bowl we can walk right into the compound."

"Won't we be seen?"

"He said there will be ranchers around and since we're foreigners they'll be aware of us, but he doubts they'll sound an alarm. The Elgen have a lot of foreigners come through their area—especially lately."

"Why lately?" I asked.

"He told us that the one they call *el doctor* is holding a big conference with all the guards."

"*El doctor?*" I asked.

"I think he means Hatch," Ostin said.

"Just like they warned us in the letter," I said.

"They've had to work extra hours to bring meat in for the kitchen, so he says the camp is in complete chaos right now. Our timing is perfect."

"Perfect or perfectly awful?" Taylor said.

"We'll find out soon enough," I said. "Let's go."

"What about the ranchers?" Taylor asked. "We can't just leave them here. It's the jungle. Something will, like, eat them."

"If they work for Hatch, they deserve it," Zeus said.

"No," I said. "They might be victims of the Elgen too. But if we let them go, they could alert the Elgen."

"I vote that we bring Raúl with us," Ostin said. "He could help us. Then, when we're done, he can come back on his own and free them."

I thought over the idea. "You trust him that much?"

Ostin nodded. "I do."

I looked at Taylor. "How about you?"

"Me too," she said.

I was doubtful but said, "Let's talk with him."

35

The Compound

"He understands a little bit of English," Ostin said.

"Can you help us get in?" I asked.

Raúl nodded.

"If you help us, we'll let you come back and free the others. Do you understand?"

He nodded again.

I looked at Taylor, and she nodded. "All right." I pulsed and melted through Raúl's ropes, which seemed to both intrigue and frighten him. Ostin gave him back his clothes and waited for him to dress. "Let's go," I said.

"*Vámonos,*" Ostin said.

The four of us walked back over to the others. They were surprised to see the rancher with us. "Raúl knows the way, so he's going to drive the first truck. Jack, you follow us."

Jack looked at Raúl suspiciously. "You sure you can trust him?"

"Taylor read his mind. She trusts him."

"Ostin," Jack said. "Translate this." He pointed at Raúl. "You betray us, I'll make sure you go down with us. Understand?"

Ostin translated. Raúl frowned.

Zeus added to the threat. "Tell him that if he turns us in, I'll electrocute him *first*. Make sure he understands that."

Ostin nodded and translated that as well.

Raúl looked as indignant as he was afraid. *"Los odio también,"* he said.

"He says he hates the Elgen too," Ostin said.

"We'll see," Jack said.

"Raúl will drive the first truck," I said to Jack. "You, Zeus, Ian, Abi, and McKenna follow us. Stay close."

The warning lights on the electric fence still hadn't come on, so I checked it once more, then we all climbed through and walked to the trucks.

Raúl said something to Ostin, who seemed to be nodding his head in agreement.

"What did he say?" I asked.

"He says we should bring back the bull. Otherwise it will look suspicious."

I looked over at the dead animal. "Good idea."

Raúl got in the truck and finished hoisting the bull into the truck bed.

The ranch was nearly five miles in diameter and was composed of hilly terrain. We drove for several minutes before we could even see the compound. The sight of it filled us all with dread.

We drove on, crossing diagonally across the main road to avoid other cars and trucks.

As Raúl had explained, the compound was surrounded by two large fences with guard towers perched high on the corners, the silver barrels of their mounted machine guns glistening in the sun. The place reminded me of the pictures I'd seen in my history book of World War II German prison camps, though this place was clearly much more high-tech.

The compound's checkpoint was a hive of activity, with trucks, cars, and buses backed up for more than a hundred yards and dozens of guards, many with leashed dogs, checking the vehicles that awaited entry. The dogs were large and muscular, and I wondered what breed they were.

"Rottweilers," Ostin said, as if reading my mind.

"What?"

"That's what type of dogs those are. Very powerful. I wonder if they're electric."

The guards were wearing the same Elgen uniforms as the guards who had attacked our safe house.

As we got closer to the compound my tics increased and I began to gulp, something I didn't notice until Taylor started gently rubbing my back. The compound was bigger than I expected and reminded me a little of the Boise State University campus, without the football stadium.

The Starxource plant, at the east end of the compound, was by far the largest of the buildings. I guessed it had to be nearly a hundred yards in diameter. Above it were three large exhaust pipes from which white smoke billowed into the air.

"Look at all that pollution," Taylor said. "I thought this was supposed to be clean energy."

"It is," Ostin said. "Those are cooling towers. That's steam emission. I'd bet my frontal lobe that's where the rats are."

Raúl pointed to a small gate near the plant and said, "There."

"There's the entrance," I said. "Be alert."

"*Todo el tiempo esta allá,*" Raúl said.

"What's that?" I asked.

"He said the guard's there," Ostin said.

"Should we turn back?" I asked.

Ostin asked Raúl, then said, "He says no. That would be too suspicious looking."

"I'll take care of him," Zeus said.

"No," Taylor said. "Let me try first."

Raúl pulled the truck slowly up to the gate. The man at the gate, a stocky Peruvian man nearly as wide as he was tall, looked at us sternly. He said to Raúl, *"Quiénes son estos gringos? Dónde están Cesar y Alvaro?"*

Suddenly the man bent over, grimacing and holding his head.

Taylor said to Ostin, "Tell him that he's been expecting us, and we've just brought the bull back that was causing the problems."

Ostin translated.

The man blinked a few times, then waved us on. *"Sí. Adelante."*

I turned to Taylor. "That was cool."

"Thanks," she said.

Raúl pulled through the gate. I motioned to Jack to follow us.

"Whoa," Ian said. "You won't believe what I'm seeing."

"The bowl?" Ostin said.

"Yeah, it's full of rats. Millions of them. And they're glowing like us. Only brighter and sort of an orange-red."

Raúl drove the truck up to the first of three metal doors. Even though we couldn't see anyone, the door slowly began to rise. Raúl said something to Ostin.

"This is where they take the meat to be processed," Ostin said. "We have to pull in here. It's their procedure, and it would look suspicious not to."

I looked into the dark entrance. Five men in ranchers' uniforms were waiting on the side of the concrete slip. Raúl slowly backed up into the space until a light came on. Jack pulled the second truck up to the side of the door.

"No," Raúl said. He began saying something very quickly to Ostin.

"He can't park there," Ostin said. "He needs to pull up next to the other trucks."

I hopped out of the truck, squeezing between the concrete wall and the vehicle until I was outside the building and close to Jack. "Raúl says to park there," I said, pointing. "But back in, just in case we need to make a run for it. Then meet us inside the building."

"Got it," Jack said.

When I returned, everyone was out of the truck and Raúl was talking to some of the ranchers who were inspecting the bull.

"What's going on?" I asked.

"They're trying to decide whether to use the bull to feed the guards or the rats. If it's the guards they'll send it to the butcher. If it's the rats it goes to the grid."

"What's the grid?"

Ostin pointed up. Half of the room's ceiling looked like the underside of a steel bowl. "The grid is where they make electricity from rats," he said.

The men appeared to have made a decision because an electric forklift drove up to the back of the truck and lifted the bull, then carried it over to a metallic cage connected to a hydraulic lift. The bull was carefully lowered onto the platform.

After the forklift had backed away, a yellow light began flashing, accompanied by a shrill beeping sound. The lift began to rise. When the platform was halfway to the ceiling, a hole opened above it and the platform moved perfectly into place, sealing the gap.

"That's cool," Ostin said. "I wonder what's up there."

I turned to him. "Has anyone asked about us?"

He nodded. "The older guy with the mega-mustache is in charge. He asked Raúl where the other ranchers are, and Raúl told him they're still out repairing the fence. He said they sent him back with the bull so a jaguar wouldn't get it."

"How'd he explain us?"

"He said one of the Elgen guards flagged him down near the checkpoint and made him bring us over to the ranch square. He said we're ranchers from an American Starxource plant and we've been brought here to observe their operations."

"Raúl's pretty clever," I said. "I almost believe his story."

"Let's hope mega-mustache does too."

Jack and the others came inside, and we gathered together in the corner of the room, trying to keep out of sight, though not successfully. The ranch hands kept glancing over at us, though they were just interested in the girls.

"There are cameras everywhere," Ostin said. "Not good. Not good."

"I'd like to blow a few of them out," Zeus said. "Just for fun."

"What do you see, Ian?" I asked. "What is this building?"

"It's their power plant. This corner is where they feed the rats. There's a butchery to the right, with a refrigeration room. In front of us there's a series of tunnels and a lot of water pipes and conveyor belts. Directly under the bowl is a huge funnel."

"For the rat droppings," Ostin said. "If there's really a million rats up there, they're going to be moving several tons of droppings a day. That's why there's a manure processing plant outside." He shook his head. "Man, I'd die for a look inside that bowl."

"I'm sure Hatch would be happy to arrange both," Taylor said.

"There are water pipes everywhere," Ian said. "Like hundreds of them."

"Cooling pipes," Ostin said. "The bowl is like a nuclear reactor. With that much heat it would need a giant cooling system to keep it from melting down. Kind of like a car's radiator."

Ian turned a little to the west. Looking up, he said, "There's an observatory up there, so they can see inside the bowl. On this level on the other side of the building it looks nearly identical to the laboratories back at the academy. Except in one of the rooms there are rows of cages filled with rats."

"Probably where they breed and electrify them," Ostin said.

Ian continued panning the room. "Over there are more offices." He turned to his left. "Hmm. They aren't offices. It's a jail. Along this wall are five cells. The three closest are empty, the fourth one has an older man in it, and there's someone in the fifth, but I can't tell what they look like."

"Is it my mother?"

Ian shook his head. "No. It's a guy. And whoever it is, he's glowing. He's one of us."

"Maybe it's Bryan," Zeus said. "He was always getting in trouble. But he'd just cut through the door. Does he have any of those wires on him?"

"He's wired," Ian said.

"That explains it," Zeus said. "Gotta be Bryan."

"Maybe he'll join us," Taylor said. "We could use him."

Zeus shook his head. "No. He won't join us. Those guys are loyal to Hatch."

"Maybe he'll change his mind like you did," Taylor said.

Zeus looked at her. "Maybe. But I doubt it."

"I want to know who it is," I said. "If Hatch is losing control of his kids, I want to know why. What type of locks are on the doors?"

"Old-fashioned kind," Ian said.

"So we need a key."

"Or explosives," Ostin said.

"Or Bryan," Zeus said.

"What do you see outside the building?" I asked.

"More buildings. The building closest to us looks like a prison or jail. A lot of bars."

"The Reeducation facility," Ostin said. "It's next to the assembly hall. Is there a bigger building next to it?"

Ian nodded. "Yeah. The guards are eating lunch in there. There's got to be more than a thousand guards in there right now."

"That's the assembly hall, all right," Ostin said. "North of it should be the dormitories."

"Yep. Bunk rooms. A lot of them. There're guards in there, too. How do you know this?"

"I studied the plans. What else do you see?"

"Past it, on the other side, there are maybe forty or fifty tents. There are guards in all of them."

"Temporary shelter for the visiting guards," Ostin said.

"This place is crawling with guards," Ian said. "They're every-where."

"Good," I said. "Once we find some guard outfits, we can move freely around the complex."

Raúl walked back to Ostin and started speaking. Ostin listened intently and asked a few questions before turning to us. "Raúl says that his boss told him to give us a tour of their operations. He also says we need to be careful because there are three Elgen guards assigned to the ranch house. Two of them are new here, so they'll be easy to fool, but it's best if we don't talk to the guards at all."

"Will the other ranchers tell the guards about us?" I asked.

Ostin asked Raúl, then said, "He doesn't think so. They don't like the guards."

"Where are the guards now?" I asked.

"He said they're at lunch."

"We can jump them for their uniforms when they get back," Jack said.

"With all these cameras around, that's risky," Ostin said.

"Being here is risky," Taylor said.

"Maybe we don't have to jump them," I said. "Ostin, ask Raúl if he knows if the guards have a uniform locker around here."

Ostin translated. Raúl's answer was surprisingly long, and Ostin looked very interested in what he had to say. When Raúl finished speaking, Ostin said, "He says they have a guard room over there by the door, but the ranchers are not allowed near it. But he knows where there are some Elgen guard uniforms no one will miss."

I couldn't believe our good fortune. "Really?"

"He said that when they built the compound they put in emergency drainage pipes. The pipes are always empty and large enough for a man to crawl through. They run underground below the compound and fence and empty about a hundred yards out into the jungle.

"The guards aren't allowed into town alone, but some of them have Peruvian girlfriends, so they uncapped one of the pipes, and every night a few of them sneak out. They secretly call it the Weekend Express. The guards don't wear their uniforms in town because the other guards might report them and the townspeople sometimes attack them if they're alone, so they change their clothes and leave their uniforms inside. A few of the guards have left and never come back, so their uniforms are still there."

"How many?"

"He remembers seeing three."

"Where are these pipes?"

"In a mechanical room behind the butchery and refrigeration."

"Can he take us to them?"

Raúl understood the question and said, *"Sí. Más adelante."*

"Later," Ostin said.

Raúl led us to the southeast corner of the room, stopping again near the cage lift, which had lowered back down without the bull. Raúl put on a show, giving us a demonstration of how the lift worked, while mega-mustache watched us from his corner. Afterward, Raúl led us to the butchery and the refrigeration room, where large slabs of meat hung from overhead hooks. It was so cold we could see our breath.

Ostin said, "Raúl says on really hot days the guards hang out in here."

Jack began pummeling a hanging beef like a punching bag. "Look, I'm Rocky."

Taylor shook her head.

At the back of the refrigeration room were green metal doors. Raúl said something to Ostin.

"He says it's best that we don't all go back to the mechanical room. There are three uniforms there, so we should decide who is changing into them."

"I need to decide who's coming with me to find my mother," I said. I turned to Ian. "I'm going to need you."

"I'm there," he said.

"Who else wants to come with me?"

Jack, Zeus, and Taylor raised their hands.

"You know they'll spot you a mile away," I said to Taylor.

"I know. I just want to help."

"You can help back here." I looked at Jack and Zeus. "Jack, you come."

Zeus started to protest, but I cut him off. "Look, if things turn bad, we're going to need you to get everyone out. Besides, I don't

want you anywhere near Hatch. I think you're the only one Hatch
hates more than me."

He nodded. "You're right." He looked at Jack, and I braced myself
for another argument. Instead Zeus raised his hand. "Bring them back."

Jack hit it. "I'll do my best."

I breathed out in relief. "Let's go."

Jack, Ostin, Ian, and I followed Raúl into the mechanical room.
The room was dim enough that my and Ian's glow could be seen.

Raúl looked at us in wonder. *"Ustedes extraterrestres?"*

Ostin grinned. "He wants to know if you and Ian are aliens."

"Tell him yes," I said.

Near the back of the room were four massive conduits that rose
from the ground up to the ceiling. Raúl pointed to a pipe with a
horizontal plug. It was capped with a metal lid and a locking latch.

"Is that the one?" I asked.

Raúl nodded, then gestured to another door just past the pipes.
He opened the door to reveal piles of civilian clothing.

"How many guys are sneaking out of this place?" Jack asked.

"Muchos," Raúl said.

We found four uniforms in the closet instead of the expected
three.

Raúl looked concerned and pulled one of the uniforms to him.
"Sudor," he said.

Ostin touched the uniform. "It's sweaty. The guy is still out
there."

"Not for long," Ian said, pointing to the ground. "He's coming
back up." Suddenly we heard the sound of someone in the pipe.

"I guess our guard's coming home," I said.

"We could lock him out," Jack said. "Or knock him out. Either
works for me."

"No," I said. "Let's see if he knows anything about my mother."

The lid suddenly opened, pushed up with one hand, and a
machete fell out to the concrete floor. Then a head appeared. The
man was starting to climb out when he saw us and froze. I could tell
he was considering fleeing back into the pipe.

Ian waved his hand, "No worries, bro. We're doing the same thing you are. Weekend Express. Our man Raúl here is hooking us up with his cousins."

The man's expression relaxed. "Oh, right."

Jack pulled the lid back for the guard, and he climbed out. He was a big man, at least an inch taller than Jack, and he picked up his machete, then walked past us to the closet, where he stripped off his street clothing. "You guys look young. What are they doing, recruiting at high schools now?"

"Better early than late," Ostin said. "We're part of the Elgen Empowering Youth program."

The man shook his head. "Never heard of it." He pulled up his pants and fastened his utility belt. "You done the tunnel before?"

"No," I said. "First time."

"Watch for snakes. Condensation forms on the pipe and the snakes like it. They hang out near the mouth. Last night I killed an eyelash pit viper on the way out."

"*Bothriechis schlegelii,*" Ostin said. "About eighteen inches long?"

He held up his stained machete. "Not anymore."

"Thanks for the warning," I said.

He sat down on a crate to pull on his boots. "No problem. But I've gotta hurry, my shift is in ten."

"Where are you stationed?" I asked.

He laced up his boots. "At the gate until a week ago. That's where I met my darlin' milkmaid," he said with a grin. "She was bringing in *leche* for the troops. Now they got me over at the Re-Ed."

"Re-Ed," Ostin said. He looked at me. "Reeducation. The *prison.*"

"Yeah," he said, standing. "Not bad duty. At least it's air-conditioned." He pulled off his shirt and donned a black Elgen one.

I took a step toward the guard. "I hear there's an American woman in there."

He looked up as he buttoned his shirt, his mouth wide in a dark grin. "Yeah, and she's all that you've heard."

"Is she?" I asked. I could feel my face turning red.

Ostin shook his head at me in warning.

"Oh yeah. But we're not allowed to go near her. She's Hatch's pet. But I keep my eye on her if you know what I mean. I've had some fun with her." He laughed. "A couple days ago I made her do a belly dance for a glass of water."

I looked at him dully, steeling my anger behind my eyes. "Sharon," I said.

"Yeah. That's her name. How'd you know that?"

I put my hand on his shoulder and looked into his eyes. "She's my mother."

His scream never made it past his lips. I had never shocked anyone that hard before, and I could feel his skin blister beneath my fingers. I didn't stop, even after he dropped to the ground and I had crouched down next to him. I was so electric that sparks were shooting at him from my knees and thighs.

"Michael," Jack said. "Bro!"

Ostin shouted, "Michael, stop it! You'll kill him!"

I stepped back, blue-white sparks still zigzagging between my fingers.

Raúl was looking at me in terror. Everyone was silent.

Ostin cautiously stepped toward me. "You okay?"

I was panting heavily. "Get his key. We just found our way in."

Ian took his key. Jack and Ian pulled off his uniform and carried him back to the pipe, dropped him in, then locked it. We dressed in the uniforms and helmets, choosing the ones that were closest to our sizes. I took a knife and cut four inches off my pants' length. Raúl took a grenade and baton from the fourth uniform.

"What's he doing?" I asked.

Ostin spoke to him. "He says he's helping us."

"He doesn't want to get mixed up in this," I said.

"He already is," Ostin said.

I looked at him, then nodded. *"Gracias."*

He nodded back.

Ostin took the fourth uniform and rolled it up.

"What's that for?" I asked.

"How else are you going to get your mother out of a prison surrounded by two thousand guards?" Ostin said.

"You are a genius, my friend."

Ostin smiled. "Tell me something I don't know. Oh, wait, you can't."

I put my arm on his shoulder. "All right. Let's get my mother."

36

The Glow

When we walked back out to the freezer, the rest of our group was huddled together, their arms wrapped around themselves against the cold. They stepped back when they saw us.

I raised my visor. "It's us."

Taylor held a hand to her chest. "Oh, you scared us. We thought you were real."

"Good," I said. "That's the idea."

"It's about time you got back," Wade said, annoyed. "We're freezing."

"Enjoy it while you can," Jack said. "Everything is about to heat up."

"We found out where my mother is," I said. "She's over in the Re-Ed."

"And we've got the key," Ian said, holding up a card.

"What's the plan?" Taylor asked.

"First, I want to see who's in that cell Ian saw. Then Ian, Jack, and I will go to the Re-Ed to find my mother. While we're gone, the rest of you need to see if you can find a way to shut down the power plant. But don't take any dumb chances. We're going to find my mom and get out of here as fast as we can." I took the GPS iPod out of my pocket and gave it to Taylor. "If things go bad, get to the jungle as fast as you can. We'll catch up to you."

"But you won't know where the pickup is," Taylor said.

"She's right," Ostin said. "How will we find you?"

"This is only in case things go bad," I said. "But if we get separated we'll make our way back to Cuzco and hide out in a hotel under Jack's name. The voice can call the hotels and find us. But don't wait for us. Promise me."

Taylor looked upset but relented. "Okay. I promise."

"Do you remember how to use the GPS?"

"Yes. Colby Cross."

We walked from the refrigeration room back out through the butchery. The three of us in guard uniforms walked out first. I could see what Raúl had meant about the ranchers hating the guards. They avoided even looking at us. Taylor and the others followed a few yards behind us. Raúl led us through a set of double doors at the side of the room that opened to a long, tiled corridor.

"The cells are there," Ian said, pointing toward a magnetic keypad next to a thick, metal door. "There's a guard inside."

"Maybe he'll let us in," I said. "Ostin, ask Raúl what the guards' names are."

Raúl did his best to pronounce the names. "Ste-ven, Kork, Sco-tt."

"Steven, Kirk, and Scott," I repeated. I hit the button on the keypad.

"Who is it?"

"It's Kirk," I said.

"What do you need?"

"We're bringing an American group through on a tour."

"I can't let you do that."

"Dr. Hatch's instructions. They are about to open a new

Starxource facility in New Mexico, and he wants them to see every inch of this place."

"You know the rules. This is a controlled access. No one comes in here without direct EGG written clearance."

"And you know that Hatch changes the rules whenever he pleases."

"And you know what he does when you break a rule. No form, no entry."

I looked at Taylor. "Try it," I whispered.

She concentrated.

"Now open the door," I said. "We're on a tight schedule."

"I don't care if you're on a tightrope," he said angrily.

Ostin stepped forward. "I have the form," he said into the intercom.

"Why didn't you just tell me," I said, playing along.

"Because I assumed we wouldn't need it," Ostin said.

"He's got it," I said. "Open up." I turned to Zeus, and he nodded.

The doorknob turned and opened. The guard, who was tall and muscular, blocked the door with his body and reached out his hand. "Let me see the—"

Zeus blasted the man so hard it knocked him back against the opposite wall. We hurried inside, shutting the door behind us. Jack grabbed the keys from the unconscious guard and opened the second cell, and he and Wade dragged the guard inside, tying him to the bed with leather restraints. They locked the door behind him.

"Which room is the Glow in?" I asked.

"Fourth one," Ian said, pointing to a cell door. Jack threw me the keys, and I unlocked the door, then slowly pushed it open. The cell was small—about half the size of my bedroom at home—and was dark and musty. There was a figure huddled under a blanket on a mat in the corner of the room. I pulled the wire out of the RESAT machine and the figure groaned a little.

"We're here to help," I said.

The figure moved, and his head slowly rose. Peering between the covers was a red-haired boy with freckles and deep blue eyes. His skin was puffy, and he was pale and trembling.

"Tanner?" McKenna said.

He looked up, his face twisted in disbelief. "McKenna?"

She went to his side. "What have they done to you?"

He dropped his head back down. "Everything."

"You know him?" I asked.

"We were captured the same week. What are you doing here?"

"Hatch locked me up."

I unfastened the RESAT from his chest and set it on the ground next to him.

He breathed a loud sigh of relief. "How did you get out of purgatory? And what is Tara doing here?" he asked, looking at Taylor.

"That's Taylor, Tara's twin, and Michael."

"In the flesh," Tanner said. "The last two. Hatch told me they found you."

"Did he tell you we shut down the Pasadena facility and escaped?" McKenna asked.

"He left that part out." He looked at Zeus. "Frank. How are you, buddy?"

"Alive and shocking," he said. "Why do they have you locked up?"

"I tried to bring down a plane."

"That's what you do," Zeus said.

Tanner smiled darkly. "The one we were flying on."

"That would do it," Zeus said.

"You tried to kill yourself?" Taylor asked.

"Yeah," he said indifferently. "I almost succeeded, too." He exhaled. "They brought me in here. The guards have this new device. It's called a RESAT." He looked at Zeus. "Since when are you on the outs with the Elgen?"

"Since I met Michael," he said. "And learned the truth."

"What truth?"

"That Hatch has been using us."

Tanner sneered. "You think?"

"What have they done to you?" Taylor asked.

"Nothing I didn't deserve," he said. "I've done bad, bad stuff."

"Whatever you did, it's not your fault," McKenna said.

Tanner grimaced. "Not my fault? Do you have any idea how many people I've killed? Thousands. I pulled the trigger. I'm one of the worst mass murderers in history. I make Jack the Ripper look like a jaywalker." He shook his head. "Not my fault."

"Let's get him out of here," I said.

"No! Stay away." His voice softened. "They're going to feed me to the rats, you know. Fitting punishment for one of the biggest mass murderers in history."

Taylor walked to his side. "May I touch you?"

"That's an odd introduction," he said. "But why not." He tried to reach out his hand but was unable to.

"I just want to help," Taylor said.

"By all means," he said, sounding almost comical. "Help away, whatever your name is, Tara's twin."

"Taylor," she said. She laid a hand on his shoulder. "Oh no."

"What are you doing?" he said. He looked at McKenna. "What is she doing?"

Taylor burst into tears. "No!"

"She's reading your mind," I said.

In spite of his weakness, Tanner pulled away from her, lifting the blanket up to his chin. "Keep out of my mind. I don't want you to see what's in my mind."

Taylor couldn't stop crying. I put my arm around her, and she laid her head on my shoulder.

Tanner glared at us. "Stay away from me!"

Abigail had been standing by the door, but now she walked up to Tanner.

"Don't touch me," he said to her.

"It's okay," McKenna said. "She's my best friend."

"Well," Tanner said sarcastically, "with that ringing endorsement. By all means." He looked at Abigail. "You one of us?"

She nodded. "I can make you feel better."

His eyes narrowed to slits. "No you can't."

Abigail looked into his eyes and held her hand up to him. "May I try?" She slowly reached out and touched him.

Almost immediately his expression changed. His eyes closed in relief and the look of pain left his face. Then he began to cry. When he could speak he said, "Thank you."

"You're welcome," Abigail said.

"Are you healing me?"

"I'm sorry. I can only do this while we're touching."

"Then don't stop touching me. Please." Tanner looked over at us as if suddenly remembering we were all in the room. "Are you rescuing me?"

"Yes," I said.

"I know some places in Italy where we can hide, if you can get me out of here."

"We're not in Italy," Taylor said.

"Where are we?"

"Peru," I said.

His eyes widened. "Peru? How did I get in Peru?"

"We don't know," I said. "But we'll take you with us. Can you walk?"

"I don't know. I thought I was still in Italy. Who knows how long they've had me hooked up to that machine."

Zeus walked over and took his arm. "C'mon, buddy. I'll help you up." He helped Tanner to his feet.

"What about the other prisoners?" Taylor asked.

"We don't have time to rescue everyone," Jack said. "We get Michael's mom and get out of here."

"He's right," I said. "Every minute we're here the more danger we're in." I turned to Taylor. "We're going to go look for my mom now. If you can find a way to shut this plant down, do it. Otherwise, be ready to go."

I looked at Ostin. "Taylor's in charge. Work together. We'll be back in less than an hour."

"Michael," Taylor said.

"Yes."

She put her arms around me. "Hurry back."

"Of course. Keep everyone safe." I lowered my visor. "Let's go, guys."

Ian and Jack pushed down their visors as well. "*Hasta luego*, baby," Jack said.

We left them standing inside the prison.

37

Reeducation

The three of us walked out of the Starxource building into the blinding Peruvian sunshine. Ian hadn't exaggerated; there were guards everywhere.

"That's the Reeducation building," I said, gesturing with my head.

"I've got the key," Ian said.

"We just don't know what it's good for," I said.

Near the Re-Ed door was a guard sitting inside a cylindrical booth.

"Ian, is there another way in?" I asked.

"Through the assembly hall, but it's worse. There are two guards at the door and about fifty just walking around."

"I say we try curtain number one," Jack said.

"What's the booth made of?"

Ian shook his head. "Plastic. All plastic."

"Great."

"Maybe he'll just let us in," Jack said.

"It's worth a try," I said.

We approached the building, pretending to be talking to one another. Out of the corner of my eye I could see the guard in the booth drinking from a metal Thermos. He set it down as we walked past him to the door. "Hey!" he shouted.

I turned back. "Yeah?"

"What are you doing?"

I looked at his name tag. "Lieutenant Cox, we're here for our shift," I said.

He stared at me dully. "There's no shift change at this hour."

"We were told to report here," Ian said. "We were just reassigned from the gate."

"Who reassigned you?"

When none of us answered, the man's eyes narrowed. "Let me guess. Anderson."

I glanced at Ian, and he shook his head.

"Come on," I said. "Don't make me name names. We're just doing as we were told."

"So it is Anderson. That's the third time this month that idiot's done this. I'm writing him up."

"All right," Jack said. "Do what you need to do, but we've got to get in before we're written up."

"All right." He pushed a button and a lock on the door buzzed. Jack quickly grabbed the door and pulled it open.

"Hold up, there. I still need your IDs."

We glanced back and forth at each other. The only ID we'd found in our guard uniforms was in Ian's pocket, and the photo was of an Asian guard.

I reached into my pocket, digging around in the empty space. "I must have left it back at the gate."

"What do you mean, you left it? No one forgets their ID. You know the penalty for not having it with you. You better find it before you're caught or I turn you in." He looked at Ian and Jack. "You two, show me yours."

Ian glanced at me. "Sure," he said. He reached into his pocket and brought out the ID. I looked back at the guard.

"C'mon," I said. "Lieutenant Cox doesn't have all day."

"You got that right."

I put Ian's ID on the counter upside down and slid it partway through the opening in the window. As Cox reached for it, I magnetically pulled his metal thermos over, spilling the liquid. The fluid rushed out over his hands and down the front of the counter, giving me the conductivity I needed. I put my hand in the liquid and pulsed as hard as I could. Electricity flashed and Cox collapsed to the ground.

I looked back at Jack and Ian. "We've got to hurry. I don't know how long he'll be out."

Jack held the door for us as we rushed inside. The interior of the building looked like a large elementary school with video monitors and screens everywhere. A strange noise played over the intercom system.

"They're in pink," Ian said, looking at a row of inmates.

"Welcome to Looneyville," Jack said.

"What kind of prison is this?" I asked.

"Reeducation," Ian said. "It's where they brainwash you. Hatch was experimenting with brainwashing at the academy."

In spite of all the cameras, we moved through the facility undisturbed. I turned to Ian. "Where is she?"

Ian casually looked around. "I think I found her. End of the second hall to our right."

My heart jumped. I couldn't believe she was so close.

"Don't stare," I said to Jack, who looked fascinated by what he was seeing.

"Don't gulp," Jack replied.

"Sorry," I said, taking a few deep breaths to calm myself. We walked slowly down the hall, then, when no one was around, strode up to the door. "This is it?" I asked Ian.

"She looks like the picture," Ian said. "Mostly."

I could guess what he meant. Ian ran the key we'd taken from the guard over the magnetic pad: A light flashed green, and we heard the sound of the lock turning.

I pulled open the door. It was dark inside, but I recognized what I was looking at—it was the same room Hatch had shown me on the monitor at the academy when I was ordered to electrocute Wade. Inside the cell was a metal cage. The prisoner huddled in the corner of the cell looked small and feeble, but there was no mistaking who she was. She was my mother.

38

Reunion

"**M**om," I said, running toward the cage.

She flinched when she saw me, then scooted herself as far back from us as possible. "Leave me alone."

I took off my helmet. "Mom. It's me."

She leaned forward, her eyes blinking rapidly. "Stop it!" she said. "Enough of your tricks."

"It's no trick. We're here to get you out."

"How dare you use my boy against me. How *dare* you?"

"Mom, I'm real. Ask me something. Ask me something no one else would know."

Her eyes narrowed. "What's my son's favorite place to eat?"

"Mac's Purple Pig Pizza Parlor and Piano Pantry," I said.

"You're a fake. My son would never call it that."

What was I thinking?

"It's PizzaMax," I said. "I call it PizzaMax. We went there on my birthday."

"So did Hatch."

"Ask me something else."

"Leave me alone."

"Mom. Please." My voice was pleading. "Please believe me."

"Quit calling me that."

"It's me. Don't you know your own son?"

Her expression softened a little. "What did I give you for your birthday?"

"Dad's watch."

She shook her head. "No. I already told you that one. I told you. What does the engraving on the watch say?"

My eyes welled up. "'I love you forever.'"

This time my answer seemed to reach her. "How do you know that?"

"Because I read it every day." I pulled back my sleeve to reveal the watch.

I saw the doubt leave her eyes. "Michael," she said.

She scooted herself forward and I ran to her, putting my arms through the cage. "Oh, Michael," she said.

"We've got to get you out of here, before they catch us."

"How? There are guards everywhere."

"We're going to dress you as a guard, then we're going to walk out the front door."

Suddenly a light started blinking on a black box on the top of the cage. A feminine automated voice said, "Code required. Please input code. Arming capacitor. Commencing countdown. Twenty-five, twenty-four, twenty-three . . ."

"What's that?" I asked.

Her eyes showed her fear. "It's an alarm, it needs to be shut off when you come in. Do you know the code?"

"No. What will it do?"

A green light turned on in the box above her cell.

"When it reaches zero it will electrocute me."

"Seventeen, sixteen, fifteen . . ."

"Ian!" I shouted. "We've got to get her out of here. Now!"

"I don't have a key."

"Find one!"

"I'm looking!" he shouted frantically. "Jack, that guard right there. He's got a key ring. Get it!"

Jack ran out into the hall and smacked the guard over the head with his baton. Jack grabbed him by the back of his collar and dragged him into the cell. Ian went after the key.

"Eight, seven . . ."

"Hurry!" I shouted.

"I'm hurrying!" Ian said. He ripped the key ring from the man's pocket. "It's gotta be one of these," he said, fumbling through them. He tried one and it didn't work.

"Three, two, one. Capacitor armed. Prepare for discharge."

My mother looked into my eyes. "Michael . . ."

"Get back!" I shouted. I grabbed the bars, pressing my entire body against the cage, and braced myself for the release. There was a bright flash and a powerful snap of electricity, the force of which threw me to the ground. Then all was quiet. The air was full of a powerful smell of ozone.

"Michael?" Ian said.

I slowly opened my eyes. Then I looked in the cage. My mother was standing against the bars staring at me, her eyes wide with panic. "Michael?"

I suddenly started to laugh.

"It fried his mind," Jack said.

I slowly climbed to my feet. "No. What a rush. Let's get out of here."

Ian continued through the rest of the keys until he found the right one. The lock slid, and he opened the door.

My mother stepped out and threw her arms around me. Tears fell down both our faces. "You shouldn't have come," she said. "You shouldn't have come."

"You can ground me when we get back to Idaho," I said.

She wiped her eyes. "I love you."

"I love you, too."

"Lots of love in here," Ian said, his voice pitched. "But out there, not so much."

"Sorry," I said, stepping back. I reached down and picked up the extra uniform. "Put this on," I said to my mother. We had saved the smallest of the Elgen uniforms for her. She quickly pulled it on. It was way too big on her, but she looked all right if you didn't look too closely.

The bigger problem was her trouble walking. She'd been kept in a cage for weeks and her legs muscles were weak and cramped. "I'm sorry," she said.

"I'd carry you if I could," I said. "But they'd notice."

"Just give me a minute," she said, leaning against the wall to stretch her legs.

"Mom," I said. "This is Jack and Ian. They're my friends. I couldn't have made it here without them."

"Thank you," she said, straightening up. "I'm ready."

"It's clear," Ian said.

Jack opened the door, and we stepped out of the cell, shutting the door behind us. We walked down the hall, back toward the doors we'd entered through.

Ian stopped abruptly. "Change of plans," he said. "Lieutenant Cox is back in action and buzzing like a mad hornet. Follow me."

We ducked down the first hall we came to just as Cox and two guards stormed past us.

"Where are we going?" I asked.

"Into the hive," Ian said.

39

Breaking Back In

The doors to the assembly hall opened automatically at our approach and we walked into a room full of hundreds of guards. Most of the guards were gathered in small clusters. Then I saw him. Hatch was standing in a corner of the room. I froze.

"What is it?" Ian asked.

"Hatch," I said.

He was surrounded by a group of guards dressed in black and red. Standing near them were three of the electric kids I had seen pictures of in my room at the academy: Quentin, Tara, and Bryan. There was also a kid I'd never seen before..

"Who's the other kid?" I asked.

"His name is Torstyn," Ian said. "You don't want to meet him."

"He's electric?"

"Yeah. He's dangerous. Let's get out of here."

I turned back. "Where's Jack?"

"Oh no," Ian said.

Jack was already twenty feet from us. He had his hand on his belt and was walking toward Hatch. I pushed through the guards, catching up to him halfway across the floor. "What are you doing?"

His jaw was clenched. "He burned down my house."

"You won't make it within twenty feet of him."

He kept walking. "I'll take my chances."

"They'll capture you."

"Let them try."

We were now only fifty feet away from Hatch.

"He'll capture *us*."

Only then did he stop.

"This isn't the time," I said. "We've got to get out of here."

Jack took a deep breath, then slowly exhaled. "This isn't over."

We turned and walked east through the assembly hall, then, meeting up with Ian and my mom, went out into the yard.

"Where are we going?" my mother asked.

"Back to the others," I said. "They're in the power plant."

"Others?"

"There are a bunch of us."

We had to walk past the Re-Ed entrance again to get to the power plant, so we waited for a large group of guards to pass by and blended in with them. When we arrived at the plant, we found a guard standing in front of the main entrance. It had been so easy getting out that I hadn't considered the difficulty of getting back in.

"Can we walk around to the ranchers' entrance?" Jack asked.

Ian shook his head. "There's a twelve-foot fence with razor wire."

"Whatever we're doing, we better decide fast," Jack said. "Cox is back and gathering a crowd."

Lieutenant Cox was talking to a dozen other guards, who were passing around an electronic tablet.

"Ian, what are they looking at?" I asked.

He turned to me with a grim expression. "Us."

"We need to create a distraction," Jack said.

As I looked at the guarded door I had an idea. "Maybe the guard can be the distraction. Ian, can you see his ID?"

"It's lying on the platform," Ian said. "Cal . . . Calvin Gunnel."

"Cal's my new best friend," I said. "Go along with me." I turned to my mother. "You better keep a few yards back. I don't think there are any female guards down here."

She looked nervous but nodded.

"Ready?" Ian said.

I took a deep breath to get my twitching under control. "Let's do it."

We walked up to the guard, a broad-shouldered man with a scar on his cheek partially concealed by a sandy beard. He reminded me of a lumberjack.

"Cal?" I said.

He looked up at me.

"Cal Gunnel?" I walked closer to him, pointing to myself with both thumbs. "It's me. Michael."

His brow furrowed. I could tell he was trying to place me.

"I've been looking for you for days. I owe you big-time, man. And don't you think I've forgotten. I never forget a favor."

"Wait," Ian said. "This is the Cal you were talking about?"

"I told you it was him." I turned back to the guard. "When's your next leave?"

The guard was glancing back and forth between us, looking more confused by the moment. "Tuesday. What—"

I didn't let him finish. "Okay. I'm going to have to trade some shifts, but you and I are going to Lima. I know this club, and let's just say you're going to be glad you did me a favor."

He stared at me for a moment, then said, "I have no idea who you are."

I faked a laugh. "Yeah, right." Then I looked into his face. "You're not kidding, are you?" I pointed to myself. "Cal, it's me."

"You sure you got the right guy?"

"I don't know," I said. "How many Cal Gunnels are there in Puerto Maldonado?"

He squinted. "Michael, right?"

"Michael. Who else? Whatever you told Anderson made the difference. I can't thank you enough for helping me."

"Anderson," he said, nodding. "It helped, huh?"

"I'll say. I don't know what you have on him, but you, my friend, have clout." I turned to Jack. "You don't want to get on Cal's bad side, you know what I mean? This guy is powerful." I turned back. "Next Tuesday. You can leave your *dinero* at home, this party is on me. I guarantee you will never forget this trip." I put out my hand. "See you then?"

"All right," he said. "Next Tuesday." He took my hand.

I dropped him like a bad habit. As I had anticipated, at least a dozen guards saw him fall.

"Get everything you can from him," I said to Jack. "But act like you're helping him."

Jack knelt down next to him, ripping the magnetic key from around his neck, then going through his pockets.

"Medic!" I shouted. "Medic!"

Guards began to move in toward us.

When there was a circle around us I said, "I think it's sunstroke."

"Clear out," one of the guards in a purple uniform said. "Give me room."

We stepped away from the crowd and the guard knelt down next to Cal, putting his fingers on the man's neck. "Heartbeat's strong. Looks like sunstroke." He stood, grabbing the phone from the podium. "We need a stretcher at Starxource west. Another sunstroke."

As the crowd milled around him, I caught my mother's eye and gestured toward the door. With more than twenty guards standing around us, the four of us opened the locked door and walked into the plant unnoticed.

At least I thought we had.

40

The Welcome

Once we were back inside the cool of the plant I asked Ian, "Where are they?"

"They're over that way," Ian said, pointing toward the center of the building. "The trick is getting to them. This place is built like a rat's maze."

"Fitting," I said. "What are they doing?"

"They're near some breaker-looking things. I think they're trying to figure out how to shut the grid down."

"It's too late for that," I said. "We've got to get out of here before they discover my mother's gone."

Almost in answer to my words, the shrill scream of a siren sounded and yellow strobes began flashing in the hallways.

"Too late," Jack said.

"Run!" Ian said.

With my mother in tow, we ran as fast as we could through

the long, vacant corridors, winding our way toward our friends. The halls were covered with a metallic, slate-colored material and were lined with stainless steel water pipes about a foot in diameter, spaced six feet apart. We caught sight of the rest of our group in a long, dark hallway halfway from the plant's entrance. Taylor was leading, with McKenna at her side providing light. They stopped when they saw us.

"Tay—" I started to say. Suddenly my head felt like it was caught in a clamp. All four of us dropped to our knees. Then Zeus shot Jack and me with electric bolts. Jack screamed out in pain, but the effect of the electricity on me was opposite. With renewed strength I took a deep breath and stood. Even Taylor's scrambling was no longer able to affect me.

"It's us!" I shouted.

"Stop!" Ostin shouted, raising his hands. "It's Michael!"

"Sorry!" Taylor said, clasping her hand over her mouth. "I'm so sorry I didn't know it was you!" She ran to me. "And there are four of you."

"Taylor?" my mother said, taking off her helmet.

"Mrs. Vey!" Taylor said. "They found you."

"What are you doing here?"

"It's a long story," Taylor said.

"Your parents are going to kill me," my mother said.

"Hi, Mrs. Vey," Ostin said.

"You too, Ostin?"

"And a good thing too," I said. "He's saved us more than once."

Ostin grinned. "Just doing my job."

Zeus walked over to Jack and put out his hand. "Dude, I'm so sorry."

"Really?" Jack said. "Again?"

"We thought you were guards," he said anxiously.

Jack looked at him, then started to laugh. He took his hand. "I would have done the same thing."

Abigail walked up to Jack and hugged him. "I'm so glad you made it."

"Me too," Jack said.

I counted the group. There were ten of us. Two were missing. "Where are Raúl and Tanner?"

"Raúl took Tanner to the mechanical room," Taylor said. "He was having trouble walking. He said if there's trouble they'll escape through the pipe."

"Where are we?" I asked.

"We're right under the bowl," Ostin said. "These pipes are all water mains to cool the grid."

"So how do we get out of here?" Zeus asked. "You can bet they've sealed off the compound. We'd never make it to the fence by car."

"I say we join Raúl at the escape pipe," I said. I turned to Ian. "How do we get there?"

"Three corridors down, on the left, there's an air duct in the ceiling that leads back to the butchery."

"All right," I said. "This way."

Suddenly the flashing lights around us stopped. Then a voice boomed from overhead speakers, echoing down the hallway. "Michael Vey. So pleased you could join us."

41

Zeus's Sacrifice

Hatch's voice continued over the speakers. "You should have told us you were coming, Michael. I would have prepared something special. As usual you've made a mess of things. And, Frank, I knew you'd come back. Couldn't resist, could you? You and I are going to have some fun. We'll bob for apples. Throw water balloons. Good times for all."

"The name's Zeus," I said.

"Inconsequential," Hatch said. "Be advised that we have you completely sealed in and surrounded. So you have a choice. You and Frank can surrender yourselves, and your friends will have reasonably humane treatment. Or you can resist and you will all die painful deaths. It's your call. Either way will amuse me."

"Eat my shorts!" Ostin shouted.

"Oh, Ostin. You just can't keep out of this, can you? Tell you what. I'll up the ante. If Michael and Frank surrender, I'll spare all of your lives and throw in a box of jelly doughnuts for Ostin. So let's see how much Michael really cares for you."

"Don't listen to him," Taylor said.

"You want us, Hatch?" I shouted. "Come and get us!"

Hatch laughed. "I was hoping you'd say that. Captain Welch, make sure the cameras are all recording, I'm going to want a replay of this. Are we set?"

"Yes, sir," a voice said. "Gate is opening."

"Wonderful. Just wonderful. You know I always enjoy feeding my pets."

From the bowels of the corridor came a loud, echoing groan like the sound of a heavy metal gate. Suddenly a high-pitched screeching echoed down the hall, shrill as a fork on a chalkboard.

"What's that sound?" Taylor asked.

Ostin turned white. "It sounds like . . . rats."

"Run to the air duct!" I shouted. I put my arm around my mother and helped her. The darkness behind us began to turn amber, the corridor distantly illuminated by some strange source of light. The first wave of rats came into view like the initial stream of a river, growing steadily heavier and thicker as the rodents began overlapping and running on top of one another, their bodies glowing like lava. They quickly closed the gap between us.

Jack threw a concussion grenade behind us, which killed a few of them but barely slowed the mass.

"Taylor, can you stop them?" I shouted.

"I'll try."

She turned and faced them, her hands on her temples. Ten yards in front of us the flow stopped as some of the rats began running in circles, confused.

"It's working," I said.

I was premature. The first wave of rats were quickly overcome by the rats behind them, as they pushed forward and climbed or jumped over them.

"There are too many of them!" Taylor shouted.

It was difficult to hear her over the squeals, which had grown in volume until the mass of them sounded like the braking of a train on metal tracks. They continued to pour toward us.

"Up the pipes!" I shouted, pointing to the walls.

Everyone grabbed onto the pipes and began climbing. I pushed my mother up the nearest pipe, and she hooked the utility belt of her uniform onto a bracket, holding her in place. I looked back down the hall. Everyone was up a pipe except Abigail, who was standing in the middle of the corridor staring at the oncoming rats, paralyzed by fear.

"Abi!" I shouted. "Climb up!"

She didn't move.

"Abi!"

Suddenly she fainted, falling to the ground.

Jack jumped down from his pipe and ran for her while Zeus began shooting at the rats heading for them, killing all he could hit. Jack lifted her and ran back to his pipe. He tried to climb with her but couldn't secure a strong enough handhold to pull them both up.

I jumped down from my pipe and ran to him. "Jack, climb up! Lift her!"

I took Abigail in my arms as Jack climbed up. He reached down and with one arm pulled her up. He hooked her blouse around a bracket to keep her from falling, then wrapped himself around her, holding them both in place.

"Michael!" Taylor shouted. "Look out!"

Zeus continued to pick off the rats, but it was like shooting rubber bands at a hive of angry hornets. Just as the first wave of rats hit my legs, I pulsed and the rodents that hit me died in a bright flash. But there were far too many. They began to swarm me, jumping higher and higher. I swatted at them, staggering to move away from them.

"Michael!" McKenna shouted, waving me to her. "Over here!" She was clinging to a pipe directly across from me. I tried to get to it, but walking was like trudging through mud. Slippery, flesh-eating mud.

Suddenly a rat about the size of a cat hit me in the chest, knocking me over. As I fell to the ground a wave of the rodents covered me. I pulsed with everything I had to keep them from eating me, but they were breaking through and I could feel their sharp teeth tearing at the Elgen uniform. My electricity was nearly exhausted. One last pulse, I told myself. Maybe I could kill enough rats to make a difference.

I wanted my last act to have some significance. I wanted my death to matter.

Just then I saw a brilliant light and felt a wave of heat. I could feel the weight of the rats lessen as they began jumping from my body. I opened my eyes to see McKenna standing next to me, raging like a blast furnace. The frenzied rats were running away from her heat.

"Get up, Michael!" she shouted.

I pulled myself up, then staggered over to a pipe and used my magnetism to climb to the top of it. McKenna climbed up after me, keeping only her legs blazing to ward off the rats. She couldn't get more than three feet from the ground. She was suffering from dehydration and looked pale and dizzy. I reached down, grabbed onto her blouse, and pulled her higher. "You need water, don't you?"

Her mouth was too dry to answer. It was cruelly ironic—we were clinging to a twelve-inch water pipe and she was about to pass out from dehydration.

Hatch's voice calmly echoed down the corridor. "I'm betting you wish you'd just stayed home about now."

With McKenna's heat gone the rats had returned tenfold, and the tile floor below us was no longer visible, just a rising sea of glowing fur.

McKenna was panting heavily, and I saw her grip on the pipe loosen.

"Hang on!" I shouted.

Her eyes were closed, and she slowly shook her head. "I can't. . . ."

I swung my body around hers, pinning her against the pipe. "I've got you."

The rats continued to pour down the hall, thousands, maybe tens of thousands, swarming below us, waiting for one of us to fall. As their numbers increased they rose like the tide, and as they got closer they started jumping at us. Most of them hit well below us, though I saw Ostin kick one off his leg. For the moment we were too high up the walls for them to reach us, but I knew it wouldn't last. Soon they would be jumping on us, one or two, then dozens, dragging us down to the undulating fur below.

I wasn't the only one who realized our predicament. Zeus, who was twenty feet ahead of me, began shooting out the hallway cameras. "If we're going to die, it's not for their entertainment!" he shouted.

Still they came. As far as I could see, the corridor glowed brilliant orange, like the inside of a toaster. I looked over at Taylor. Her eyes were wide with terror. She looked over at me and for a moment we both just stared. "They just keep coming!" she shouted. "They're like a river!"

"That's it!" Ostin shouted. "Zeus, shoot out the ceiling sprinklers!"

Zeus turned back and looked at us.

"Blow out the sprinklers!" Ostin shouted. "They can't take water. Do it or we're goners!"

Zeus looked down at the rats, then at Jack and Abigail, then over at me.

"He can't," I said, not loud enough for anyone but McKenna to hear. "He'll electrocute himself." I looked at Zeus, wondering what he was thinking. He wore an expression that seemed to be less fear than sadness. He looked once more down the hall at the rising flow of rats, then pointed his hand toward the farthest sprinkler, visible in the distance by the rats' glow.

"Don't do it!" I yelled.

My shout was too late. Fierce yellow bolts of electricity shot from Zeus's fingertips, connecting with the sprinkler head. At first nothing happened, then, like a breaking dam, water burst from the ceiling, starting from the sprinklers at the end of the hall, then, one by one, working its way toward us. I looked at Zeus, who was stoically watching the water approach. Then all the hall sprinklers blew. Water burst from the ceiling in a torrential downpour.

The rats shrieked as the water hit them, and electricity sparked wildly below us in sporadic, brilliant bursts, like camera flashes at a concert. I held tightly to McKenna as she leaned her head back and opened her mouth to catch the spray, drinking furiously.

Zeus screamed, then fell backward into the middle of the steam-ing rats.

"No!" I shouted.

In an instant Jack shouted, *"Semper Fi!"* He jumped from the wall and started running up the corridor toward Zeus, sinking thigh-deep in the squirming bodies of dying rats. By the time Jack reached him, Zeus was completely covered by the rats, a bulge in a pile of moving fur. He reached down and lifted Zeus up onto his shoulders, rats fall-ing off around him. Zeus's skin was severely blistered, and blood was streaming down his arms and legs from rat bites.

Jack struggled through the mound of rats, like he was dragging himself from a snowbank. As he pulled his legs out from the pile, rodents were still clinging to him, and he flung them off. He ran to the end of the corridor where the sprinklers hadn't been activated and pulled off Zeus's wet outer clothing. He wiped the water off Zeus's blistered body, then listened to Zeus's chest and started CPR. Zeus suddenly gasped for air, then screamed with pain.

"Abi!" Jack shouted. "I need you."

Abigail had regained consciousness just in time. She slid down the pipe and ran to Zeus's side, putting both of her hands on him.

"That was crazy brave," Jack said to Zeus. "Crazy brave."

Zeus was barely conscious and didn't respond.

I turned to McKenna. "Are you okay?"

She nodded, water dripping from her face. Her lips were pink again. "I'm okay."

"Good, because we've got to go."

We both slid down the pipe to the wet floor, which was layered with the bodies of dead rats. The carcasses squished beneath our feet. Taylor had already jumped down, and I crossed the hall and helped my mother to the ground. She was trembling with fear.

"Come on, Mom. We know a way out."

She didn't speak, but leaned into me.

"Everyone after Ian!" I shouted. I purposely didn't mention the air duct. Zeus may have blown out most of the hall cameras, but I was guessing the Elgen could still hear us.

Jack lifted Zeus onto his shoulders, and he and Abigail ran down the hall after Ian. When we reached the air vent Ian climbed up the pipe first, pushed out the vent cover, and climbed inside the duct. Then he reached down to help us up. "Come on! Hand him up!"

Jack and Ian lifted Zeus, then Abigail, Wade, and my mother.

Hatch's voice came echoing down the hallway. "Your resource-fulness never ceases to amaze me. But there's no way out. The building is surrounded by hundreds of guards. Give yourself up."

"You're a freak!" I shouted. "Come get your dead rats!"

"Don't worry, I've got plenty more. Guards," Hatch said softly, emphasizing his confidence, "get them."

Jack noticed a fire box a few yards down the hall, and he kicked it in and grabbed the ax.

"What's that for?" I asked.

"Whatever comes next."

A moment later Ian yelled, "Bunch of guards sixty yards up the hall."

"How many is a bunch?" I asked.

"Thirty? And there's twice that down the hall, waiting behind the door."

"Do they have those helmets?" Taylor asked.

"Looks like it," Ian said. "You can't help here. Give me your hand." He lifted her up.

"Your turn, Ostin," I said.

"After McKenna," he said.

"Go without me," McKenna said. "I've got an idea. Jack, can you break one of these pipes?"

"I think so." Jack lifted the ax to the closest water main, then swung at it. The blow only dented the pipe. "Hold on!" he shouted.

He pulled back and hit the pipe again and again. On his fifth strike the ax pierced the pipe and a powerful stream of water shot across the corridor, hitting the opposite wall.

"Here we go," McKenna said, turning her hands white with heat. She put them into the gushing stream. The water immediately flashed into steam, the sound echoing loudly down the hallway like the blast of a steam engine. The steam made it impossible for everyone but Ian to see.

While McKenna continued to fill the hall with steam, I helped lift Ostin up to Ian; then Jack lifted me up, and I climbed inside the duct, leaving just Jack and McKenna behind. Everyone was still clustered around the vent area.

"Taylor!" I shouted. "Get them to the mechanical room! Hurry!"

"How far down is it?"

"It's the third vent opening!" Ian shouted. "You should be able to feel the cold of the refrigeration room, it's just past that!" He turned back. "Michael, they're close! Tell McKenna and Jack to get out of there!"

I leaned out through the vent. "McKenna, Jack, you've got to come now!"

McKenna had cupped her hands in the gushing water and was drinking greedily from its spray.

"Now, McKenna!" Jack shouted.

She ran to the vent. Jack threw down the ax, then lifted McKenna up to me, and I helped pull her in. Then Jack jumped and, doing a chin-up, pulled himself up and in.

Just a few seconds after I'd replaced the vent cover the guards moved past us through the steam, none of them noticing the vent above them.

I breathed out in relief. "Just in time, guys," I said. "Now let's get out of here."

42

The Weekend Express

It took us only a few minutes to crawl to the mechanical room, though we had to stop once when a troop of guards ran underneath one of the vents. Wade was ahead of us dragging Zeus, who was still barely conscious. He was the first to reach the vent opening above the mechanical room.

"That's it!" Ian shouted to him. "It's clear below. Just Raúl and Tanner!"

Wade pulled off the vent cover. "Hey, guys! It's us!" he shouted. Then he climbed out, dropping to the concrete floor. Ian helped lower Zeus and Abigail down to Wade and Raúl, then climbed down himself.

Taylor jumped down without anyone's help—it was easy for a cheerleader—then Jack helped lower my mother, and then climbed out of the vent, lowering himself down slowly. McKenna and I were the last ones out. As I looked around, I saw that Raúl was standing next to the open pipe. Tanner was curled up near the lockers, his shirt pulled over his head.

"Where's the guard we left in there?" Jack asked Raúl.

Raúl said something to Ostin, who translated. "The guards can be executed for going AWOL, so he's probably running for his life," Ostin said.

I put a hand on my mom's arm. "I know it's crazy, but hang in there. We're going to get home again."

My mother forced a smile. "I know we are. I'm so proud of you, Michael. Your father would be proud of the man you've become."

Her words had a powerful impact on me—powerful enough that I had no idea how to reply. "Thanks," I finally said. "Now let's get out of here." I turned back to the group. "McKenna, you go first so you can light the way."

She looked nervously down into the pipe.

"Is something wrong?" Ostin asked.

"I'm just a little claustrophobic."

"Just look straight ahead," Ostin said. "And think of feathers."

"Feathers?"

"Something soft and relaxing. It will help."

McKenna smiled at him. "Feathers. Thanks." She climbed in.

Next in was Jack, who was carrying Zeus, with Abigail following closely behind, keeping a hand on him always. Raúl, Wade, my mother, Taylor, and Tanner went next.

When she was in the pipe Taylor turned back to me. "Come on."

"Go on," I said. "I'll be right there."

She looked at me nervously but obeyed, leaving just Ian, Ostin, and me. Ian went next. As he was climbing in we heard a short burst of machine gun fire.

"Ian," I said. "How close are they?"

"They're entering the butchery."

His words filled me with fear. We'd run out of time.

"Go!" I shouted. "They need you to make sure it's safe at the other end."

Ian dropped out of sight, and Ostin climbed into the pipe. He slid down the side, then said, "Come on, Michael."

"We're not going to make it," I said.

"What do you mean? We're almost out."

"They could be here any second. The guards know about the pipe. If we just disappear, they're going to figure it out. Then all they need to do is throw a grenade down the pipe or wait at the other end to catch us. We need time. We need to keep them looking."

Ostin looked at me with an anxious expression. "I don't like where this is going," he said. "What are you thinking?"

"Anacondas," I said. "Hatch wants me. If he follows me, everyone else can get out. Taylor's got the GPS, she can get you to the pickup point. "

"You can't do this," Ostin said. "If we need a distraction it should be me."

"Hatch doesn't care about you."

Ostin stared at me blankly. There was another burst of machine gun fire, closer this time.

"We don't have time to debate this. You know I'm right."

"They'll catch you."

"Think, Ostin. It's the logical choice. This way everyone else gets out and I still have a chance."

"Dude . . ."

"You know it's the logical thing! Now get out of here. I'm locking the pipe behind you, so there's no turning back. I'll lose the guards, then I'll join you."

"But you don't know where we're going."

"Remember plan B. Find me in Cuzco."

There was a crash just outside the door. My heart froze. "Go! Now!"

Ostin looked at me one last time, and his eyes watered. "Don't get caught!"

"I don't plan to. Go!"

Ostin disappeared down into the pipe, the last of McKenna's light just barely visible behind him. I capped the lid and locked it. Then

I pushed some crates around the pipe and laid a chain over its cap. I figured that if one of the guards was familiar with the pipe, he would think we couldn't have escaped through it.

I gathered grenades from the locker—three concussion and two smoke grenades—then I put my ear to the door. The guards were close, but as far as I could tell, they hadn't entered the refrigeration room yet. I pulled the pins from both a smoke and a concussion grenade, threw them into the refrigeration room, then locked the mechanical room door.

The concussion grenade exploded with a loud boom. A minute later I heard the guards enter the refrigeration room, their heavy boots clomping on the concrete floor. As their footsteps came closer to the mechanical room, I hid behind a stack of boxes next to an air duct. When someone tried the door, I pulled down my visor, then set off a smoke grenade, filling the room with smoke.

Just seconds later there was a loud blast as the door blew in. The guards shouted as they blindly stormed the smoke-filled room. I stood up and joined the chaos, my visor pulled down over my face.

"Where are they?" someone shouted.

I pointed up toward the vent. "Look."

A guard shouted, "They're in the air shaft!"

"We'll flush them out," the captain said. He lifted a communicator from a strap on his chest. "Targets are in the air ducts. I repeat, targets are in the air ducts. Position guards at all vents. We'll hold at east corridor and send a deuce in." He replaced the communicator, then pulled out an electronic tablet, summoning up a complete diagram of the Starxource duct system. "Schulz, Berman, go after them. You are only cleared to use RESATs. We're too close to the bowl for guns."

"Yes, sir," the two guards said almost in unison. The first guard stepped on the crate, then jumped up, grabbing both sides of the vent. He lifted himself up with the dexterity of a gymnast. As the second guard stepped up on the crate, the captain said, "Wait." He took from his utility belt a handheld device that resembled a television remote. "Track them with this."

He turned it on and the machine immediately started to scream. The captain looked at the reading, then back up with a bewildered expression. He slowly panned the machine the length of the ceiling, then down across the room, stopping at me. For a moment we both stared at each other.

"Gentlemen," he said, replacing the device in his belt, "the chase is over." He pulled his helmet off and smiled at me. "Finally we meet, Mr. Vey."

I produced a lightning ball in each hand and simultaneously threw them in the faces of the guards closest to me, dropping them both to the ground. Then I lunged at the captain as he reached for his RESAT.

I never made it. Two darts hit me in the back, followed by a third, taking my breath away. As I dropped to my knees, three more darts hit me. I think it was three. At least that's as many as I could remember before blacking out.

PART 4

43

The End of the Pipe

The escape pipe was smooth and sloped slightly, so even at a distance of more than a hundred yards, it was an easy crawl. It reminded Ostin of a slide at a water park.

The end of the pipe was deemed clear by Ian, so McKenna jumped down about five feet to the spongy forest ground below. The ground and foliage beneath the pipe were trampled and littered with cigarette butts, revealing the pipe's steady traffic.

As McKenna looked around, Jack jumped down, then turned and helped Zeus, who was now more conscious, which meant in more pain.

Jack laid Zeus on the ground a few yards from the pipe, then helped Abigail, who immediately knelt down next to Zeus, running her hand over his forehead. She pulled back the shirt they had put on him, revealing second- and third-degree burns over half his body.

"We've got to get him help," Abigail said. "If it gets infected he could die."

"We'll get help," Jack said.

Wade and Raúl helped Mrs. Vey out of the pipe, then Raúl came over and knelt beside Zeus. His forehead creased in concern. "*Sábila,*" he said, nodding. "Need *sábila.*"

Jack looked at Abigail. "What's *sábila?*"

She shrugged.

"*Sábila,*" Raúl said again, lifting his hands in a flourish as if describing what he was saying.

"We'll ask Ostin," Abigail said.

Mrs. Vey was standing next to the pipe's mouth when Taylor climbed out. After Taylor had caught her breath, she put her hand on Mrs. Vey's shoulder. "Are you okay?"

Mrs. Vey nodded, even though she was weak and emaciated. "Where's Michael?"

"He'll be here in a second. He's bringing up the rear."

Tanner carefully jumped down, followed by Ian. It was another five minutes before Ostin stuck his head out, panting from the long crawl. He looked around, then scooted on his butt until he was sitting on the rim of the pipe and jumped down.

As Ostin dusted off his knees, Mrs. Vey walked over to the pipe and looked inside. "Where's Michael?"

Taylor also looked inside the pipe. "Michael!" Her voice echoed in the darkness, but there was no response. "Ian, where is he?"

"He was right behind us," Ian said. He looked at the pipe. "He's not there."

"What?" Taylor and Mrs. Vey said in unison.

Ostin looked up with a pained expression. "He didn't come."

Taylor blanched. "What do you mean, he didn't come?"

Everyone's eyes turned to Ostin, who was still catching his breath.

"The guards were too close. Michael stayed back to provide a diversion so we could escape."

Mrs. Vey stared at him in disbelief. "Michael's still inside the compound?"

"He said he had to stay," Ostin said.

"And you let him?" Taylor shouted.

"What was I supposed to do? It was the logical thing to do."

"Logical!" Taylor screamed. She put her hands on the rim of the pipe to climb back in. "I'm going after him."

"It won't do any good," Ostin said. "He locked the pipe after me."

"No!" she shouted, her voice echoing down the pipe. She turned back angrily. "We came all the way here to rescue his mother and you left him behind?"

Ostin swallowed. "I was just—"

"Being stupid?" Jack said fiercely.

"Leave him alone," McKenna said. "It's not his fault."

"Then whose is it?" Taylor said.

"It's Michael's," McKenna said. "He made a choice."

"I knew I should have waited!" Taylor shouted. She swung around, thrusting her finger in Ostin's face. "I never would have gone first if I had any idea he was thinking of leaving. We stick together."

"I'm sorry," Ostin said.

"Sorry?" Taylor said. "I thought you were smart."

For a moment no one spoke.

Then Abigail said, "So what are we supposed to do now?"

Ostin said meekly, "Michael said that Taylor has the GPS; she's supposed to lead us to the pickup site."

"That's not going to happen," Taylor said. "I didn't come all this way to leave Michael. Do you have any idea what Hatch will do to him if he catches him?" She turned to Ian. "Can you see him?"

Ian looked back for a moment, then said, "He's with the guards."

"They've captured him?"

"No. He's standing with them, talking. They must think he's one of them."

"He stayed back to cause a diversion so we could get away," Ostin said. "He said after he led them away he'd sneak back down through the pipe. But he wanted us to hurry toward the pickup site before they figured out how we escaped."

"I'm not leaving without my son," Mrs. Vey said.

"And *if* he gets out," Taylor said, "just how exactly is he supposed to find us?"

"He said he'd go to Cuzco."

"How? It's at least a week by foot, with no food or water—if something in the jungle doesn't kill him first."

"He's more powerful than anything in the jungle," Ostin said.

"Even when he's sleeping? Or is he supposed to go a week without sleep, too?"

Ian suddenly groaned. "Oh no."

"What?" Taylor asked.

"They just captured Michael."

His words stunned everyone. Taylor gasped, and Mrs. Vey sat down on a fallen log and began to cry.

"I'm so sorry," Ostin said, his eyes filling with tears. "I thought it was the right thing to do. I couldn't have made him come if I wanted to."

"Did you even try?" Taylor asked.

"Yes," he said.

Taylor looked at him in disgust. "I'll bet. And he thought you were his best friend."

Ostin hung his head.

"Enough!" McKenna said, walking up to Taylor. "Leave him alone. It's not his fault."

Mrs. Vey looked up, her cheeks wet with tears. "She's right. It's not Ostin's fault. Michael would have done this anyway. He would do anything to save his friends."

"No," Ostin said, shaking his head. "Taylor's right. I should have tried harder. I let him down. It's all my fault." He put his head down and walked away from the group.

Taylor turned toward him. "Ostin, come back."

Ostin continued walking off into the jungle until he was out of sight.

"Thanks," McKenna said angrily, then ran after Ostin.

A haze of despair fell over the group. After a few minutes Jack said, "We're not leaving him."

No one answered. The impossibility of saving Michael was obvious to everyone. The silence was broken by Zeus's groan. Raúl looked at Zeus, then pointed to Jack's knife. *"Cuchillo."*

"You want my knife?" Jack asked.

Raúl nodded. *"Por favor."*

"That means please," Abigail said.

Jack pulled his knife from its sheath and handed it to him. Raúl took it, then ran off into the forest.

"Where do you think he's going?" Abigail asked.

"I have no idea," he said. "But does it matter?"

44

The Betrayal

I awoke buckled tightly to a cot only slightly larger than the one I'd been strapped to in the back of the Elgen truck. There were wires connected to me coming from a white metal box about the size of a deck of cards strapped to my chest. It was a RESAT box, the same device I had pulled off Tanner when we'd freed him. The top of the box had a single knob and several flashing red and green diodes registering its power diffusion. It also had a small antenna, which made me believe my suffering was being controlled by remote. I felt dizzy, and my thoughts were blurred, nearly as hazy as my vision. Above me was a large light fixture, and the light from it blinded and hurt my eyes, making me blink as hard as I ever have, which is probably why I didn't notice Taylor until she spoke.

"Michael."

I squinted, looking up into her face. *I must be dreaming*, I thought.

She leaned over and kissed me on the forehead. "How are you?"

"What are you doing here? You've got to get out, before they catch you."

"It's okay," she said. "We're safe."

My forehead was wet with perspiration. "We're not safe. Pull off these wires. We've got to get out of here."

Taylor just smiled. "Why would I want to escape?"

"What?"

Her smile grew. "I want to tell you a secret." She leaned close to my ear and whispered, "The whole boyfriend-girlfriend thing, it's not real. I made it up to get you down here for Dr. Hatch. I delivered you to him. And in return Dr. Hatch gave me this beautiful diamond bracelet." She dangled the bracelet in front of my face. "You know how we girls love bling. I just thought you'd like to know that." She stood up and walked out of the room.

Tears fell down the sides of my face. *This must be a nightmare*, I told myself.

Ten minutes later someone else walked into the room, stopping at the side of my cot. It was Dr. Hatch. "Welcome back, Michael," he said.

I closed my eyes. I didn't want to look at him.

"You've been crying. So you must have learned the truth about Taylor. Unrequited love always hurts. You didn't really think that a girl as beautiful as Taylor would be interested in someone as pathetic as you, did you?"

I said nothing.

"Not speaking, I see." He slowly exhaled. "No matter." He pulled a stool up to the side of my cot and sat down. "Michael the oath breaker. That's what we call you around here. What do you think of that?"

"I don't care what you call me," I said.

Hatch's voice turned more serious. "How did you get down here?"

I didn't answer.

He grabbed my face, squeezing my cheeks. "I asked you a question."

"I walked."

He let go of me but remained close enough that I could feel his breath on my face. His voice dropped. I knew Hatch well enough to know that that was his way. Most people's voices rise when they're angry. Hatch's voice softened. "Let's try this one," he said slowly. "Where are your friends, Michael?"

I didn't answer.

Hatch waited nearly a full minute before he said, "Oh please. Don't be so cliché with the 'I'm going to be the hero and protect my friends' routine. We both know that I could throw you in Cell 26, our new and improved Peruvian version of your suite in the academy, and get it out of you."

The idea of being sent to the cell sent chills through me, but I also knew that my mother and friends would be back in America before the Elgen broke me.

Hatch leaned forward. "Apart from Taylor, you don't know where your 'friends' are, do you? Maybe they're not really friends. If they were, wouldn't they have tried to rescue you? They haven't, you know. We haven't heard a peep out of them. I'm a little surprised that they deserted you in your hour of need. Aren't you?"

I clenched my jaw.

"Or maybe you just don't want to accept the truth that after all you did for her, even your mother didn't care enough to stick around. That must hurt even more than Taylor's betrayal." His voice fell almost to a whisper. "No one cares about you, Michael. You're all alone in this world."

In spite of the pain, I forced a defiant smile. "They got away," I said, finding relief in his words. "That's all that matters."

Hatch sneered. "Yes, they got away, for now. But that's all right. We'll get them. We'll hunt them down one by one. And in the meantime, we have you. The big kahuna. President of the electro*clam* or whatever ridiculous name you gave your group."

"Electroclan," I said.

"It doesn't matter. The club has been disbanded. But you were worth all the trouble you and your little club caused. At least I thought you were." He reached over to the box on my chest and turned a knob. Increased pain shot through my body, and I groaned out. "Then you went and made things . . . difficult. You changed your destiny for the worse. Only one thing can save you now. Do you want to know what that is?"

I was gritting my teeth with pain. "Yes."

He reached over and turned the knob back down. The pain lessened.

"Humility, Michael. Humility." He sat back as if giving me time to contemplate his words. "I wonder if you even know what it is? It's a lost virtue. Kids these days are all swagger. They think they have all the answers. But they're just a new generation of fools.

"Humility is the wisdom of accepting the truth that you might just be wrong. Unfortunately, for most it comes too late—after the game is lost, if you know what I mean. Humility comes when you've hit rock bottom. When your best friends have deserted you. When you have nothing more to lose. Like you. So just put away your arrogant ways and join us, like Taylor did, completely and without reservation, or I have no choice but to dispose of you."

"You're not going to kill me," I said. "You need me."

"Not exactly," Hatch said. "We need your DNA, a few pints of blood, and some of your tissue. But we don't need *you*." He lingered on the word "you" like it left a bitter taste in his mouth.

"Honestly, I wouldn't have minded keeping you around for a while. I had planned on it. But then you went and ruined the party. Now I have no choice but to make an example of you.

"You see, I have eight very promising and powerful young men and women who I am grooming for future leadership in my organization. These young people are impressionable and they have seen you defy me. If I let that slide, they'll think I'm soft. Then it's just a matter of time before one, or all of them, tries the same thing. Not right away of course, these things need time to culture, but, like a virus, dissension will grow." Hatch's eyes flashed with anger. "*That* is not an option. They need to know that being special does not mean they're indispensable.

"So, after our scientists have taken what they need from you, you're going to help me teach my youths a vital lesson about the importance of obedience and fidelity. And in this way, your worthless little life, which until now has only served to annoy me, will actually do me some good.

"How will I do this, you ask?" He ran his finger up my arm. "I can see from these bites that you've had a taste of our rats. Or," he said darkly, "vice versa. They're going to get another helping of you. Only this time there will be no one to save you. Do you have any idea how carnivorous those little things are? I've seen them strip a bull to bones in less than two minutes. I can't imagine the pain, the sheer agony, as a thousand little teeth devour your flesh.

"I'll give you some time to consider your fate, Michael. Can you be humble?" Hatch leaned close to my ear. "Before I go I'd like to confide in you. Parents sometimes say it's the child who stands up to them who they respect the most. I admit there is some truth to this. You have shown tremendous leadership with your little group of miscreants. I'm just sorry it's not going to take you anywhere but the bowl." He stood. "Au revoir, Michael. The next time I see you will be suppertime. Not for you, of course."

"Wait," I said.

Hatch smiled. "Yes?"

"Tell Tara that I know she and Taylor are identical twins, but she's really not as pretty. Sorry."

Hatch scowled at me, then turned and walked out of the room.

45

Dynamite

Ostin was sitting by himself nearly a hundred yards away from the camp, leaning against a tree. He was drawing in the dirt with a stick, doing mathematical equations, something he did when he was upset. He didn't notice McKenna until she was standing a few yards from him.

"May I sit down?" McKenna asked.

"Free world," Ostin said. "At least until the Elgen take over."

McKenna sat down cross-legged a few feet from him. She picked up a rock and rolled it in her hands. For a long time neither of them spoke.

"They estimate that there are seven and a half trillion trees in the Amazon rain forest," Ostin said. "That one right there is called a strangler fig. The Peruvians call it *matapalo*, the killer tree. It starts when a bird drops its seed up in a tree and the strangler fig grows down to the ground until it chokes out the host tree and takes its place."

"That's interesting," McKenna said. After another moment she said, "It's not your fault, you know."

"I let my best friend down. I wasn't loyal."

"Did you want him to stay?"

He looked up angrily. "No! Of course not."

"Then you honored his wishes even when you didn't want to. That's loyalty, isn't it?"

Ostin couldn't answer.

"Taylor doesn't really think it's your fault either."

"You could have fooled me."

"Sometimes people are like that. When we're upset at someone and they're not around, we take it out on whoever is close. Even people we love. Taylor's afraid for Michael and so she's upset. And since he isn't here, she took it out on you. Does that make sense?"

Ostin sighed. "I guess so."

"The truth is, no matter what anyone said back there, if it wasn't for you, we'd all still be locked up at the academy. All of us, including Michael." Ostin looked up to see her gazing at him. "You're the smartest person I've ever met. And you're smarter than any of us. You're our only hope of saving Michael." She looked at him for a moment, then leaned forward, staring him directly in the eyes. "Michael needs you. So stop feeling sorry for yourself and *save* him."

"You think I can save him?"

"I *know* you can save him. And I know you can save us." She leaned back.

Ostin stared at the ground for a moment. When he lifted his head his expression had changed. He looked like himself again.

"Let's break down our situation into its individual components. We're hiding in a tropical rain forest next to a seemingly impenetrable fortress with two thousand armed guards, huge electric fences, and ubiquitous camera surveillance. Our original way into the compound through the ranch entrance is no longer an option, and our second route was locked off by Michael.

"Our foe seems all-powerful, but if history has taught us any-thing, it's that everyone and everything has a weakness—you just have to find it. My weakness is jelly doughnuts. Your weakness is dehydration, or lack of water." His brow furrowed. "Zeus's weakness is also water." Suddenly his face animated. "That's it!" He clapped his hands together. "That's their weakness!"

"What?" McKenna asked.

"Water! They built protection around the power plant but not their water source." He jumped up. "I know how to shut them down."

"Explain," McKenna said, smiling at his enthusiasm.

"To power two million homes, their plant would have to create nearly twenty billion kilowatt hours of electricity. That's twice the energy of a standard nuclear power plant. Given that the Elgen's power creation is three times more efficient than a steam-turbine system, I'm guessing that the rats are generating heat close to one thousand degrees Fahrenheit. That's why they built the plant next to a river—without water the bowl would melt down in a matter of minutes. Or even if it didn't, the heat would kill the rats. No rats, no electricity. No electricity, no lights, no cameras, no electric locks, and no electric fences." Ostin grabbed McKenna's hand and pulled her to her feet. "Come on, we've got to tell the others."

In Ostin's absence, the group had moved a couple of hundred feet from the pipe to a more concealed location. Everyone was sitting or lying down when Ostin and McKenna rushed into the clearing.

"I know how we can save Michael!" Ostin shouted.

Taylor stood. "How?"

"Everyone gather round," Ostin said, standing next to Zeus. They formed a crescent around him, McKenna holding on to Ostin's arm.

"Here's the gist of it," Ostin said. "Just north of the compound is the Elgen pump house. That's where they bring in the water from the river to cool the Starxource plant. It's outside of the compound. If we blow up the pump house, their grid will heat up to a thousand degrees within minutes. So even if the grid doesn't melt down, the heat will kill all the rats and still shut down their power. The entire compound is electric, so if they lose their power they lose their cameras, alarms, intercoms, and light. Which means the prisoners can escape."

"Don't they have backup power?" Zeus asked.

"They have two backup generators run by diesel," Ostin said. "But even if they could get their generators up, it would take at least five to ten minutes to get them online. And they would only create enough power for the compound. The rest of Peru would go dark."

Suddenly a grin crossed Ostin's face. "Wait, I've got an even better idea. We also blow the generators! All that diesel fuel would create a massive explosion that would set fire to the camp. It will take hundreds of guards to fight it. Between that and all the escaping prisoners, we'll practically be able to walk in and get Michael."

"Brilliant," Ian said.

"But how do we blow the pump house?" Taylor asked.

"Dynamite," Ostin said.

"Last I checked we're completely out," Wade said sardonically.

"Where do we get dynamite?" Taylor asked.

"I don't know," Ostin said. "But this is the jungle and jungle people use dynamite for clearing trees and mining. I'm hoping that Raúl knows where to find some." He looked around. "Where is Raúl?"

"We don't know," Abigail said. "No one could understand him. He took Jack's knife and ran out into the forest."

Ostin looked puzzled. "Did he say anything?"

Jack looked at Abigail. "Something like saliva."

Ostin's brow furrowed. "Saliva?"

Abigail said, "No, it was more like . . . saliba. Salvia. Maybe, sabila."

"*Sábila*," Ostin repeated. "Of course. For Zeus."

"He was looking at Zeus when he said it," Abigail said.

"He must know where he can find some."

"Find what?" Jack asked.

"Aloe vera. It's a cactuslike plant that grows in Peru and is useful for treating burns," Ostin said. "While we're waiting for Raúl we need to make our plan. Ian, the generators are on the north side of the plant. There should be some big fuel tanks."

"I think I see them," Ian said, standing up and looking toward the compound. "There are two huge tanks aboveground, then a couple dozen oil barrels stacked near them."

"Can you tell if they're full?"

"All except two."

"Perfect," Ostin said. "So first we set the dynamite at the pump. The generators are going to be trickier because they're behind the fence."

"We could throw the dynamite," Jack said. "If it's not too far."

"It's not," Ian said. "But then how do we detonate it?"

"Zeus could do it," Jack said. "Couldn't you?"

Zeus nodded weakly. "If I can get there, I can. Back at the academy I used to set off firecrackers all the time."

"I'll get you there," Jack said.

Ostin continued, "While the guards are trying to put out the fire, we'll blow the pump house. Then the bowl will melt down, the power will go out, and in all the confusion, Ian, McKenna, Taylor, and I will slip in through the east fence to save Michael."

"Where am I while this is happening?" Jack asked.

"After we blow the pump house, you and Zeus will stay with the rest of the Electroclan. If something goes wrong, you get them to the village. Raúl knows his way through the jungle. In the village he can hide you."

Jack nodded. "Good plan."

"When do we do it?" Taylor asked.

"Tomorrow, after dark. It's also best if we wait until their feeding time—that's when the bowl will be at its hottest." Ostin looked at them all. "Are you with me?"

"I'm with you," McKenna said.

"Me too," Taylor said.

"I'm in," Jack said. "So is Wade."

"It could work," Ian said. "What do we do first?"

"First thing we need to do is get the dynamite. Let's just hope Raúl knows where to find some."

"Let's just hope Raúl comes back," Jack said.

*   *   *

Raúl returned to the camp about a half hour later carrying half a dozen large, dull-green serrated leaves. He set them down on the ground near Zeus, then knelt beside him.

"Yep, aloe vera," Ostin said. "It's a natural remedy for burns."

Zeus looked at the moist leaves fearfully. "It may burn me more," he said.

"Let me try just a little," Ostin said. He took a leaf from Raúl, squeezed some salve from it onto his finger, then lightly touched it to Zeus's skin. There was no electric reaction. "Looks good," Ostin said.

"All right," Zeus said.

Ostin nodded to Raúl. "Okay."

"Okay," Raúl said. He split a leaf, then began applying the salve to Zeus's burned flesh, murmuring something to Ostin as he worked.

"He said this will help," Ostin said.

"Let's hope so," Jack said.

Abigail continued to hold Zeus's hand.

"How are you holding up?" Zeus asked Abigail. She was weary from her constant exertion, but she forced a smile. "Still better than you."

As Raúl worked, Ostin explained his plan, then the two of them had a long discussion. When it was over, Ostin said, "Raúl knows where we can find dynamite. It's about a three-hour walk from here. But he'll need help carrying it."

"Someone's going to carry dynamite for three hours through a slippery jungle?" Wade said. "That sounds like a death wish."

"Wade and I will go," Jack said.

"What?" Wade said.

"Someone's got to do it," Jack said. "We'll do it."

Wade just shook his head.

Raúl handed Jack's knife back to him, then pointed to Jack and Wade and said something.

"He said you should leave a little before sunrise," Ostin said.

Jack nodded. "*Sí.*"

Wade looked distressed. "Great. I won't even get a last meal."

*   *   *

As darkness fell, Mrs. Vey approached Ostin, who was sketching out a map of the compound in the dirt. "Ostin?"

He looked up. "Yes, Mrs. Vey?"

"It's really a great plan you came up with."

Ostin blushed. "Thank you."

She kissed Ostin on the forehead. "You're a good friend to Michael. That's why he loves you so much. And when we get back to Idaho, I'm making you waffles."

Ostin pumped his fist. "Yes!"

Ostin was still smiling when Taylor approached him a few minutes later.

"Hey," she said.

Ostin looked up.

"About your idea," Taylor said. "It's brilliant."

"Thanks."

She took a deep breath. "Look, I'm sorry about what I said earlier. It wasn't your fault. I was just upset."

"I know," Ostin said.

"You do?"

He nodded.

"I was afraid you wouldn't know that. I mean, you're so smart about everything except girls. Well, girls and pretty much anything social . . ."

"McKenna explained it to me," Ostin said.

"Oh," Taylor said. "I feel awful about what I said about you being a bad friend. You're not. You're a great friend." She looked into his eyes. "Can you forgive me?"

"Yes."

"I know I tease you a lot, but I'm glad we're friends, too."

"Really?" Ostin asked.

Taylor nodded. "Really."

Ostin put out his fist. "Bones?"

Taylor smiled and put out hers. "Bones."

46

Nighttime in the Jungle

The group huddled together for the night, sleeping on the dirt. The Amazonian floor receives less than 2 percent of the sunlight, so very little grows, making it soft, like a decaying mulch pile.

The night air was moist and a little too cool for comfort, but they didn't dare make a fire or even let McKenna light herself up for fear that they'd be discovered by an Elgen patrol—it was dangerous enough that most of them glowed naturally.

Everyone was thirsty. Raúl took Ostin with him into the jungle, and when they came back Ostin was holding a tan, tennis-ball-size glob from which he pinched out pieces, rolled them into small balls, and handed them out to everyone.

"What is this?" Taylor said.

"It's gum," Ostin said. "It will make you less thirsty."

"Where did you find gum?"

"It's called chicle. It comes from the sap of the sapodilla tree. That's how they make gum."

"Chicle. Chiclets," McKenna said.

"*Exacto,*" Ostin said. "That's where it got its name."

Taylor put some in her mouth and chewed. "It's kind of sweet. But it tastes like gum you've already chewed for ten hours."

"It's tree sap," Ostin said. "What did you expect, Bazooka bubble gum?"

Taylor shrugged. "That would be nice."

The jungle came alive at night, as noisy and bustling as Times Square. Maybe noisier. As exhausted as he was, Ian volunteered to stand guard. It wasn't as difficult as he thought it would be, as observing the jungle at night was like watching a live presentation of the Discovery Channel. He watched two scorpions, locked in combat, battle to the death. He saw a jaguar climb a tree to catch a monkey, and an entire colony of vampire bats emerge from a rotted tree to seek blood. Everything in the jungle seemed engaged in a life-and-death struggle. Just like them.

No one, outside of Raúl, got much sleep. Between their growing thirst, the symphony of insects, and the continuous assault of mosquitoes, everyone was miserable.

In the middle of the night the sound of thunder rolled across the forest accompanied by the excited chatter of monkeys. Even though they could hear the sound of rain hitting the trees, the thick, lush canopy of leaves kept them dry. Ian found a stream of water rolling down a tree and let it gather in a leaf to drink.

Tanner woke up three times in the night screaming. On the third occasion, Mrs. Vey went to his side and comforted him, gently stroking his forehead. He broke down crying, and she held him, rocking him like a baby.

The only thing that really concerned Ian was when he spotted a guard sneaking back to the pipe. *Isn't he going to be surprised?* Ian thought.

A half hour later, the guard, having found the cap locked,

reemerged from the pipe's mouth and ran back in the direction he had come from.

Ian was still awake when Raúl, Jack, and Wade left at the first hint of dawn.

Ostin awoke an hour later covered with mosquito and spider bites. "I can't spend another night here," he said, scratching his arm.

"I know what you mean," Ian said.

"Did Jack and Raúl already leave?"

"And Wade."

"I hope they make it."

"Me too," Ian said. Then added, "It's a jungle out there."

The three didn't return until late afternoon. They were carrying large, overstuffed packs. Jack had two, one strapped to his front as well as his back, and Raúl was carrying a bag in his hand in addition to his pack. Wade was a physical and emotional wreck and his clothes were soaked through with sweat. He took off his pack and carefully set it on the ground, overjoyed to be free of it.

"You made it," Taylor said to them.

"That was farther than I thought it was," Jack said. "Nice hike."

Taylor turned to Wade. "So how was it?"

"It was a death march," he said. "Nothing like carrying death on your back through a dangerous, death-filled jungle."

"The good thing is that if the dynamite had gone off you'd never even know it," Jack said.

"Comforting," Wade said.

"Well," Taylor said, "if you gotta go, that's the way to go. Oblivious."

"Just like my great-grandfather," Jack said. "He died in his sleep. Much more peacefully than the screaming passengers in the car he was driving."

"You just made that up, didn't you?" Taylor said.

Jack grinned. "Yep." He lifted one of the packs and tossed it to her. It landed on the ground a few feet in front of her.

Taylor jumped back. "What are you doing?"

Jack laughed. "It's not dynamite. I brought back some food and water. Also some gauze for Zeus."

Taylor opened the pack. Inside were a dozen bottles of water, four large, crusted loaves of bread, and green fruits that were slightly smaller than a grapefruit, with the texture of an avocado. She drank some water, then took one of the fruits from the pack.

"What's this?" she asked.

"No idea," Jack said. "He said it was a cherry or something. But it's pretty good."

"Cherimoya," said Raúl, who was eating one a few yards away.

"I'll take your word for it," Taylor said. She grabbed two more bottles of water, three fruits, and a loaf of bread to take to Mrs. Vey and Tanner.

Jack walked around distributing food and water. McKenna was so happy when she saw the water that she started to cry. "Water."

"I got two bottles for you," Jack said. "I know how you need it."

"Thank you, thank you, thank you," she said, opening a bottle. "You're my hero."

"I thought I was," Ostin said.

McKenna drank half the bottle, then said, "You still are."

Relieved, Ostin asked, "Are those cherimoyas?"

"Something like that," Jack said, tossing him one. "Is there anything you don't know?"

"The meaning of life," Ostin said. "And how girls think." He peeled back the fruit's glossy green skin and took a bite, juice dribbling down his chin. "Oh man. That's good."

"What does it taste like?" McKenna asked.

"The flavor falls somewhere between strawberry and bubble gum."

"I want one," she said.

"Mark Twain called the cherimoya the most delicious fruit known to man," Ostin said.

"I definitely want one," McKenna said.

Jack handed her a fruit.

"Me too," Ian said. "Toss one this way."

Raúl laughed and said to Ostin, *"Vendes muy bien. Puedes trabajar en el carro de frutas de mi mamá."*

Ostin laughed.

"What did he say?" McKenna asked.

"He said I'm a good salesman. And I can have a job at his mother's fruit cart."

Jack took water and food to Abigail and Zeus. The night before, at the first sound of thunder, Jack and Abigail had carried Zeus into the sloping, deep roots of a kapok tree, then covered him with an additional canopy of brush. Jack handed Abigail a bottle and she took a quick drink, then held it to Zeus's lips.

Zeus raised his hand. "I can hold it," he said.

"How are you feeling?" Jack asked.

"I think the aloe vera is helping."

Jack brought out a crusted loaf of bread and offered it to Abigail. "I brought this."

She tore off a piece and handed it to Zeus, then took a piece for herself. "I'm so hungry," she said.

"Try this," Jack said, handing her a cherimoya.

"What is it?" she asked. "Actually, never mind, I don't care what it is. I'll eat anything."

Jack peeled a fruit for Zeus and handed it to him.

"I've had one of these before," he said. "In Costa Rica. Thanks."

"No problem," Jack said.

After the food was gone Jack handed Abigail the gauze. "We should wrap him in this. It will help keep his burns from getting infected."

"Thank you," Zeus said. He turned to Abigail. "Could you give Jack and me a moment to talk?"

She looked at him quizzically. "But your pain . . ."

"I can take it for a few minutes. And you need the rest."

"Okay." She stood up. "Bye." She walked over to McKenna.

When she was gone Zeus said to Jack, "Why are you being so nice to me? I shocked you twice."

Jack grinned. "Yeah, but what did I call you? Lightning stink? I deserved to get shocked."

Zeus looked at him somberly. "I'm serious. Abi told me what you did in the compound. How you ran through the rats to save me."

Jack sat down next to Zeus. "Not something I hope to do again soon."

Zeus just looked at him. "Really, why did you do it?"

Jack didn't answer immediately, though his expression turned more serious. When he spoke his voice was low and sincere. "We may have our differences—or maybe they're really our similarities—but anyone who's willing to sacrifice his life for his friends is a true hero. I'd award you the Medal of Honor if I could."

For a moment Zeus was speechless. Then he said, "About Abi . . ."

Jack lifted his hand. "We don't have to talk about her."

"I know. But if you want a shot at her, I'll step aside."

Jack looked down at him. "I don't think she's going to be leaving your side anytime soon," he said. "Besides, that's not really our choice, is it?"

"I'm just saying, I owe you."

"No you don't. But I'd be proud to be your friend."

"Me too," Zeus said. They clasped hands and Zeus grimaced a little, hiding his pain.

Jack stood. "I'll get Abi."

"Thank you."

He took a few steps, then turned back. *"Semper Fi."*

Zeus smiled. *"Semper Fi."*

After everyone had eaten, Taylor and Ostin called the group together. Jack and Abigail helped Zeus over, though he insisted on walking himself.

In the center of their camp Ostin had drawn a diagram of the Elgen compound in the dirt, using rocks and leaves to designate buildings.

"This is where we are," Ostin said, pointing to a spot a few inches from the compound, using a long, slender stick. "And this is where we came from the pipe. Over here, about four hundred yards from us, is the pump house. Earlier today Ian and I sneaked over to take a look at it. Even though it's outside the compound it's still within view of the guard towers, which means we'll have to camouflage ourselves to get to it. Right here is the side where the water is controlled."

"There's also a barbwire fence around it," Ian said. "But it's easy to climb over."

"Or under," Ostin said. "When we blow this thing, it's going to be like a fire hydrant on steroids. We'll be hiding over here behind these rocks when we set off the dynamite. The northeast guard tower is only fifty yards from the pump house and it's equipped with two fifty-caliber Browning machine guns. Those bad boys spit bullets longer than my foot and can pretty much mow down anything in the jungle, so hiding behind a tree won't do much good. Stay clear until the place goes dark."

"I'll explain the next part," Taylor said. "After the sun sets we'll split up into three groups. Ian, McKenna, Ostin, and I are in group one. We'll set the dynamite at the pump house and keep an eye on the bowl. Ian will tell us when it's time to blow the pump and the generators.

"Group two is Jack, Zeus, Abi, and Wade." She looked at Jack. "Your job is to blow the fuel and diesel generators. You won't be able to get close, so you'll have to throw the dynamite, and Zeus will have to set it off. The oil drums are about thirty yards behind the fence. What's the farthest you can hit, Zeus?"

"I can hit them," Zeus said.

"Good," Taylor said. "Ian will be watching for when the bowl is hottest, which is at feeding time. When we tell you, you'll blow the pumps. Ian's been able to confirm that there are eighteen forty-two-gallon drums as well as the tanks connected to the generator. There are fourteen sticks of dynamite in each pack, so you'll each take one pack. Combined with all that oil, that's going to make one big explosion. The generator is only fifty yards from the guard barracks, so with some luck we'll set them on fire as well."

Ostin jumped in. "Diesel puts out a lot of thick smoke, so it will help create confusion and panic, but it has one potential problem— it's not as flammable as gasoline, so it's going to be harder to get this right. Remember, our primary goal is to shut down the generator. So make sure that the dynamite is close to the generator and blows up the tanks first. Just hitting the barrels might not be enough. Are you clear on that?"

"Got it," Jack said. "Hit the generator and hope the barrels come along for the ride."

"Exactly. As soon as we hear your explosion, we'll blow the pump house. We'll be close enough to lay a fuse, which McKenna will light. Without water the power plant should go down within three to five minutes."

"One question," Zeus said. "How are you going to signal me when it's time to blow our dynamite?"

Taylor looked at Ostin. "We didn't think of that," she said. "Maybe we could do a bird call."

"The guards are closer to you than we are," Jack said. "They'll hear."

Ostin squeezed his chin. "Hmm."

"I have an idea," McKenna said. "Didn't you say there's a barbwire fence outside of the compound?"

"Yes," Ostin said. "But don't worry, it will be easy to get through."

"I'm not worried about that," McKenna said. "How long is the fence?"

"It extends almost the whole length of the north side," Ian said. "How come?"

"What I'm thinking is that Taylor should switch to group two, and then she and Ian could both hold on to the wire. When it's time to blow, Ian just thinks that it's time, then Taylor hears his thoughts and signals Zeus. That way there's no sound or anything that might alert the guards."

Ostin just gaped at her. "That's brilliant."

"Thank you," she said with a slight smile.

"That is a good idea," Taylor said. "So maybe Wade and I should switch places."

Wade nodded. "I'm good with that."

"Then what?" Abigail asked.

"After we've blown the dynamite," Ostin said, "we'll regroup halfway between the pump house and the generator, then Taylor, Ian, McKenna, and I will climb through the fence and rescue Michael. Ian thinks that Michael is being held in the same place Tanner was."

"What about the rest of us?" Mrs. Vey said.

Taylor turned. "You, Tanner, and Raúl are group three. Since you and Tanner are still recovering, we decided it's best that you get an early start to our meeting point. Raúl will lead you back to where we entered the compound."

Ostin added, "We left some of Raúl's friends tied up there and we need to free them."

Taylor nodded. "After we've got Michael, we'll meet you there, then we'll all hike together to the pickup point. Sound good?"

Mrs. Vey nodded.

"I almost forgot," Ostin said, looking at Tanner. "The Elgen have four helicopters. If they put any up, you take them down."

"With pleasure," he said. "I hope they come after us."

"We're kicking their hive," Ostin said. "I think you can count on it."

47

The Offer

There was a video monitor in my prison cell that played a continuous loop of the rats at feeding time. The Elgen guards were generally cruel, but I'm sure this was done on Hatch's orders. He would do anything he could to increase my suffering. And he'd enjoy it. I think that deep inside he was sorry he had to kill me, but only because he couldn't do it more than once.

I had been in the cell (in the same cellblock where we had found Tanner) for less than twenty-four hours, but it felt much longer. Security around me was tight, with a guard outside my door and two inside. The truth was, they didn't even need a locked door. Drained of my electricity, I couldn't even leave the cot, let alone my cell.

The RESAT box still fastened to me was like having Nichelle sitting on my chest, drawing out all my energy—only the box was much more powerful than Nichelle was. The only bodily functions that seemed undisturbed by the machine were my tics, which, unfortunately, never seemed to take a break. Especially now. My eyes stung from all my blinking.

Then a thought came to me—a small spark of hope. Maybe the Elgen had locked me up not to keep me in the cell but to keep my friends out. *Maybe my friends are still trying to save me after all.* I had mixed feelings about this. Of course I wanted to be rescued. I was terrified by what was to come. But, realistically, there was no way they could save me—and the only thing worse than dying would be to watch everyone I loved suffer and die too. I couldn't think about that option. I hoped they had followed my instructions and made it to the pickup site. At least then my death would have mattered for something.

That morning I had visitors. Tara, Bryan, Quentin, and Torstyn. This time Tara came as herself. I had seen Bryan and Quentin at the academy, but I had seen Torstyn only when Ian pointed him out as we escaped from Re-Ed through the assembly hall.

I knew there were other electric kids, seventeen in all, but Hatch had told me the last four were dead. But here was Torstyn—so Hatch was lying after all.

The guard opened the door, and Tara was the first in, her lip curled in a mocking sneer. "Oh, Michael, you're so cute. I'm so in love with you." She laughed. "So you're all kissy with my pathetic sister?"

Bryan shook his head. "What an idiot."

Quentin walked up to my side, his mouth stretched in a confident grin. "You really thought you could take us on? You're delusional, man. You're getting what you deserve."

I turned away from them. Torstyn grabbed my chin and pulled my head back. "I didn't say you could look away from us. You want me to fry you, lover boy?"

In spite of my weakness I said, "Try."

The other youths looked at Torstyn, wondering if he would. He just stared at me. "You know I would if Hatch let me."

"Your master won't let you?" I said. "Maybe he'll let you lick his shoes."

Torstyn scowled. "Watch your mouth or I'm gonna mess you up, man."

"Real tough threatening me when I'm locked up. Let me out and you can show everyone how tough you really are."

Torstyn looked stumped, caught between his ego and his fear of Hatch.

"Don't worry about it, Torstyn," Quentin said. "The rats will take care of him."

"That's your name?" I said. "Torstyn? They named you after a wrench?"

Torstyn turned red. When he finally spoke he said, "You're stupid."

"Wow," I said. "Is that your superpower? Your brilliant vocabulary?"

Torstyn blushed again.

Quentin intervened. "Hey, Vey, you're going to love this. We just talked to the dudes at the chute. They said they can slow the conveyor belt, so we can prolong the fun. The rats can eat you a couple of inches at a time."

"Awesome," Bryan said. "Wouldn't it be cool if Dr. Hatch, like, made a game of it and let him run across the bowl? They could even make it a contest. If he gets to the other side and back, he can go free. It would be like dropping a grasshopper on an anthill. We could, like, make bets on how far he gets."

"Hey, Bryan, wouldn't it be cool if you had half a brain?" I said. "Did you know these guys all think you're an idiot? Zeus told me all about it."

Bryan looked back and forth between them. "No, they don't. They're my boys."

"Really? Is that why Quentin put dog poop in your bed?"

Bryan looked at Quentin. "*You* did that?"

Quentin shoved him. "He's just messing with your head, man."

"Yeah, he did it. Zeus watched him."

Bryan glared at him.

"I didn't do it," Quentin said. "That was Tanner."

"Tanner was in England," Bryan said.

"I told you," I said. "They're always making fun of you behind your back."

Bryan stormed out of my cell. I turned my attention to Torstyn. "C'mon, tough guy, let me out. Let's see how tough you are."

For a moment he looked as if he actually might do it. I didn't know if I had any chance against him, I didn't even know what his powers were, but I figured he couldn't be worse than a million rats.

"He's messing with you, too," Tara said. "Enough of this loser. Let's get out of here."

"You know, your sister is so much cooler than you are," I said. "In Meridian she has like a million friends. I guess beauty really is more than skin deep."

"So are rats," Tara said.

"That doesn't even make sense," I said.

Quentin said, "We thought watching the bulls get eaten was sick. You getting eaten is going to be epic."

"Enjoy it. Your turn's coming soon. Someday Hatch will be feeding you to something," I said.

"That shows how little you know," Quentin said. "Dr. Hatch is like a father to us. He'd never hurt one of us."

"Yeah, Tanner thought that too," I said.

My reply stumped him.

Tara said, "Tanner was a screwup."

"Then you better hope you don't screw up," I said. "Because, father or not, Hatch is afraid of you. Do you know why he's executing me? He told me he's afraid that if he doesn't, one of you will someday take him down."

Suddenly a beeper went off on my RESAT and a wave of pain passed through my body, freezing me. I grimaced. Through clenched teeth I said, "I guess someone doesn't want me telling you the truth."

A guard walked briskly into the room. "It's time to leave," he said. "The prisoner is getting agitated."

"Hatch is getting agitated," I said.

The guard quickly ushered them out. Tara turned back at the door. "Enjoy the bowl."

"You too," I said.

Hours later Hatch walked into my room wearing his sunglasses. He came to the side of my cot and sat down but didn't say anything. They hadn't turned down the RESAT, so I was still struggling to breathe.

"Twelve," he said.

The pain dropped immediately—not completely, but enough for me to take a deep breath. I turned toward him.

"It's that easy," Hatch said. "Just one word and the pain goes away."

"I don't think your kids' visit went the way you planned."

Hatch didn't answer, but I saw his jaw tighten.

"I met Torstyn. You said that the other four kids had died."

"Truth is relative."

"Then I'm not dying?"

"You're dying—just not from cancer. You're actually quite healthy, you oath-breaking, insignificant bug." Hatch looked down at his watch. "It's almost time. It's a shame it had to end this way. There are few things sadder in life than squandered opportunity. You could have been great. I could have made you a god."

"You must be dyslexic," I said. "I think you meant to say 'dog.'"

He leaned in close. "In spite of your continual insolence, it's not too late, Michael. One word and I can still save you."

"Why would you want to save an insignificant bug?"

"Don't try me!" Hatch shouted. "I'm giving you a chance at salvation." He calmed himself. "I don't think you've ever really thought this through. You've seen how we live—how our youths live. They have whatever they want. I know you're not the materialistic type, and I honestly admire that. I too am a man of principles. But what principles allow you to watch your mother suffer every day of her life and do nothing about it? There she is, working herself to the bone, just trying to put food on the table, trying to take care of *you*. That's not a life, Michael, that's an existence—and a poor one at that. If you joined us, really joined us, your mother wouldn't have to work another day for the rest of her life. She could see the world, dine at fancy restaurants, drive a new car, wear nice clothing, live in a beautiful home. Doesn't she deserve that? Don't you want that for her? Don't you love her enough to give that to her?"

"My mother deserves everything you just said," I replied. "But there's more to life than things."

"Of course there is. There's happiness. And is she happy?"

"Most of the time," I said.

"She acts that way for you, Michael. Because she loves you. Don't you love her? Wouldn't she be happier without all the stress and worry? Be honest, Michael."

"Not at the price you're asking."

"What price?" he said. "My offer to you is free."

"Nothing is free," I said. "The price is my allegiance to you."

"And is that too much to ask? You will never be raised higher than when you are kneeling to me."

I lay there quietly for a moment, then said, "I'd rather kneel to a rat."

His expression turned to rage. "So you shall," he said. "You fool. Again I have offered you the world and you spit it back at me." He looked up at a camera and said, "Make it twenty."

Immediately the RESAT buzzed, and pain racked my body. I gasped, my eyes welling up from the pain.

"It's time," Hatch said to the guard. "Take him to the chute." He turned back to me, leaning in close enough that I could feel his breath. "You have no idea how much I'm going to enjoy this." He stood and walked away.

Immediately the two guards were by my side. They checked my shackles and wires, pulled out my IV, and unplugged my RESAT from the wall.

Two more guards walked in. One came behind my cot, knelt down, and unlocked the wheels on my gurney; the other pulled out a plastic handle from the front and pulled me forward. The two guards who were already in the room walked behind the bed until I was outside the cell door, then they came to my side and walked in formation, slowly and at attention, like a color guard. I was wheeled from my cell through a long, concrete-floored corridor with tiled walls.

I had a flashback to the time I was seven years old and was taken to the hospital to have my tonsils removed, my mother and father had walked next to me as I was wheeled to the operating room. I found out later that I had shocked the doctor while he was operating.

Why am I thinking about this? Maybe that's what the mind does when it can't face its own reality—it searches for another one. It was safer to be seven again.

I was in such excruciating pain that everything seemed nightmarishly unreal. The walls blurred past me, partially hidden by the guards, who moved without a word, steady and emotionless like robots, their heavy boots echoing through the hallway. We stopped, waited for a double set of doors to open, then entered a different room with high ceilings. *I've been here before*, I thought. I heard Spanish being spoken in whispers, and above me I could see the curve of the bowl. I was in the ranch entrance, the room where we had entered the power plant. Of course I was. They were taking me to the lift Raúl had shown us, where they brought the bulls to feed to the rats.

Time was running out. If I was going to escape it had to be now. I had to think of something—but even thinking seemed impossible. My mind felt like it was on a long string, like a kite, floating away from me, connected by nothing but a quivering line. I was helpless. I couldn't think. I couldn't move. I was going to die.

The cart stopped, and the guards lifted my bed and set it on the lift. I must have blacked out from pain for a few seconds because the next thing I knew I was already high up in the air, approaching an open trapdoor in the ceiling.

This was it. Doubt began to creep in. Hatch's words returned to me, mocking me. *Where are your friends now, Michael?* Was he right?

Had they deserted me? I fought Hatch's lies. *I* had left *them*. I had locked the pipe behind me. Of course they would have come for me if I hadn't made it impossible. I had told them to run, to escape. If they didn't try to save me, it was my fault, not theirs.

The lift stopped abruptly. I tried to look around, but I could barely move my head. I was in a dark room lit by dim, amber lights flickering like candles. There were people there. Guards? Ranchers? No. They were dressed all in black like the guards, but they were executioners.

Thoughts of my loved ones came flooding into my mind: Taylor and her beautiful eyes. I wondered if they would cry for me. I thought about Ostin and the time he blew up his parents' new microwave because he was sure he could create cold fusion in a Tupperware container.

Mostly, I thought of my mother. I had read somewhere that grown men, dying on the battlefield, cried out for their mothers. I understood that. I wanted to be with her again. At least she was safe, I told myself. Tears fell down both sides of my cheeks.

The executioners were methodical and quiet, not even speaking among themselves. I was grateful for this. The Elgen guards would have mocked me. They would have laughed at my tears, then slapped me a few more times before sending me off to my end. Perhaps the executioners had seen too much death. There were two, maybe three in the room. I couldn't see their faces. Were they wearing hoods? It was hard to tell. Whatever they wore over their faces was stiff and resembled a mask. They all wore the same disguise, making them anonymous. *Do they feel anonymous? Are they wearing their masks for me or for themselves?*

I was unstrapped from the cot, lifted, and set on a conveyor belt. A strap, made from the same rubberized material that my shackles were, was pulled around my chest, next to the RESAT, and my bound wrists were lifted and buckled to it.

Is Ian watching me? Or were they already on their way back to America? Part of me felt relief that I wouldn't have to fight anymore. The fight was theirs now. I had given all I could.

An executioner turned a knob on the RESAT, and I groaned as my body convulsed with more pain. At first I thought he had done this out of cruelty, but as my thoughts became more blurred I realized that he was probably acting in mercy, dulling me to the impending agony of being eaten alive.

Alive. I was too young to die! I wanted to live and fall in love and someday have children of my own. I had wondered if they would be electric too. My Tourette's could be passed on, why not my electricity? And what if I married Taylor? Would our children possess multiple powers?

What if. What if I had just gone with them? Maybe we could have made it. Maybe we would all be together. Or maybe we would all be together in here. There was no use second-guessing what I couldn't know. I had made my decision. What was done was done.

One of the executioners began spraying something on me from a hose, soaking my clothing and skin. *What is this? It smells sweet.*

There was suddenly a loud beep like the sound a garbage truck makes when it's backing up. From its echo I guessed it was coming from the bowl itself. I didn't think about its meaning, as I was certain it had something to do with feeding time. A thin, tinny voice from an intercom spoke to the executioners. I couldn't understand what was said, nor did I try. One of the executioners grunted a response then pushed a button. A loud, stoic, female voice began counting down from ten.

"Ten, nine, eight, seven . . ."

My executioners put on earphones. "Five, four, three . . ."

On the wall ahead of me, near my feet, a door slid open and the color of the room immediately changed, lit by an amber glow like the flickering of a fire. The rats. They were waiting.

"Two, one. Commence feeding."

The beeping suddenly stopped, replaced by a single long tone. There was no rescue coming. I had run out of time.

A light above me began to flash, then the conveyor started to move beneath me. My heart froze. "No . . . ," I said.

I was so weak. There was nothing I could do but wait. At least it wouldn't take long. Soon everything would be over.

48

Fireworks

The hours waiting for night-
time passed quietly. The bread, water, and fruit were long gone, and
everyone was thirsty, tired, and hungry. As darkness fell over the
jungle Ostin gathered everyone together to review the plan one
more time. Just sitting together in the darkness already revealed a
flaw in their plan. "The guards in the towers are going to see your
glow," Ostin said. "They'll shoot you through the trees."

"Easy fix," Taylor said. "Everyone who's electric follow me." She
led them over to a spot near the edge of their camp where the
ground was still wet from the rain the night before. She scooped up
a handful of moist dirt and rubbed it over her hands and face. With
the exception of Zeus, the rest of them covered one another with the
dark soil. Jack and Wade said they were rubbing mud on for solidar-
ity, but the truth was they loved the commando look.

As soon as the last of the light had vanished, they said a quick good-bye to Mrs. Vey, Tanner, and Raúl, then set off through the jungle in single file, Ian and Taylor leading the group. Zeus slowed their pace considerably. He was finally walking on his own, but he had to lean heavily on Jack. Had they not needed his power they would have sent him off with Raúl. Wade, Ostin, and McKenna walked at the rear of the column, carrying the dynamite.

They traveled east in an ellipse, making a wide swing into the jungle to avoid being spotted by the tower guards at the northeast corner of the interior fence. When they were past the compound they circled back in, crouching at the perimeter of the barbwire fence just thirty-five yards from the pump house.

The pump house was a simple adobe-brick structure with a tin roof and barred windows. A large pipe, nearly three feet in diameter, was visible on the east side of the structure. It rose up from the ground forming a loop.

"There it is," Ostin whispered. He turned to Taylor. "Is group two ready?"

"Ready," Taylor said.

"We're ready," Jack said.

Ostin looked at Zeus. "You okay?"

He was clearly still in a lot of pain but nodded. "Let's shut them down."

"We should test the wire," Taylor said.

"Good idea," Ian said. He and Taylor grabbed the barbwire about six feet apart.

"What number am I thinking of?" Ian asked.

"You're not," Taylor said. "You're thinking about that fruit."

"It works," Ian said, releasing the wire.

"All right," Ostin said. "See you after the fireworks. Good luck, everyone."

While Taylor led group two back into the jungle, Ostin, Wade, McKenna, and Ian covered themselves with branches, then crawled on their stomachs under the barbwire closer to the pump house. Ian and Wade carried the dynamite on their backs but had to take their packs off to slide them through the fence. They all stopped about fifteen yards from the house.

"What's going on in there?" Ostin asked Ian.

"There's a guy sitting at a console."

"Just one guy?"

"Yes."

"Is he armed?"

"No. He looks more like a tech." He turned back. "He looks like he's sleeping."

"He's about to get the wake-up call of his life," Ostin said. "What else do you see?"

"The right side of the house is nothing, just a kitchen and bathroom. On the other side there's the end of that pipe with a bunch of lights and switches."

"How thick is the pipe?"

"About three feet."

"I mean the walls of the pipe."

"Oh." He looked closer. "Maybe an inch and a half."

Ostin thought this over. "Dynamite blows down, so we should put the packs on top of the pipe, but it's much more powerful in a confined space." He did the math in his head. "For maximum explosive effect we need to stack the packs *inside* the loop."

Ian and Wade pulled a coil of fuse out of each pack, and McKenna wrapped the ends of the fuse around her hand.

Ostin looked at McKenna. "You don't ever just spontaneously ignite, do you?"

"Only a few times a day," McKenna said, staring ahead.

"Really?"

She looked at him. "No."

"Sorry," he said.

Wade turned to Ostin. "Now?"

"Do it," Ostin said. "Don't forget to check the fuses."

"I won't." Wade slid his arms through both packs, then McKenna and Ostin covered them with brush.

"Good luck," Ostin said.

Wade crawled on his stomach toward the pipe, moving about as fast as a turtle. In the darkness he looked like a slow-moving bush.

"Can't he go faster?" McKenna said.

"He's just being careful," Ostin said. "We've got one shot at this."

When Wade reached the pipe he looked back at Ian, who gave him the thumbs-up. Wade checked the fuse connections again, then placed the packs in between the looped pipe and crawled back, though much faster. The four of them dropped back into the jungle, McKenna feeding the fuse out from her hand as they went.

"How's our sleeper?" Ostin asked Ian.

"Still snoozing."

"Good. Have you found Michael?"

"No. He's not in the cells anymore."

"What's going on in the bowl?"

Ian strained. "It's hard to see with all the electrical interference. But something must be going on. There's a large crowd gathered up in the observation deck. The chute's extended, so it must be feeding time." He shook his head. "That's strange, I don't see a bull. Let me see what's in the feeding station." His expression changed. He quickly grabbed the barbwire. "We've got to blow it. Now!"

"What's going on?" Ostin asked. "What's in the feeding station?"

"Michael."

49

Return of Power

The conveyor belt moved me slowly toward the open door leading to the bowl. As I approached the opening I was overcome by the shrill scream of a million rats echoing in the metal collector—far louder and more horrific than the sound of the rats in the hallway. I can't describe the terror of that sound, though I had once heard something like it. A few years earlier Ostin played for me something he had downloaded from the Internet—a radio program claiming that Russian scientists conducting deep-hole drilling experiments in Siberia had recorded the sounds of hell. The recording was proven a hoax, but if there was such a place as hell, it couldn't be worse than this—the shrieking of a million hungry rats climbing on top of one another to eat me alive. Even the stench was torture, and I started gagging.

The belt moved slowly, like a roller coaster about to take its first plunge. My heart raced, fueled by adrenaline. My mind and my body felt numb. I wished I could pass out.

Then I felt something else. As my feet cleared the door, they began to tingle. Powerfully. As I slowly passed through the opening in the wall the sensation moved up my body. *What's happening to me?* To my surprise I was able to lift my feet. It felt like energy was washing over me. Of course it did. I was being carried out over the largest electrical field ever created—millions of kilowatts were bombarding my body. The RESAT that had been sucking the energy from me couldn't possibly handle that much current. A thousand of them couldn't.

As my chest approached the opening I was able to sit up and look down. My feet were beginning to glow. What I saw past my feet, at the bottom of the chute, was horrific. Until you see the rats you can't possibly imagine how terrible they look, bubbling like a vast sea of lava. At the sight of me, the rats' ravenous, collective shriek grew in intensity, and I could see a wave of rodents swelling toward me.

My thighs were now glowing. I strained at my bonds. I couldn't break free yet, but I was still absorbing electricity. My head passed through the opening, and I was looking directly down the chute, lying on the metal rollers. This is where I was supposed to roll down. I waited for it, but I didn't move. I wasn't sliding anywhere. Of course I wasn't. These were metal rollers and I was magnetic again, only a hundred times more.

The RESAT started to make a high-pitched squeal, then popped as it blew, a thin wisp of smoke rising from it. My skin was now as bright as an incandescent lightbulb. I was just lying there on the chute, a few yards past the trap door, immovable and growing brighter by the second, brighter than I had ever experienced. I looked down at my feet, but they were now too bright to look at. I wasn't melting through my bands; my bands were just gone. I lifted the RESAT from my chest and threw it down at the grid.

I could hear shouting coming from the intercom in the execution room. Then the chute began to lower. I guessed that if I wasn't going to the rats, they were going to bring the rats to me. The trapdoor shut behind me, and the chute continued lowering until it was within a few feet of the grid. The ravenous rats began jumping onto the chute, pouring up the trough like a flash flood in reverse.

I had been covered by the rats before—in the hallway—but I hadn't felt this way then. The bowl was designed to collect and focus energy toward a collector, and I had become the center of that focus, channeling the pure energy of a million rats.

The first rats didn't come within six feet of me before they burned up like meteors entering the Earth's atmosphere. I was becoming even more electric. I *was* lightning. I was *pure energy*. Then I wasn't burning the rats anymore; I was vaporizing them. For the first time, I felt more electric than human. I wondered if I would vaporize too.

As the metal rollers began to glow beneath me, I slowly stood and walked, on an incline, down the chute, my feet clinging to the metal. The rats began running from me, scrambling as if they were fleeing a burning ship. I walked to the end of the chute, then stepped down onto the grid.

I looked up at the observation window. Hatch was pressed against the glass. Even with his glasses on I could see his astonishment. Standing next to him were his kids: Tara, Quentin, Torstyn, Bryan, and Kylee, with at least a dozen guards at attention behind them. I stepped over the sweep and walked closer to the observation window so I could observe them.

I formed a brilliant ball of electricity in my hand and threw it right at Hatch. Hatch, and everybody else, dove out of the way as the ball exploded against the thick glass, blasting a hole in it large enough for my mom's car to drive through. When the smoke cleared, only Torstyn's head popped up. I formed another ball in my hand.

"Hey, tough guy!" I shouted. "Want to play ball?"

He ran.

I noticed that the sound the rats were making had begun to change. I turned to see the rodents pressed up against the opposite side of the bowl. Thousands of them were on their backs, twitching. A loud alarm sounded. That's when I noticed that the color of the bowl was also changing. The bowl was heating up. Even in my state, I could feel its heat. All around me, rats were dying by the thousands.

Am I doing this? Then the rats began to burst into flames, like stuffed animals thrown into a furnace. A robotic female voice echoed across the bowl: "Danger. Evacuation protocol. Bowl meltdown imminent."

I didn't want to stick around to see what that might look like. I ran to the side of the bowl and jumped across a three-foot trough, magnetically sticking to the bowl's metal side.

That's when the power went out.

50

Darkness

Everything stilled. A dying alarm echoed across the bowl, and the only light came from me and the burning carcasses of rats. I slowly lowered myself down the metal side, below the grid. I was free, at least for the time being, but I wasn't sure how to get from where I was to the mechanical closet.

Michael?

The voice sounded as if it had come from someone standing next to me. It sounded like Taylor's. I looked around but couldn't see anyone. *Taylor?*

Good, you hear me! she said.

I realized that I wasn't hearing a voice but thoughts.

Where are you? I asked.

I'm outside the building. Are you touching the bowl?

Yes.

Me too. You're reading my thoughts.

Where is everyone?

In the jungle.

Is everyone okay? Is my mother?

She's fine. Raúl took her and Tanner to our rendezvous point, where the bull got caught in the fence.

The power's out. The bowl melted down.

I know. We blew up their water supply so the bowl would melt down.

Ostin's idea?

Of course. How are you getting out? Taylor asked.

The pipe. If I can find it. Is Ian around?

Yes.

Ask him how I get to the pipe.

Just a minute. Ian, how does Michael get to the pipe?

Tell him to climb down to the ground below and go right to the first door. That hallway will take him back to the air duct we crawled through. Did you hear that, Michael?

(It's a little weird listening to someone's thoughts when they're listening to someone else speak, almost like an echo.) *Yes. I'll lose contact with you when I drop down from the bowl. I'll meet you at the rendezvous point.*

We'll see you there. I'll see you soon.

I couldn't help but smile. *I'll see you soon.*

I climbed down the sloping metal of the bowl as far as I could, which wasn't far enough, as there was still a twelve-foot drop to the dark ground below—the floor barely illuminated by my glow. I let go, dropping hard to the concrete.

"My ankle," I groaned. I looked down at my foot. My right foot had landed on a wrench and twisted as I hit. As I stood, a shock of pain shot through my ankle. It felt like a sprain. I limped along the wall until I found the door Ian had told me about and opened it to the corridor we'd escaped from. The hall had some illumination, as the battery-powered emergency lights had been activated. I looked both ways, then hobbled out into the hall.

I could hear running, heavy Elgen boots, but it was coming from somewhere else in the maze. I limped down the hall until I found the vent cover. I climbed the water pipe next to it into the duct, then replaced the cover behind me.

My glow had increased tenfold, illuminating the duct almost as brightly as McKenna had. I crawled as quickly as I could until I felt the cold of the refrigeration room. I crawled slowly to the next vent and put my ear to it. I could hear movement. Then I saw the beam of a flashlight. There was someone in the mechanical room. I pulled back, afraid that they might notice my glow through the vent, but the sound didn't stop. I crept up and looked out the vent again. There was a guard below. He was in uniform, standing near the pipe. I couldn't tell if he was coming or going. He lifted the cap off the pipe and dropped his flashlight in, answering my question. He was escaping too.

I gave him time to disappear down the pipe, then I removed the vent cover. I looked around and then climbed out, lowering myself as much as possible, then dropped to the floor, trying to absorb as much of the fall as I could on my good foot. I hobbled over to the pipe and lifted the cap. I could hear the echo of the guard moving inside. I put both hands on the pipe and pulsed, knocking the guard out. I climbed into the pipe, then slid down, crawling out of the compound as fast as I could.

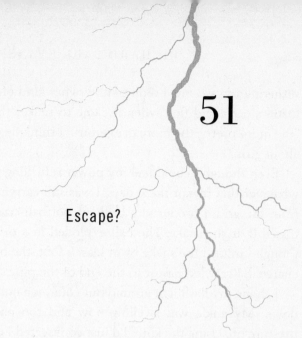

51

Escape?

I caught up to the unconscious guard just a hundred feet from the pipe's entrance. I took his weapons, mostly so he couldn't use them on me. He was carrying the standard Elgen weaponry and ordnance: a concussion grenade, a smoke grenade, a special ops knife, and a 9mm pistol. I took everything, including his flashlight. Then I cuffed his hands behind his back. I didn't want him following me. I wondered how many other guards were taking the opportunity to escape.

I hurried on as fast as I could, wondering how the rest of the Electroclan were doing. They had just shut down the Elgen's largest power plant and blackened out the country's largest cities. I could only imagine how angry Hatch was. He would spare nothing to catch us before we left the country. He would be out for blood.

As I neared the end of the pipe, I saw something move. I pointed the flashlight toward the pipe's mouth. A brightly colored snake was slithering toward me. I didn't know what kind of serpent it was, but Ostin always said that when it came to snakes the rule of thumb is "the more pretty, the more dangerous." I think he said the same thing about girls.

Even though I could feel my power returning to its normal levels, whatever that meant these days, I was still carrying excess electricity from the grid. I produced a brilliant, softball-size lightning ball and tossed it at the snake. The ball exploded in a bright flash, and even though I missed the snake by at least a foot, the ball still burned it to charcoal. I crawled past it to the end of the pipe.

I shone my flashlight around but could see nothing, so I let myself down. My ankle was swelling now and too painful to put much pressure on. Using the knife I'd just confiscated I cut away part of my shirt, then wrapped my ankle with it. I looked back at the compound. I could hear shouting and an occasional gunshot but no machinery of any kind. There were no electric lights, but in the moonlight I could see a column of smoke rising from behind the power plant. My Electroclan had wreaked some serious chaos. I was so proud of them.

I knew it would be just a matter of time before the Elgen came looking for me outside the compound. I had to get to the meeting point as quickly as possible. Forgetting my ankle, I started to run and nearly fell. I didn't want my friends to have to wait for me. But they were traveling with wounded as well, so I might not hold them back too much.

I hurried on, concealed in the darkness of the jungle but close enough to keep my eye on the fence for navigation. The last thing I wanted to do was get lost in the jungle. I was glad I had given Taylor the GPS. At least I didn't have to worry about everyone else getting lost.

I had limped along for about a half hour when I heard the sound of approaching helicopters. As they got closer I heard another noise that I couldn't distinguish until I saw the fire. The helicopters were burning the forest with flamethrowers.

In spite of my pain, I started moving faster, heading deeper into the jungle. But they kept coming as if they knew exactly where I was. *How did they find me?* Then I remembered the el-readers, like the handheld one they had caught me with in the mechanical room. With the Elgen's love for technology I had no doubt that they had developed bigger, more powerful el-readers that had a range of hundreds of yards.

The sound of the rotors just got louder, and it didn't matter how deep I was in the jungle, how dark the night, or how thick the canopy, they were clearly following me. Then I heard the blast of the flames again, this time followed by the screeching of birds and monkeys. A black jaguar ran past me.

Thirty feet in front of me was an orange-yellow wall of fire, taking out everything in its path and clearing a smoldering swath in the jungle nearly twenty feet wide. Then I heard the blast of a flamethrower behind me as well.

Huddled in the trees, I couldn't tell how many helicopters there were—at least three. They were flying in circles around me, cutting back the jungle with their flames—the circle closing in on me until the heat was intense enough that it was hard to breathe. They didn't have to burn me—they could just suck all the oxygen out of the area and suffocate me. Smoke and fumes stung my eyes and throat and I was covered with ash. Within minutes they had left me in a small circle of trees, an island in an inferno of fire and soot. Then one of the helicopters broke off and hovered directly over me. A voice boomed out from its amplifier.

"You can't escape, Vey. We have you surrounded. If you run we'll open fire. You have five seconds to step out from the canopy or we'll burn you alive."

I said nothing, weighing my chances of running through the charred and burning swath to the jungle beyond without getting mowed down by their machine guns. But really, there was no point to it. They'd just find me again.

"One. Two . . ."

"Okay!" I shouted. "I'm coming out."

I limped out into the smoldering black clearing, my arms raised, my body illuminated by their spotlights. There were four helicopters, bobbing above me in the night like they were on strings. One was directly over me, maybe just fifty feet above the tops of the trees, another was to my left, and the other two were slowly circling, their spotlights and machine guns all pointing at me.

The voice said, "Get on your knees."

I looked at the steaming ground, then slowly knelt down.

The helicopter to my left began to descend when it suddenly started to wobble. It yawed violently to one side, veering directly into the path of another helicopter. Their blades collided and both helicopters exploded.

Then the third and fourth helicopters dropped to the ground. I sprang to my feet and, ignoring the pain in my ankle, sprinted out of the way as one of the helicopters fell just twenty yards from where I had been kneeling and burst into flames.

I looked back only once to see the clearing completely engulfed in fire, then ran headlong into the jungle as fast as I could.

"Wherever you are, Tanner," I said, "thank you."

52

Shadows and Nose Bones

My friends are close. Close enough at least to drop the helicopters. Not that that knowledge did me much good. I was utterly lost. In fleeing the helicopters I had run even deeper into the jungle. I had no idea how far I was from the meeting point or even what direction to walk in. If I were Ostin I could look at the stars and figure it out, but I wasn't Ostin and, even if I were, under the thick canopy, I couldn't even see the stars. I had to somehow find my bearings. If I could get above the canopy I could find the compound and head back toward the fence. My ankle was throbbing now, and I hopped on one foot until I found a tall, lichen-covered tree hung with vines as thick as rope. I tested one of the larger vines, and it easily held me, so I began to climb.

I was tired and weak and the climbing was difficult, but I continued on, knowing that the Electroclan was nearby. Monkeys and birds

329

screeched around me as I invaded their domain. A black-and-white monkey about the size of a squirrel jumped on my head. It started pulling at my ears so I pulsed a little, and it shrieked and jumped off, scolding me as it swung to a nearby limb.

It took me about a half hour to make it to the emergent level above the canopy. I was panting and drenched with sweat, but the air was cooler and fresh and I sucked it in like water. The velvet night sky was brilliant with stars and, for the first time since I'd come, I realized that it wasn't the same sky we saw at home. There was no Big or Little Dipper down here, no North Star. In this part of the world they looked to the Southern Cross.

From my vantage point I could see for miles around in all directions. I could see the moon reflecting off the river, winding through the jungle like a snake through grass.

On the opposite side of the valley the Elgen compound was still dark, lit only by sporadic fires. Smoke was billowing into the sky. This made me unspeakably happy.

I found the electric fence. Its yellow warning lights were dead but I could see the moon glisten off its metal lines. I had gone farther into the forest than I had thought, and I could now see that I was at least a quarter mile from the fence and a couple of miles from what I guessed to be our meeting place.

As I looked out over the compound I saw them coming. Shadows. They were everywhere. There were more than a thousand of them, silently moving toward the jungle. The guards had been sent out to find us.

I quickly climbed back down below the canopy, afraid that my glow might have given me away. I had no doubt that they were equipped with el-readers and night vision goggles. My optimism vanished, replaced with dread. I couldn't go to our meeting place even if I could find it. The meeting place. My mother was there. Raúl could guide them through the jungle. *Had the rest of the Electroclan already caught up to them? Had Ian seen the Shadows coming?*

A few minutes later I heard something crashing through the foliage below me. As I turned to see what it was, I heard a gunshot and something smashed against the tree less than three feet from my head, splintering wood around me. Then I saw the brilliant green flash of laser pointers on my body. Three Elgen guards had their guns trained on me. "Come down from the tree!" one shouted. "Or we'll shoot you down!"

I had no doubt they would, though I wondered if I would be better off taking the bullet here. Hatch would not be so merciful. But the rest of the Electroclan was somewhere nearby and they had to have heard the gunshot. They could take out these three. "All right," I said. "I'm coming."

My back was to them as I climbed down the tree. I was afraid. Part of me expected a bullet at any second. When I reached the ground I put my hands in the air and slowly turned around. "Don't shoot."

To my surprise, all three guards were lying facedown on the ground, motionless. I couldn't figure out what had happened. I hadn't heard a thing. I looked around but couldn't see anyone.

I knelt down next to one of the men and saw a small, feathered dart stuck in his neck. I swallowed as I slowly looked up. Just yards away from me, concealed in the darkness, were at least a dozen Amazon tribesmen. The lower halves of their faces were painted bloodred, and the upper halves, just above their noses, were painted black, making them look like they wore masks. They wore simple loincloths and headdresses of freshly plaited leaves, perfect camouflage for the jungle. They were armed with blow darts and spears.

I slowly stood. I had no idea what to do. If they had wanted to kill me, they could have easily done it as I climbed down the tree, just as they had the three Elgen guards. I remembered what Jaime had said about the tribes—that they hated the Elgen. *White devils*, they called them. Maybe the tribesmen were still trying to figure out what I was. If the Elgen were hunting me, maybe they would think I was good. You know, my enemy's enemy is my friend.

One of the natives approached me. His face was painted like the others', and he wore a chest plate made of bamboo laced together with dyed twine and a necklace with jaguar claws and bird talons. There were bones through his nose and ears. He slowly reached out and cautiously touched me, probably intrigued by my glow. For a second it crossed my mind that if I gave him a small shock, he might think I was a god or something, but I decided it was too risky. I had clearly watched too many movies.

He took my hands and crossed them at my wrists, then another one of the natives stepped forward and tied them together with twine. I could have easily dropped them both, but I was sure that I would answer for it with a dozen poison darts and arrows.

One of them made a peculiar clicking noise with his tongue and the rest began mimicking him, then they started off, leading me deeper into the black jungle. Even in the darkness they knew where they were going. We walked all night. My ankle throbbed with pain, and a few times I had to stop, which was met with a lot of shouting and shoving. It took a great deal of self-control not to shock them.

After hiking for miles through the dense terrain, we finally stopped at a village on a cliff overlooking the river. It was still dark and I guessed it was probably around four in the morning. I was moving on sheer adrenaline.

In spite of the hour, there was a great deal of excitement at my arrival, and even children, about two dozen of them, ran out to look at me. Old, gray-haired men came from their huts, their bodies painted in white and red. The women were also painted and wore layers of bright blue beads around their necks.

From what I could see, the village consisted of about thirty thatch-roofed huts. The tribesmen led me to an elderly man who, from the natives' gestures, I guessed was a person of authority—a chief or shaman. His face was painted white with a few black lines and his gray hair was cut short. He also had a bone through his nose. He wore a necklace made of piranha jaws and a headdress made from brightly colored parrot feathers. He looked me over, touched me, then said, *"Shr ta."*

His pronouncement was met with a loud whoop from the tribesmen.

"Pei ta dau fangdz chyu. Ma shang," the old man said.

"Ma shang," they echoed.

"Chyu," my guard said to me.

"Chew what?" I said. "I don't speak cannibal."

The man grabbed my arm, and I was taken to a small hut and my hands were untied. As I rubbed my wrists the guard said, *"Chyu. Chyu."* I looked at him blankly, and he pushed me inside the hut. *"Schwei jau,"* he said.

"I don't understand a word you're saying," I said.

He pointed to a large fur on the ground and closed his eyes. *"Sch-wei jau."*

"Sleep," I said. "I can do that. Gladly."

I sat down on the fur. The bed was on a dirt floor covered by mats made of woven leaves. It wasn't any worse than the Elgen's prison cot. In spite of my fear, I immediately fell asleep.

At daylight, I opened my eyes to an elderly man with a bone sticking through his nose, staring into my face. I jumped back.

He laughed.

"You think that's funny?" I said. "How would you like a shock? We'll see how funny that is." I was pretty angry, and I felt at ease to speak my mind because I was certain they couldn't understand me.

The man stared at me for another moment, then he made a clicking noise and left my hut. I sat up on the fur, reminded of my ankle. After last night's hike it was swollen to almost twice its size. I rubbed it for a minute, then lay back down. My mind was reeling. What was going to happen? My mother used to say, "Better the devil you know than the one you don't." I finally understood what she meant. At least, with the Elgen, I knew what they wanted. I had no idea what these people were about. For all I knew I was their main entrée for dinner tonight.

I wondered about my mother and the rest of the Electroclan. Had they made it to the pickup point? Were they still waiting for me? No, they couldn't be. Not with the guards searching for us.

A few minutes later an older woman walked into my hut. She

carried a wooden bowl with something inside that resembled a greenish-brown oatmeal, which she handed to me along with a gourd filled with water. I drank thirstily, then, using my fingers, tried the food in the bowl. It tasted unlike anything I had ever eaten before. It wasn't all bad and I told myself it was some kind of fruit, but it could have been smashed bug larvae or monkey brains for all I knew. The woman then knelt down by my feet and took my sprained ankle in her hands and began rubbing it. I took this as a good sign, as I doubted they would spring for massages for people they planned to eat. Or maybe this was just how they tenderized their meat.

Nearly an hour later two young tribesmen came into the hut. I thought I recognized them from the night before, but from the way they were painted, I couldn't tell. They said something to the woman, and she stopped rubbing my ankle and stood. I looked at my ankle. The swelling had gone down considerably. "Thank you," I said to her. The woman didn't look at me as she left but said, *"Buy-ong she,"* and walked out.

"Jan chi lai!" the older of the two shouted at me. I guessed that he was telling me to stand. I lifted myself up, slowly putting weight on my bad foot, testing it. My ankle had improved. Not enough that I could outrun anyone, but I had never considered that an option anyway. In the jungle I was definitely at a disadvantage.

The men escorted me back out into the center of the village. The old man, Mr. Important Guy, was standing in the exact same place he had been the night before. He was waiting for me.

"Womun dai ta," one of the tribesmen said to him.

"Ta yo mei yo schwei jau," the important guy said.

"Schwei le."

"Yo mei yo ting chi tade ren?"

"Mei yo."

I listened to them banter for a while, then finally I said, "Listen, if you're going to eat me, you're not going to like the way I taste."

To my surprise the men stopped talking. The old man's face twisted with a peculiar expression, then he started to laugh.

"I'm not your enemy," I said. "I just want to go home."

The old man stopped laughing. He looked at me for a long time, his dark gray eyes locked onto mine. Then he said in perfectly clear English, "Michael Vey. That is not your path. You are not going home."

For Michael Vey trivia, sneak peeks, and events in your area,
follow Michael and the rest of the Electroclan at:
WWW.MICHAELVEY.COM

For contests, advance peeks, and fun fan interaction,
Join the official Michael Vey Facebook page!
Facebook.com/MichaelVeyOfficialFanPage

Join the ELECTROCLAN on Facebook!
For those 18 years and younger only, the Electroclan page
has weekly contests, fan fiction, and fun interaction
with all the Electroclan members! Don't miss out!
Facebook.com/TheElectroclan

Follow Michael Vey on Twitter!
Twitter.com/MichaelVey